# THE PROSE WORKS OF
# *W*ILLIAM *B*YRD
# OF *W*ESTOVER

# THE PROSE WORKS OF
# WILLIAM BYRD
# OF WESTOVER:

*Narratives of a Colonial Virginian*

*Edited by*

Louis B. Wright

THE BELKNAP PRESS OF

HARVARD UNIVERSITY PRESS

*Cambridge, Massachusetts*

1966

# $\mathcal{P}$REFACE

$\mathcal{A}$ NEW edition of the literary prose works of William Byrd II of Westover has long been needed. For many years an edition collated with the original Westover Manuscripts was impossible because that document was in private hands and could not be seen. But in 1962 the Virginia Historical Society acquired the folio volume of the Westover Manuscripts from the owners and immediately made it available. The present editor wishes to thank the Virginia Historical Society for its courtesy in providing a microfilm copy of the manuscripts for purposes of comparison. Mr. John Jennings, the director of the Virginia Historical Society, has been particularly helpful.

In preparing the text for publication, we have modernized eccentricities of spelling, punctuation, and capitalization, but we have changed no words nor tampered with Byrd's grammar. The text is as precisely accurate as human fallibility permits. Although we cannot be certain that we have not erred in interpreting Byrd's handwriting here and there, we have made every effort to achieve accuracy.

The spelling of proper names has raised problems, for Byrd himself was not consistent. Where proper names have a modern accepted form, we have followed the practice of regularizing them. But where Byrd's spelling indicates a variation in pronunciation, or a form different from the modern word (as distinct from a mere eccentricity of spelling), we have retained the form as Byrd wrote it.

The notes prepared by William K. Boyd identifying persons mentioned in the *Secret History*, which Boyd edited in 1929, are still valid, and we have reprinted many of them verbatim with proper credit to him.

A study of the provenance and relations of the manuscripts, made by Mrs. William Leonard, is reproduced in the Appendix. I am indebted to Mrs. Leonard for her careful study of these manuscripts. Mr. Whitfield Bell of the American Philosophical Society and Mr. Francis Berkeley of the University of Virginia have supplied information and data useful in explaining the relationship of the various manuscripts. I am grateful to the staff of Harvard University Press for their invariable helpfulness. I am greatly in the debt of Miss Virginia LaMar, chief editor of the Folger Publications, for assistance in solving various problems and in the preparation of the notes. To Mrs. John Bates and to Mrs. John Hendrickson I wish to express my appreciation for their transcription of manuscripts and the typing of difficult copy.

LOUIS B. WRIGHT

*February 5, 1965*

# CONTENTS

# ILLUSTRATIONS

# INTRODUCTION

# WILLIAM BYRD AS A
# MAN OF LETTERS

$\mathcal{O}$NE of the most urbane writers of the colonial period in British America was William Byrd of Westover in Virginia, the second of his name in the colony, whose narrative, *The History of the Dividing Line betwixt Virginia and North Carolina, Run in the Year of Our Lord 1728*, has become a classic of early American literature. Byrd never permitted this account to be printed in his lifetime, but he allowed various friends in both Virginia and England to read it in manuscript. This document, along with others written by Byrd, remained unpublished until 1841, when Edmund Ruffin brought out at Petersburg, Virginia, a volume bearing the title *The Westover Manuscripts: Containing the History of the Dividing Line betwixt Virginia and North Carolina; A Journey to the Land of Eden, A.D. 1733; and A Progress to the Mines. Written about 1728 to 1736, and Now First Published.*

Although Ruffin was the first to print Byrd's principal prose writings, they were known to some of the author's contemporaries and to others in a later period. Thomas Jefferson, for example, interested himself in trying to have the Westover Manuscripts published. Byrd was not one to hide his light under a bushel, but he was a perfectionist about his writing, and he was unwilling to turn over the manuscript to a publisher until he had given it an ultimate polishing. As a proud and dandified colonial gentleman, eager to retain the good opinion of aristocratic friends in England, he felt a certain diffidence about rushing into print like any common scribbler. As was the way of dilettantes of letters, he preferred to have his writings circulate genteelly in manuscript until such time as he could bring them out in a manner befitting a gentleman.

He may also have enjoyed arousing the curiosity of his friends about his literary efforts. For example, Peter Collinson, the English naturalist and virtuoso, who corresponded with many Americans, was eager to see Byrd's narrative, which he had heard about, and wrote to ask if he could borrow a copy. In a letter written in 1736, Byrd made an excuse that the treatise was not yet finished, but he would send him the journal if he promised to let only Sir Charles Wager see it. Another naturalist, Mark Catesby, however, saw a copy and praised Byrd for it, to which the author replied in 1737: "I am obliged to you for the compliment you are pleased to make to my poor performances. 'Tis a sign you never saw them that you judge so favorably . . . It will seem like a joke when I tell you that I have not time to finish that work. But 'tis very [certain] I have not, for I am always engaged on some project for improvement of our infant colony. The present scheme is to found a city at the falls of the James River, and plant a colony of Switzers on my land upon Roanoke." [1]

That Byrd was hoping to publish his book appears from a letter that he wrote to Collinson on July 5, 1737, saying that he expected to finish his history during the next winter; he asked Collinson's aid in having illustrations made of animals that he described. We do not know why Byrd did not complete the manuscript and send it to press. For a man who was constantly reading and writing, it is incredible that he could not find time to put the last finishing touches on the document. Either his sense of perfection or his aristocratic notions about committing his work to print prevented the publication.

William Byrd's attitude toward his writings was conditioned by his social milieu and his own personal predilections. Few men of his generation so perfectly reflected the society in which they moved as did William Byrd of Westover, one of the most cultivated members of the landed ruling class of Virginia and a social aspirant in the drawing rooms of the aristocrats of early Georgian England. Byrd was wealthy, well-read, well-traveled, and socially acceptable in any society. He chose to be a social climber in England and to cultivate the friendship of titled Englishmen. But the social aspirations which he displayed in his years in England were not merely evidences of personal vanity; the contacts that he so sedulously cultivated were neces-

[1] Cited by John Spencer Bassett, *The Writings of Colonel William Byrd of Westover in Virginia* (New York, 1901), p. lxxix.

sary to him as the agent for the colony of Virginia, an office that he held on various occasions. And they were useful to him in his search for a rich wife, a pursuit that occupied some of his time abroad. It was necessary for him to be mindful of those things expected of a gentleman and a beau in the reigns of the first two Georges.

William Byrd the writer was the son of William Byrd I, himself a wealthy planter, landowner, and Indian trader. The father had come to Virginia sometime before 1670, in which year, as a youth of eighteen, he inherited from his uncle, Thomas Stegge, Jr., a considerable estate which Stegge had acquired by way of trade. Trade was in the blood, for William Byrd I's father had been a goldsmith of London, and Stegge had probably induced his nephew to come to Virginia to help him with his own trade with the Indians. Certainly the nephew quickly adapted himself to the life that his uncle had planned for him and became one of the most important traders in Virginia. He employed pack trains to travel to the back country with trading goods — beads, pots, pans, blankets, rum, guns, lead for bullets, and anything else in demand from the natives — and these pack trains brought back a rich freight of beaver skins, mink, otter, and other furs, as well as deerskins and an occasional buffalo robe. How far Byrd's traders penetrated into the interior can never be known, for these pioneers were closemouthed about their activities, but it is fairly certain that they reached the mountain region. With his profits, Byrd added land to his estate.

Always with an eye on the main chance, William Byrd I made a good match in 1673 with Mary Horsmanden, daughter of Warham Horsmanden, a royalist from East Anglia. Mary was already the widow of Samuel Filmer. The couple's first child, a son born on March 28, 1674, was named William after his father. In time Mary bore Byrd three other children, all daughters. All of the children were sent to England to be educated under the direction of their maternal Grandfather Horsmanden, of Purleigh, in Essex. The youngest, Ursula, at the age of seventeen married Robert Beverley, the historian, and died at the birth of her first child.

The future author of the *Dividing Line* left for England when he was a child of seven and did not return until 1696, when he was a young man of twenty-two. Thus in education he was an Englishman. During his formative youth he lived through the later years of Charles II's reign, saw the events of the Glorious Revolution of 1688, and remained in London until the middle years of William III's reign. His education was that of a son of a prosperous family well connected with the gentry. His grandfather placed him in Felsted Grammar School in Essex under a famous schoolmaster, Christopher Glasscock. It was this school that Oliver Cromwell had chosen for his sons, not because of its political point of view but because of its reputation for sound classical learning. Byrd's grandfather, though a royalist, evidently concurred in this faith in the school, and Byrd's father wrote to the headmaster to express his own "hearty thanks" for the lad's excellent instruction. The elder Byrd hoped that the boy would not "be discouraged in his fair proceedings." That young Byrd received a good grounding in the classics and acquired a taste for learning was demonstrated throughout his life. In his later diaries he constantly reports reading Latin, Greek, and Hebrew and occasionally mentions his own efforts at translating something from the classics. Christopher Glasscock found an apt pupil and left a profound impression upon him.

Byrd's father, a realistic businessman as well as a member of the aristocratic landed class in Virginia, had no notion of making a mere scholar of his son and heir. He realized that when the youth eventually inherited his estate he would have heavy responsibilities that required a knowledge of business as well as the cultivation expected of a gentleman. In this period, Virginia had no towns, and each great tobacco planter shipped tobacco directly from his own docks to his factor in London or Bristol; furthermore, he frequently bought tobacco from small farmers and sold them goods imported from England. Added to these normal transactions, William Byrd I had the responsibility of an extensive Indian trade that he had developed. All of these multifarious duties would in time devolve upon his only son, who had to be trained for his tasks. To this end, when William was sixteen, Byrd instructed his London factors, the merchant house of Perry & Lane, to send the boy to Holland for additional experience in business and trade. Apparently young Byrd did not like Holland, for he wrote his father asking permission to return to London. Whereupon Byrd replied that he had instructed Perry & Lane "to employ you about business wherein I hope you will endeavor to acquaint yourself that you may be no stranger to it when necessity will require you to attend to it." [2]

For two years after his return from Holland in 1690, young Byrd employed his time in the countinghouse of Perry & Lane learning what he could about the tobacco trade and the ways of business in the later years of the seventeenth century. But since his father did not intend his heir to become merely another London merchant, he saw to it that the youth entered the Middle Temple in April 1692, where in due course he was admitted to the bar.

The life of an incipient lawyer in one of the Inns of Court in the last decade of the seventeenth century was not dedicated exclusively to poring over Coke's *Reports* and other volumes interpreting English law. Some of the most illustrious families in Great Britain were represented in the membership of the Inns of Court, and many writers and other intellectuals of the day frequented the Inns, where they formed lasting friendships.

Byrd found the life congenial. Not only did he meet many Englishmen whose acquaintance served his ends in later years, but he found there other colonials with whom he formed useful friendships. Many years later, in 1735, Byrd wrote to Benjamin Lynde of Salem, Massachusetts, then a dignified judge, to recall their mutual escapades in the Middle Temple:

If I could persuade our captain of the guard ship to take a cruise to Boston at a proper season, I would come and beat up your quarters at Salem. I want to see what alteration forty years have wrought in you since we used to intrigue together in the Temple. But matrimony has atoned sufficiently for such backslidings, and now I suppose you have so little fellow feeling left for the naughty jades that you can order them a good whipping without any relenting. But though I should be mistaken, yet at least I hope

---

[2] Cited in Louis B. Wright, *The First Gentlemen of Virginia* (San Marino, Calif., 1940; paperback edition, University Press of Virginia, 1964), p. 321. This volume gives an account of the social background of Byrd and his contemporaries in Virginia.

your conscience with the aid of threescore-and-ten has gained a complete victory over your constitution, which is almost the case of, sir, your, &c.[3]

Almost but not quite, in Byrd's case, one should note incidentally, for in his diary for February 25, 1741, when he was sixty-seven, he notes that he "played the fool with Sarah, God forgive me. However, I prayed and had coffee." Other similar entries indicate that the habits of the gay life that he led at the Middle Temple lingered into old age.

Byrd's life at the Middle Temple served as a sort of literary apprenticeship, for, although he himself was not actively pursuing the profession of letters, he made the acquaintance at this time of several important writers, among them Charles Boyle (later the Earl of Orrery), William Congreve, William Wycherley, and Nicholas Rowe. Rowe was to become the first biographer of Shakespeare and the editor of his works. With such companions as these Byrd could hardly have avoided developing a taste for contemporary literature and the theater. We know from entries in his diaries that he frequently went to see plays, though, unlike Samuel Pepys, he rarely mentions the name of the play or his reaction to the performance.

Among his friends and acquaintances were also some who were interested in science, and Byrd managed to get himself elected to membership in the Royal Society on April 29, 1696. That a youth of twenty-two not yet known for any scientific accomplishments or literary activities should have been elected to this body of virtuosi argues some influence in high place, which, indeed, was true, for Byrd had cultivated the friendship of Sir Robert Southwell, Principal Secretary of State for Ireland, who served as president of the Royal Society from 1690 until 1696.

Byrd had a peculiar genius for picking the right people to be his friends, and his choice of Southwell illustrated this skill in the young Virginian. It was through Southwell's influence that Byrd met Sir Hans Sloane, Sir William Petty, and other scientific minds of the day. Byrd himself had a curiosity about natural philosophy and found

[3] Cited by Louis B. Wright in the introduction to *William Byrd of Virginia: The London Diary, 1717–1721*, edited by Louis B. Wright and Marion Tinling (New York, 1958), pp. 9–10. This introduction provides a succinct life of William Byrd incorporating recent discoveries concerning his career and background.

## William Byrd As a Young Man

*(This painting, by an unknown artist, is believed to be the earliest of the known portraits of Byrd; it may have been painted in London between 1692 and 1695, while Byrd was a member of the Middle Temple. Formerly at Westover, it now hangs in the Capitol at Williamsburg.)*

Westover As It Appears Today

Bookplate of William Byrd II

association with these men to his liking. He valued highly his membership in the Royal Society, and was much distressed in later years when his name happened to be omitted from a published list of members. To complain of this slight, he wrote to Sir Hans Sloane in 1641:

I take it a little unkindly, Sir, that my name is left out of the yearly list of the Royal Society, of which I have the honor to be one of its ancientest members. I suppose my long absence has made your secretaries rank me in the number of the dead, but pray let them know I am alive and by the help of ginseng hope to survive some years longer.[4]

Soon after his election, Byrd felt a compulsion to demonstrate his own qualifications by submitting a paper entitled "An Account of a Negro Boy That Is Dappled in Several Places of His Body with White Spots. By Will. Byrd, Esq., F.R.S.," which he read to the Society on November 17, 1697, and had published in the *Philosophical Transactions* (XIX, 781–782, London, 1698). It is not recorded that his essay made any important contribution to an understanding of albinism, but it did give evidence of his concern with natural phenomena.

During his years at the Middle Temple, Byrd probably tried his hand at writing light verse and translating bits from the classics, for we have evidence in the diaries of a later date that he amused himself from time to time in this way. At any rate, in one of his notebooks in the University of North Carolina Library he has left a short translation of the story of the Matron of Ephesus from the *Satyricon* of Petronius Arbiter. He may have been the collaborator of William Burnaby, a Middle Temple colleague, in the translation of Petronius published in 1694, *The Satyr of Titus Petronius Arbiter, a Roman Knight, with Its Fragments Recovered at Belgrade, 1688, Made English by Mr. Burnaby of the Middle Temple, and Another Hand.* In view of Byrd's long-continued interest in Petronius, as evidenced by his entries in the diaries, his may have been the other hand.

Besides these literary and scientific friends, Byrd also cultivated other men of prominence, including Charles Wager, knighted in 1709 and created First Lord of the Admiralty in 1733; John Campbell, who in 1703 became the second Duke of Argyll and in 1715 commanded

[4] Cited *ibid.*, p. 10.

the Hanoverian troops against the Jacobite rebels in Scotland; and John Percival, created Earl of Egmont in 1733 and an associate of General James Oglethorpe in the development of the colony of Georgia. With these and other important English aristocrats, Byrd kept up a correspondence long after his student days in London. Later he had the portraits of some of his titled English friends painted so that he could hang their likenesses in his house at Westover and impress his Virginia neighbors.

The education available to a well-bred young Virginian backed by a county family in Essex extended far beyond books and moot courts at the Middle Temple. Moving in the most sophisticated circles of London society, Byrd acquired the cultivation, the polish, the manners, and the vices of the beaux of his time. He also made the contacts that later would prove invaluable to him when he was appointed to represent his colony before the Board of Trade and other official bodies in England.

The senior William Byrd back in Virginia, anxious about his heir who had been absent so long, in 1696 called him home. To establish him properly among the best people, he contrived to have his son elected to the House of Burgesses as a representative from Henrico County. The young lawyer from the Middle Temple, more Englishman than Virginian, showed a quality of easy adaptation to his new environment that was characteristic of Byrd throughout his life. However much he enjoyed London and England, and though he spent many years there in his youth and afterward, he was able to resume plantation life without any evidence of unhappiness.

A Virginian with so many useful contacts in London could not hope to remain long at home, for the colonials had frequent need of an advocate in England. Consequently Byrd found himself on the way back to London in 1697, within a few months after he had served his first term in the House of Burgesses. The journey was dictated by a combination of personal business for his father and political activities for the Virginia Assembly and Governor Edmund Andros of Virginia. In April 1697 he presented an address from the Virginia Assembly to the Board of Trade, and in December he served as attorney for

Andros at a hearing called at Lambeth Palace by the Archbishop of Canterbury and the Bishop of London to consider complaints made by James Blair, Commissary of the Bishop of London in Virginia, that the Governor was blocking the Commissary's efforts to support the College of William and Mary and to improve the clergy in his jurisdiction.[5] This was the beginning of a long feud with James Blair, a stubborn Scot, who managed to get Andros recalled despite an able defense made by the twenty-three-year-old attorney.

During the next few years Byrd remained in London and, as agent for the colony, carried out various political missions. In a long controversy between the colony and Governor Francis Nicholson involving the respective prerogatives of the Virginia Assembly and the Governor, Byrd represented the Assembly against Nicholson,[6] who at last in 1705 was recalled. Nicholson during his governorship aroused the indignation of the Virginians by opposing the growing and processing of cotton and flax, which he feared might injure the English market for textiles. The Virginians, on their part, claimed that shipping was so difficult in time of war that they stood in danger of going naked unless they themselves took steps to produce textiles. Byrd and his brother-in-law, Robert Beverley the historian, both argued in behalf of the Virginia point of view, and Byrd made representations before the Board of Trade, but the London mercantilists were obdurate in their opposition. Though Byrd was not altogether successful in his efforts in behalf of the colony, he gained useful experience. Nicholson, however, achieved a modicum of revenge upon Byrd by dividing the office of auditor and receiver-general of quitrents, an office that the senior Byrd had held for years and had expected his son to inherit; this action resulted in a financial loss to the Byrds.

Although young Byrd was more at home in London than in Virginia, he was obliged to return to the place of his birth in 1705 to look after the inheritance that his father left at his death on December 4,

---

[5] For an account of this affair, see Louis B. Wright, "William Byrd's Defense of Sir Edmund Andros," *The William and Mary Quarterly*, 3rd Ser., 2:47–62 (January 1945).

[6] Details of this episode may be found in Louis B. Wright, "William Byrd's Opposition to Governor Francis Nicholson," *The Journal of Southern History*, 11:68–79 (February 1945).

1704. It was a princely estate that included more than twenty-six thousand acres of land. The home plantation at Westover alone contained fourteen thousand acres, with a comfortable manor house of wood, which William Byrd II rebuilt in brick. In addition to the land on the James at Westover, Byrd owned land farther up the river on the present site of Richmond.

The heir of this legacy quickly assumed the responsibilities and the privileges that had been his father's. He obtained the office of receiver-general of the colony's revenues and in 1709 took his seat on the Council of State, the highest official body in the colony and the goal of every member of the aristocratic ruling class.

In the meantime, on May 4, 1706, he married Lucy Parke, daughter of Daniel Parke, Governor of the Leeward Islands, a marriage that mingled affection with stormy quarrels. Parke had married a daughter of Philip Ludwell and owned land in Virginia. Lucy's sister Frances, who married John Custis, proved such a shrew that Custis had engraved on his own tombstone an epitaph declaring that his bachelor days were the only peace he knew before death. Byrd's father-in-law, who was killed in an insurrection in the Leeward Islands, left to Byrd's wife a legacy of £1,000, but to Custis' wife he bequeathed his lands, which Byrd had hoped to get. All his life, William Byrd was greedy for land.

Parke also left debts which had to be paid for out of the sale of a portion of his estate. Seeing an opportunity to obtain at least part of Parke's Virginia land, Byrd agreed to obligate himself to pay Parke's debts in exchange for the lands that would have to be sold. This agreement was a disaster for Byrd, who did not bother to ascertain in advance the extent of Parke's indebtedness. As a result he found himself burdened with financial obligations that persisted through most of his life.

For this period, when Byrd was adapting himself to the life of a Virginia planter, we have ample documentation in the first portion of his diary covering the years 1709–1712.[7] In the daily entries we can

[7] *The Secret Diary of William Byrd of Westover, 1709–1712*, edited by Louis B. Wright and Marion Tinling (Richmond, Va., 1941). An abridgment of this

follow the routine of a young married man eager to establish himself as a member of the ruling hierarchy with all the material wealth that went with his position. He is conscientious about his duties to the commonwealth, ambitious to improve his estate, attentive to all the details of managing his plantation, and concerned with maintaining his intellectual and literary interests. A passage for June 4, 1709, picked at random, illustrates his routine:

I rose at 5 o'clock and read a chapter in Hebrew and some Greek in Josephus. I said my prayers and ate milk for breakfast. I danced my dance [setting-up exercises that he took regularly]. My man Jack was pretty well. We made some wine of the common cherry for an experiment. It was extremely hot this day. I was out of humor with my wife for not minding her business. I ate roast shoat and sallet for dinner. In the afternoon I read some Latin and some Greek in Homer. In the evening Mr. C—s came to see me, who is a man of good understanding, and Ned Randolph brought me a letter from Mr. Bland in which he told me that the Lord Lovelace was dead at New York. We took a walk. I said my prayers and had good health, good thoughts, and good humor, thanks be to God Almighty.

This entry, like hundreds of others in his diaries, shows Byrd's devotion to learning, for throughout a long lifetime he kept up his Hebrew, Latin, and Greek, besides French, Italian, and Dutch, which he also read. In addition, it suggests an innate piety that remained with him through life, whatever his occasional lapses from moral rectitude may have been. His prayers were constant, and he had a taste for sermons as reading matter. For example, on Christmas night, 1710, he notes, "In the evening I read a sermon in Mr. Norris but a quarrel which I had with my wife hindered my taking much notice of it. However we were reconciled before we went to bed, but I made the first advance."

In August of 1709 Byrd notes that he is busy arranging books in his library, which was already one of the best in the colonies. Clearly he had spent many hours in England visiting bookshops. Eventually he collected more than 3,600 titles, a number only equaled at this time by the library of Cotton Mather in Boston. Curiously, these two men, so alien from one another in most ways, bought and read many

---

volume appears as *The Great American Gentleman: William Byrd of Westover in Virginia. His Secret Diary for the Years 1709-1712* (New York, 1963).

books on the same subjects. Byrd's library contained some 150 works of divinity, about the same as the number of his law books. Of Greek and Roman classics, in their original languages, he had nearly 300 titles, and he had probably the best collection of belles lettres, including contemporary drama, in the British colonies. Like other colonial libraries, Byrd's collection also had a number of utilitarian books, including an assortment of medical and scientific works. He fancied himself something of a physician and was constantly prescribing some remedy for his servants and neighbors. Byrd's library was the source of much pleasure and pride; he sometimes expressed annoyance because a chance visitor took him from his books; at other times he was delighted to show off his library, as on July 12, 1710, when he noted a visit by Dr. William Cocke and added, "The Doctor, who is a man of learning, was pleased with the library."

Byrd was too busy with plantation affairs and politics to turn his attention to many literary efforts during these years, but on at least one occasion his facility with the pen got him into trouble. During a meeting of the House of Burgesses in Williamsburg in November 1710, Byrd took it upon himself to write a satire of some of the members and their actions. On November 24, 1710, he notes:

I directed a letter to Nat Burwell with a lampoon in it and threw it into the capitol and Mr. [John] Simons found it and gave it him, which put the House of Burgesses into a ferment, but I discovered to nobody that I had a hand in it . . . About 4 o'clock we went to dinner and I ate boiled pork. Then we went to the coffeehouse where I played at cards and I lost my money but was diverted to see some of the burgesses so concerned at the lampoon.

The peace of anonymity and the enjoyment of the Burgesses' discomfiture ended with an untoward incident on November 26, which disclosed the authorship of the satire. After a session at the coffeehouse, Byrd writes: "Before we had been there long, in came George Mason [grandfather of the author of the Virginia Bill of Rights] very drunk and told me before all the company that it was I that wrote the lampoon and that Will Robertson dropped it. I put it off as well as I could but it was all in vain for he swore it." Previously the Burgesses had voted "that a scandalous paper lately found be privately kept by the clerk and that the author thereof, if discovered, be liable to the censure of this House."[8] The clerk kept the document so privately that this evidence of Byrd's literary quality has been lost to posterity.

Byrd's political ambitions led him in 1710 to attempt to procure the office of lieutenant governor for himself. The titular governor was the Earl of Orkney, who, like many who held colonial sinecures, was an absentee who ruled by deputy. The lieutenant governor of Virginia was therefore actually *de facto* governor, and the office was worth a high fee. An age which regarded as commonplace the sale of commissions in the army and navy and the auction of almost any office in the government saw nothing improper in William Byrd's bid of £1,000 for the lieutenant governorship of Virginia. Unhappily, the Duke of Marlborough, a veteran of the wars, declared that none but a soldier ought to govern a plantation overseas, and Byrd was disappointed. The appointment went to Alexander Spotswood, with whom Byrd had many political and personal controversies but at last managed to establish a friendship.

By late 1714 or early 1715 Byrd was again in England. Personal and public business dictated the journey; Byrd went with a mandate from some of the ruling hierarchy to complain to the Board of Trade about Spotswood's alleged usurpation of the rights of the colonists. A constant battle went on in Virginia between the Burgesses and Council and the Crown's representative concerning the respective prerogatives of each.

Byrd found quarters in a flat off the Strand and sent for his wife, who died the next year, 1716, of smallpox. A year later, his daughter Evelyn came over, followed by her younger sister, Wilhelmina, in 1719. Because a widower's quarters in London were not suitable for two daughters, he placed them with friends and relatives, but he himself carefully supervised their bringing-up. Byrd remained in England until late in 1720. These years are also well documented by an extant diary.

[8] *Journals of the House of Burgesses of Virginia*, edited by H. R. McIlwaine (Richmond, Va., 1918–19), volume for 1702–1712, p. 281.

Much of Byrd's energy in this period was expended in pursuit of an heiress. Between fortune-hunting by day and the search for less honorable game by night, Byrd managed to lead a full life — which he carefully records in his diary, even to the occasional rebuffs that he suffered.

The heiress whom Byrd selected as the most promising was one Mary Smith, daughter of John Smith, a commissioner of excise, a wealthy and proud citizen of London with lands in Lincolnshire. She lived in Beaufort Street, across from Byrd's own quarters, from which he could occasionally wave to the elusive object of his affection and interest. The course of this courtship can be charted in the diary and in a series of faintly disguised letters in which Byrd designates Mary as Sabina and her father as Vigilante. The ardent lover of forty-three reveals in his letters the conventional swing between happiness and dejection, depending upon the expression of favor or coolness shown by the coquettish Mary. In the end her father demanded a financial statement from her colonial suitor and rejected him outright in favor of a more opulent baronet. Byrd's envious disappointment was not eased when Mary's father died three days after her marriage and the baronet came into possession of her fortune.

During this period of courtship, Byrd was not without other, less reticent feminine consolation, as he often notes in his diary. For a time he kept as mistress a certain Mrs. A-l-c, to whom he paid a fee of two guineas a visit, until at last he brought himself to dismiss her for infidelity. Not one to waste an opportunity for an amour, on October 4, 1718, he makes this entry: "Then I went to visit Mrs. A-l-n and committed uncleanness with the maid because the mistress was not at home. However when the mistress came I rogered her and about 12 o'clock went home and ate a plum cake for supper. I neglected my prayers, for which God forgive me." With no more discrimination than James Boswell was later to show, Byrd was not above picking up a stray wench in St. James's Park and consummating the affair in the weeds nearby. As a result he was forced to undergo a course of treatment for gonorrhea, but even this only temporarily curbed his zest for illicit amours.

Although Byrd was consistently promiscuous during his years in London, he was not without conscience and, after recording some notable encounter, he frequently appends this phrase, "may God forgive me." And in spite of his amorous activities, he was extraordinarily busy about other matters. He carefully cultivated politicians who could be of help to Virginia and Virginians and was a frequent visitor to coffeehouses where merchants and politicians could be found, the Virginia Coffeehouse, Will's Coffeehouse, and St. James's Coffeehouse being his favorite haunts. He also took part in various social affairs, masquerade balls, theater parties, and visits to the Spanish Ambassador's, where there was habitual gambling. Byrd does not appear to have been lucky, and records more losses than winnings. He also conscientiously visited his daughters and was periodically engaged in business conversation with Micajah Perry, the leading merchant in the Virginia trade and Byrd's own factor. On November 17, 1718, as agent for the colony of Virginia, Byrd had an audience with King George I.

Byrd had been earnestly laying petitions before the Board of Trade and had made an appeal to the Crown to prevent Governor Spotswood from establishing courts of oyer and terminer and appointing the judges, a move that the Virginia ruling class believed would curtail their own rights and liberties. In the end the King upheld Spotswood, and Byrd had to agree that the Council would quit feuding and make peace with the lieutenant governor. Spotswood was anxious to have Byrd removed from the Council on the grounds of his long absence from Virginia, but Byrd received assurances that as the price of peace he would have the support of the Board of Trade in keeping his place on the Council.

The diary for 1717–1721 frequently records that Byrd was writing something, although the writer usually does not specify what form of composition was engaging his interest. On June 18, 1718, he notes:

Then we went to Mrs. D-n-s where we drank tea and ate sweet biscuits. I read several things to them out of my book and we stayed till 10 o'clock and then took leave. Then we went to the coffeehouse and read the news and about eleven I went home and said my prayers.

The next day he recorded that "after dinner I wrote some English till five." He was busy "writing English" during this period, but what he put into "his book" remains a matter of conjecture.

During a stay at the fashionable watering place of Tunbridge Wells in the summer of 1719, however, Byrd was slightly more specific about his literary activities. On August 24, 1719, he makes this entry in his diary:

I rose about 7 o'clock and read a chapter in Hebrew and some Greek. I neglected my prayers, and had milk for breakfast. I danced my dance and read some English and then wrote some verses upon four ladies . . . About 10 o'clock I took a walk and met with a woman and kissed her exceedingly. Then I went home and said my prayers.

The verses that he was writing appeared under the pseudonym of "Mr. Burrard," in a thin little volume entitled *Tunbrigalia: or, Tunbridge Miscellanies, For the Year 1719* (London, 1719). Ladies to whom Byrd addressed compliments in verse in this volume included the Duchess of Montague, Lady Hinchinbrooke, Lady Percival, Lady Ranelagh, and other fashionable visitors to Tunbridge Wells.[9] Much of his effort in this period was devoted to satirical and occasional verse. On August 4, 1719, he notes: "I wrote some verses to ridicule Mr. Buckhurst's panegyrics." On several consecutive days, August 16–19, he continued to report that he "wrote some English," without specifying what, but on August 25 he

wrote verses all the morning till 1 o'clock and then went upon the Walk . . . After dinner Molly the fruit girl came and Mr. C-r-v-n and I kissed her. Then I went home and wrote some English till six and then returned to the Walk and won a little at the ace of hearts . . . About twelve I went home and neglected to say my prayers.

Some of Byrd's literary efforts in this period were evidently devoted to a prose description of Virginia, for on November 20, 1719, he made this comment: "I went to Lord Islay's where I stayed till 12 o'clock and then went to the Duke of Argyll's but he was from home; but I

[9] These verses have been reprinted in *Another Secret Diary of William Byrd of Westover, 1739–1741*, edited by Maude H. Woodfin and Marion Tinling (Richmond, Va., 1942), pp. 397–409.

left the description of Virginia for him and gave my Lord Islay another." Islay was the Duke of Argyll's brother, and Byrd was cultivating both of them assiduously. In the preface to the 1741 edition of John Oldmixon's *The British Empire in America*, the author states that he has used a history of Virginia "written with a great deal of spirit and judgment by a gentleman of the province, . . . Colonel Byrd, whom I knew when I was in the Temple." A number of years after Byrd left his description of Virginia with the Duke of Argyll, Samuel Jenner published in Berne, Switzerland, a descriptive volume on Virginia, based on notes provided by Byrd and bearing the title *Neu-gefundenes Eden* (1737), which has been translated and published by R. C. Beatty and W. J. Mulloy as *William Byrd's Natural History of Virginia* (Richmond, 1940). This book, frankly a promotional tract to lure settlers to Byrd's lands on the North Carolina border, may have been an adaptation of the work that he supplied the Duke of Argyll and John Oldmixon. At any rate, Byrd was interested in writing about Virginia even before his longest extant narrative, the account of running the dividing line between Virginia and North Carolina, was composed.

Although Byrd must have found it hard to tear himself away from the pleasant life of London and Tunbridge Wells, at length he found it necessary to think of Virginia, and on November 24, 1719, he embarked at Dover with two English maids, Annie and Hannah, upon whom from time to time he laid amorous hands. On February 2, 1720, his ship rounded the Virginia capes and came to anchor. Weary of the sea and unwilling to wait until a favorable wind might take them to his own dock at Westover, Byrd had the captain put him ashore and traveled overland to Westover, which he reached on February 13.

During the next year, Byrd busied himself with many details of plantation life. His garden and his library were his particular delights, and he apparently spent considerable effort in restoring or remodeling the plantation house, for the diary mentions the arrival of a shipload of shingles and the payment to a bricklayer for his work. As a member of the Council, Byrd took part in the political affairs of the colony and during this period managed to patch up his relations with Governor Spotswood, with whom he had long conducted a political feud.

The diary continued to note that the author was "writing English," and we know from specific entries that Byrd was engaged in preparing a treatise on the plague. On March 26, 1721, for instance, Colonel Nathaniel Harrison came over for Sunday morning breakfast at Westover and Byrd "read some of my plague book to him." On April 4, 1721, he turned over the manuscript to a ship captain bound for London, with instructions to deliver it to his agent, Micajah Perry, who apparently saw to its publication. That year there appeared in London *A Discourse Concerning the Plague with Some Preservatives Against It. By a Lover of Mankind*, "printed for J. Roberts near the Oxford Arms in Warwick Lane." From the style it is evident that the "Lover of Mankind" who wrote the *Discourse* was William Byrd. If this indeed is Byrd's treatise, it is the only complete book that he saw through the press during his lifetime.

*The Discourse Concerning the Plague* must have been pleasing to Virginia tobacco planters, for it concludes with an eloquent declaration of the virtue of tobacco as a panacea against infection. "I am humbly of opinion," the author writes,

that when there is any danger of pestilence, we can't more effectually consult our preservation than by providing ourselves with a reasonable quantity of fresh, strong scented tobacco. We should wear it about our clothes and about our coaches. We should hang bundles of it round our beds, and in the apartments wherein we most converse. If we have an aversion to smoking, it would be very prudent to burn some leaves of tobacco in our dining rooms lest we swallow infection with our meat. It will also be very useful to take snuff plentifully made of the pure leaf to secure the passages to our brain. Nor must those only be guarded but the pass to our stomachs should be also safely defended by chewing this great antipoison very frequently.[10]

In 1721 Byrd received another appointment as agent for the colony of Virginia, and in the summer of that year he sailed again for England, where, as it turned out, he would remain for the next five years. Since we have no diary entries for these years, we cannot follow him

[10] *Ibid.*, p. 442.

closely, but a few records and letters indicate his activities. He made representations before the Board of Trade on various matters and was busy about his own affairs, particularly about his father-in-law's debts that he had agreed to pay. He also renewed his search for an heiress, but in the end, after pursuing various prospects, he married Maria Taylor, of Kensington, who brought him no fortune. Nevertheless, she made him a good wife, displayed a far more equable disposition than his first wife, Lucy, and bore him four children, including William, his son and heir.

In 1726 Byrd came back to Westover, where he remained for the rest of his life. Again, although he was thoroughly at home in England, he showed no reluctance to resuming his life on a Virginia plantation and quickly fell into the routine of a member of the ruling aristocracy of the province. To his friends in London he described his life as something approaching a pastoral idyl. "Thus, my Lord," he wrote to the Earl of Orrery on July 5, 1726, "we are very happy in our Canaans if we could but forget the onions and fleshpots of Egypt." His daughters, Evelyn and Wilhelmina, whom he also brought back to Virginia, found it somewhat harder to adjust; Byrd comments in a letter on February 2, 1727, "My young gentlewomen like everything in the country except the retirement; they can't get the plays, the operas, and the masquerades out of their heads; much less can they forget their friends." [11]

As a duty to the colony of Virginia, Byrd accepted in 1728 the headship of a commission appointed to settle a long-standing boundary dispute between Virginia and North Carolina. The Virginia commissioners planned to meet a similar commission appointed by North Carolina and actually to survey the line and make a map plainly showing the border. The survey was made in the spring and autumn of 1728, and it was upon the experiences of this expedition that Byrd based *The History of the Dividing Line betwixt Virginia and North Carolina, Run in the Year of Our Lord 1728*, his most extensive literary work.

This account, published by Edmund Ruffin in 1841 from a manu-

[11] Cited in *London Diary*, p. 38.

script copied by an amanuensis and corrected by Byrd himself, was expanded from rough notes that Byrd made on the spot. Other members of the party perhaps kept notes that Byrd may have consulted in the preparation of his own narrative. He also wrote another literary account of the expedition with the title *The Secret History of the Line*, which was not published until W. K. Boyd's edition in 1929 from the original manuscript preserved in the library of the American Philosophical Society in Philadelphia.[12] In this version Byrd is franker in some of his comments than in the *History*. In the *Secret History* he uses descriptive pseudonyms for the participants in the expedition, and this gives him license to report their shortcomings with considerably more freedom than he employs in the *History*.

Two other, much briefer reports, hardly more than rough notes, exist in manuscript. They apparently were sent to London as early reports on the survey. One, called "a Journal of the Dividing line . . . [by] Colo. Byrd & Others," is preserved in the British Museum, and the second, entitled "A Journal of the proceedings of the Commissioners . . . ," is in the Public Record Office in London. Neither is in Byrd's handwriting. The first, by "Colonel Byrd and others," is short, ungrammatical, and much abbreviated. The second, the "Journal of the Proceedings," appears to be a somewhat expanded version of the first and must have been the official report submitted by Byrd. A study of these two reports indicates that Byrd used them in expanding his account into the two "literary" narratives, the *History* and the *Secret History*.

In the present edition of Byrd's literary prose, the editor has made an effort to eliminate corruptions that crept into earlier texts. Ruffin's edition was carelessly printed on cheap newsprint paper. The next edition, that by Thomas H. Wynne, *History of the Dividing Line and Other Tracts from the Papers of William Byrd of Westover, in Virginia, Esquire* (2 vols., Richmond, 1866), was more carefully compared with the manuscript, but it too has many errors that have been perpetuated in later editions, even the editions by Boyd and the

[12] *William Byrd's Histories of the Dividing Line betwixt Virginia and North Carolina*, edited by William K. Boyd (Raleigh, N.C., 1929).

handsomely printed version edited by John Spencer Bassett, *The Writings of Colonel William Byrd of Westover in Virginia* (New York, 1901). Although no editor can hope to avoid misreadings, the present edition at least has had a careful collation with the earliest extant version of Byrd's writings, known as the Westover Manuscripts, acquired in 1962 by the Virginia Historical Society, and with the manuscript of the *Secret History* in the American Philosophical Society. A hiatus in the *Secret History* manuscript has been supplied by the collation of two fragments, one in the Huntington Library and another in the Blathwayt Papers at Colonial Williamsburg. Another manuscript of the *History* exists in the American Philosophical Society, evidently a fair copy made by an amanuensis, probably from a lost original. The two manuscript versions of the *History*, that in the Westover Manuscripts and that in the American Philosophical Society, have many slight variations in phraseology. Corrections in the Westover Manuscripts in a hand that looks like Byrd's indicate that the author himself revised this version. It is this manuscript that is the basis of the present edition.

An attempt was made by the American Philosophical Society beginning about 1816 to publish Byrd's *History of the Dividing Line*. The project originated with the gift to the Society in 1815 of a manuscript of the *History*, presented by Mrs. E. C. Izard, a great-granddaughter of the author. The task was undertaken by the Literary Committee, consisting of Peter S. DuPonceau, J. Correa de Serra, and Dr. Caspar Wistar, who recommended its publication because of the "important and curious information that it affords" and the information on "the state of civilization of these states about the middle of last century."[13] Since the Committee discovered that their manuscript had several pages missing, they sought the help of Mrs. Izard and Thomas Jefferson in locating other copies of the document that might supply the missing pages. On January 27, 1817, Jefferson wrote that he had borrowed a manuscript and would supply the gaps, but it turned out that the manuscript in his possession was that of the *Secret*

---

[13] A more detailed discussion of the manuscripts in the American Philosophical Society and the early plans for publication will be found in the Appendix.

*History*; later he forwarded this manuscript to the Society with the permission of the *de facto* executor of the Byrd estate, Benjamin Harrison, who offered to help find a copy of the *History* that might supply the lost leaves. The manuscript of the *Secret History* was never returned and remains to this day in the library of the American Philosophical Society. In January 1818, Harrison wrote Jefferson that he had located the manuscript of the *History* in the possession of George Evelyn Harrison at Brandon and would lend it to Jefferson to copy the required pages, provided that Jefferson would undertake not to let it leave his hands. Whereupon Jefferson again wrote to DuPonceau that he would have the pages copied, which he did. For reasons that do not appear, the American Philosophical Society did not carry through its intention of publishing the *History of the Dividing Line* and the matter was allowed to drop, to be revived in 1834, when a committee was appointed to determine whether any portion of the Byrd material might be published in the Society's *Transactions*. After reading the documents, the committee reported that "the style and manner in which they are written forbid their publication as a whole, and . . . even extracts or a review of them, though they might amuse elsewhere, would not be in their place in the *Transactions* of our Society." Someone, whether this committee or an earlier editor, went through the manuscript and "improved" the diction by substituting more elegant words for homely expressions. Even so, the style was too racy for the staid dignity of the American Philosophical Society in the year 1834.

The document that the philosophers of 1834 found improper for their transactions is indeed a brisk, uninhibited, entertaining, and sometimes satirical account of the joint expedition of the Virginia and North Carolina commissioners who surveyed the boundary in 1728. As one would expect from the pen of a man who had been the friend and associate of writers of Restoration and Augustan London, Byrd's prose is sophisticated and urbane. It reads as if it might have been written by a Londoner, for Byrd automatically chooses similes that are reminiscent of his life in England. For example, in describing a bivouac, he says the men lay around their campfire "like so many

Knights Templars," a figure suggested by the effigies on the tombs in the Temple Church, where he had walked many times while a resident in the Middle Temple; two horses that had strayed were found standing "as motionless as the equestrian statue at Charing Cross." These similes came naturally to one who had had long experience in England; furthermore Byrd was probably consciously writing with an English audience in mind.

His satirical commentary on some of his fellow commissioners from North Carolina and upon North Carolinians generally has not endeared the writer to sensitive citizens of that commonwealth. When the North Carolina commissioners arrived, Byrd observed that they had come "better provided for the belly than the business" and "not above two men . . . would put their hands to anything but the kettle and the frying pan." His commentary upon the laziness of the North Carolinians has been often cited:

Surely there is no place in the world where the inhabitants live with less labor than in North Carolina. It approaches nearer to the description of Lubberland than any other, by the great felicity of the climate, the easiness of raising provisions, and the slothfulness of the people . . . The men, for their parts, just like the Indians, impose all the work upon the poor women. They make their wives rise out of their beds early in the morning, at the same time that they lie and snore till the sun has risen one-third of his course and dispersed all the unwholesome damps. Then, after stretching and yawning for half an hour, they light their pipes, and, under the protection of a cloud of smoke, venture out into the open air; though if it happen to be never so little cold they quickly return shivering to the chimney corner. When the weather is mild, they stand leaning with both their arms upon the cornfield fence and gravely consider whether they had best go and take a small heat at the hoe but generally find reasons to put it off till another time. Thus they loiter away their lives, like Solomon's sluggard, with their arms across, and at the winding up of the year scarcely have bread to eat. To speak the truth, 'tis a thorough aversion to labor that makes people file off to North Carolina, where plenty and a warm sun confirm them in their disposition to laziness for their whole lives.

Of Edenton, Byrd is equally satirical:

There may be forty or fifty houses, most of them small and built without expense. A citizen here is counted extravagant if he has ambition enough to aspire to a brick chimney. Justice herself is but indifferently lodged, the courthouse having much the air of a common tobacco house. I believe this is the only metropolis in the Christian or Mahometan world where there is neither church, chapel, mosque, synagogue, or any other place of worship of any sect or religion whatsoever. What little devotion there may happen to be is much more private than their vices. The people seem easy without a minister as long as they are exempted from paying him. Sometimes the Society for Propagating the Gospel has had the charity to send over missionaries to this country; but, unfortunately, the priest has been too lewd for the people, or, which often happens, they too lewd for the priest. For these reasons these reverend gentlemen have always left their flocks as arrant heathen as they found them.

Byrd's narrative displays the keen and amused observations of a man interested in the world about him. Indeed, wherever he found himself, whether in the center of London society or on the borders of the Dismal Swamp, Byrd was never bored; he always found something in his environment to attract his attention, to entertain him, and to be worth a comment. As a member of the Royal Society and a virtuoso himself, he was fascinated by the curiosities of nature that he encountered on the survey of the border. His observations are still of use to students concerned with the plant and animal ecologies of colonial Virginia and North Carolina. When Byrd discovered some new or interesting animal or plant, it usually called forth a comment that reflected his past reading and his stored knowledge. From Pliny, Olaus Magnus, and other writers, he had picked up traditional lore about animals that found its way into the *History*. For instance, he tells a tale that had often appeared in earlier writers of the squirrel's ingenuity in crossing a stream by launching a chip and hoisting its tail as a sail; and he relates a bit of ancient lore about the alligator, which swallows rocks in order to sink to the bottom more readily.

As a practical explorer and planter, Byrd was eager to find good land for exploitation, minerals that would be profitable, and plants and animals that might prove beneficial. After describing a buffalo that the party's hunters discovered, Byrd commented: "Buffaloes may be easily tamed when they are taken young . . . If we could get into a breed of them they might be made very useful, not only for the dairy, by giving an ocean of milk, but also for drawing vast and cumbersome weights by their prodigious strength."

Of all the plants that Byrd found on the survey, he became more enthusiastic about ginseng than any other. Indeed, he remained for the rest of his life an advocate of ginseng as a sort of panacea and restorative. At one point in the *History*, he remarked:

Though practice will soon make a man of tolerable vigor an able footman, yet, as a help to bear fatigue, I used to chew a root of ginseng as I walked along. This kept up my spirits and made me trip away as nimbly in my half-jack boots as younger men could do in their shoes. This plant is in high esteem in China, where it sells for its weight in silver. Indeed, it does not grow there but in the mountains of Tartary, to which place the Emperor of China sends ten thousand men every year on purpose to gather it. But it grows so scatteringly there that even so many hands can bring home no great quantity. Indeed, it is a vegetable of so many virtues that Providence has planted it very thin in every country that has the happiness to produce it . . . It grows also on the northern continent of America, near the mountains, but as sparingly as truth and public spirit . . . Its virtues are that it gives an uncommon warmth and vigor to the blood and frisks the spirits beyond any other cordial. It cheers the heart even of a man that has a bad wife and makes him look down with great composure on the crosses of the world. It promotes insensible perspiration, dissolves all phlegmatic and viscous humors, that are apt to obstruct the narrow channels of the nerves. It helps the memory and would quicken even Helvetian dullness . . . However, 'tis of little use in the feats of love, as a great prince once found, who, hearing of its invigorating quality, sent as far as China for some of it, though his ladies could not boast of any advantage thereby.

Byrd's language is simple, direct, concrete, and idiomatic; his sentences are usually short and unencumbered with awkward constructions; and his paragraphs frequently build up to some striking statement or humorous comment. For instance, a routine account of the party's arrival at a lone farmhouse where they planned to spend the night gives a crisp and entertaining bit of information in a short paragraph:

We had but two miles more to Captain Embry's, where we found the housekeeping much better than the house. Our bountiful landlady had set her oven and all her spits, pots, gridirons, and saucepans to work to diversify our entertainment, though after all it proved but a Mahometan feast, there being nothing to drink but water. The worst of it was we had unluckily outrid the baggage and for that reason were obliged to lodge very sociably in the same apartment with the family, where, reckoning women and children, we mustered in all no less than nine persons, who all pigged lovingly together.

Byrd's commentary on the Indians that the party met holds more than passing interest, for in it he argues for miscegenation as the way to solve the Indian problem, an argument that his brother-in-law Robert Beverley also made in the *The History and Present State of Virginia* (1705). Speaking of the poor success of the whites in Christianizing the Indians, Byrd remarks:

I am sorry I can't give a better account of the state of the poor Indians with respect to Christianity, although a great deal of pains has been and still continues to be taken with them. For my part, I must be of opinion, as I hinted before, that there is but one way of converting these poor infidels and reclaiming them from barbarity, and that is charitably to intermarry with them, according to the modern policy of the Most Christian King in Canada and Louisiana. Had the English done this at the first settlement of the colony, the infidelity of the Indians had been worn out at this day with their dark complexions, and the country had swarmed with people more than it does with insects. It was certainly an unreasonable nicety that prevented their entering into so good-natured an alliance. All nations of men have the same natural dignity, and we all know that very bright talents may be lodged under a very dark skin. The principal difference between one people and another proceeds only from the different opportunities of improvement. The Indians by no means want understanding and are in their figure tall and well proportioned. Even their copper-colored complexion would admit of blanching, if not in the first, at the farthest in the second, generation. I may safely venture to say, the Indian women would have made altogether as honest wives for the first planters as the damsels they used to purchase from aboard the ships. 'Tis strange, therefore, that any good Christian should have refused a wholesome, straight bedfellow when he might have had so fair a portion with her as the merit of saving her soul.

Both for content and style, Byrd's *History* is a landmark in colonial writing. Few other contemporary documents are so "civilized," so entertaining, and so modern in tone and point of view.

The *Secret History* is hardly more than half as long as the *History* and was probably written first and designed for a more restricted group of readers. Although it disguises the names of the participants under such names as Steddy (Byrd himself), Meanwell (William Dandridge, one of the Virginia commissioners), Firebrand (Richard Fitzwilliam, another of the Virginia commissioners), and Dr. Humdrum (Peter Fontaine, the chaplain), the document is much more explicit than the *History* about the characteristics of the individuals taking part in the expedition, their quarrels and conflicts of interest, and various episodes including incidents involving violence to women on the frontier. The *Secret History* contains some preliminary letters exchanged between the Virginia and North Carolina commissioners and other documents not included in the *History*.

That the Virginians and North Carolinians would not work in harmony might have been predicted from the beginning. For one thing, they were trying to settle a long-standing quarrel: the controversy over the boundary that had exacerbated feelings on both sides for many years. Both Virginia and North Carolina claimed certain territory in the border region, and both jurisdictions had from time to time tried to collect taxes from the inhabitants of the disputed territory.[14] The second charter granted to North Carolina (1665) declared that the boundary should run "from the north end of Currituck River or Inlet upon a straight westerly line to Weyanoke Creek, which lies within or about the degrees of 36 and 30' northern latitude, and so west in a direct line as far as the South Seas." The problem in 1728 was to locate "Weyanoke" Creek, which had lost its identity with the passage of years. It was finally agreed that Nottoway River was meant, and the survey was run that way. But this agreement did not come without argument, which is related in the *Secret History*.

The *Secret History* shares with the *History* its racy quality and idiomatic expression. The uninhibited frankness gives additional

[14] Boyd, *William Byrd's Histories*, pp. xvi ff, gives a succinct account of the boundary dispute.

piquancy to this narrative, particularly in Byrd's characterization of his associates. For instance:

We found Shoebrush [John Lovick, one of the North Carolina commissioners] a merry good-humored man, and had learnt a very decent behavior from Governor Hyde, to whom he had been *valet de chambre*, of which he still carried the marks by having his coat, waistcoat, and breeches of different parishes. Puzzlecause [William Little, another North Carolina commissioner] had degenerated from a New England preacher, for which his godly parents designed him, to a very wicked but awkward rake.

Byrd's observations during this survey whetted his appetite for frontier land to such a degree that he obtained from North Carolina 20,000 acres at the confluence of the Dan and Irvin rivers. Much later he acquired another 6,000 acres adjoining this property. To this territory he gave the name of the Land of Eden. Between 1730 and 1738, Byrd acquired 5,211 acres at the confluence of the Dan and Staunton rivers. Finally, in 1742 he took up 105,000 acres of frontier land on the borders of North Carolina and about the same time bought a plantation on the Meherrin River consisting of 2,429 acres. By the time of his death in 1744, Byrd was the owner of a total of 179,440 acres; to the end of his life, the appetite for land remained unsatisfied. He even conceived a project to drain the Great Dismal Swamp and turn it into a vast plantation for hemp and other products. To advance this project Byrd wrote, apparently soon after the completion of the survey of the dividing line, "A Description of the Dismal," which was published by Edmund Ruffin at Petersburg in the *Farmer's Register*, IV (1836). At the time, Ruffin reported that "The manuscript, in our charge, is the original, in the handwriting of the author — and though time worn, and requiring much care to handle without injury, is perfectly legible. It is here copied literally." Apparently the fragile manuscript has been lost. Ruffin's version was edited in 1922 by Dr. Earl Gregg Swem and issued in an edition of sixty-one copies by Charles F. Heartman of Metuchen, New Jersey. The whole document consists of only thirty-two pages of large print. Byrd includes descriptive material that he used in the *History of the Dividing Line* and adds some estimates of cost, with a copy of a petition to the King asking him to grant to the petitioners the "large bog . . . that corrupts the air of all the neighboring country by the noxious vapors that perpetually ascend from it." After estimating the expense in money and slaves, Byrd remarks that "we may safely conclude that each share will then [after the draining of the swamp] be worth more than ten times the value of the original subscription, besides the unspeakable benefit it will prove to the public."

Nothing came of Byrd's project to drain the Dismal Swamp, but the scheme continued to excite the activity of his heirs and successors. George Washington was concerned with a plan to drain the swamp which was under discussion both before and after the Revolution. In fact, it was the continued talk of draining the Dismal Swamp that prompted Edmund Ruffin to take an interest in Byrd's manuscripts and to print the first edition of the *History of the Dividing Line*. His initial intention was evidently to extract only those portions dealing with the Dismal Swamp, but his interest was captured by the document as a whole.

Two shorter pieces of prose from Byrd's pen, similar in tone to the *History of the Dividing Line*, have appeared in editions of Byrd's works since Ruffin's time. They are *A Journey to the Land of Eden in the Year 1733* and *A Progress to the Mines in the Year 1732*. The previous versions of Byrd's prose have printed them in this reverse chronological order, which is the way they appear in the Westover Manuscripts. In the present edition they are printed in their chronological order.

In the early autumn of 1732 Byrd made the journey that he described in *A Progress to the Mines*. On September 18, he set out from Westover accompanied by Mrs. Byrd and their young son "in the chariot." After a picnic lunch on the road, his companions turned back and Byrd continued alone on horseback to the site of Richmond, where he found his water mills idle because of a drought. He continued his journey by easy stages to Fredericksburg and Germanna, where Colonel Alexander Spotswood, the former governor and Byrd's political rival, was operating iron mines which Byrd wished to see.

He writes in an easy, gossipy manner of his adventures along the way. At Tuckahoe, the Randolph plantation near Richmond, he was graciously received by the Widow Randolph, who told him a sad story of her daughter's elopement with an uncle's overseer, an Irishman without "one visible qualification except impudence to recommend him to a female's inclination." Marooned at Tuckahoe by a three days' rainstorm, he found a copy of *The Beggar's Opera* in the Randolph library and read it aloud to the family. "Thus we killed the time and triumphed over the bad weather," he adds.

His next stop after leaving Tuckahoe was at the house of Charles Chiswell, "a sensible, well-bred man, and very frank in communicating his knowledge of the mystery of making iron, wherein he has had long experience." Byrd's interest was now in the smelting of iron, but some years before he had other designs on the Chiswell family. In his diary for November 2, 1709, he had noted:

I played at [r–m] with Mrs. Chiswell and kissed her on the bed till she was angry and my wife also was uneasy about it, and cried as soon as the company was gone. I neglected to say my prayers, which I should not have done because I ought to beg pardon for the lust I had for another man's wife.

Now, nearly a quarter of a century later, he comments sadly on the ravages of time, perhaps recalling that earlier romantic moment:

I had not seen Mrs. Chiswell in twenty-four years, which, alas! had made great havoc with her pretty face and plowed very deep furrows in her fair skin. It was impossible to know her again, so much the flower was faded. However, though she was grown an old woman, yet she was one of those absolute rarities, a very good old woman.

Byrd no longer had eyes for Mrs. Chiswell, but he talked earnestly with his friend Mr. Chiswell about iron smelting, a secret to stop the fermentation of any liquor, and a method of keeping weevils out of wheat and other grain. He enjoyed the hospitality of the Chiswells and "after saying some very civil things to Mrs. Chiswell for my handsome entertainment, I mounted my horse and Mr. Chiswell his phaeton, in order to go to the mines at Fredericksville [Fredericksburg]."

Byrd's destination was Colonel Spotswood's home at Germanna, which he reached on September 27.

This famous town consists of Colonel Spotswood's enchanted castle on one side of the street and a baker's dozen of ruinous tenements on the other, where so many German families had dwelt some years ago, but are now removed ten miles higher, in the fork of Rappahannock, to land of their own,

he comments. The hospitality of Colonel and Mrs. Spotswood was unbounded, and Byrd enjoyed his stay at Germanna visiting a man with whom he was now happily reconciled and on terms of intimate friendship. The passages telling of his days at Germanna provide a charming picture of life in Virginia in the first third of the eighteenth century.

Byrd was prompted to write *A Journey to the Land of Eden in the Year 1733* by his experiences in surveying lands that he had acquired in the border region. During the survey of the dividing line, he had had an opportunity to observe the quality of the terrain on the border, and the sight had aroused his land-hunger. From the North Carolina commissioners, who had received frontier land in payment for their services, Byrd bought the 20,000 acres at the confluence of the Dan and Irvin rivers which he christened "the Land of Eden." It was to survey this estate that he set out with a party of friends on September 11, 1733. From this time onward until the end of his life he was eagerly seeking to acquire more frontier land and trying to induce colonists to settle on his holdings.

The people whom Byrd preferred for his lands were Swiss, and he made persistent efforts to lure Swiss settlers to his new Eden. In the years following the acquisition of land on the Dan River on the North Carolina side of the border, he had taken up even larger holdings on the Virginia side in the Dan and Roanoke valleys, and it was for these lands that he sought colonists. Byrd was emphatic in his preference for Swiss instead of the Scotch-Irish who were threatening to swarm down from Pennsylvania "like the Goths and Vandals of old." [15] A

[15] Richmond C. Beatty and William J. Mulloy (eds.), *William Byrd's Natural History of Virginia or The Newly Discovered Eden*, edited and translated from a German version (Richmond, Va., 1940), p. xxii.

correspondence with a certain Mr. Ochs about Swiss colonists began hopefully, but Ochs was not able to deliver any Switzers.

A more promising effort was made in July 1736, when Byrd made a contract with Samuel Jenner, of Berne, an authorized agent of the Helvetian Society, for the sale of 33,400 acres on the Roanoke River. He gave a receipt to Samuel Tschiffeli on January 9, 1737, for £3,000 in payment for this land. To promote the enterprise, Byrd supplied Jenner with notes for the description of Virginia that was published in Berne in 1737 with the title *Neu-gefundenes Eden*. Byrd's name was translated in Jenner's document as Wilhelm Vogel. His description of the delights of life in Virginia and the prosperity to be expected in so fruitful a country would do credit to the most zealous real estate promoter. Some 250 emigrants left Switzerland in the winter of 1738, but they suffered shipwreck off the coast of Virginia and only a few "unhappy wretches," Byrd reported, survived to reach his lands. Although he again tried to get Swiss or German settlers, he failed to attract an appreciable number of these colonists and was at last driven to seek Scots.

The narrative of his visit to the border lands in *A Journey to the Land of Eden* is informative, lively, and entertaining. The party surveyed Byrd's North Carolina holdings and then explored his other lands on the Roanoke River. On September 19, after a strenuous day of paddling up and down the river, Byrd returned to camp and apparently spent the evening drawing plans for cities that he expected to create on the James and Appomattox rivers. "When we got home," he comments,

we laid the foundation of two large cities: one at Shacco's, to be called Richmond, and the other at the point of Appomattox River, to be called Petersburg. These Major Mayo offered to lay out into lots without fee or reward. The truth of it is, these two places, being the uppermost land of [the] James and Appomattox rivers, are naturally intended for marts where the traffic of the outer inhabitants must center. Thus we did not build castles only, but also cities in the air.

While Major Mayo was out with a surveying party, Byrd and some of his other companions spent time in camp occupying themselves as best they could. On October 9 the author comments that he "never spent a day so well during the whole voyage," for on that day he managed to pull "an impertinent tooth" in his upper jaw, as he explains in some detail:

Toothdrawers we had none amongst us, nor any of the instruments they make use of. However, invention supplied this want very happily, and I contrived to get rid of this troublesome companion by cutting a caper. I caused a twine to be fastened round the root of my tooth, about a fathom in length, and then tied the other end to the snag of a log that lay upon the ground in such a manner that I could just stand upright. Having adjusted my string in this manner, I bent my knees enough to enable me to spring vigorously off the ground as perpendicularly as I could. The force of the leap drew out the tooth with so much ease that I felt nothing of it, nor should have believed it was come away unless I had seen it dangling at the end of the string . . . This new way of toothdrawing, being so silently and deliberately performed, both surprised and delighted all that were present, who could not guess what I was going about.

Byrd possessed a sense of satirical humor that found expression in much of his writing. The foibles of his associates on the expedition to survey the dividing line, the qualities of the people whom he observed in London or in Virginia, the shortcomings of those who incurred his disfavor, might become the subject of commentary in one of his journals or in letters that he carefully composed as if for purposes of publication.

Byrd's letters are particularly interesting, not only for their biographical significance but for their literary quality. Although he did not intend to publish his correspondence, he obviously was so unwilling to see these manifestations of his literary skill perish that he carefully copied them. In a notebook in the University of North Carolina library, reproduced by Miss Maude H. Woodfin in her edition of *Another Secret Diary*, Byrd preserved a considerable body of his correspondence, but he disguised the names of the persons addressed under such fanciful appellations as "Charmante," "Sabina," "Vigilante," "Cleora," "Erranti," "Belinda." Miss Woodfin managed to identify a number of these addressees. Some of the letters are cast in the form of the eighteenth-century "character," essentially an informal descriptive essay, and included among the letters are two or three characters that are strictly literary exercises. One of these, entitled "Inamorato L'Oiseaux,"[16] is a self-portrait of Byrd himself. Miss Woodfin thinks the use of the plural form, "L'Oiseaux" was a slip of Byrd's pen when he copied it in his notebook.

The character that Byrd painted of himself is revealing and substantially accurate. He begins with a description of his amorous nature that is confirmed by his diaries. "Never did the sun shine upon a swain who had more combustible matter in his constitution than the unfortunate Inamorato. Love broke out upon him before his beard, and he could distinguish sexes long before he could the difference between good and evil," he comments at the beginning of the little essay. "This foible has been an unhappy clog to all his fortunes and hindered him from reaching that eminence in the world which his friends and abilities might possibly have advanced him to," he adds. Unwilling to subdue his spirit to the requirements of ambition, he recognizes the limitations upon his attainments that the pursuit of pleasure has imposed. "Diligence gives wings to ambition by which it soars up to the highest pitch of advancement. These wings Inamorato wanted, as he did constancy, which is another ingredient to raise a great fortune." This passage helps to explain why Byrd made no more of his literary efforts than he did. His interest in his writing flagged, and he did not have the drive required to make him complete any great work. He was willing to content himself with pretty little essays, light verses, and satirical pieces to entertain his friends. He remained essentially a dilettante of letters, albeit a brilliant one.

One characteristic bit of light foolery is reprinted by Miss Woodfin from a manuscript in the Huntington Library. Entitled "The Female Creed,"[17] it dates from about 1725 and is a satire on the credulities and weaknesses of women, with veiled references to particular women whom Byrd knew in London. A somewhat ribald piece without much merit, it was probably written to entertain some of Byrd's English

[16] Woodfin, *Another Secret Diary*, pp. 276–282.
[17] *Ibid.*, pp. 447–475.

cronies. Nevertheless it is revealing as an example of the type of composition that Byrd found pleasure in writing.

That he was an inveterate writer is abundantly evident from the
surviving pieces from his pen: his diaries, which he evidently kept
throughout his life, though many portions have been lost; his numerous
letters, which he took care to preserve; his notebooks, like the ones at
the University of North Carolina which Miss Woodfin has edited;
and his commonplace books, which we now have evidence that he
kept.

Why Byrd — or anyone — should keep the kind of diaries that he
kept remains a mystery of human nature. In them he entered the
stark and banal doings of each day with a minimum of comment upon
them. He also recorded the intimate details of his sex life in as matter-
of-fact a manner as he would mention the arrival and departure of
guests. For reasons that puzzle us, Byrd felt a compulsion to write,
even to write down his most trivial or most intimate actions. He also
felt impelled to keep everything that he wrote. Unhappily, large sections of his diaries have been lost and may never be recovered, and
notebooks containing letters and memoranda have disappeared.

A commonplace book that Byrd kept between the years 1722 and
1732 has recently come to light and has been acquired by the Virginia
Historical Society. Through the kindness of the Director, Mr. John
Jennings, it has been made available for study. In Byrd's own handwriting, it reveals matters that caught his interest in reading or in
chance conversations. Here he jotted down the items that he wanted
to remember, perhaps for his own conversational purposes or for use
in his writing. The book is a hodgepodge of miscellaneous quotations
and curious information, much of it ribald. It contains proverbs, words
of advice, anecdotes, recipes, cures for venereal diseases, rules for
good health, pious moralizing, gossip about Charles II and other
prominent characters, bits of verse, quotations from Greek and Roman
writers, and almost anything that Byrd thought worth remembering.
It also contains four letters dating from 1722 and addressed to "Charmante," whom Miss Woodfin identified as Lady Elizabeth Lee, grand-
daughter of Charles II; Byrd had sought in vain to persuade her to

marry him, but she chose to marry in 1731 Edward Young, the poet and the author of *Night Thoughts.*

Elizabeth Lee's refusal of Byrd's hand infuriated him and moved him to write this message to posterity at the end of the last letter copied in his commonplace book:

These passionate billets were writ to a lady who had more charms than honor, more wit than discretion. In the beginning she gave the writer of them the plainest marks of her favor. He did not only hint his passion to her but also confirmed it by many a close hug and tender squeeze, which she suffered with the patience of a martyr. Nay, that she might have no doubt of his intentions, he put the question to her in the plainest terms, which she seemed to agree to, not only by a modest silence but by permitting the same familiarities for more than a month afterwards.

Byrd continues in this vein and blames his bad fortune upon a rival who found it necessary "to work underground and blow him up by a mine." Elizabeth Lee did not marry Young for his virtue, Byrd suggests, but

for the worst quality any husband can have — for his wit. That I own he has his share of, yet so overcharged and encumbered with words that he does more violence to the ear than a ring of bells, for he's altogether as noisy, without having so many changes. But if he had never so much wit, a wife may be sure the edge of it will be turned mostly against herself.

This comment prompts Byrd to make some observations upon the hazards of displaying too much wit.

Wit is a dangerous quality, both for the owner and everyone that has the misfortune to belong to him. He that is curst with wit has commonly too much fire to think, too much quickness to have any discretion . . . In one word, wit rarely makes a man either happier or better, and much seldomer makes him rich than immortal. Wit in a man, like beauty in a woman, may please and divert other people but never does its owner any good.[18]

The commonplace book is filled with facts, anecdotes, and curious bits of lore that Byrd gleaned in his reading. Some of it is ribald and bawdy, some of it is pious and moralistic, and all of it reflects the diversity of his reading. As in the diaries, he rarely specifies the title

[18] Commonplace Book, Virginia Historical Society, pp. 91–92.

of the book that is the source of the information that he copies. An entry that may reflect Byrd's own hesitancy about publishing his work reads: "Socrates had a modesty which would much better become most of our modern authors, for, being asked why he would not oblige the world with some of his works, replied, ''Twould be a pity to spoil so much paper.'" In another characteristic passage on the same page of the commonplace book, he quotes Aristotle but gives no source: "Aristotle had a despicable opinion of human nature, by saying that man was the very center of frailty, the jest of fortune, the emblem of inconstancy, the prey of time, and the shuttlecock of envy and compassion, and for the rest, nothing but phlegm and melancholy." This observation is followed by a short paragraph reading: "Approach not the tremendous throne of God with any petition for prosperity, but pray for such a portion of grace and wisdom as may enable you in all conditions to behave in a manner suitable to the dignity of your nature and the firmness of your dependence." [19]

This commonplace book is a revelation of the diversity of Byrd's interests and his curiosity about everything, ranging from abstract matters of religion to practical questions affecting life on a Virginia plantation. He describes the diagnostic skill of Dr. John Radcliffe, the most eminent physician in the reign of Queen Anne, and provides some sensible rules of health (which his diaries indicate that he tried to follow). As he indicated in his character of himself, he recognized his own amorous proclivities and was fascinated by these manifestations in others, as entries in the commonplace book show. The contemplation of the frailties of men and women results in a curious jumble of quotations, proverbs, advice, and even recipes in the commonplace book. "In matters of love, the only sure way to conquer is to run away, according to Cato," Byrd observes. "'In spite of all the virtue we can boast, / The woman that deliberates is lost.' Nor is this the case with the women only, but the men find it as true as they in every instance of temptation." He cites various methods by which men have sought to gain supremacy over their emotions. Some have worn "a leaden girdle upon their loins and strewed their

[19] *Ibid.*, p. 40.

37

beds with white roses," he states. "They have also eat sour lemons and abundance of lettuce to cool their concupiscence." [20] This problem constantly occupied Byrd's attention and resulted in a variety of curious entries in the commonplace book.

This collection of miscellaneous observations and quotations provides additional insights into Byrd's character, his tastes, and his literary interests. In itself it is not a literary document of much value, but it supplies clues to an understanding of one of the most entertaining men in colonial America. The study of Byrd's writings makes us wish that he had shown less of the modesty that he recommended for "our modern authors" and had devoted more of his time to writing for publication. If he had, we can be certain that colonial literature would have been much richer — and far more amusing.

[20] *Ibid.*, p. 84.

# THE SECRET HISTORY

# OF THE LINE

$T$HE Governor and Council of Virginia in the year 1727 received an express order from His Majesty to appoint commissioners who, in conjunction with others to be named by the government of North Carolina, should run the line betwixt the two colonies. The rule these gentlemen were directed to go by was a paper of proposals formerly agreed on between the two governors, at that time Spotswood and Eden.[1] It would be a hard thing to say of so wise a man as Mr. Spotswood thought himself that he was overreached, but it has appeared upon trial that Mr. Eden was much better informed how the land lay than he. However, since the King was pleased to agree to these unequal proposals, the government of Virginia was too dutiful to dispute them. They therefore appointed Steddy[2] and Merryman[3] commissioners on the part of Virginia to execute that order and Astrolabe[4] and Capricorn[5] to be the surveyors. But Merryman dying, Firebrand[6] and Meanwell[7] made interest to fill his place. Most of

[1] See the Appendix, pp. 322–336.      [2] William Byrd.

[3] Boyd (*William Byrd's Histories of the Dividing Line betwixt Virginia and North Carolina*, edited by William K. Boyd [Raleigh, N.C., 1929]): "Nathaniel Harrison (1677–1727) of Wakefield, Surry County, member of the House of Burgesses (1699–1706) and of the Council (1713–1727), County Lieutenant of Surry and Prince George in 1715 and after, and Auditor of Virginia in 1724."

[4] William Mayo. Boyd: Mayo was "a native of Wiltshire, England, who arrived in Virginia about 1723 from the Barbadoes, whither he had migrated prior to 1712. During 1717–1721 he made a survey of the Barbadoes and also a map, preserved in the library of King's College. He was one of the justices of Goochland County and was very active as a surveyor in that county and the colony at large, laying off for Byrd the City of Richmond and aiding in establishing the boundaries of the Northern Neck. He died in 1744. Mayo's River is named for him. See Brown's *The Cabells and Their Kin*."

[5] John Allen. Boyd: "See 'Virginia Council Journals,' Sept. 12, 1727. (*Virginia Magazine of History and Biography*, Vol. XXXII, p. 242.) He was probably that John Allen of Surry County who married Elizabeth Bassett, daughter of William Bassett of the Virginia Council, and sometime a student of William and Mary. His will was proved in 1741. See 'Allen Family of Surry County' in *William and Mary College Quarterly*, Vol. VIII, p. 110."

[6] Richard Fitzwilliam. Boyd: "In 1719 he was Collector of Customs for the Lower District of James River. (*Calendar of Treasury Books and Papers, 1714–1719*, p. 481.) On November 21, 1727, he was appointed 'Surveyor General of all the Duties and Importations' for the Carolinas, Maryland, Virginia, Pennsylvania, the Bahama Islands and Jamaica. (*Ibid.*, 1729–30, p. 470.)"

[7] William Dandridge. He was a partner of Governor Spotswood in commercial

the Council inclined to favor the last, because he had offered his services before he knew that any pay would belong to the place. But Burly,[8] one of the honorable board, perceiving his friend Firebrand would lose it if it came to the vote, proposed the expedient of sending three commissioners upon so difficult and hazardous an expedition. To this a majority agreed, being unwilling to be thought too frugal of the public money. Accordingly, they were both joined with Steddy in this commission. When this was over, Steddy proposed that a chaplain might be allowed to attend the commissioners, by reason they should have a number of men with them sufficient for a small congregation and were to pass through an ungodly country where they should find neither church nor minister; that, besides, it would be an act of great charity to give the gentiles of that part of the world an opportunity to christen both them and their children. This being unanimously consented to, Dr. Humdrum[9] was named upon Steddy's recommendation.

Of all these proceedings notice was dispatched to Sir Richard Everard, Governor of North Carolina, desiring him to name commissioners on the part of that province to meet those of Virginia the spring following. In consequence whereof that government named Jumble,[10] Shoebrush,[11] Plausible,[12] and Puzzlecause,[13] being the flower

---

enterprises in 1717 and in 1740 took part in the naval operations against the Spanish at St. Augustine. In 1728 he was a member of the Virginia Council.

[8] Boyd: "Rev. James Blair, Commissary of the Bishop of London in Virginia from 1685 until his death in 1743. A veritable 'King Maker,' for he was responsible for the recall of three governors, Andros, Nicholson, and Spotswood. In 1697 Byrd represented Governor Andros before the Archbishop of Canterbury and the Bishop of London in the controversy between Andros and Blair, and lost his case."

[9] Boyd: "Rev. Peter Fontaine (1691-1757), one of the six children of James Fontaine, a Huguenot refugee . . . Peter was educated at Dublin, Ireland, and after officiating at Wallingford, Weyanoke, Martin's Brandon, and Jamestown, became rector of Westover Parish, Charles City County, of which Byrd was a parishioner."

[10] Christopher Gale. Boyd: "Chief Justice, a native of Yorkshire, England, and eldest son of Rev. Miles Gale, rector of Wighby . . . By 1703 he was a Justice of the General Court and in 1712 was appointed Chief Justice, an office which he held until 1731, except for an intermission from 1717 to 1722 when he was in England, and a briefer one in 1724-25 . . . He was Collector of the Customs at Edenton."

[11] John Lovick. A deputy of the Proprietors and a member of the Council from 1718 to 1731; secretary to the Council and also Secretary of the province from

and cream of the Council of that province. The next step necessary to be taken was for the commissioners on both sides to agree upon a day of meeting at Currituck Inlet in order to proceed on this business, and the fifth of March was thought a proper time, because then Mercury and the moon were to be in conjunction.

It was desired by Sir Richard that the commissioners might meet on the frontiers sometime in January to settle preliminaries, and particularly, that it might be previously agreed that the present possessors of land in either government should be confirmed in their possession, though it should not happen to fall within the government that granted it. This the Governor of Virginia disagreed to, not thinking it just that either the King or the Lords Proprietors should grant away land that did not belong to them. Nor was this proposal made on the part of Carolina purely out of good nature, but some of the Council of that province found their own interest concerned; and particularly the Surveyor General must in justice have returned some of his fees, in case the people should lose the land he surveyed for them as belonging to the Proprietors when in truth it belonged to the King.

Soon after the commissioners for Virginia wrote the following letter to the worthy commissioners of North Carolina:

Gentlemen:
We are sorry we can't have the pleasure of meeting you in January next, as is desired by your governor. The season of the year in which that is proposed to be done, and the distance of our habitation from your frontiers,

---

1722 to 1730. He held other governmental posts including that of Surveyor General, to which he was appointed in 1732.

[12] Edward Moseley. Boyd: Moseley was "a member of the boundary commission of 1710, the preeminent political leader of North Carolina from his appearance in public affairs in 1705 until his death in 1749 . . . He was a member of the Council under four administrations, being President of that body and Acting Governor in 1725 . . . He was one of the commissioners chosen in 1709 to establish the boundary, and in 1723 he was made Surveyor General. Later he was one of the commissioners to establish the South Carolina boundary and also the boundary of the Granville District."

[18] William Little. Boyd: "a native of Massachusetts and a graduate of Harvard, class of 1710. While visiting in England he met Chief Justice Gale and was persuaded by him to move to North Carolina. He settled at Edenton and in 1726 married Justice Gale's daughter, Penelope. In 1725 he was appointed Attorney General and in 1726 Receiver General of Quit Rents. He was also Clerk of the General Court and in 1732 became Chief Justice, an office he held for one year."

we hope will make our excuse reasonable. Besides, His Majesty's order marks out our business so plainly that we are persuaded that there can be no difficulty in the construction of it. After this, what imaginable dispute can arise amongst gentlemen who meet together with minds averse to chicane and inclinations to do equal justice both to His Majesty and the Lords Proprietors? in which disposition we make no doubt the commissioners on both sides will find each other.

We shall have full powers to agree at our first meeting on what preliminaries shall be thought necessary, which we hope you will likewise be, that an affair of so great consequence may have no delay or disappointment.

It is very proper to acquaint you in what manner we intend to come provided, that so you gentlemen who are appointed in the same station may, if you please, do the same honor to your government. We shall bring with us about twenty men, furnished with provisions for forty days. We shall have a tent with us and a marquee for the convenience of ourselves and servants. We shall be provided with as much wine and rum as just enable us and our men to drink every night to the success of the following day. And because we understand there are many gentiles on your frontier who never had an opportunity of being baptized, we shall have a chaplain with us to make them Christians. For this purpose we intend to rest in our camp every Sunday, that there may be leisure for so good a work. And whoever of your province shall be desirous of novelty may repair on Sundays to our camp and hear a sermon. Of this you may please to give public notice, that the charitable intentions of this government may meet with the happier success.

Thus much, gentlemen, we thought it necessary to acquaint you with and to make use of this first opportunity of signifying with how much satisfaction we received the news that such able commissioners are appointed for that government, with whom we promise ourselves we shall converse with prodigious pleasure and execute our commissions to the full content of those by whom we have the honor to be employed.

We are, gentlemen, your most humble servants,

Firebrand          Steddy

Meanwell

Williamsburg
The 16th of December, 1727

To this letter the commissioners of Virginia the latter end of January received the following answer:

Gentlemen:

We have the honor of your favor from Williamsburg, dated the sixteenth of December, in which you signify that the proposals already agreed on are so plain that you are persuaded there can no difficulty arise about the construction of them. We think so too; but if no dispute should arise in construing them, yet the manner of our proceeding in the execution we thought had better be previously concerted, and the end of the meeting we proposed was to remove everything that might lie in the way to retard the work, which we all seem equally desirious to have amicably concluded. We assure you, gentlemen, we shall meet you with a hearty disposition of doing equal justice to either government; and as you acquaint us you shall come fully empowered to agree at our first meeting to settle all necessary preliminaries, we shall endeavor to have our instructions as large. Your governor in his last letter to ours was pleased to mention our conferring with you by letters about any matters previously to be adjusted. We therefore take leave to desire by this messenger you will let us know after what manner you purpose to run the line — whether you think to go through the Great Swamp, which is near thirty miles through and thought not passable; or, by taking the latitude at the first station, to run a due-west line to the swamp and then to find the said latitude on the west side the swamp and continue thence a due-west line to Chowan River; or to make the second observation upon Chowan River and run an east line to the Great Swamp. We shall also be glad to know what instruments you intend to use to observe the latitude and find the variation with in order to fix a due-west line. For we are told the last time the commissioners met their instruments varied several minutes, which we hope will not happen again, nor any other difficulty that may occasion any delay or disappointment after we have been at the trouble of meeting in so remote a place and with such attendance and equipage as you intend on your part. We are at a loss, gentlemen, whether to thank you for the particulars you give us of your tent, stores, and the manner you design to meet us. Had you been silent, we had not wanted an excuse for not meeting you in the same manner; but now you force us to expose the nakedness of our country and tell you we can't possibly meet you in the manner our great respect to you would make us glad to do, whom we are not emulous of outdoing, unless in care and diligence in the affair we came about. So all we can answer to that article is that we will endeavor to provide as well as the circumstances of things will admit; and what we want in necessaries we hope will be made up in spiritual comfort we expect from your chaplain, of whom we shall give notice as you desire and

45

doubt not of making a great many boundary Christians. To conclude, we promise to make ourselves as agreeable to you as possibly we can; and we beg leave to assure you that it is a singular pleasure to us that you gentlemen are named on that part to see this business of so great concern and consequence to both governments determined, which makes it to be undertaken on our parts more cheerfully, being assured your characters are above any artifice or design.

We are your most obedient, humble servants,

| Plausible | Jumble |
| Puzzlecause | Shoebrush |

This letter was without date, they having no almanacs in North Carolina, but it came about the beginning of January. However, the Virginia commissioners did not return an answer to it till they had consulted their surveyor, honest Astrolabe, as to the mathematical part. When that was done, they replied in the following terms:

Gentlemen:

We should have returned an answer sooner had not the cold weather and our remote situation from one another prevented our meeting. However, we hope 'tis now time enough to thank you for that favor and to assure you that though we are appointed commissioners for this government we incline to be very just to yours. And as the fixing fair boundaries between us will be of equal advantage to both, you shall have no reason to reproach us with making any step either to delay or disappoint so useful a work. If the Great Swamp you mention should be absolutely impassable, we then propose to run a due-west line from our first station thither and then survey round the same till we shall come on our due-west course on the other side, and so proceed till we shall be again interrupted. But if you shall think of a more proper expedient, we shall not be fond of our own opinion. And though we can't conceive that taking the latitude will be of any use in running this line, yet we shall be provided to do it with the greatest exactness. In performing which, we shall on our part use no graduated instrument,[14] but our accurate surveyor, Astrolabe, tells us he will use a method that will come nearer the truth. He likewise proposes to discover, as near as possible, the just variation of the compass, by means of a true meridian to be found by the North Star. We shall bring

[14] Boyd: "The 'graduated instrument' was doubtless the surveyor's pole, 16½ feet long. By sighting the north star with this, latitude could be crudely calculated. The 'better method' referred to was perhaps the astrolabe."

with us two or three very good compasses, which we hope will not differ much from yours, though if there should be some little variance, 'twill be easily reconciled by two such skillful mathematicians as Astrolabe and Plausible.

In short, gentlemen, we are so conscious of our own disposition to do right to both colonies, and at the same time so verily persuaded of yours, that we promise to ourselves an entire harmony and good agreement. This can hardly fail when justice and reason are laid down on both sides as the rule and foundation of our proceeding. We hope the season will prove favorable to us, but, be that as it will, we intend to preserve fair weather in our humor, believing that even the Dismal may be very tolerable in good company.

We are without the least artifice or design, gentlemen, your most humble servants,

S. F. M.

It was afterwards agreed by the commissioners on both sides to meet on the north shore of Currituck Inlet on the fifth day of the following March in order to run the dividing line. In the meantime, those on the part of Virginia divided the trouble of making the necessary preparations. It fell to Steddy's share to provide the men that were to attend the surveyors. For this purpose, Mr. Mumford [15] recommended to him fifteen able woodsmen, most of which had been Indian traders. These were ordered to meet at Warren's Mill, armed with a gun and tomahawk, on the twenty-seventh of February, and furnished with provisions for ten days. Astrolabe came on the twenty-sixth in order to attend Steddy to the place of rendezvous.

[27.] [16] The next day they crossed the river, having first recommended all they left behind to the divine protection. Steddy carried with him two servants and a sumpter horse for his baggage. About twelve o'clock he met the men at the new church near Warren's Mill. He drew them out to the number of fifteen, and, finding their arms in good order, he caused them to be mustered by their names as follows:

[15] Boyd: "Robert Mumford (Munford), Justice and Colonel of Militia in Prince George County, vestryman of Bruton Parish, and member of the House of Burgesses in 1720–22." He acted as Byrd's lawyer and business manager.

[16] The date has been added from the *History* (p. 171).

| | | |
|---|---|---|
| Peter Jones | Thomas Jones | John Ellis |
| James Petillo | Charles Kimball | John Evans |
| Thomas Short | George Hamilton | Robert Hix |
| Thomas Wilson | Steven Evans | Thomas Jones, Jr. |
| George Tilman | Robert Allen | John Ellis, Jr. |

Here, after drawing out this small troop, Steddy made them the following speech:

Friends and fellow travelers:

It is a pleasure to me to see that we are like to be so well attended in this long and painful journey. And what may we not hope from men who list themselves not so much for pay as from an ambition to serve their country. We have a great distance to go and much work to perform, but I observe too much spirit in your countenances to flinch at either. As no care shall be wanting on my part to do every one of you justice, so I promise myself that on yours you will set the Carolina men whom we are to meet at Currituck a constant pattern of order, industry, and obedience.

Then he marched his men in good order to Capricorn's elegant seat,[17] according to the route before projected, but found him in doleful dumps for the illness of his wife. She was really indisposed, but not so dangerously as to hinder a vigorous man from going upon the service of his country. However, he seemed in the midst of his concern to discover a secret satisfaction that it furnished him with an excuse of not going upon an expedition that he fancied would be both dangerous and difficult. Upon his refusing to go for the reason above-mentioned, Steddy wrote to the Governor how much he was disappointed at the loss of one of the surveyors and recommended Astrolabe's brother[18] to supply his place. At the same time he dispatched away an express to young Astrolabe to let him know he had named him to the Governor for his service. But, not knowing how it would be determined, he could promise him nothing; though if

[17] Bacon's Castle. This seventeenth-century house, built about 1650, was never occupied by Nathaniel Bacon, despite the name. At the time of Bacon's Rebellion it was the home of Major Arthur Allen, grandfather of Capricorn, but it was seized and fortified by one of Bacon's followers. The name was given it at a later date. It still stands, the only Jacobean house in Virginia. See Richard L. Morton, *Colonial Virginia* (Chapel Hill, 1960), I, 273–274 and n. 44.

[18] Boyd: "Joseph Mayo, of 'Powhatan Seat,' on the James River, below Richmond."

he would come to Norfolk at his own risk he should there be able to resolve him. This was the best expedient he could think of for the service at that plunge, because Capricorn had in the bitterness of his concern taken no care to acquaint the Governor that he was prevented from going. However, Dr. Arsmart,[19] who had been to visit Mrs. Capricorn, let the Governor know that he was too tender a husband to leave his spouse to the mercy of a physician.

Upon this notice, which came to the Governor before Steddy's letter, it was so managed that the learned Orion[20] was appointed to go in his room. This gentleman is professor of the mathematics in the College of William and Mary but has so very few scholars that he might be well enough spared from his post for a short time. It was urged by his friends that a person of his fame for profound learning would give a grace to the undertaking and be able to silence all the mathematics of Carolina. These were unanswerable reasons, and so he was appointed. The Reverend Doctor Humdrum came time enough to bless a very plentiful supper at Capricorn's. He treated his company handsomely, and by the help of a bowl of rack punch his grief disappeared so entirely that if he had not sent for Arsmart it might have been suspected his lady's sickness was all a farce. However, to do him justice, the man would never be concerned in a plot that was like to cost him five pistoles.[21]

28. The table was well spread again for breakfast, but, unfortunately for the poor horses, the key of the cornloft was mislaid; at least the servant was instructed to say as much. We marched from hence in good order to the Widow Allen's,[22] which was twenty-two

[19] The fragment of the "Secret History" in the Huntington Library has the name "Dr. Nicolas" crossed out, with "Dr. Arsmart" written above it. This would probably be Dr. George Nicholas, who emigrated to Williamsburg from Lancashire in 1700 after training as a surgeon. He married Elizabeth Carter Burwell, daughter of Robert "King" Carter and widow of Nathaniel Burwell. See *Dictionary of American Biography* under Robert Carter Nicholas, the doctor's eldest son.

[20] Alexander Irvine, professor of mathematics at the College of William and Mary (1729–1732).

[21] A pistole was a Spanish gold coin worth 16s. 6d. to 18s.

[22] Boyd: "The maiden name of this hospitable lady was Bray. She was thrice married: first to Arthur Allen, second to Arthur Smith, finally to —— Stith. In 1753 she donated £125 for a free school in the upper part of Isle of Wight County and her will revealed a bequest of £120, the interest from which was to be used for the education of 'any six poor children.' See *William and Mary College Quarterly*, Vol. VI, pp. 77–78."

miles. She entertained us elegantly and seemed to pattern Solomon's housewife, if one may judge by the neatness of her house and the good order of her family. Here Firebrand and Meanwell had appointed to meet Steddy but failed; however, the tent was sent hither under the care of John Rice, of the kingdom of Ireland, who did not arrive till twelve o'clock at night. This disorder at first setting out gave us but an indifferent opinion of Firebrand's management.

29. From hence Steddy sent a letter to the Governor with an account of his march to that place and of the steps he had taken about Astrolabe's brother. At ten in the morning he thanked the clean widow for all her civilities and marched under the pilotage of Mr. Baker to Colonel Thomas Godding's.[23] By the way Steddy was obliged to be at the expense of a few curses upon John Rice, who was so very thirsty that he called at every house he passed by. The cavalcade arrived at Colonel Godding's about four o'clock after a pleasant journey of thirty miles. But Steddy found himself exceedingly fatigued with the march.

In passing through the upper part of the Isle of Wight, Mr. Baker remarked the dismal footsteps made by the hurricane, which happened in August, 1626. The violence of it did not extend in breadth above a quarter of a mile but in that compass leveled all before it. Mr. Baker's house was so unlucky as to stand in its way, which it laid flat to the ground and blew some of his goods above two miles.

Colonel Godding was very hospitable, both to man and beast, but the poor man had the misfortune to be deaf, which hindered him from hearing any parts of the acknowledgments that were made to him; he pressed everybody very kindly to eat, entreating 'em not to be bashful, which might be a great inconvenience to travelers. The son and heir of the family offered himself as a volunteer the overnight[24] but dreamt so much of danger and difficulties that he declared off in the morning.

[23] Boyd: "The Baker family was prominent in Isle of Wight County, Lawrence Baker being a vestryman of New Port Parish from 1724 to 1737 and James Baker, Clerk of the County Court, 1732–1734. Colonel Thomas Godding was Colonel Thomas Godwin of Nansemond County."
[24] The night before.

MARCH

1. About nine in the morning the Colonel was so kind as to set all his guests over the south branch of Nansemond River, which shortened their journey seven or eight miles, and from thence his son conducted them into the great road. Then they passed for several miles together by the north side of the Great Dismal and after a journey of twenty-five miles arrived in good order at Major Crawford's [25] over against Norfolk Town. Just before they got hither, the lag commissioners overtook them and all the men were drawn up to receive them. Meanwell was so civil as to excuse his not meeting Steddy at Mr. Allen's as had been agreed, but Firebrand was too big for apology.

It was agreed to leave the men and the heavy baggage at Major Crawford's (having made the necessary provision for it) and pass over to Norfolk only with the servants and portmantles,[26] that the townsmen might not be frightened from entertaining them. Here they divided their quarters, that as little trouble might be given as possible, and it was Steddy's fortune, after some apprehensions of going to the ordinary,[27] to be invited by Colonel Newton.[28] To show his regard to the church, he took the chaplain along with him.

Mrs. Newton provided a clean supper without any luxury about eight o'clock and appeared to be one of the fine ladies of the town and, like a true fine lady, to have a great deal of contempt for her husband.

2. This morning old Colonel Boush [29] made Steddy a visit with the tender of his service. There was no soul in the town knew how the land lay betwixt this place and Currituck Inlet, till at last Mr. William Wilkins,[30] that lives upon the borders, drew a rough sketch

[25] Boyd: "Major William Crawford, a member of the County Court of Norfolk in 1728. See *Lower Norfolk County, Virginia, Antiquary*, Vol. I, p. 80."

[26] Portmanteaux, baggage.

[27] Tavern or inn.

[28] Boyd: "George Newton, Lieutenant-Colonel of Militia in Norfolk County, one of the trustees of the Town of Norfolk in the transfer of land owned by the town to Norfolk Academy. In 1744 he was a member of the County Court of Norfolk (*Lower Norfolk County, Virginia, Antiquary*, Vol. I, pp. 78–81, 117.)"

[29] Boyd: "Samuel Boush, member of the County Court of Norfolk in 1728. Today there is a Boush Avenue in Norfolk."

[30] Boyd misread the last name as "Williams," but at a later mention of the man he identifies him as "probably William Wilkins, Justice of Norfolk County in 1728."

that gave a general notion of it. The light given by this draft determined the commissioners to march to the landing of Northwest River and there embark in a piragua [31] in order to meet the commissioners of Carolina at Currituck.

It was really a pleasure to see twelve or fourteen sea vessels riding in the harbor of this city and several wharves built out into the river to land goods upon. These wharves were built with pine logs let into each other at the end, by which those underneath are made firm by those which lie over them. Here the commissioners were supplied with two kegs of wine and two of rum, 178 pounds of bread, and several other conveniencies.

Our good landlord entertained Steddy and the chaplain at dinner, but Firebrand refused because he was not sent to in due form. In the evening the commissioners were invited to an oyster and a bowl by Mr. Sam Smith, a plain man worth £20,000. He produced his two nieces, whose charms were all invisible. These damsels seemed discontented that their uncle showed more distinction to his housekeeper than to them.

We endeavored to hire two or three men here to go along with us but might for the same price have hired them to make a trip to the other world. They looked upon us as men devoted, like Codrus [32] and the two Decii,[33] to certain destruction for the service of our country. The parson and I returned to our quarters in good time and good order, but my man Tom broke the rules of hospitality by getting extremely drunk in a civil house.

3. This being Sunday, we were edified at church by Mr. Marston [34] with a good sermon. People could not attend their devotion for staring at us, just as if we had come from China or Japan. In the meantime, Firebrand and Astrolabe, not having quite so much regard for the Sabbath, went to the Northwest Landing to prepare vessels for our

[31] A type of canoe. The manuscript spells this word "periagua" or "periauga."
[32] A legendary king of Sparta, who sacrificed his life rather than allow it to be the price of his country's surrender to Dorian invaders.
[33] Presumably Gaius Messius Quintus Trajanus Decius, Roman Emperor A.D. 249–251, and his son, both of whom were killed in a battle with the Goths.
[34] Boyd identifies him as the Reverend Richard Marsden, of Lynnhaven Parish, Princess Anne County.

transportation to Currituck. I wrote to the Governor an account of our progress thus far, with a billet-doux to my wife. The wind blew very hard at southwest all day; however, in the evening Steddy ordered the men and horses to be set over the South Branch [35] to save time in the morning. My landlady gave us tea and sweetened it with the best of her smiles. At night we spent an hour with Colonel Boush, who stirred his old bones very cheerfully in our service. Poor Orion's horse and furniture were much disordered with the journey hither. His instrument would not traverse nor his ball rest in the socket. In short, all his tackle had the air of distress. Over against the town is Powder Point,[36] where a ship of any burden may lie close to and the men-of-war are used to careen.

4. About eight o'clock in the morning we crossed the river to Powder Point, where we found our men ready to take horse. Several of the grandees of the town, and the parson among the rest, did us the honor to attend us as far as the great bridge over South River. Here we were met by a troop under the command of Captain Wilson,[37] who escorted us as far as his father's castle near the Dismal. We halted about a quarter of an hour and then proceeded to Northwest Landing. Here Firebrand had provided a dinner for us, served up by the master of the house, whose nose seemed to stand upon very ticklish terms.

After dinner we chose ten able men and embarked on board two piraguas under the command of Captain Wilkins,[38] which carried us to the mouth of Northwest River. By the way we found the banks of the river lined with myrtles and bay trees, which afforded a beautiful prospect. These beautiful plants dedicated to Venus and Apollo grow in wet ground, and so does the wild laurel, which in some places is intermixed with the rest. This river is in most places about one hun-

[35] Of Elizabeth River, on which Norfolk is located.
[36] Now a suburb of Norfolk called Berkeley.
[37] Boyd suggests Captain Willis Wilson, Jr., who was in 1744 a member of the County Court of Norfolk, but Byrd later mentions a Captain James Wilson (p. 84), and further references to Captain Willis Wilson suggest that he is a different man.
[38] One cannot be certain whether this is the same man as the William Wilkins mentioned earlier or, indeed, whether the name is a mistake for Wilson.

dred yards over and had no tide till the year 1713, when a violent tempest opened a new inlet about five miles to the southward of the old one, which is now almost closed up and too shallow for any vessel to pass over. But the new inlet is deep enough for sloops.

We were four hours in rowing to the mouth of the river, being about eighteen miles from the landing. Here we took up our lodging at one Andrew Duke's, who had lately removed, or rather run away, hither from Maryland. We were forced to lie in bulk upon a very dirty floor that was quite alive with fleas and chinches and made us repent that we had not brought the tent along with us. We had left that with the rest of the heavy baggage at Captain Wilson's under the guard of seven men. There we had also left the Reverend Doctor Humdrum, with the hopes that all the gentiles in the neighborhood would bring their children to be christened, notwithstanding some of them had never been christened themselves. Firebrand had taken care to board his man Tipperary with Captain Wilson, because by being the squire of his body he thought him too much a gentleman to diet with the rest of the men we left behind. This indignity sat not easy upon their stomachs, who were all honest housekeepers in good circumstances.

5. At break of day we turned out, properly speaking, and blest our landlord's eyes with half a pistole. About seven we embarked and passed by the south end of Knott's Island, there being no passage on the north. To the southwards at some distance we saw Bell's and Church's Islands. About noon we arrived at the south shore of old Currituck Inlet, and about two we were joined by Judge Jumble and Plausible, two of the Carolina commissioners; the other two, Shoebrush and Puzzlecause, lagged behind, which was the more unlucky because we could enter on no business for want of the Carolina commission which these gentlemen had in their keeping. Jumble was brother to the late Dean of York,[39] and if His Honor had not formerly been a pirate himself, he seemed intimately acquainted with many of them. Plausible had been bred in Christ's Hospital and had a tongue

[39] This is not literally true. The purport of Byrd's remark is not clear. See *Dictionary of National Biography* under Thomas Gale, Dean of York, and Miles Gale (father of the Chief Justice).

as smooth as the Commissary, and was altogether as well qualified to be of the Society of Jesus. These worthy gentlemen were attended by Boötes[40] as their surveyor, a young man of much industry but no experience.

We had now nothing to do but to reconnoiter the place. The high land ended in a bluff point, from which a spit of sand extended itself to the southeast about half a mile. The inlet lies between this spit and another on the south side, leaving a shoal passage for the sea not above a mile over. On the east are shoals that run out two or three miles, over which the breakers rise mountains high with a terrible noise. I often cast a longing eye toward England and sighed.

This night we lay for the first time in the woods, and, being without the tent, we made a bower of the branches of cedar, with a large fire in front to guard us from the northwester, which blew very smartly. At night young Astrolabe came to us and gave great jealousy to Orion. His wig was in such stiff buckle that if he had seen the devil the hair would not have stood on end. This night we found the variation to be 3° west, by a due meridian taken from the North Star.

6. We were treated at breakfast by the commissioners of Carolina, who, coming from home by water, were much better provided for the belly than the business. At noon we found the latitude to be 36° 31′, according to Astrolabe, but Orion, to prove his skill in the mathematics by flat contradiction, would needs have it but 36° 30′. Captain Wilkins furnished us with excellent oysters, as savory and well-tasted as those in England.

About three o'clock Messrs. Shoebrush and Puzzlecause made a shift to come to us, after calling at every house where they expected any refreshment; after the necessary compliments and a thousand excuses for making us wait for them so long, we began to enter upon business. We had a tough dispute where we should begin; whether at the point of high land or at the end of the spit of sand, which we with good reason maintained to be the north shore of Currituck Inlet, ac-

[40] Boyd identifies him as Samuel Swann (1704–1772), son of Major Samuel Swann and nephew of Edward Moseley. He was a member of the North Carolina Assembly from Perquimans County from 1725 to 1734, from Onslow County, 1734–1762, and was Speaker from 1742 to 1762.

cording to the express words of His Majesty's order. They had no argument to support our beginning at the high land but because the former commissioners for Virginia submitted to it. But if what they did was to be a rule for us, then we ought to allow no variation of the compass because those gentlemen allowed of none.

This controversy lasted till night, neither side receding from its opinion. However, by the lucky advice of Firebrand, I took Plausible aside and let him know the government of Virginia had looked upon him as the sole obstacle to the settling the bounds formerly, and if we should break off now upon this frivolous pretense he would surely bear the blame again. At the same time I showed him a representation made to the late Queen by Colonel Spotswood greatly to his disadvantage. This worked so powerfully upon his politic that he without loss of time softened his brethren in such a manner that they came over to our opinion. They were the rather persuaded to this by the peremptory words of our commission, by which we were directed to go on with the business though the Carolina commissioners should refuse to join with us therein. However, by reason of some proof that was made to us by the oaths of two credible persons that the spit of sand was advanced about two hundred yards to the southwards since the year 1712, when the proposals between the Governors Eden and Spotswood were agreed upon, we thought it reasonable to allow for so much and accordingly made our beginning from thence.

Upon the high land we found one kind of silk grass and plenty of yaupon, which passes for tea in North Carolina, though nothing like it. On the sands we saw conch shells in great number, of which the Indians make both their blue and white peak,[41] both colors being in different parts of the same shell.

7. We drove down a post at our place of beginning and then crossed over to Dosier's Island, which is nothing but a flat sand with shrubs growing upon it. From thence we passed over to the north end of Knott's Island, our line running through the plantation of William Harding. This man had a wife born and bred near Temple Bar and still talked of the walks in the Temple with pleasure. These poor people bestowed their wood and their water upon us very freely.

[41] A variant of "peag" or "wampum"; see pp. 178 and 218.

We found Shoebrush a merry, good-humored man and had learnt a very decent behavior from Governor Hyde, to whom he had been *valet de chambre*, of which he still carried the marks by having his coat, waistcoat, and breeches of different parishes. Puzzlecause had degenerated from a New England preacher, for which his godly parents designed him, to a very wicked but awkward rake.

I had almost forgot to mention a marooner [42] who had the confidence to call himself an hermit, living on the south shore of Currituck near the Inlet. He has no other habitation but a green bower or arbor, with a female domestic as wild and as dirty as himself. His diet is chiefly oysters, which he has just industry enough to gather from the neighboring oyster banks; while his concubine makes a practice of driving up the neighbor's cows for the advantage of their milk.

Orion seemed to be grievously puzzled about plotting off his surveyor's work and chose rather to be obliged to the Carolina commissioners than to Mr. Mayo for their instruction, which it was evident to everybody that he wanted. The truth of it is, he had been much more discreet to loiter on at the College and receive his salary quietly (which he owes to his relation to the pious Commissary) than to undertake a business which discovered he knew very little of the matter.

8. We quitted our camp about seven and early dispatched away the large piragua, with the heavy baggage and most of the men, round the south end of Knott's Island. About nine we embarked ourselves on board the lesser piragua, under the pilotage of Captain Wilkins, and steered our course toward the north end of the island. This navigation was so difficult by reason of the perpetual shoals that we were often fast aground, but Firebrand swore us off again very soon. Our pilot would have been a miserable man if one half of that gentleman's curses had taken effect. It was remarkable to see how mild and unmoved the poor man was under so much heavy displeasure, insomuch that the most passionate expression that escaped him was, "Oh, forever and after!" which was his form of swearing.

We had been benighted in that wide water had we not met a canoe that was carrying a conjurer from Princess Anne to Carolina. But, as all conjurers are sometimes mistaken, he took us at first for pirates,

[42] Buccaneer or pirate, hence a disreputable person.

and, what was worse for him, he suspected afterwards that we were officers that were in pursuit of him and a woman that passed for his wife. However, at last being undeceived in both these points, they suffered us to speak with them and directed us in the course we were to steer. By their advice we rowed up a water called the Back Bay as far as a skirt of pocosin [43] a quarter of a mile in breadth. Through this we waded up to the knees in mud and got safe on the firm land of Princess Anne County.

During this voyage, Shoebrush, in champing a biscuit, forced out one of his teeth, which an unlucky flux had left loose in his head. And though one of his feet was inflamed with the gout, yet he was forced to walk two miles as well as the rest of us to John Heath's, where we took up our quarters. Amongst other spectators came two girls to see us, one of which was very handsome and the other very willing. However, we only saluted [44] them, and if we committed any sin at all, it was only in our hearts.

Captain White, [45] a grandee of Knott's Island, and Mr. Moss, a grandee of Princess Anne, made us a visit and helped to empty our liquor. The surveyors and their attendants came to us at night, after wading through a marsh near five miles in breadth which stretches from the west side of Knott's Island to the high land of Princess Anne. In this marsh several of the men had plunged up to the middle; however, they kept up their good humor and only made sport of what others would have made a calamity.

9. In the morning we walked with the surveyors to the line, which cut through Eyland's plantation, and came to the banks of North River. Hither the girls above-mentioned attended us, but an old woman came along with them for the security of their virtue. Others rose out of their sickbeds to see such rarities as we were.

One of our piraguas set the surveyors and five men over North River. They landed in a miry marsh, which led to a very deep pocosin. Here they met with beaver dams and otter holes which it was not

[43] Swamp, a word of Algonquian origin.
[44] Kissed.
[45] Boyd: "Reference is doubtless to Capt. Solomon White of Princess Anne County. There is no record of a Moss family in that County."

practicable to pass in a direct line, though the men offered to do it with great alacrity, but the surveyors were contented to make a traverse.

While they were struggling with these difficulties, we commissioners went in state in the other piragua to Northwest River and rowed up as high as Mr. Merchant's.[46] He lives near half a mile from the river, having a causeway leading through a filthy swamp to his plantation. I encamped in his pasture with the men, though the other commissioners indulged themselves so far as to lie in the house. But it seems they broke the rules of hospitality by several gross freedoms they offered to take with our landlord's sister. She was indeed a pretty girl, and therefore it was prudent to send her out of harm's way. I was the more concerned at this unhandsome behavior because the people were extremely civil to us and deserved a better treatment.

The surveyors came to us at night, very much jaded with their dirty work, and Orion slept so sound that he had been burnt in his blanket if the sentry had not been kinder to him than he deserved.

10. This being Sunday, we rested the men and surveyors, though we could not celebrate the Sabbath as we ought for want of our chaplain. I had a letter from him informing me that all was well, both soul and body, under his care. Captain Wilkins went home to make his wife a visit and brought me a bottle of milk, which was better than a bottle of Tokay. Firebrand took all occasions to set Orion above Astrolabe, which there was no reason for but because he had the honor to be recommended by him. I halted as bad as old Jacob, without having wrestled with anything like an angel. The men were concerned at it and had observed so much of Firebrand's sweet temper that they swore they would make the best of their way home if it pleased God to disable me from proceeding on the business. But I walked about as much as I could and thereby made my hip very pliable.

We found Captain Willis Wilson here, whose errand was to buy pork, which is the staple commodity of North Carolina and which with pitch and tar makes up the whole of their traffic. The truth of it

---

[46] Boyd: "There was a Willoughby Merchant, justice of Princess Anne, at this time."

is, these people live so much upon swine's flesh that it don't only incline them to the yaws [47] and consequently to the downfall of their noses, but makes them likewise extremely hoggish in their temper, and many of them seem to grunt rather than speak in their ordinary conversation.

11. We ordered the surveyors early to their business, with five of the men to attend them. They had a tiresome day's work of it, wading through a deep pocosin near two miles over, in which they frequently plunged up to the middle. In the meantime, we commissioners rowed up the river in our piragua much more at our ease and dropped anchor at Mossy Point, near a deserted pork store belonging to Captain Willis Wilson. After the men had swept out a cartload of dirt, we put our baggage into it for fear of rain. Then we sent our piragua in quest of the surveyors; and Firebrand, believing nothing could be well done without him, went in it himself, attended by Puzzlecause, though he did no other good but favor us with his room instead of his company.

In the meanwhile, Shoebrush and I took a walk into the woods and called at a cottage where a dark angel surprised us with her charms. Her complexion was a deep copper, so that her fine shape and regular features made her appear like a statue *en bronze* done by a masterly hand. Shoebrush was smitten at the first glance and examined all her neat proportions with a critical exactness. She struggled just enough to make her admirer more eager, so that if I had not been there, he would have been in danger of carrying his joke a little too far.

The surveyors found us out in the evening very much fatigued, and the men were more off their mettle than ever they had been in the whole journey, though without the least complaint. I took up my lodging in the camp but was driven into the house about midnight without my breeches, like Monsieur Broglie,[48] by a smart shower of rain. Here we all lay in bulk the rest of the night upon a dirty and wet floor without taking cold.

[47] A contagious disease, common in warm and tropical climates, somewhat resembling syphilis.

[48] Byrd possibly refers to François Marie, duc de Broglie, who served in the French army during the War of the Spanish Succession and in later battles in Italy. On the night of September 14, 1734, his quarters on the Secchia were raided and he narrowly escaped capture. If Byrd has this incident in mind, the reference was obviously added much later than the original composition of his narrative.

12. Complaint was made to me this morning that the men belonging to the piragua had stole our people's meat while they slept. This provoked me to treat them *à la dragon*, that is, to swear at them furiously, and by the good grace of my oaths I might have passed for an officer in His Majesty's guards. I was the more out of humor because it disappointed us in our early march, it being a standing order to boil the pot overnight that we might not be hindered in the morning.

This accident and necessity of drying our bedclothes kept us from decamping till near twelve o'clock. By this delay the surveyors found time to plot off their work and to observe the course of the river. Then they passed it over against Northern's Creek, the mouth of which was very near our line. But the commissioners made the best of their way to the bridge and, going ashore, walked to Mr. Ballance's plantation.

I retired early to our camp at some distance from the house, while my colleagues tarried withindoors and refreshed themselves with a cheerful bowl. In the gaiety of their hearts, they invited a tallow-faced wench that had sprained her wrist to drink with them, and when they had raised her in good humor they examined all her hidden charms and played a great many gay pranks. While Firebrand, who had the most curiosity, was ranging over her sweet person, he picked off several scaps as big as nipples, the consequence of eating too much pork. The poor damsel was disabled from making any resistance by the lameness of her hand; all she could do was to sit still and make the fashionable exclamation of the country, "Flesh alive and tear it!" and, by what I can understand, she never spake so properly in her life.

One of the representatives of North Carolina made a midnight visit to our camp, and his curiosity was so very clamorous that it waked me, for which I wished his nose as flat as any of his porcivorous countrymen.

13. In the morning our chaplain came to us and with him some men we had sent for to relieve those who had waded through the mire from Currituck. But they begged they might not be relieved, believing they should gain immortal honor by going through the Dismal. Only Petillo desired to be excused on the account of his eyes. Old Ellis petitioned to go in the room of his son, and Kimball was deprived from

that favor by lot. That grieved him so that he offered a crown to Hamilton to let him go in his room, which the other would not listen to for ten times the money.

When this great affair was settled, we dismissed all the men to their quarters at Captain Wilson's except the nine Dismalites. Of these we sent five with the surveyors, who ran the line to the skirts of the Dismal, which began first with dwarf reeds and moist, uneven grounds. We discharged our piraguas, and about noon our good friend Captain Wilkins conducted us to his own house and entertained us hospitably. We made the necessary disposition for entering the Dismal next morning with nine of our men and three of Carolina, so many being necessary to attend the surveyors and for carrying the bedding and provisions. The men were in good spirits, but poor Orion began to repent and wish he had slept in a whole skin at the College rather than become a prey to the turkey buzzard. These reflections sunk his courage so low that neither liquor nor toast could raise it. I hardly knew how to behave myself in a bed, after having lain a week in the open field and seeing the stars twinkle over my head.

14. This morning early the men began to make up the packs they were to carry on their shoulders into the Dismal. They were victualed for eight days, which was judged sufficient for the service. These provisions, with the blankets and other necessaries, loaded the men with a burden of fifty or sixty pounds for each. Orion helped most of all to make these loads so heavy by taking his bed and several changes of raiment, not forgetting a suit for Sundays, along with him. This was a little unmerciful, which with his peevish temper made him no favorite.

We fixed them out about ten in the morning, and then Meanwell, Puzzlecause, and I went along with them, resolving to enter them fairly into this dreadful swamp, which nobody before ever had either the courage or curiosity to pass. But Firebrand and Shoebrush chose rather to toast their noses over a good fire and spare their dear persons.

After a march of two miles through a very bad way, the men sweating under their burdens, we arrived at the edge of the Dismal, where the surveyors had left off the night before. Here Steddy thought proper to encourage the men by a short harangue to this effect: "Gentlemen, we are at last arrived at this dreadful place, which till now has been thought unpassable, though I make no doubt but you will convince everybody that there is no difficulty which may not be conquered by spirit and constancy. You have hitherto behaved with so much vigor that the most I can desire of you is to persevere unto the end. I protest to you, the only reason we don't share in your fatigue is the fear of adding to your burdens (which are but too heavy already), while we are sure we can add nothing to your resolution. I shall say no more but only pray the Almighty to prosper your undertaking and grant we may meet on the other side in perfect health and safety." The men took this speech very kindly and answered it in the most cheerful manner with three huzzas.

Immediately we entered the Dismal, two men clearing the way before the surveyors to enable them to take their sight. The reeds, which grew about twelve feet high, were so thick and so interlaced with bamboo briers that our pioneers were forced to open a passage. The ground, if I may properly call it so, was so spongy that the prints of our feet were instantly filled with water. Amongst the reeds here and there stood a white cedar, commonly mistaken for juniper. Of this sort was the soil for about half a mile together, after which we came to a piece of high land about one hundred yards in breadth.

We were above two hours scuffling through the reeds to this place, where we refreshed the poor men. Then we took leave, recommending both them and the surveyors to Providence. We furnished Astrolabe with bark and other medicines for any of the people that might happen to be sick, not forgetting three kinds of rattlesnake root made into doses in case of need.

It was four o'clock before we returned to our quarters, where we found our colleagues under some apprehension that we were gone with the people quite through the Dismal. During my absence Firebrand was so very careful in sending away the baggage that he forgot the candles.

When we had settled accounts with our landlord, we rode away to Captain Wilson's, who treated us with pork upon pork. He was a great lover of conversation, and rather than it should drop, he would repeat the same story over and over. Firebrand chose rather to litter the floor than lie with the parson, and, since he could not have the best bed, he sullenly would have none at all. However, it broiled upon his stomach so much that he swore enough in the night to bring the devil into the room, had not the chaplain been there.

15. We sent away the baggage about eight o'clock under the guard of four men. We paid off a long reckoning to Captain Wilson for our men and horses, but Firebrand forgot to pay for the washing of his linen, which saved him two shillings at least. He and his flatterer, Shoebrush, left us to ourselves; intending to reach Captain Meade's [49] but, losing their way, they took up at Mr. Pugh's, after riding above fifty miles, and part of the way in the dark. How many curses this misadventure cost them I can't say, though at least as many as they rode miles. I was content to tarry to see the men fixed out and jog on fair and softly along with them, and so were Meanwell and Puzzlecause. One of our men had a kick on the belly by a horse, for which I ordered him to be instantly blooded, and no ill consequence ensued. We left Astrolabe's Negro sick behind us.

About eleven we set off and called at an ordinary eight miles off, not far from the great bridge. Then we proceeded eight miles farther to honest Timothy Ives's,[50] who supplied us with everything that was necessary. He had a tall, straight daughter of a yielding, sandy complexion, who having the curiosity to see the tent, Puzzlecause gallanted her thither, and might have made her free of it had not we come seasonably to save the damsel's chastity. Here both our cookery and bedding were more cleanly than ordinary. The parson lay with Puzzlecause in the tent to keep him honest or, peradventure, to partake of his diversion if he should be otherwise.

16. We marched from hence about nine, always giving our baggage the start of us. We called at John Ives's for a taste of good water, which is as rare in these parts as good doctrine. We saw several pretty girls

[49] Boyd: "Andrew Meade . . . a member of the House of Burgesses, 1727–1734, and of the County Court, and . . . Senior Captain of Militia. See Baskerville's *Andrew Meade of Ireland and Virginia*."

[50] The last name is Ivy in the *History* (p. 192). In the American Philosophical Society manuscript of the "History" the name has been corrected from Ives's to Ivy's. The scribe may have been influenced by the John Ives mentioned below.

here as wild as colts, though not so ragged, but dressed all in their own industry. Even those could not tempt us to alight, but we pursued our journey with diligence.

We passed by Mr. O'Shield's and Mr. Pugh's, the last of which has a very good brick house, and arrived about four at Captain Meade's. Here amongst other strong liquors we had plenty of strong beer, with which we made as free as our libertines did with the parson. The Carolina commissioners did not only persecute him with their wit but with their kisses too, which he suffered with the patience of a martyr. We were no sooner under the shelter of that hospitable house but it began to rain, and so continued to do great part of the night, which put us in some pain for our friends in the Dismal. The journey this day was twenty-five miles, yet the baggage horses performed it without faltering.

17. It rained this morning till ten o'clock, which filled us all with the vapors. I gave myself a thorough wash and scrubbed off a full week's dirt, which made me fitter to attend the service which our chaplain performed.

I wrote to the Governor a particular account of our proceedings and had the complaisance to show the letter to my colleagues. These worthy gentlemen had hammered out an epistle to the Governor, containing a kind of remonstrance against paying the Burgesses in money, and prevailed with our landlord to deliver it.

At night we had a religious bowl to the pious memory of St. Patrick, and, to show due regard to this saint, several of the company made some Hibernian bulls, but the parson unhappily outblundered all, which made his persecutors merry at his cost.

18. It was not possible to get from so good a house before eleven o'clock, nor then neither for our servants. When Firebrand asked his man why he lagged behind, he expressed himself with great freedom of his master, swearing he cared for no mortal but his dear self and wishing that the devil might take him if he ever attended him again in any of his travels.

We made the best of our way to Mr. Thomas Speight's,[51] who ap-

[51] Boyd: "Mr. Thomas Speight, of Perquimans County, member of the North Carolina Assembly in 1725 and Associate Justice of the General Court, 1726-28."

peared to be a grandee of North Carolina. There we arrived about four, though the distance could not be less than twenty-five miles. Upon our arrival our poor landlord made a shift to crawl out upon his crutches, having the gout in both his knees. He bid us welcome, and a great bustle was made in the family about our entertainment. We saw two truss [52] damsels stump about very industriously, that were handsome enough upon a march.

Our landlord gave us much concern by affirming with some assurance that the Dismal could not be less than thirty miles in breadth. All our comfort was that his computation depended wholly on his own wild conjecture. We ordered guns to be fired and a drum to be beaten to try if we could be answered out of the desert, but we had no answer but from that prating slut, Echo.

The servants tied the horses so carelessly that some of them did our landlord much damage in his fodder. I was the more concerned at this because the poor man did all he could to supply our wants.

Firebrand and the parson lay single, while some were obliged to stow three in a bed. Nor could lying soft and alone cure the first of these of swearing outrageously in his sleep.

19. We dispatched men to the north and south, to fire guns on the edge of the Dismal by way of signal, but could gain no intelligence of our people. Men, women, and children flocked from the neighborhood to stare at us with as much curiosity as if we had been Morocco ambassadors. Many children were brought to our chaplain to be christened, but no capons, so that all the good he did that way was gratis. Major Alston and Captain Baker made us a visit and dined with us.

My landlord's daughter, Rachel, offered her service to wash my linen and regaled me with a mess of hominy, tossed up with rank butter and glyster sugar. [53] This I was forced to eat to show that nothing from so fair a hand could be disagreeable. She was a smart lass, and, when I desired the parson to make a memorandum of his christenings that we might keep an account of the good we did, she asked me very

[52] Shapely.
[53] Probably a scribal error for "caster sugar."

pertly who was to keep an account of the evil? I told her she should be my secretary for that if she would go along with me. Mr. Pugh and Mr. O'Shield helped to fill up our house, so that my landlady told us in her cups that now we must lie three in a bed.

20. No news yet of our Dismalites, though we dispatched men to every point of the compass to inquire after them. Our visitors took their leave, but others came in the evening to supply their places. Judge Jumble, who left us at Currituck, returned now from Edenton and brought three cormorants along with him. One was his own brother,[54] the second was brother to Shoebrush,[55] and the third, Captain Genneau, who had sold his commission and spent the money. These honest gentlemen had no business but to help drink out our liquor, having very little at home. Shoebrush's brother is a collector and owes his place to a bargain he made with Firebrand. Never were understrappers[56] so humble as the North Carolina collectors are to this huge man. They pay him the same colirt[57] they would do if they held their commissions immediately from his will and pleasure, though the case is much otherwise, because their commissions are as good as his, being granted by the same commissioners of His Majesty's Customs. However, he expects a world of homage from them, calling them his officers. Nor is he content with homage only, but he taxes them, as indeed he does all the other collectors of his province, with a hundred little services.

At night the noble captain retired before the rest of the company and was stepping without ceremony into our bed, but I arrived just time enough to prevent it. We could not possibly be so civil to this free gentleman as to make him so great a compliment, much less let him take possession, according to the Carolina breeding, without invitation. Had Ruth or Rachel, my landlord's daughters, taken this liberty, we should perhaps have made no words, but in truth the captain had no charms that merited so particular an indulgence.

21. Several persons from several parts came to see us, amongst which

---

[54] Edmund Gale.
[55] Boyd: "Thomas Lovick, of Chowan County, Collector of the Customs."
[56] Underlings.
[57] Probably a scribal misreading for "courtesy."

was Mr. Baker and his brother, the surveyor of Nansemond, but could tell us no tidings from the Dismal. We began to be in pain for the men who had been trotting in that bog so long, and the more because we apprehended a famine amongst them. I had indeed given them a warrant to kill anything that came in their way in case of necessity, not knowing that no living creature could inhabit that inhospitable place.

My landlord thought our stay here as tedious as we did, because we eat up his corn and summer provisions. However, the hopes of being well paid rendered that evil more supportable. But complaint being made that the corn grew low, we retrenched the poor men's horses to one meal a day.

In the evening Plausible and Puzzlecause returned to us from Edenton, where they had been to recover the great fatigue of doing nothing and to pick up new scandal against their governor.

22. Our disagreeable Carolina visitors were so kind as to take their leave; so did Mr. O'Shield and Captain Foot, by which our company and my landlord's trouble were considerably lessened. We went out several ways in the morning and could get no intelligence. But in the afternoon Boötes brought us the welcome news that the surveyors and all the people were come safe out of the Dismal. They landed, if one may so call it, near six miles north of this place about ten this morning, not far from the house of Peter Brinkley. Here they appeased their hungry stomachs and waited to receive our orders. It seems the distance through the desert where they passed it was fifteen miles. Of this they had marked and measured no more than ten but had traversed the remainder as fast as they could for their lives. They were reduced to such straits that they began to look upon John Ellis' dog with a longing appetite, and John Evans, who was fat and well-liking,[58] had reason to fear that he would be the next morsel.

We sent Astrolabe's horses for him and his brother, and Firebrand ordered Peter Jones, with an air of authority, to send his horse for Orion, but he let him understand very frankly that nobody should ride his horse but himself. So, not finding his commands obeyed by

[58] Thriving.

the Virginians, he tried his power amongst the Carolina men, who were more at his devotion and sent one of their horses for his friend, to save his own. He also sent him a pottle [59] bottle of strong beer particularly,[60] without any regard to Astrolabe, though the beer belonged to the other commissioners as much as to him.

We also sent horses for the men, that they might come to us and refresh themselves after so dreadful a fatigue. They had, however, gone through it all with so much fortitude that they discovered as much strength of mind as of body. They were now all in perfect health, though their moist lodging for so many nights and drinking of standing water, tinged with the roots of juniper, had given them little fevers and slight fluxes in their passage, which as slight remedies recovered.

Since I mentioned the strong beer, it will be but just to remember Captain Meade's generosity to us. His cart arrived here yesterday with a very handsome present to the commissioners of Virginia. It brought them two dozen quart bottles of excellent Madeira wine, one dozen pottle bottles of strong beer, and half a dozen quarts of Jamaica rum. To this general present was added a particular one to Meanwell of Naples biscuit from Mrs. Meade. At the same time we received a very polite letter, which gave a good grace to his generosity and doubled our obligation. And surely never was bounty better timed, when it enabled us to regale the poor Dismalites, whose spirits needed some recruit. And indeed we needed comfort as well as they, for though we had not shared with them in the labors of the body, yet we made it up with the labor of the mind, and our fears had brought us as low as our fatigue had done them. I wrote a letter of thanks to our generous benefactor, concluding with a tender of the commissioners' service and the blessing of their chaplain.

23. The surveyors described the Dismal to us in the following manner: that it was in many places overgrown with tall reeds interwoven with large briers, in which the men were frequently entangled, and that not only in the skirts of it but likewise toward the middle. In

[59] Half-gallon.
[60] That is, for Orion particularly, and for no one else.

other places it was full of juniper trees, commonly so called though they seem rather to be white cedars. Some of these are of a great bigness, but, the soil being soft and boggy, there is little hold for the roots, and consequently any high wind blows many of them down. By this means they lie in heaps, horsing upon one another and bristling out with sharp snags, so that passage in many places is difficult and dangerous. The ground was generally very quaggy, and the impressions of the men's feet were immediately filled with water. So, if there was any hole made, it was soon full of that element, and by that method it was that our people supplied themselves with drink. Nay, if they made a fire, in less than half an hour, when the crust of leaves and trash were burnt through, it would sink down into a hole and be extinguished. So replete is this soil with water that it could never have been passable but in a very dry season. And, indeed, considering it is the source of six or seven rivers without any visible body of water to supply them, there must be great stores of it underground. Some part of this swamp has few or no trees growing in it but contains a large tract of reeds, which being perpetually green and waving in the wind, it is called the Green Sea. Gallbushes grow very thick in many parts of it, which are evergreen shrubs bearing a berry which dyes a black color like the galls of the oak, and from thence they receive their name.

Abundance of cypress trees grow likewise in this swamp and some pines upon the borders toward the firm land, but the soil is so moist and miry that, like the junipers, a high wind mows many of them down. It is remarkable that toward the middle of the Dismal no beast or bird or even reptile can live, not only because of the softness of the ground but likewise because 'tis so overgrown with thickets that the genial beams of the sun can never penetrate them. Indeed, on the skirts of it cattle and hogs will venture for the sake of the reeds and roots, with which they will keep themselves fat all winter. This is a great advantage to the bordering inhabitants in that particular, though they pay dear for it by the agues and other distempers occasioned by the noxious vapors that rise perpetually from that vast extent of mire and nastiness. And a vast extent it is, being computed at a medium ten miles broad and thirty miles long, though where the line passed it 'twas completely fifteen miles broad. However, this dirty Dismal is in many parts of it very pleasant to the eye, though disagreeable to the other senses, because there is an everlasting verdure which makes every season look like the spring. The way the men took to secure their bedding here from moisture was by laying cypress bark under their blankets, which made their lodging hard but much more wholesome.

It is easy to imagine the hardships the poor men underwent in this intolerable place, who, besides the burdens on their backs, were obliged to clear the way before the surveyors and to measure and mark after them. However, they went through it all not only with patience but cheerfulness, though Orion was as peevish as an old maid all the way, and the more so because he could persuade nobody to be out of humor but himself. The merriment of the men and their innocent jokes with one another gave him great offense; whereas if he had had a grain of good nature he should have rejoiced to find that the greatest difficulties could not break their spirits or lessen their good humor. Robin Hix took the liberty to make him some short replies that discomposed him very much: particularly, one hot day, when the poor fellow had a load fit for a horse upon his back, Orion had the conscience to desire him to carry his greatcoat. But he roundly refused it, telling him frankly he had already as great a burden as he could stagger under. This Orion stomached[61] so much that he complained privately of it to Firebrand as soon as he saw him but said not one syllable of it to me. However, I was informed of it by Astrolabe but resolved to take no notice, unless the cause was brought before us in form, that the person accused might have the English liberty of being heard in his turn. But Firebrand said a gentleman should be believed on his bare word without evidence and a poor man condemned without trial, which agreed not at all with my notions of justice.

I understood all this at second hand, but Meanwell was let into the secret by the parties themselves with the hopes of perverting him into their sentiments; but he was stanch and they were not able to

[61] Resented.

71

make the least impression upon him. This was a grievous balk, because if they could have gained him over, they flattered themselves they might have been as unrighteous as they pleased by a majority. As it happens to persons disappointed, it broiled upon our gentlemen's stomachs so much that they were but indifferent company, and I observed very plain that Firebrand joked less adays and swore more anights ever after. After these misfortunes, to be formally civil was as much as we could afford to be to one another. Neither of us could dissemble enough to put on a gay outside when it was cloudy within. However, these inward uneasinesses helped to make the rest of our sufferings the more intolerable. When people are joined together in a troublesome commission, they should endeavor to sweeten by complacency [62] and good humor all the hazards and hardships they are bound to encounter and not, like married people, make their condition worse by everlasting discord. Though in this, indeed, we had the advantage of married people, that a few weeks would part us.

24. This being Sunday, the people flocked from all parts, partly out of curiosity and partly out of devotion. Among the female part of our congregation there was not much beauty; the most fell to Major Alston's daughter, who is said to be no niggard of it. Our chaplain made some Christians but could persuade nobody to be married, because every country justice can do that job for them. Major Alston and Captain Baker dined with us.

In the afternoon I equipped the men with provisions and dispatched them away with Astrolabe and Boötes to the place where they were to return into the Dismal, in order to mark and measure what they had left unfinished. Plausible and Shoebrush took a turn to Edenton and invited us to go with them, but I was unwilling to go from my post and expose the men to be ill treated that I left behind. Firebrand had a flirt at Robin Hix, which discovered much pique and no justice, because it happened to be for a thing of which he was wholly innocent.

25. The air was chilled with a northwester, which favored our Dismalites, who entered the desert very early. It was not so kind to

[62] Complaisance, courtesy.

Meanwell, who unseasonably kicked off the bedclothes and catched an ague. We killed the time by that great help to disagreeable society, a pack of cards.

Our landlord had not the good fortune to please Firebrand with our dinner, but, surely, when people do their best, a reasonable man would be satisfied. But he endeavored to mend his entertainment by making hot love to honest Ruth, who would by no means be charmed either with his persuasion or his person. While the master was employed in making love to one sister, the man made his passion known to the other; only he was more boisterous and employed force when he could not succeed by fair means. Though one of the men rescued the poor girl from this violent lover but was so much his friend as to keep the shameful secret from those whose duty it would have been to punish such violations of hospitality. Nor was this the only one this disorderly fellow was guilty of, for he broke open a house where our landlord kept the fodder for his own use, upon the belief that it was better than what he allowed us. This was in compliment to his master's horses, I hope, and not in blind obedience to any order he received from him.

26. I persuaded Meanwell to take a vomit of ipecacuanha, which worked very kindly. I took all the care of him I could, though Firebrand was so unfriendly as not to step once upstairs to visit him. I also gave a vomit to a poor shoemaker that belonged to my landlord, by which he reaped great benefit. Puzzlecause made a journey to Edenton and took our chaplain with him to preach the Gospel to the infidels of that town and to baptize some of their children. I began to entertain with my chocolate, which everybody commended but only he that commends nothing that don't belong to himself. In the evening I took a solitary walk that I might have leisure to think on my absent friends, which I now grew impatient to see. Orion stuck as close to his patron Firebrand as the itch does to the fingers of many of his country folks.

27. Though it threatened rain both yesterday and today, yet Heaven was so kind to our friends in the Dismal as to keep it from falling. I persuaded Meanwell to take the bark, which he did with good effect,

though he continued very faint and low-spirited. He took Firebrand's neglect in great dudgeon and, amidst all his good nature, could not forbear a great deal of resentment; but I won his heart entirely by the tender care I took of him in his illness. I also gained the men's affection by dressing their wounds and giving them little remedies for their complaints. Nor was I less in my landlord's books for acting the doctor in his family, though I observed some distempers in it that were past my skill to cure. For his wife and heir apparent were so inclined to a cheerful cup that our good liquor was very unsafe in their keeping. I had a long time observed that they made themselves happy every day before the sun had run one third of his course, which no doubt gave some uneasiness to the old gentleman, but custom, that reconciles most evils, made him bear it with Christian patience.

As to the young gentleman, he seemed to be as worthless as any homebred squire I had ever met with and much the worse for having a good opinion of himself. His good father intended him for the mathematics, but he never could rise higher in that study than to gauge a rum cask. His sisters are very sensible, industrious damsels, who, though they see gentlemen but seldom, have the grace to resist their importunities and, though they are innocently free, will indulge them in no dangerous liberties. However, their cautious father, having some notion of female frailty from what he observed in their mother, never suffers them to lie out of his own chamber.

28. I had a little stiffness in my throat, I fancy by lying alone, for Meanwell, being grown restless by his indisposition, chose to lie by himself. The time passed heavily, which we endeavored to make lighter by cards and books. The having nothing to do here was more insupportable than the greatest fatigue, which made me envy the drudgery of those in the Dismal.

In the evening we walked several ways, just as we drew in the day, but made a shift to keep within the bounds of decency in our behavior. However, I observed Firebrand had something that broiled upon his stomach, which though he seemed to stifle in the day, yet in the night it burst out in his sleep in a volley of oaths and imprecations.

yet in the Night it burst out in his Sleep in a Volley
of Oaths & Imprecations. This being my Birth day, I
adored the Goodness of Heaven, for having indulg'd me
with so much Health & uncommon happiness, in
the Course of 54 Years in which my Sins have been
many, & my Sufferings few, my Opportunitys great,
but my Improvements small. Firebrand & Meanwell
had very high Words, after I went to Bed, concerning
Astrolabe, in which Conversation Meanwell shew'd
most Spirit, & Firebrand most Arrogance & Ill Nature.

29. I wrote a Letter to the Governor which I had the Complaisance to shew to my Colleagues to prevent Jealousies &
Fears. We receiv'd Intelligence that our Surveyors & people finish'd their business in the Dismal last Night, &
found it no more than 5 Miles from the Place where
they left off. Above a Mile before they came out, they were
led up to the Knees in a Pine Swamp. We let them rest
this day at Peter Brinkley's, & sent Orders to them to proceed the next Morning. Bootes left them & came to
us with intent to desert us quite, & leave the rest of the
Drudgery to Plausible, who had indulged his Old Bones
hitherto. Our Parson return'd to us with the Carolina
Commissioners from Edenton, where he had preach't in
their Court-house, there being no Place of Divine Worship in that Metropolis. He had also Christen'd 19
of their Children, & pillag'd them of some of their
Cash, if Paper Money may be allow'd that Appellation.

30. This Morning all the ill-humour that Firebrand
had so long kept broiling upon his Stomach broke out.
First he insisted that Young Astrolabe might go no
longer with the Surveyors to be a Spy upon Orion,

A Page from the Manuscript of *The Secret History of the Line*
in the American Philosophical Society Library

This being my birthday, I adored the goodness of Heaven for having indulged me with so much health and very uncommon happiness in the course of fifty-four years, in which my sins have been many and my sufferings few, my opportunities great but my improvements small.

Firebrand and Meanwell had very high words after I went to bed concerning Astrolabe, in which conversation Meanwell showed most spirit and Firebrand most arrogance and ill nature.

29. I wrote a letter to the Governor, which I had complaisance to show to my colleagues to prevent jealousies and fears.

We received intelligence that our surveyors and people finished their business in the Dismal last night and found it no more than five miles from the place where they left off. Above a mile before they came out, they waded up to the knees in a pine swamp. We let them rest this day at Peter Brinkley's and sent orders to them to proceed the next morning. Boötes left them and came to us with intent to desert us quite and leave the rest of the drudgery to Plausible, who had indulged his old bones hitherto.

Our parson returned to us with the Carolina commissioners from Edenton, where he had preached in their courthouse, there being no place of divine worship in that metropolis. He had also christened nineteen of their children and pillaged them of some of their cash, if paper money may be allowed that appellation.

30. This morning all the ill-humor that Firebrand had so long kept broiling upon his stomach broke out. First he insisted that young Astrolabe might go no longer with the surveyors to be a spy upon Orion. I told him that volunteers were always employed upon the side, that he was very useful in assisting Orion, who had reason to be satisfied with having his defects so [well] [63] supplied. Then he complained of the rudeness of Robin Hix to Orion and proposed he might be punished for it. To this I answered that if Orion had any accusation to make against Robin Hix, it had been fair to make it openly before all the commissioners, that the person accused might have an opportunity to make his defense, and ought not to whisper his complaints in pri-

[63] So illegible that the reading is doubtful.

vate to one gentleman, because it looked like suspecting the justice of the rest. That word "whispering" touched him home and made him raise his voice and roll his eyes with great fury, and I was weak enough to be as loud and choleric as he. However, it was necessary to show that I was not to be dismayed either with his big looks or his big words, and, in truth, when he found this, he cooled as suddenly as he fired. Meanwell chimed in with my sentiments in both these points, so that we carried them by a fair majority. However, to show my good humor and love of peace, I desired young Astrolabe to concern himself no more with the surveying part, because it gave uneasiness, but only to assist his brother in protracting and plotting of the work. After this storm was over, Firebrand went with Shoebrush to Mr. O'Shield's for some days, and his going off was not less pleasing to us than the going off of a fever.

31. This was Sunday, but the people's zeal was not warm enough to bring them through the rain to church, especially now their curiosity was satisfied. However, we had a sermon and some of the nearest neighbors came to hear it. Astrolabe sent word that he had carried the line seven miles yesterday but was forced to wade up to the middle through a mill swamp. Robins sent his mate hither to treat with my landlord about shipping his tobacco; they roll it in the night to Nansemond River, in defiance of the law against bringing of tobacco out of Carolina into Virginia, but 'twere unreasonable to expect that they should obey the laws of their neighbors who pay no regard to their own. Only the masters of ships that load in Virginia should be under some oath or regulation about it.

Sunday seemed a day of rest indeed, in the absence of our turbulent companion, who makes every day uneasy to those who have the pain of his conversation.

## APRIL

1. We prepared for a march very early, and then I discharged a long score with my landlord and a short one with his daughter Rachel for some smiles that were to be paid for in kisses. We took leave in form of the whole family and in eight miles reached Richard Par-

ker's, where we found young Astrolabe and some of our men. Here we refreshed ourselves with what a neat landlady could provide and christened two of her children, but did not discharge our reckoning that way. Then we proceeded by Somerton Chapel (which was left two miles in Virginia) as far as the plantation of William Speight, that was cut in two by the line, taking his tobacco house into Carolina. Here we took up our quarters and fared the better for a side of fat mutton sent us by Captain Baker. Our lodging was exceedingly airy, the wind having a free circulation quite through our bedchamber, yet we were so hardy as to take no cold, though the frost was sharp enough to endanger the fruit. Meanwell entertained the Carolina commissioners with several romantic passages of his life with relation to his amours, which is a subject he is as fond of as a hero to talk of battles he never fought.

2. This morning early Captain Baker came to make us a visit and explained to us the reason of the present of mutton which he sent us yesterday. It seems the plantation where he lives is taken into Virginia, which without good friends might prejudice him in his surveyor's place of Nansemond County. But we promised to employ our interest in his favor.

We made the best of our way to Chowan River, crossing the line several times. About a mile before we came to that river we crossed Somerton Creek. We found our surveyors at a little cottage on the banks of Chowan, over against the mouth of Nottoway River. They told us that our line cut Blackwater River about half a mile to the northward of that place, but, in obedience to His Majesty's order in that case, we directed them to continue the line from the middle of the mouth of Nottoway River. Accordingly, the surveyors passed Chowan there and carried the line over a miry swamp, more than half a mile through, as far as an Indian old field.

In the meantime, our horses and baggage were ferried over the river a little lower to the same field, where we pitched our tent, promising ourselves a comfortable repose; but our evil genius came at night and interrupted all our joys. Firebrand arrived with his most humble servant, Shoebrush, though, to make them less unwelcome, they brought a present from Mr. O'Shield's of twelve bottles of wine and as many of strong beer. But to say the truth, we had rather have drunk water the whole journey to have been fairly quit of such disagreeable company.

Our surveyors found by an observation made this night that the variation was no more than 2° 30′ westerly, according to which we determined to proceed in the rest of our work toward the mountains.

Three of the Meherrin Indians came hither to see us from the place where they now live about seven miles down the river, they being lately removed from the mouth of Meherrin. They were frightened away from thence by the late massacre committed upon fourteen of their nation by the Catawbas. They are now reduced to a small number and are the less to be pitied because they have always been suspected to be very dishonest and treacherous to the English.

3. We sent away the surveyors about nine o'clock and followed them at ten. By the way Firebrand and Shoebrush, having spied a house that promised good cheer, filed off to it and took it in dudgeon that we would not follow their vagaries. We thought it our duty to attend the business in hand and follow the surveyors. These we overtook about noon, after passing several miry branches where I had like to have stuck fast. However, this only gave me an opportunity to show my horsemanship, as the fair-spoken Plausible told me.

After passing several dirty places and uneven grounds, we arrived about sunset on the banks of Meherrin, which we found thirteen and a quarter miles from the mouth of Nottoway River. The county of Isle of Wight begins about three miles to the east of this river, parted from Nansemond by a dividing line only. We pitched our tent and flattered ourselves we should be secure from the disturber of our peace one night more; but we were mistaken, for the stragglers came to us after it was dark, with some danger to their necks because the low grounds near the river were full of cypress snags as dangerous as so many *chevaux de frise*.[64] But this deliverance from danger was not enough to make Firebrand good humored, because we had not been so kind as to rejoice at it.

[64] Defensive barriers, often made of sharpened stakes.

4. Here we called a council of war whether we should proceed any farther this season, and we carried it by a majority of votes to run the line only about two miles beyond this place. Firebrand voted for going on a little longer, though he was glad it was carried against him. However, he thought it gave him an air of industry to vote against leaving off so soon, but the snakes began to be in great vigor, which was an unanswerable argument for it.

The river was hardly fordable and the banks very steep, which made it difficult for our baggage horses to pass over it. But thank God we got all well on the other side without any damage.

We went to a house just by the riverside, belonging to a man who learnedly called himself Carolus Anderson, where we christened his child. Then we proceeded to Mr. Kinchen's, a man of figure in these parts, and his wife a much better figure than he. They both did their utmost to entertain us and our people in the best manner. We pitched our tent in the orchard, where the blossoms of the apple trees mended the air very much. There Meanwell and I lay, but Firebrand and his flatterers stuck close to the house.

The surveyors crossed this river three times with the line in the distance of two and a half miles and left off about half a mile to the northward of this place.

5. Our surveyors made an elegant plat of our line from Currituck Inlet to the place where they left off, containing the distance of seventy-three miles and thirteen poles.[65] Of this exact copies were made and, being carefully examined, were both signed by the commissioners of each colony. This plat was chiefly made by Astrolabe, but one of the copies was taken by Plausible; but Orion was content with a copy which the parson took for him. However, he delivered me the minutes which he had kept of our proceedings by order of the commissioners.

The poor chaplain was the common butt at which all our company aimed their profane wit and gave him the title of "Dean Pip," because instead of a pricked line he had been so maidenly as to call it a pipped line. I left the company in good time, taking as little pleasure

---

[65] A pole is a measure identical with a rod (16½ feet). The *History* (p. 216) says seventy-three miles and thirteen chains (a measure of four rods).

in their low wit as in their low liquor, which was rum punch. Here we discharged six of the men, who were near their own habitations.

6. We paid our scores, settled our accounts, and took leave of our Carolina friends. Firebrand went about six miles with us as far as one Corker's, where we had the grief to part with that sweet-tempered gentleman and the burr that stuck to him, Orion. In about ten miles we reached a muster field near Mr. Kindred's house, where Captain Gerald was exercising his company. There were girls enough come to see this martial appearance to form another company and beauties enough among them to make officers of.

Here we called and christened two children and offered to marry as many of the wenches as had got sweethearts, but they were not ripe for execution. Then we proceeded ten miles farther to Bolton's Ferry, where we passed Nottoway River at Mr. Symonds' quarter. From hence we intended to proceed to Nottoway Town to satisfy the curiosity of some of our company, but, losing our way, we wandered to Richard Parker's plantation, where we had formerly met with very kind entertainment. Our eyes were entertained as well as our stomachs by the charms of pretty Sally, the eldest daughter of the family.

7. This being Sunday, we had a sermon, to which very few of the neighbors resorted, because they wanted timely notice. However, some good Christians came and amongst them Molly Izard, the smartest damsel in these parts. Meanwell made this girl very vain by saying sweet things to her, but Sally was more engaging, whose wholesome flesh and blood neither had nor needed any ornament. Nevertheless, in the afternoon we could find in our hearts to change these fair beauties for the copper-colored ones of Nottoway Town.

Thither we went, having given notice by a runner that we were coming, that the Indians might be at home to entertain us. Our landlord showed us the way, and the scouts had no sooner spied us but they gave notice of our approach to the whole town by perpetual whoops and cries, which to a stranger sound very dismal. This called their great men to the fort, where we alighted and were conducted to the best cabins. All the furniture of those apartments was hurdles covered with clean mats. The young men had painted themselves in a hideous manner, not for beauty but terror, and in that equipage entertained us with some of their war dances. The ladies had put on all their ornaments to charm us, but the whole winter's dirt was so crusted on their skins that it required a strong appetite to accost them. Whatever we were, our men were not quite so nice but were hunting after them all night. But though Meanwell might perhaps want inclination to these sad-colored ladies, yet curiosity made him try the difference between them and other women, to the disobligation of his ruffles, which betrayed what he had been doing.

Instead of being entertained by these Indians, we entertained them with bacon and rum, which they accepted of very kindly, the ladies as well as the men. They offered us no bedfellows, according to the good Indian fashion, which we had reason to take unkindly. Only the Queen of Weyanoke told Steddy that her daughter had been at his service if she had not been too young.

Some Indian men were lurking all night about our cabin, with the felonious intent to pilfer what they could lay their hands upon, and their dogs slunk into us in the night and eat up what remained of our provisions.

8. When we were dressed, Meanwell and I visited most of the princesses at their own apartments, but the smoke was so great there, the fire being made in the middle of the cabins, that we were not able to see their charms. Prince James's princess sent my wife a fine basket of her own making, with the expectation of receiving from her some present of ten times its value. An Indian present, like those made to princes, is only a liberality put out to interest and a bribe placed to the greatest advantage.

I could discern by some of our gentlemen's linen, discolored by the soil of the Indian ladies, that they had been convincing themselves in the point of their having no fur.

About ten we marched out of the town, some of the Indians giving us a volley of small arms at our departure. We drank our chocolate at one Jones's, about four miles from the town, and then proceeded over Blackwater Bridge to Colonel Henry Harrison's,[66] where we

---

[66] Boyd: "Henry Harrison (1691–1732) . . . member of the House of Burgesses in 1715 and later years, and of the Council in 1730."

were very handsomely entertained and congratulated one another upon our return into Christendom.

9. We scrubbed off our Indian dirt and refreshed ourselves with clean linen. After a plentiful breakfast, we took our leave and set our faces toward Westover. By the way we met Bowler Cocke and his lady, who told me my family was well, Heaven be praised.

When we came to the new church near Warren's Mill, Steddy drew up his men and harangued them in the following manner: "Friends and fellow travelers, it is a great satisfaction to me that after so many difficulties and fatigues you are returned in safety to the place where I first joined you. I am much obliged to you for the great readiness and vigor you have showed in the business we went about, and I must do you all the justice to declare that you have not only done your duty but also done it with cheerfulness and affection. Such a behavior, you may be sure, will engage us to procure for you the best satisfaction we can from the government. And besides that, you may depend upon our being ready at all times to do you any manner of kindness. You are now, blessed be God, near your own dwellings and, I doubt not, willing to be discharged. I heartily wish you may, every one, find your friends and your families in perfect health, and that your affairs may have suffered as little as possible by your absence."

The men took this speech very kindly and were thankful on their part for the affectionate care we had taken of them during the whole journey. Upon the whole matter, it was as much as we could do to part with dry eyes. However, they filed off to Prince George court, where they entertained their acquaintance with the history of their travels; and Meanwell with the two Astrolabes passed over the river with me to Westover, where I had the pleasure of meeting all my family in perfect health, nor had they been otherwise since I left them. This great blessing ought to inspire us all with the deepest sentiments of gratitude, as well as convince us of the powerful effect of sincere and hearty prayers to the Almighty in all our undertakings.

Thus ended our progress for this season; and it should be remembered that before we parted with the commissioners of North Carolina we agreed to meet again at Kinchen's on the tenth of September to continue the line from thence toward the mountains — upon this condition, nevertheless, that if the commissioners on either side should find it convenient to alter the day, they should give timely notice to the other.

I had been so long absent from home that I was glad to rest myself for a few days, and therefore went not down to Williamsburg till the seventeenth of April. And then I waited upon the Governor to give an account of my commission but found my reception a little cooler than I thought my behavior in the service had deserved. I must own I was surprised at it, till I came to understand that several stories had been whispered by Firebrand and Orion to my disadvantage.

Those gentlemen had been so indiscreet as to set about several ridiculous falsehoods, which could be proved so by every man that was with us, particularly that I had treated Orion not only without ceremony but without justice, denying him any assistance from the men and supporting them in their rudeness to him. And because they thought it necessary to give some instance of my unkindness to that worthy gentleman, they boldly affirmed that I would not send one of the men from Captain James Wilson's to Norfolk Town for his horse, which he had left there to be cured of a sore back. The Father of Lies could not have told one more point-blank against the truth than this was, because the author of it knew in his own conscience that I had ordered one of the men to go upon this errand for him, though it was more than fifty miles backward and forward, and though his own servant might as well have gone, because he had at that time nothing to hinder him, being left behind at Wilson's where the men were and not attending upon his master. And this I could prove by Meanwell, who wrote the order I signed for this purpose, and by Dr. Humdrum, who received it and thereupon had sent one of the men to Norfolk for him.

Nor were these gentlemen content with doing this wrong to me, but they were still more and more unjust to Astrolabe, by telling the Governor that he was ignorant in the business of surveying, that he had done nothing in running of the line but Orion had done all, which was as opposite to truth as light is to darkness or modesty to impudence. For, in fact, Astrolabe had done all and Orion had done nothing but what exposed not only his awkwardness in the practice but his ignorance in the theory. Nor was this a bare untruth only with regard to Astrolabe, but there was malice in it; for they had so totally prepossessed the Commissary with his being ignorant in the art of surveying that, contrary to his promise formerly given, he determined not to make him surveyor of Goochland, nor had he yielded to it at last without the interposition of the Governor. So liable is human nature to prepossession that even the clergy is not exempt from it.

They likewise circulated a great many other ridiculous stories in the gaiety of their hearts, which carried a keener edge against themselves than Steddy and therefore merited rather my contempt than resentment. However, it was very easy when Meanwell and I came to town not only to disprove all their slander but also to set everything in a true light with regard to themselves. We made it as clear as noonday that all the evidence they had given was as much upon the Irish [67] as their wit and their modesty. The Governor was soon convinced and expressed himself very freely to those gentlemen and particularly to Orion, who had with great confidence imposed upon him. He was also so fully persuaded of Astrolabe's abilities that he perfectly constrained the Commissary to appoint him surveyor of Goochland, to the mortification of his adversaries.

As soon as I could complete my journal, I sent it to Firebrand for his hand if he found it right, but after many days he returned it to me unsigned, though he could make no objection.[68] I gave myself no further trouble about him but desired Mr. Banister [69] to give it to the Governor, subscribed by Meanwell and me. Upon his asking Firebrand why he would not grace the journal with his hand, his invention could find no other reason but because it was too poetical. However, he thought proper to sign this poetical journal at last, when he found it was to be sent to England without it.

[67] In the manner of the Irish.
[68] This is the "Journal of the Proceedings," in the Public Record Office, P.R.O. CO5/1321.
[69] Boyd: "John Banister, collector of the Customs for the Upper James District, son of Rev. John Banister, naturalist and entomologist, who arrived in Virginia about 1678. The Banister plantation was near Petersburg."

Sometime in June, Plausible made me a visit and let me know in the name of his brother commissioners of North Carolina that it was their common request that our meeting to continue the line might be put off to the twentieth of September and desired me to communicate their sentiments to the other commissioners for Virginia. I begged he would make this request in writing by way of letter, lest it might be called in question by some unbelievers. Such a letter he wrote, and a few days after I showed it to Firebrand and let him know Meanwell and I had agreed to their desire and intended to write them an answer accordingly. But he, believing this alteration of the day to have been made in compliment to me (because he knew I had always been of this opinion), immediately sent away a letter, or rather an order, to the commissioners for Carolina, directing them to stick to their first day of meeting, being the tenth of September, and to disown their order to Plausible to get it put off. A precept from so great a man, three of these worthy commissioners had not the spirit to disobey but meanly swallowed their own words and under their hands denied they had ever desired Plausible to make any such motion. The renegade letter of these sycophants was afterwards produced by Firebrand to the Governor and Council of Virginia. In the meantime, I sent them an epistle signed by Meanwell and myself that we, in compliance with their desire delivered by Plausible, had agreed to put off our meeting to the twentieth of September. This servile temper in these three Carolina commissioners showed of what base metal they were made and had discovered itself in another pitiful instance not long before.

Firebrand, despairing of a good word from his Virginia colleagues, with great industry procured a testimonial from his Carolina flatterers, as well for himself as his favorite Orion. And because the compliment might appear too gross if addressed to himself, it was contrived that the gentlemen above-mentioned should join in a letter to the Commissary (with whom, by the way, they had never before corresponded), wherein without rhyme or reason they took care to celebrate Firebrand's civility and Orion's mathematics.

This certificate was soon produced by the good Commissary to

our Governor, who could not but see through the shallow contrivance. It appeared ridiculous to him but most abject and monstrous to us, who knew them to be as ill judges of the mathematics
as a deaf man could be of music. So that, to be sure, it was a great
addition to the character of our professor to have the honor of their
testimonials. And though we should allow men of their education to
be critics in civility, yet at first these very men complained of Firebrand's haughty carriage, though now they have the meanness to
write to the Commissary in commendation of his civility. These are
such instances of a poor spirit as none could equal but themselves in
other passages of their behavior.

And though the subject be very low, yet I must beg leave to mention another case in which not only these but all the Council of
North Carolina discovered a submission below all example. They
suffered this Firebrand to come in at the head of their Council, when
at his first admission he ought to have been at the tail. I can't tell
whether it was more pretending in him to ask this precedence or more
pitiful in them to submit to it. He will say, perhaps, that it befitted
not a gentleman of his noble family and high station to sit below a
company of pirates, vagabonds, and footmen; but, surely, if that be
their character, he ought as little to sit among them at all. But what
have they to say in their excuse for prostituting the rank in which
the Lords Proprietors had placed them, since the person to whom
they made this compliment has no other title to the arms he bears
and the name he goes by but the courtesy of Ireland? And then for
his office, he is at most but a publican and holds not his commission
from His Majesty but from the Commissioners of the Customs. So
they had no other reason to give this man place but because their
own worthlessness flew in their faces.

Sometime in July, I received a letter from Firebrand, in which he
accused me of having taken too much upon me in our last expedition by pretending to a sole command of the men, that then the
number of our men was too great and brought an unnecessary charge
upon the public, that nine or ten would be sufficient to take out with
us next time, of which he would name three. This was the sum and

substance of his letter, though there were turns in it and some raillery which he intended to be very ingenious and for which he belabored his poor brains very much. I did not think this epistle worth an answer but fancied it would be time enough to dispute the points mentioned therein at our next council.

It happened in August, upon the news of some disturbance among the Indians, that the Governor called a small council composed only of the councilors in the neighborhood, judging it unnecessary to give us the trouble of a journey who lived at a greater distance. At this council assisted only Firebrand, the Commissary, and three other gentlemen. Neither Meanwell nor I were there nor had any summons or the least notice of it. This Firebrand thought a proper occasion to propose his questions concerning the reduction of the number of our men and the day when we were to meet the Carolina commissioners. He was seconded by his friend the Commissary, who surprised the rest of the council into their opinion, there being nobody to oppose them nor any so just as to put off the question till the two commissioners that were absent might be heard in a matter that concerned them.

However, these unfair and shortsighted politics were so far from prospering that they turned to the confusion of him that contrived them. For, having quickly gained intelligence of this proceeding, I complained of the injustice of it in a letter I wrote to the Governor, and he was so much convinced by my reasons that he wrote me word he would call a general council the week following to overhaul that matter again. Indeed, he had been so prudent at the little council as to direct the clerk not to enter what had been there determined upon the council books, that it might not stand as an order but only as matter of advice to us commissioners.

Upon receipt of this letter, I dispatched an express to Meanwell, acquainting him with this whole matter and entreating him to call upon me in his way to the next council. When he came, we consulted what was fittest for us to do after such treatment; and, upon weighing every circumstance, we resolved at last that since it was not possible for us to agree with Firebrand we would absolutely refuse to go with him upon the next expedition lest His Majesty's service might suffer by our perpetual discord.

Full of this resolution, we went down to Williamsburg and begged the Governor that he would be pleased to dispense with our serving any more with Firebrand in running the line, because he was a person of such uneasy temper that there were no hopes of preserving any harmony amongst us. The Governor desired we would not abandon a service in which we had acquitted ourselves so well but finish what we had began, though he owned we were joined by a gentleman too selfish and too arrogant to be happy with him. I replied that since he did me the honor to desire me to make another journey with him, I would do it, but hoped I might have twenty men and have the sole command of them to prevent all disputes upon that chapter. He thought what I asked was so reasonable that if I would propose it to the Council, I might easily carry it.

According to the Governor's advice, Meanwell and I yielded to put it to the Council; and when it was met and our business entered upon, I delivered myself in the following terms: "I humbly conceive that the business of running the line toward the mountains will require at least twenty men if we intend to follow it with vigor. The chain carriers, the markers, and the man who carries the instrument after the surveyor must be constantly relieved. There must be five in number always upon duty, and where the woods are thick, which will frequently be the case, there should be two more men to clear the way and open the prospect to the surveyors. While this number is thus employed, their arms must be carried and their horses led after them by as great a number. This will employ at least ten men constantly, and, if we must have no more, who must then take care of the baggage and provisions, which will need several horses, and in such pathless woods each horse must be led by a careful man or the packs will soon be torn off their backs. Then, besides all these, some men should be at leisure to hunt and keep us in meat, for which our whole dependence must be upon the woods.

Nor ought we in an affair of so much consequence be tied down to so small a number of men as will be exactly requisite for the daily business; some may be sick or lame or otherwise disabled. In such an exigence must we return home for want of spare hands to supply such misfortune? Ought we not to go provided against such common disasters as these? At this rate we should lose more in the length of time than we should save by the shortness of our number, which would make our frugality, as it often happens, an extravagant expense to us.

Nor would it be prudent or safe to go so far above the inhabitants without a competent number of men for our defense. We shall cross the path which the northern Indians pass to make war upon the Catawbas and shall go through the very woods that are frequented by those straggling savages, who commit so many murders upon our frontiers. We ought therefore to go provided with a force sufficient to secure us from falling into their hands.

It may possibly be objected that the Carolina men will increase our number, which is certain, but they will very little increase our force. They will bring more eaters than fighters, at least they did so the last time, and, if they should be better provided with arms now, their commissioners have so little command over the men that I expect no good from them if we should be so unfortunate as to be attacked.

From all which I must conclude that our safety, our business, and the accidents that attend it will require at least twenty men. And, in order to make this number more useful, there ought to be no confusion in the command. We are taught both by reason and experience that when any men in arms are sent on an expedition they ought to be under the command of one person only. For should they be commanded by several claiming equal power, the orders given by so many might happen to be contradictory, as probably they would happen to be in our case. The consequence of which must follow that the men would not know whom to obey. This must introduce an endless distraction and end in defeating the business you are sending us about.

It were ridiculous to say the command ought to rest in the majority, because then we must call a council every time any orders are to be issued. It would be still more absurd to propose that such persons claiming equal power should command by turns, because then one commander may undo this day what his colleague had directed the day before, and so the men will be perplexed with a succession of jarring orders. Besides, the preference and distinction which these poor fellows might have reason to show to one of these kings of Brentford [70] may be punished by the other when it comes to his turn to be in power. This being the case, what men of spirit or common sense would list themselves under such uncertain command where they could not know whom to please or whom to obey?

For all which reasons, sirs, I must conclude that the command of the men ought to rest in one person, and if in one, then without controversy in him who has the honor to be first in commission."

The Council, as well as the Governor, was convinced by these arguments and unanimously voted twenty men were few enough to go out with us and thought it reasonable that the command of them should be given to me as being the first in commission. Firebrand opposed each of these points with all his eloquence, but to little purpose, nobody standing by him — not so much as his new ally, the Commissary. He seemed at first to befriend him with a distinction which he made between the day of battle and a day of business, but, having no second, he ran with the stream. However, in pure compassion to poor Firebrand, for fear he should want somebody to run of his errands for him, it was agreed he should have three men to fetch and carry for him.

I had the same success in getting the day of meeting which the Carolina commissioners desired might be put off till the twentieth of September, notwithstanding Firebrand produced letters from Messrs. Jumble and Shoebrush that they had not desired their colleague Plausible to procure our rendezvous to be deferred. I confronted these letters with that epistle I had from Plausible which flatly contradicted them. Thus it was evident there was a shameful untruth on one side or the other; but if we consider the characters of the men and the

[70] In Buckingham's play *The Rehearsal* there are two kings of Brentford ruling simultaneously. The character Bayes (author of the play within the play, a satire on John Dryden) explains in Act I, sc. ii: "The chief hinge of this play, upon which the whole plot moves and turns . . . is that I suppose two kings of the same place; as, for example at Brentford . . . Now the people have the same relation to 'em both, the same affections, the same duty, the same obedience, and all that; are divided among themselves in point of devoir and interest, how to behave themselves equally between 'em: these kings differing sometimes in particular, though in the main they agree."

influence of Firebrand over those two, whose brothers were collectors, one may guess where it lies, especially since this was not the first time their pens had been drawn in his service.

However, these letters did no service. But the Governor declared he would write to Sir Richard Everard that we should meet the commissioners of his government on the twentieth of September with twenty men. How much the pride of Firebrand was mortified by so entire a defeat in every one of his points may be easily guessed by the loud complaint he made afterwards how inhumanely the Council had treated him and by the pains he took with the Governor to get the order of Council softened with relation to the command. But remembering how unjustly he had reproached me with having taken too much upon me in our former trip, I insisted upon the order of Council in the fullest extent. Upon seeing me so sturdy, he declared to the Governor he could not go on such dishonorable terms and swore to others he would not; but interest got the better of his oath and honor too, and he did vouchsafe to go at last, notwithstanding all the disgraces which he thought had been put upon him. From hence we may fairly conclude that pride is not the strongest of his passions, though strong enough to make him both ridiculous and detestable.

After these necessary matters were settled, I ordered one thousand pounds of brown biscuit and two hundred pounds of white to be provided and six baggage horses to carry it, at the rate of three bags containing two hundred pounds each horse. As for meat, I intended to carry none but to depend entirely upon Providence for it. But because the game was not like to be plentiful till we got above the inhabitants, I directed all the men to find themselves with ten days' provision. I augmented my number of men to seventeen, which, together with three which Firebrand undertook to get, made up the complement of twenty. For these I provided ammunition after the rate of two pounds of powder a man, with shot in proportion. On the sixteenth of September, Meanwell and Astrolabe came to my house in order to set out with me the day following toward the place of rendezvous.

SEPTEMBER

17. About ten in the morning I, having recommended my wife and family to the protection of the Almighty, passed the river with Messrs. Meanwell and Astrolabe to Mr. Ravenscroft's landing.[71] He was so complaisant as to accompany us as far as the new church,[72] where eight of our men were attending for us, namely, Peter Jones, George Hamilton, James Petillo, Thomas Short, John Ellis, Jr., Richard Smith, George Tilman, and Abraham Jones. The rest were to meet us at Kinchen's, which lay more convenient to their habitations. Only I had ordered three of them who were absent to convoy the bread horses thither the nearest road they could go, namely, Thomas Jones, Thomas Jones, Jr., and Edward Powell, to the last of which the bread horses belonged.

We proceeded with the eight men above-mentioned to Colonel Henry Harrison's, where our chaplain, Dr. Humdrum, was arrived before us. We were handsomely entertained and after dinner furnished ourselves with several small conveniences out of the store. Then we took a turn to the cold bath, where the Colonel refreshes himself every morning. This is about five feet square and as many deep, through which a pure stream continually passes, and is covered with a little house just big enough for the bath and a firing room. Our landlord, who used formerly to be troubled both with the gripes and the gout, fancies he receives benefit by plunging every day in cold water. This good house was enough to spoil us for woodsmen, where we drank rack punch while we sat up and trod on carpets when we went to bed.

18. Having thanked the Colonel for our good dinner, we took leave about ten, not at all dismayed at the likelihood of rain. We traveled after the rate of four miles an hour, passing over Blackwater

---

[71] Boyd: "Reference is to the Maycox plantation, across the James from Westover, which was purchased in 1723 by Thomas Ravenscroft. In the late eighteenth century it passed into the ownership of David Meade who made it one of the famous show places of Virginia. See Tyler, *Cradle of the Republic*, p. 212."

[72] Boyd suggests that this was a chapel built in 1723, the contractor being a Mr. Thomas Jefferson, and cites William Meade, *Old Churches, Ministers, and Families* (Philadelphia, 1857), I, 440.

Bridge and, ten miles beyond that, over another called Assamoosick Bridge. Then we filed off to Richard Parker's plantation, where we had been kindly used in our return home. We found the distance twenty-four miles, going a little astray for want of a guide, and there fell a sort of Scots mist all the way. We arrived about five o'clock and found things in much disorder, the good woman being lately dead and those that survived sick. Pretty Sally had lost some of her bloom by an ague but none of her good humor. They entertained us as well as they could, and what was wanting in good cheer was made up in good humor.

19. About ten this morning we wished health to Sally and her family and forded over Nottoway River at Bolton's Ferry, the water being very low. We called upon Samuel Kindred again, who regaled us with a beefsteak and our men with cider. Here we had like to have listed a mulatto wench for cook to the expedition, who formerly lived with Colonel Ludwell.[73] After halting here about an hour, we pursued our journey, and in the way Richard Smith showed me the star root,[74] which infallibly cures the bite of the rattlesnake.

Nine miles from thence we forded over Meherrin River near Mr. Kinchen's, believing we should be at the place of meeting before the rest of the commissioners. But we were mistaken, for the first sight my eyes were blest with was that of Orion and, finding the shadow there, I knew the substance could not be far off.

Three commissioners on the part of North Carolina came that night, though Jumble and Puzzlecause were ordered by their governor to stay behind lest their General Court might be delayed. But they came notwithstanding, in the strength of their interest with the Council, but seemed afraid of being pursued and arrested. They put on very gracious countenances at our first greeting, but yet looked a little conscious of having acted a very low part in the epistles they had written. For my part, I was not courtier enough to disguise the sentiments I had of them and their slavish proceeding and therefore

[73] Colonel Philip Ludwell II, of Green Springs, James City County, member of the Council, trustee of the College, and vestryman of Bruton Parish.
[74] The star grass or colicroot, a shrub bearing white or yellow flowers, the roots of which were used medicinally.

could not smile upon those I despised. Nor could I behave much better to Firebrand and his echo, Orion; nevertheless, I constrained myself to keep up a stiff civility.

The last of these gentlemen, remembering the just provocation he had given me, thought it necessary to bring a letter from the Governor recommending him to my favor and protection. This, therefore, had the air of confessing his former errors, which made me, after some gentle reproofs, assure him he should have no reason to complain of my treatment. Though I carried fair weather to Firebrand, yet Meanwell could not, but all ceremony, notice, and conversation seemed to be canceled betwixt them. I caused the tent to be pitched in the orchard, where I and my company took up our quarters, leaving the house to Firebrand and his faction.

20. This morning Meanwell was taken a-purging and vomiting, for which I dosed him with veal broth and afterwards advised him to a gallon of warm water, which finished his cure. We herded very little with our brother commissioners, and Meanwell frankly gave Jumble to understand that we resented the impertinent letters he and some of his colleagues had writ to Virginia. He made a very lame apology for it, because the case would not bear a good one.

He and his brethren were lamentably puzzled how to carry their baggage and provisions. They had brought them up by water near this place and had depended on fortune to get horses there to carry them forward. I believe too they relied a little upon us to assist them, but I was positive not to carry one pound weight. We had luggage enough for our own horses, and, as our provisions lightened, the shortness of their provenders would require them to be lightened too. I was not so complaisant to these worthy gentlemen as Firebrand, for he brought a tent for them out of the magazine at Williamsburg to requite the dirty work they had been always ready to do for him. At last they hired something like a cart to carry their lumber as far as it could go toward Roanoke River.

In the evening six more of our men joined us, namely, Robert Hix, John Evans, Stephen Evans, Charles Kimball, Thomas Wilson, and William Pool, but the three men that conducted the bread horses came not up as yet, which gave me some uneasiness though I concluded they had been stopped by the rain. Just after sunset Captain Hix and Captain Drury Stith [75] arrived and made us the compliment to attend us as far as Roanoke. The last of these gentlemen, bearing some resemblance to Sir Richard Everard, put Messrs. Jumble and Puzzlecause into a panic lest the knight was come to put a stop to their journey.

My landlord had unluckily sold our men some brandy, which produced much disorder, making some too choleric and others too loving, so that a damsel who came to assist in the kitchen would certainly have been ravished if her timely consent had not prevented the violence. Nor did my landlady think herself safe in the hands of such furious lovers and therefore fortified her bedchamber and defended it with a chamber pot charged to the brim with female ammunition. I never could learn who the ravisher was, because the girl had walked off in the morning early, but Firebrand and his servant were the most suspected, having been engaged in those kind of assaults once before.

21. In the morning Meanwell joined us. We sent away the surveyors about nine, who could carry the line no more than three and a half miles, because the low grounds were covered with thickets. As soon as we had paid a very exorbitant bill and the Carolina men had loaded their vehicle and disposed of their lumber, we mounted and conducted our baggage about ten miles. We took up our quarters at the plantation of John Hill, where we pitched our tent with design to rest there till Monday. This man's house was so poorly furnished that Firebrand and his Carolina train could not find in their hearts to lodge in it, so we had the pleasure of their company in the camp. They perfumed the tent with their rum punch and hunted the poor parson with their unseemly jokes, which turned my stomach as much as their fragrant liquor. I was grave and speechless the whole evening and retired early; by all which I gave them to understand I was not fond of the conversation of those whose wit, like the commons at the university and Inns of Court, is eternally the same.

[75] Boyd: "Colonel Drury Stith, Sheriff of Charles City County in 1719–20 and 1724–25. He removed to Brunswick County and was its first County Clerk."

22. This being Sunday, we had a large congregation, and though there were many females, we saw no beauty bright enough to disturb our devotions. Our parson made eleven Christians. Mr. Hill made heavy complaint that our horses did much damage to his cornfield; upon which I ordered those that were most vicious that way to be tied up to their good behavior. Among these, Humdrum's and Astrolabe's were the greatest trespassers. After church I gave John Ellis a vomit for his ague, with good success, and was forced myself to soften my bowels with veal broth for a looseness. I also recommended warm water to Captain Stith for the colic, which gave him immediate ease.

In the afternoon our three men arrived with the six bread horses, having been kept so long behind by the rain, but thank God it had received no damage. I took a walk with Plausible and told him of the letters his colleagues had writ to falsify what he had told me concerning their request to put off the time of our meeting. He justified his own veracity but showed too much cold blood in not being piqued at so flagrant an injury.

Firebrand and his followers had smelt out a house about half a mile off, to which they sent for the silver bowl and spent the evening by themselves, both to their own satisfaction and ours. We hoped to be rid of them for all night, but they found the way to the camp just after we were gone to bed, and Firebrand hindered us from going to sleep so soon by his snoring and swearing.

23. We continued in our camp and sent the surveyors back to the place where they left off. They could run the line no more than four miles by reason that it was overgrown with bushes.

I sent several of the men out a-hunting, and they brought us four wild turkeys. Old Captain Hix killed two of them, who turned his hand to everything notwithstanding his great age, disdaining to be thought the worse for threescore-and-ten. Beauty never appeared better in old age, with a ruddy complexion and hair as white as snow.

It rained a little in the evening but did not hinder our rum commissioners from stepping over to John Hill's to swill their punch, leaving the tent clear to us. After midnight it rained very hard, with a storm of thunder and lightning, which obliged us to trench in our tent to cast off the water. The line crossed Meherrin five times in all.

24. So soon as the men could dry their blankets, we sent away the surveyors, who made a shift to carry the line seven miles. But we thought it proper not to decamp, believing we might easily overtake the surveyors before tomorrow night. Our shooters killed four more wild turkeys. Meanwell and Captain Stith pretended to go a-hunting, but their game was eight fresh-colored wenches, which were not hard to hunt down. The neighbors supplied us with pretty good cheese and very fat mutton. I ordered a view of John Hill's damage in his corn-field and paid him for six barrels on that account.

Firebrand instructed one of the three men which he listed on the public service to call him master, thereby endeavoring to pass him on the Carolina commissioners for his servant, that he might seem to have as many servants as Steddy; but care was taken to undeceive them in this matter and expose his vanity. The Carolina men lived at rack [76] and manger without any sort of economy, thereby showing they intended not to go very far with us, though we took care to set them a better example.

Our chaplain had leave to go home with Robert Hix, who lived no more than six miles from this place, to christen his child, and the old Captain went along with them. We had the comfort to have the tent to ourselves, the Knights of the Rum Cask retiring in the evening to the house and wasting the liquor and double-refined sugar as fast as they could.

25. Our surveyors proceeded to run little more than seven miles. Firebrand and his gang got out this morning before us on pretense of providing our dinner; but they outrid the man that carried the mutton, and he, not knowing the way, was lost, so that instead of having our dinner sooner, we run a hazard of having none at all. We came up to them about four o'clock and thanked them for the prudent care they had taken. This was a sample of these gentlemen's management whenever they undertook anything.

We encamped near Beaver Pond Creek, and on our way thither Peter Jones killed a small rattlesnake. The surveyors made an end

[76] A "rack" was a framework to hold fodder for animals.

very near where we lay. Orion was exceedingly awkward at his business, so that Astrolabe was obliged to do double duty. There being no house at hand to befriend us, we were forced to do penance at the tent with the topers.

26. This morning we dispatched the surveyors early, and they ran about ten and a half miles. By the way the men that were with him killed two large rattlesnakes. Will Pool trod upon one of them without receiving any hurt, and two of the chain carriers had marched over the other, but he was so civil as to bite neither of them; however, one of these vipers struck at Wilson's horse and missed him. So many escapes were very providential, though the danger proves that my argument for putting off our business was not without foundation.

We marched upon the line after the surveyors and about four o'clock encamped upon Cabin Branch, which is one of the branches of Fontaine Creek.

Before we set off this morning, we christened two children. One of them was brought by a modest lass, who, being asked how she liked Captain Stiff, replied, "Not at all, nor Captain Limber neither," meaning Orion.

We saw abundance of ipecacuanha in the woods and the fern rattlesnake root,[77] which is said to be the strongest antidote against the bite of that viper. And we saw St.-Andrew's-cross [78] almost every step we went, which serves for the same purpose. This plant grows on all kinds of soil everywhere at hand during the summer months, when the snakes have vigor enough to do mischief. Old Captain Hix entertained us with one of his trading songs, which he quavered out most melodiously, and put us all into a good humor. *159855*

27. We sent away the surveyors before ten o'clock and followed with the baggage at eleven. But Firebrand thought proper to remain with three of the Carolina commissioners till their cart came up and took it ill that we tarried not with them likewise. But I could not compliment away our time at that rate. Here they made broad hints

[77] Boyd: "An herb of the chicory family. Its milky juice was taken internally and its leaves when steeped were applied externally in the treatment of snake wounds."
[78] Boyd: "A small plant of the St. Johns-wort family, so called because its petals open into shape like the St. Andrews cross."

to carry some of their luggage for them; I would put not such hardships upon our men, who had all enough to carry of their own, so we left them there to make the best shift they could and followed the line with all diligence.

We passed Pea Hill Creek and, sometime after, Lizard Creek, which empties itself into Roanoke River. Here we halted till our chaplain baptized five children. Then we proceeded to Pigeon Roost Creek, where we took up our quarters, having carried the line above nine miles.

28. We hurried away the surveyors, who could run no more than six miles because of the uneven grounds near Roanoke River. We did not follow with the baggage till ten, being stayed to christen six children and to discourse a very civil old fellow, who brought us two fat shoats for a present. The name of our benefactor was Epaphroditus Bainton, who is young enough at sixty years of age to keep a concubine and to walk twenty-five miles in a day. He has forsworn ever getting on a horse's back, being once in danger of breaking his neck by a fall. He spends most of his time in hunting and ranging the woods, killing generally more than one hundred deer in a year. He pretends to skill in the virtues of many plants, but I could learn nothing of that kind from him.

This man was our guide to Major Mumford's plantation, under the care of Miles Riley, where we were regaled with milk, butter, and many other refreshments. The Major had ordered some wine to be lodged here for us and a fat steer to be at our service, but the last we refused with a great many thanks.

From hence we continued our journey to the canoe landing upon Roanoke River, where young Mumford and Mr. Walker met us. Here we ferried over our baggage and our persons, ordering the men with the horses to the ford near a mile higher which leads to the trading path. Here my old friend Captain Hix took his leave, committing us to our kind stars.

We were set ashore at another plantation belonging to Major Mumford, under the management of a man they called Nat. Here was another fat steer ordered for us, which we thankfully accepted of for the sake of the men. We pitched the tent near the house, which supplied all our wants. Poor Miles Riley received a kick from one of the horses, for which I ordered him to be instantly blooded and hindered all bad consequences. I interceded with Plausible in behalf of the Virginians whose land was left by the line in Carolina, and he promised to befriend them. George Hamilton killed a snake with eleven rattles, having a squirrel in his belly which he had charmed and only the head of it was digested. Also the chain carriers killed another small one the same day.

29. Being Sunday, we had a sermon, but 'twas interrupted with a shower of rain which dispersed our congregation. A little before noon the Carolina baggage came up, and the servants blessed us with the news that their masters would come in the evening. They also informed us they lay last night at John Young's and had hired him and his brother to assist them upon the line; that for want of horses to carry their luggage they had left some of it behind.

Our chaplain baptized five children, and I gave Thomas Wilson a vomit that worked powerfully and carried off his fever. I wrote to the Governor a full and true account of all our proceedings and sent the letter by Mr. Mumford, who took his leave this evening.

About four in the afternoon Firebrand and his Carolina guards came to us, as likewise did some of the Saponi Indians. I had sent Charles Kimball to Christanna [79] to persuade two of their most able huntsmen to go the journey to help supply us with meat. I had observed that our men were unfortunate gunners, which made me more desirous to have some that had better luck. Out of five which came I chose Bearskin and another, who accepted the terms I proposed to them. From this time forward the Carolina men and their leader honored us with their company only at dinner, but mornings and evenings they had a distinct fire, to our great comfort, at which they toasted their noses. Indeed, the whole time of our being together, our dear colleague acted more like a commissioner for Carolina than Virginia

[79] A fort established by Governor Spotswood in 1714 on the south side of Meherrin River between Emporia and Lawrenceville in what is now Brunswick County. Here the Saponi Indians were to be introduced to Christianity under the instruction of Charles Griffin, as Byrd mentions in the *History* (p. 220).

and not only herded with them perpetually but in every instance joined his politics with theirs in their consultations. No wonder then they acted so wisely in their conduct and managed their affairs with such admirable prudence. It rained the whole night long and held not up till break of day.

30. The tent and baggage was so wet that we could not get them dry till twelve o'clock, at which hour we sent the surveyors out and they carried the line about four and a half miles, which we computed was as high as any inhabitants. But we moved not till two with the baggage. We passed over Hawtree Creek two miles from our camp, marching over poisoned fields. By the way a very lean boar crossed us and several claimed the credit of killing it, but all agreed 'twas stone-dead before Firebrand fired, yet he took the glory of this exploit to himself, so much vanity he had that it broke out upon such paltry occasions.

Before we set off this morning, Orion came to me with a countenance very pale and disordered, desiring that Astrolabe might have orders never to concern himself when it was his turn to survey, because, when he needed to be relieved, he chose rather to be beholden to Boötes than to him. I could by no means agree to this request, telling him that none was so proper to assist one Virginia surveyor as the other. I let him know too that such a motion savored more of pique and peevishness than reason. However, I desired him to ask the opinion of the other commissioners, if he was not satisfied with mine, but he found it proper to ask no more questions.

Puzzlecause had a sore throat which incommoded him very much indeed, for he could not swallow so much as rum punch without pain. But I advised him to part with twelve ounces of blood, which opened the passage to his stomach. I recommended the bark to Boötes for an ague and gave one of the Carolina men a dose of ipecacuanha for the same distemper as I did to Powell, one of our own men.

### OCTOBER

1. We sent out the surveyors early, and by the benefit of clear woods and even ground they carried the line twelve miles and twelve

poles. One of our baggage horses being missing, we decamped not till noon, which gave Firebrand and his crew an opportunity to get the start of us about an hour. However, we came up with the surveyors before them. We forded over Great Creek not far from the place where we encamped and passed Nutbush Creek about seven miles from thence. And five miles further we quartered near a branch which we called Nutbush Branch, believing it ran into the creek of that name. One of the Indians killed a fawn, which, with the addition of a little beef, made very savory soup. The surveyors, by the help of a clear night, took the variation and found it something more than 2° 30′; so that it did not diminish by approaching the mountains, or by advancing toward the West, or increasing our distance from the sea, but continued much the same we found it at Currituck.

2. The surveyors got out about nine o'clock and advanced the line about nine miles. We followed with the baggage at eleven and passed at three miles distance from our camp Massamony Creek, an Indian name signifying "Paint Creek," from red earth found upon the banks of it, which in a fresh tinges the water of that color. Three miles farther we got over Yapatsco or Beaver Creek with some difficulty, the beavers having raised the water a great way up. We proceeded three and a quarter miles beyond this and encamped on the west side of Ohimpamony Creek, an Indian name which signifies "Fishing Creek."

By the way Firebrand had another occasion to show his prowess in killing a poor little wildcat, which had been crippled by two or three before. Poor Puss was unhappily making a meal on a fox squirrel when all these misfortunes befell her. Meanwell had like to have quarreled with Firebrand and his Carolina squadron for not halting for me on the west side of Yapatsco, having been almost mired in crossing that creek, while they had the fortune to get over it at a better place. The Indians killed two deer and John Evans a third, which made great plenty and consequently great content in Israel.

3. We hurried away the surveyors by nine, who ran something more than eight and a half miles. We followed them at eleven and crossed several branches of excellent water. We went through a large level of very rich, high land, near two miles in length and of unknown

breadth. Our Indian killed one deer and William Pool another, and this last we graciously gave to the Carolina men, who deserved it not because they had declared they did not care to rely upon Providence.

We encamped upon Tewahominy or Tuscarora Creek. We saw many buffalo tracks and abundance of their dung, but the noise we made drove them all from our sight. The Carolina commissioners with their leader lagged behind to stop the cravings of their appetites; nor were we ever happy with their conversation but only at dinner, when they played their parts more for spite than hunger.

4. The surveyors got to work a little after nine and extended the line near eight miles, notwithstanding the ground was very uneven. We decamped after them about eleven, and at five miles distance crossed Bluewing Creek, and three miles beyond that we forded Sugartree Creek and pitched our tent on the west side of it. This creek received its name from many sugar trees which grow in the low grounds of it. By tapping the sugar tree in the spring, a great quantity of liquor flows out of it, which may be boiled up into good sugar. It grows very tall and the wood of it is very soft and spongy.

Here we also found abundance of spice trees, whose leaves are fragrant and the berry they bear is black when dry and hot like pepper. Both these trees grow only in a very rich soil.

The low ground upon this creek is very wide, sometimes on one side, sometimes on the other, but on the opposite side the high land advances close to the creek. It ought to be remembered that the commissioners of Carolina made a compliment of about two thousand acres of land lying on this creek to Astrolabe, without paying any fees.

Robert Hix saw three buffaloes but, his gun being loaden only with shot, could do no execution. Boötes shot one deer, and the Indians killed three more and one of the Carolina men four wild turkeys. Thus Providence was very plentiful to us and did not disappoint us who relied upon it.

5. This day our surveyors met with such uneven ground and so many thickets that with all their diligence they could not run the

line so far as five miles. In this small distance it crossed over Hycoo-tomony Creek[80] no less than five times. Our Indian, Ned Bearskin, informed us at first that this creek was the south branch of Roanoke River, but I thought it impossible, both by reason of its narrowness and the small quantity of water that came down it. However, it passed so with us at present till future experience could inform us better.

About four o'clock this afternoon Jumble advanced from the rest of his company to tell me that his colleagues for Carolina wanted to speak with me. I desired, if they had anything to communicate, that they would please to come forward. It was some time before I heard any more of these worthy gentlemen, but at last Shoebrush, as the mouth of the rest, came to acquaint me that their government had ordered them to run the line but thirty or forty miles above Roanoke, that they had now carried it near fifty and intended to go no further. I let them know it was a little unkind they had not been so gracious as to acquaint us with their intentions before; that it had been neighborly to have informed us with their intentions before we set out how far they intended to go, that we might also have received the commands of our government in that matter; but since they had failed in that civility, we would go on without them, since we were provided with bread for six weeks longer. That it was a great misfortune to lose their company, but that it would be a much greater to lose the effect of our expedition by doing the business by halves. That though we went by ourselves, our surveyors would continue under the same oath to do impartial right both to His Majesty and the Lords Proprietors; and though their government might choose perhaps whether it would be bound by our line, yet it would at least be a direction to Virginia how far His Majesty's land extended to the southward.

Then they desired that the surveyors might make a fair plat of the distance we had run together, and that of this there might be two copies signed by the commissioners of both governments. I let them know I agreed to that, provided it might be done before Monday

[80] Now Hyco River.

noon, when, by the grace of God, we would proceed without loss of time because the season was far advanced and would not permit us to waste one moment in ceremony to gentlemen who had showed none to us. Here the conversation ended till after supper, when the subject was handled with more spirit by Firebrand. On my repeating what I had said before upon this subject, he desired a sight of our commission. I gave him to understand that since the commissioners were the same that acted before, all which had heard the commission read, and since those for Carolina had a copy of it, I had not thought it necessary to cram my portmanteau with it a second time, and was therefore sorry I could not oblige him with a sight of it. He immediately said he would take a minute of this, and, after being some time in scrabbling of it, he read to this effect: that being asked by him for a sight of my commission, I had denied it upon pretense that I had it not with me; that I had also refused the commissioners of Carolina to tarry on Monday till the necessary plats could be prepared and exchanged but resolved to move forward as soon as the tent should be dry, by which means the surveyors would be obliged to work on the Sunday. To this I answered that this was a very smart minute, but that I objected to the word "pretense," because it was neither decent nor true that I denied him a sight of our commission upon any pretense but for the honest reason that I had it not there to show. Most of the company thinking my objection just, he did vouchsafe to soften that expression by saying I refused to show him the commission, alleging I had not brought it.

Soon after, when I said that our governor expected that we should carry the line to the mountains, he made answer that the Governor had expressed himself otherwise to him and told him that thirty or forty miles would be sufficient to go beyond Roanoke River. Honest Meanwell, hearing this and, I suppose, not giving entire credit to it, immediately lugged out his pencil, saying in a comical tone that since he was for minutes, egad, he would take a minute of that. The other took fire at this and without any preface or ceremony seized a limb of our table, big enough to knock down an ox, and lifted it up at Meanwell while he was scratching out his minutes. I, happening to see him brandish this dangerous weapon, darted toward him in a moment to stop his hand, by which the blow was prevented; but while I hindered one mischief, I had like to have done another, for the swiftness of my motion overset the table and Shoebrush fell under it, to the great hazard of his gouty limbs. So soon as Meanwell came to know the favor that Firebrand intended him, he saluted him with the title he had a good right to, namely, of son of a w — e, telling him if they had been alone he durst as well be damned as lift that club at him. To this the other replied with much vigor that he might remember, if he please, that he had now lifted a club at him.

I must not forget that when Firebrand first began this violence, I desired him to forbear or I should be obliged to take him in arrest. But he telling me in a great fury that I had no authority, I called to the men and let him know if he would not be easy I would soon convince him of my authority. The men instantly gathered about the tent ready to execute my orders, but we made a shift to keep the peace without coming to extremities. One of the people, hearing Firebrand very loud, desired his servant to go to his assistance. "By no means," said he, "that's none of my business, but if the gentleman will run himself into a broil, he may get out of it as well as he can."

This quarrel ended at last, as all public quarrels do, without bloodshed, as Firebrand has experienced several times, believing that on such occasions a man may show a great deal of courage with very little danger. However, knowing Meanwell was made of truer metal, I was resolved to watch him narrowly to prevent further mischief. As soon as this fray was composed, the Carolina commissioners retired very soon with their champion, to flatter him, I suppose, upon the great spirit he had showed in their cause against those who were joined with him in commission.

6. This being Sunday, we had prayers but no sermon, because our chaplain was indisposed. The gentlemen of Carolina were all the morning breaking their brains to form a protest against our proceeding on the line any further without them. Firebrand stuck close to them and assisted in this elegant speech, though he took some pains to persuade us he did not. They were so intent upon it that we had not their good company at prayers.

The surveyors, however, found time for their devotions, which helped to excuse their working upon their plats when the service was over. Besides, this, being a work of necessity, was the more pardonable.

We dined together for the last time, not discovering much concern that we were soon to part. As soon as dinner was over, the protesters returned to their drudgery to lick their cub into shape. While I was reading in the tent in the afternoon, Firebrand approached with a gracious smile upon his face and desired to know if I had any commands to Williamsburg, for that he intended to return with the Carolina commissioners; that it was his opinion we had no power to proceed without them, but he hoped this difference of sentiment might not widen the breach that was between us; that he was very sorry anything had happened to set us at variance and wished we might part friends. I was a little surprised at this condescension but humored his inclinations to peace, believing it the only way to prevent future mischief. And as a proof that I was in earnest, I not only accepted of these peaceable overtures myself but was so much his friend as to persuade Meanwell to be reconciled to him. And at last I joined their hands and made them kiss one another.

Had not this pacification happened thus luckily, it would have been impossible for Meanwell to put up the indignity of holding up a club at him, because in a court of honor the shaking of a cudgel at a gentleman is adjudged the same affront as striking him with it. Firebrand was very sensible of this and had great reason to believe that in due time he must have been called to an account for it by a man of Meanwell's spirit. I am sorry if I do him wrong, but I believe this prudent consideration was the true cause of the pacific advances he made to us, as also of his returning back with his dear friends of Carolina, though there might have still been another reason for his going home before the General Court. He was, it seems, left out of the instructions in the list of councilors, and as that matter was likely to come upon the carpet at that time, he thought he might have a better chance to get the matter determined in his favor when two of his adversaries were absent. Add to this the lucre of his attendance during the General Court, which would be so much clear gain if he could get so much interest as to be paid as bountifully for being out four weeks as we for being ten out upon the public service. This I know he was so unconscionable as to expect, but without the least shadow of reason or justice.

Our reconciliation with Firebrand naturally made us friends with his allies of Carolina, who invited us to their camp to help finish their wine. This we did, as they say, though I suspect they reserved enough to keep up their spirits in their return, while we that were to go forward did from henceforth depend altogether upon pure element.

7. This morning I wrote some dispatches home, which Firebrand was so gracious as to offer to forward by an express so soon as he got to Williamsburg. I also wrote another to the Governor, signifying how friendly we parted with our brother commissioner. This last I showed to my colleagues to prevent all suspicion, which was kindly taken.

The plats were countersigned about noon, and that which belonged to Virginia we desired Firebrand to carry with him to the Governor. Then the commissioners for Carolina delivered their protest, signed by them all, though I did not think Plausible would have joined in so ill-concerted a piece. I put it up without reading, to show the opinion I had of it, and let the gentlemen know we would endeavor to return an answer to it in due time. But that so fine a piece may be preserved, I will give both that and the answer to it a place in my journal. The protest is in the following words:

We, the underwritten commissioners for the government of North Carolina, in conjunction with the commissioners on the part of Virginia, having run the line for the division of the two colonies from Currituck Inlet to the southern branch of Roanoke River, being in the whole about 170 miles and near 50 miles without the inhabitants, being of opinion we had run the line as far as would be requisite for a long time, judged the carrying of it farther would be a needless charge and trouble. And the grand debate, which had so long subsisted between the two governments about Weyanoke River or Creek, being settled at our former meeting in the spring, when we were ready on our parts to have gone with the line to the outmost inhabitants (which if it had been done, the line at any time after might have been continued at an easy expense by a surveyor on each side, and if at any time hereafter there should be occasion to carry the line on farther than we have now run it, which we think will not be in an age or two, it may be done in the same easy manner without the great expense that now attends it); and on a conference of all the commissioners, we, having communicated our sentiments thereon, declared our opinion that we had gone as far as the service required and thought proper to proceed no farther; to which it was answered by the commissioners for Virginia that they should not regard what we did, but if we desisted, they would proceed without us. But we, conceiving by His Majesty's order in council they were directed to act in conjunction with the commissioners appointed for Carolina, and having accordingly run the line jointly so far and exchanged plans, thought they could not carry on the bounds singly, but that their proceedings without us would be irregular and invalid and that it would be no boundary, and thought it proper to enter our dissent thereto. Wherefore for the reasons aforesaid, in the name of His Excellency the Palatine and the rest of the true and absolute Lords Proprietors of Carolina, we dissent and disallow of any farther proceedings with the bounds without our concurrence and, pursuant to our instructions, do give this our dissent in writing.

Plausible     Jumble
Puzzlecause     Shoebrush

October 7th, 1728

To this protest the commissioners for Virginia made the following answer:

Whereas on the seventh day of October a paper was delivered to us by the commissioners of North Carolina in the style of a protest against our carrying any farther without them the dividing line between the two governments, we, the underwritten commissioners on the part of Virginia, having maturely considered the reasons offered in the said protest why those gentlemen retired so soon from that service, beg leave to return the following answer.

They are pleased to allege in the first place by way of reason that, having run the line near fifty miles without the inhabitants, it was sufficient for a long time and in their opinion for an age or two. To this we answer that they, by breaking off so soon, did very imperfectly obey His Majesty's order, assented to by the Lords Proprietors. The plain meaning of that order was to ascertain the bounds betwixt the two governments as far toward the mountains as we could, that neither the King's grants may hereafter encroach upon the Lords Proprietors nor theirs on the right of His Majesty. And though the distance toward the mountains be not precisely determined by the said order, yet surely the west line should be carried as near to them as may be, that both the land of the King and of the Lords may be taken up the faster, and that His Majesty's subjects may as soon as possible extend themselves to that natural barrier. This they will do in a very few years when they know distinctly in which government they may enter for the land, as they have already done in the more northern parts of Virginia; so that 'tis strange the Carolina commissioners should affirm that the distance of fifty miles beyond the inhabitants should be sufficient to carry the line for an age or two, especially considering that a few days before the signing of this protest Astrolabe had taken up near two thousand acres of land, granted by themselves, within five miles of the place where they left us. Besides, if we reflect on the goodness of the soil in those parts and the fondness of all degrees of people to take up land, we may venture to foretell, without the spirit of divination, that there will be many settlements much higher than these gentlemen went in less than ten years and perhaps in half that time.

The commissioners of North Carolina protested against proceeding on the line for another reason: because it would be a needless charge and trouble, alleging that the rest may be done by one surveyor on a side in an easy manner when it shall be thought necessary. To this we answer that frugality of the public money is a great virtue, but when the public service must suffer by it, it degenerates into a vice, and this will ever be the case when gentlemen execute the orders of their superiors by halves. But had the Carolina commissioners been sincerely frugal for their government, why did they carry out provisions sufficient to support themselves and their men for eight weeks when they intended to tarry out no longer than half that time? This they must confess to be true, since they had provided five hundred pounds of bread and the same weight of beef and bacon, which was sufficient allowance for their complement of men for two months if it had been carefully managed. Now after so great an expense in their preparations, it had been but a small addition to their charge if they had endured the fatigue a month longer. It would have been at most no more than what they must be at whenever they finish their work, even though they think proper to entrust it to the management of a surveyor, who must have a necessary strength to attend him both for his attendance and defense.

These are all the reasons these gentlemen think fit to mention in their protest, though in truth they had a much stronger argument for their retiring so abruptly, which because they forgot, it will be but neighborly to help them out and remind them of it. The provisions they brought along with them, for want of providing horses to carry it, was partly left behind upon a high tree to be taken down as they returned, and what they did carry was so carelessly handled that after eighteen days, which was the whole time we had the honor of their company, they had by their own confession no more left than two pounds of bread for each man to carry them home.

However, though in truth this was an invincible reason why they left the business unfinished, it was none at all to us who had at that time biscuit sufficient for six weeks longer. Therefore, lest their want of management should put a stop to His Majesty's service, we conceived it our duty to proceed without them and have extended the dividing line so far west as to leave the mountains on each hand to the eastward of us. This we have done with the same fidelity and exactness as if those gentlemen had continued with us. Our surveyors acted under the same oath which they had taken in the beginning and were persons whose integrity will not be called in question. However, though the government of North Carolina should not hold itself bound by the line we made in the absence of its commissioners, yet it will continue to be a direction to the government of Virginia how far the King's lands reach toward Carolina and how far His Majesty may grant them away without injustice to the Lords Proprietors. To this we may also add that, having the authority of our commission to act without the commissioners of North Carolina in case of their disagreement or refusal, we thought it necessary on their deserting to finish the dividing line without them, lest His Majesty's service might suffer by any neglect or mismanagement on their part. Given under our hands the seventh of December, 1728.

Meanwell        Steddy

Though the foregoing answer was not immediately returned to the protest, as appears by the date, yet it can't be placed better in this journal than next to it, that the arguments on each side may be the better compared and understood.

Thus, after we had completed our business with our dear friends of Carolina and supplied 'em with some small matters that could be spared, they took their leave and Firebrand with them, full of professions of friendship and good will — just like some men and their wives who, after living together all their time in perpetual discord and uneasiness, will yet be very good friends at the point of death when they are sure they shall part forever.

A general joy discovered itself through all our camp when these gentlemen turned their backs upon us; only Orion had a cloud of melancholy upon his face for the loss of those with whom he had spent all his leisure hours. Before these gentlemen went, he had persuaded Puzzlecause to give him a certificate concerning the quarrel betwixt Firebrand and Meanwell, not because he was ignorant how it was, because he was sitting by the fire within hearing all the time of the fray, but because he should not be able to tell the truth of the story for fear of disobliging his patron, and to disguise and falsify the truth, besides making himself a liar, would give just offense to Meanwell. In this dilemma he thought it safest to persuade Puzzlecause to be the liar by giving him a certificate which softened some things and left out others and so, by his New England way of cooking the story, made it tell less shocking on the side of Firebrand. This was esteemed wonderful politic in Orion, but he was as blameable to circulate an untruth in another's name and under another's hand as if it had been altogether his own act and deed, and was in truth as much resented by Meanwell when he came to hear it.

Because Firebrand desired that one of the men might return back with him, I listed one of the Carolina men to go on with us in his room, who was indeed the best man they had. One of our horses being missing, we quitted not our camp till two o'clock. This and the thick woods were the reason we carried the line not quite three miles. We crossed Hycootomony Creek once more in this day's work and encamped near another creek that runs into it called Buffalo Creek,[81] so called from the great signs we saw of that shy animal.

Now we drank nothing but the liquor Adam drank in Paradise and found it mended our appetite, not only to our victuals, of which we had plenty, but also to women, of which we had none. It also promoted digestion, else it had been impossible to eat so voraciously, as most of us did, without inconvenience.

Tom Short killed a deer, and several of the company killed turkeys. These two kinds of flesh, together with the help of a little rice or French barley, made the best soup in the world. And what happens

---

[81] Buffalo Mineral Springs, in Halifax County, is believed to have received its name from Byrd's description of the buffalo he saw nearby.

very rarely in other good things, it never cloys by being a constant dish. The bushes, being very thick, began to tear our bread bags so intolerably that we were obliged to halt several times a day to have them mended. And the Carolina men pleased themselves with the joke of one of the Indians, who said we should soon be forced to cut up our house (meaning the tent) to keep our bags in repair. And what he said in jest would have happened true in earnest if I had not ordered the skins of the deer which we killed to be made use of in covering the bags. This proved a good expedient, by which they were guarded and consequently our bread preserved.

I could not forbear making an observation upon our men, which I believe holds true in others, that those of them who were the foremost to stuff their guts were ever the most backward to work and were more impatient to eat their supper than to earn it. This was the character of all the Carolina men without exception.

8. We hurried the surveyors out about nine and followed ourselves with the baggage about eleven, yet the woods were so thick we could advance little better than four miles. I spirited up our men by telling them that the Carolina men were so arrogant as to fancy we could make no earnings of it without them.

Having yet not skins enough to cover all our bread bags, those which had none suffered much by the bushes, as in truth did our clothes and our baggage, nor indeed were our eyes safe in our heads. Those difficulties hindered Tom Jones from coming up with some of the loaded horses to the camp where we lay. He was forced to stop short about a mile of us, where there was not a drop of water, but he had the rum with him, which was some comfort. I was very uneasy at their absence, resolving for the future to put all the baggage before us.

We were so lucky as to encamp near a fine spring, and our Indian killed a fat doe, with which Providence supplied us just time enough to hinder us from going supperless to bed. We called our camp by the name of Tear-Coat Camp by reason of the rough thickets that surrounded it. I observed some of the men were so free as to take what share of the deer they pleased and to secure it for themselves while

others were at work, but I gave such orders as put a stop to those ir-
regularities and divided the people into messes, among which the
meat was fairly to be distributed.

9. The surveyors went to work about nine, but because the bushes
were so intolerably thick, I ordered some hands to clear the way before them. This made their business go on the slower; however, they
carried the line about six miles by reason the thicket reached no
farther than a mile and the rest of the way was over clear woods and
even grounds. We tarried with the rear guard till twelve for our absent
men, who came to the camp as hungry as hawks, for, having no water
to drink, they durst not eat for fear of thirst, which was more uneasy
than hunger.

When we had supplied our wants, we followed the track of the surveyors, passing over two runs of excellent water, one at three and the
other at four miles' distance from our last camp. The land was for the
most part very good, with plenty of wild angelica growing upon it.
Several deer came into our sight but none into our quarters, which
made short commons and consequently some discontent. For this
reason some of the men called this Bread-and-Water Camp, but we
called it Crane Camp, because many of those fowls flew over our
heads, being very clamorous in their flight. Our Indian killed a mountain partridge, resembling the smaller partridge in the plumage but as
large as a hen. These are common toward the mountains, though we
saw very few of them, our noise scaring them away.

10. We began this day very luckily by killing a brace of turkeys
and one deer, so that the plenty of our breakfast this morning made
amends for the shortness of our supper last night. This restored good
humor to the men, who had a mortal aversion to fasting. As I lay in my
tent, I overheard one of them, called James Whitlock, wish that he
were at home. For this I reproved him publicly, asking him whether
it was the danger or the fatigue of the journey that disheartened him,
wondering how he could be tired so soon of the company of so many
brave fellows. So seasonable a reprimand put an effectual stop to all
complaints, and nobody after that day was ever heard so much as to
wish himself in Heaven.

A small distance from our camp we crossed a creek which we called Cockade Creek, because we there began to wear the beards of wild turkey cocks in our hats by way of cockade. A little more than a mile from thence we came to the true southern branch of Roanoke River, which was about 150 yards over, with a swift stream of water as clear as crystal. It was fordable near our line, but we were obliged to ride above 100 yards up the river to the end of a small island and then near as far back again on the other side of the island before we could mount the bank. The west side of this fine river was fringed with tall canes a full furlong in depth, through which our men cleared a path broad enough for our baggage to pass, which took up a long time. The bottom of the river was paved with gravel, which was everywhere spangled with small flakes of mother-of-pearl that almost dazzled our eyes. The sand on the shore sparkled with the same. So that this seemed the most beautiful river that I ever saw. The difficulty of passing it and cutting through the canes hindered us so much that we could carry the line little more than three miles.

We crossed a creek two and a half miles beyond the river, called Cane Creek from very tall canes which lined its banks. On the west side of it we took up our quarters. The horses were very fond of those canes, but at first they purged them exceedingly and seemed to be no very heartening food.

Our Indian killed a deer and the other men some turkeys, but the Indian begged very hard that our cook might not boil venison and turkey together because it would certainly spoil his luck in hunting and we should repent it with fasting and prayer. We called this south branch of Roanoke the Dan, as I had called the north branch the Staunton before.

11. We hurried away the surveyors at nine and followed with the baggage about eleven. In about four and a half miles we crossed the Dan the second time and found it something narrower than before, being about 110 yards over. The west banks of it were also thick set with canes, but not for so great a breadth as where we passed it first. But it was here a most charming river, having the bottom spangled as before, with a limpid stream gently flowing and murmuring among

the rocks, which were thinly scattered here and there to make up the variety of the prospect. The line was carried something more than two miles beyond the river, in which distance the thickets were very troublesome. However, we made a shift to run six and a half miles in the whole, but encamped after sunset. I had foretold on the credit of a dream which I had last Sunday night that we should see the mountains this day, and it proved true, for Astrolabe discovered them very plain to the northwest of our course, though at a great distance. The rich land held about a mile broad on the west side the river. Tom Jones killed a buck and the Indian a turkey, but he would not bring it us for fear we should boil it with our venison against his ridiculous superstition. I had a moderate cold, which only spoiled my voice but not my stomach. Our chaplain, having got rid of his little lurking fevers, began to eat like a cormorant.

12. The surveyors were dispatched by nine, but the thick woods made the horses so hard to be found that we did not follow with the baggage till after twelve. The line was extended something more than five miles, all the way through a thicket. We judged by the great number of chestnut trees that we approached the mountains, which several of our men discovered very plainly. The bears are great lovers of chestnuts and are so discreet as not to venture their unwieldy bodies upon the smaller branches of the trees which will not bear their weight. But after walking upon the limbs as far as is safe, they bite off the limbs, which falling down, they finish their meal upon the ground. In the same cautious manner they secure the acorns that grow on the outer branches of the oak. They eat grapes very greedily, which grow plentifully in these woods, very large vines wedding almost every tree in the rich soil. This shows how natural the situation of this country is to vines.

Our men killed a bear of two years old which was very fat. The flesh of it hath a good relish, very savory, and inclining nearest to that of pork. The fat of this creature is the least apt to rise in the stomach of any other. The men for the most part chose it rather than venison; the greatest inconvenience was that they eat more bread with it. We, who were not accustomed to eat this rich diet, tasted it at first with some squeamishness but soon came to like it. Particularly, our chaplain loved it so passionately that he would growl like a wildcat over a squirrel.

Toward the evening the clouds gathered thick and threatened rain, and made us draw a trench round the tent and take the necessary precautions to secure the bread, but no rain fell. We remembered our wives and mistresses in a bumper of excellent cherry brandy. This we could afford to drink no oftener than to put on a clean shirt, which was once a week.

13. This being Sunday, we rested from our fatigue and had a sermon. Our weather was very louring, with the wind hard at northwest with great likelihood of rain. Every Sunday I constantly ordered Peter Jones to weigh out the weekly allowance of bread to each man, which hitherto was five pounds. This with plenty of meat was sufficient for any reasonable man, and those who were unreasonable I would by no means indulge with superfluities. The rising ground where we encamped was so surrounded with thickets that we could not walk out with any comfort; however, after dinner several of the men ventured to try their fortune and brought in no less than six wild turkeys. They told us they saw the mountains very distinctly from the neighboring hills.

In the evening I examined our Indian, Ned Bearskin, concerning his religion, and he very frankly gave me the following account of it. That he believed there was a supreme being that made the world and everything in it. That the same power that made it still preserves and governs it. That it protects and prospers good people in this world and punishes the bad with sickness and poverty. That after death all mankind are conducted into one great road, in which both the good and bad travel in company to a certain distance where this great road branches into two paths, the one extremely level and the other mountainous.[82] Here the good are parted from the bad by a flash of lightning, the first filing to the right, the other to the left.

[82] William Strachey's relation of the beliefs of the Powhatan Indian tribes concerning an afterlife has some points of resemblance with Bearskin's religion. See William Strachey, *Historie of Travell into Virginia Britania*, edited by Louis B. Wright and Virginia Freund (London, 1953), pp. 102–103.

The right-hand road leads to a fine warm country where the spring is perpetual and every month is May. And, as the year is always in its youth, so are the people, and the women beautiful as stars and never scold. That in this happy climate there are deer innumerable, perpetually fat, and the trees all bear delicious fruit in every season. That the earth brings forth corn spontaneously, without labor, which is so very wholesome that none that eat of it are ever sick, grow old, or die. At the entrance into this blessed land sits a venerable old man, who examines everyone before he is admitted, and if he has behaved well, the guards are ordered to open the crystal gate and let him into this terrestrial paradise.

The left-hand path is very rough and uneven, leading to a barren country where 'tis always winter; the ground was covered with snow and nothing on the trees but icicles. All the people are old, have no teeth, and yet are very hungry. Only those who labor very hard make the ground produce a sort of potato, pleasant to the taste but gives them the dry gripes and fills them full of sores which stinks and are very painful. The women are old and ugly, armed with sharp claws like a panther, and with those they gore the men that slight their passion. For it seems these haggard old furies are intolerably fond. They talk very much and very shrill, giving most exquisite pain to the drum of the ear, which in that horrid climate grows so tender that any sharp note hurts it.

On the borders sits a hideous old woman whose head is covered with rattlesnakes instead of tresses, with glaring white eyes sunk very deep in her head. Her tongue is twenty cubits long, armed with sharp thorns as strong as iron. This tongue, besides the dreadful sound it makes in pronouncing sentence, serves the purpose of an elephant's trunk, with which the old gentlewoman takes up those she has convicted of wickedness and throws them over a vast high wall, hewn out of one solid rock, that surrounds this region of misery to prevent escapes. They are received on the inside by another hideous old woman, who consigns them over to punishments proper for their crimes. When they have been chastised here a certain number of years according to their degrees of guilt, they are thrown over the wall again and driven once more back into this world of trial, where, if they mend their manners, they are conducted into the above-mentioned fine country after their death. This was the substance of Bearskin's religion, which he told us with a freedom uncommon to the Indians.

14. It began to rain about three o'clock this morning, but so gently that we had leisure to secure the bread from damage. It continued raining all night and till near noon, when it held up; the clouds looked very heavy and frightened us from all thoughts of decamping. Meanwell and I lay abed all the morning, believing that the most agreeable situation in wet weather. The wind, blowing hard at northeast, made the air very raw and uncomfortable. However, several of the men went hunting in the afternoon and killed three deer and four turkeys, so that the frying pan was not cool till next morning. The chaplain, disdaining to be useful in one capacity only, condescended to darn my stockings; he acquired that with his other university learning at the College of Dublin. At six it began to rain again and held not up till nine, when the clouds seemed to break away and give us a sight of the stars. I dreamt the three Graces appeared to me in all their naked charms; I singled out Charity from the rest, with whom I had an intrigue.

15. The weather promising to be fair, we hurried away the surveyors as early as we could but did not follow with the baggage till one o'clock, because the thick woods made it difficult to find the horses. I interposed very seasonably to decide a wager betwixt two of the warmest of our men, which might otherwise have inflamed them into a quarrel.

In about a mile's march we passed over a large creek, whose banks were fringed with canes. We called it Sable Creek from the color of its water. Our surveyors crossed the Dan twice this day. The first time was 240 poles from our camp and the second in 1 mile and 7 poles farther, and from thence proceeded with the line only 59 poles, in all no more than 1 mile and 300 poles. The difficulty they had in passing the river twice made their day's work so small.

The baggage did not cross the river at all but went round the bent of it; and in the evening we encamped on a charming piece of ground that commanded the prospect of the reaches of the river, which were about fifty yards over and the banks adorned with canes. We pitched the tent at the bottom of a mount, which we called Mount Pleasant for the beauty of the prospect from thence.

This night Astrolabe's servant had his purse cut off, in which he lost his own money and some that my man had put into his keeping. We could suspect nobody but Holmes of the kingdom of Ireland, who had watched, it seems, that night for several of the men, without which he could not have had an opportunity. He had also the insolence to strike Meanwell's servant, for which he had like to have been tossed in a blanket. Astrolabe's horse fell with him in the river, which had no other consequence but to refresh him and make the rest of the company merry. Here the low ground was very narrow, but very dry and very delightful.

16. The surveyors got to work about nine, and we followed with the baggage at eleven. They carried the line about four and a half miles and were stopped by the river, over which they could not find a ford. We passed a small creek near our camp, which had canes on each side on which our horses had feasted. The constant current in the river may be computed to run about two knots, and we discovered no falls over which a canoe might not pass.

Our journey this day was through very open woods. At three miles' distance we crossed another creek, which we called Lowland Creek from a great breadth of low ground made by this creek and the river, which ran about a fourth of a mile to the northward of us. We were obliged to go two miles higher than where our line intersected the river, because we could not find a ford.

In our way we went through several large Indian fields where we fancied the Sauro Indians [83] had formerly planted corn. We en-

---

[83] The Cheraws, also variously known as the Saraws, Saras, Sauras. This Siouan tribe lived on the Yadkin River in the seventeenth century, but in 1700 they settled on the Dan, near the southern boundary of Virginia, with a second village thirty miles higher on the south side of the Dan; the latter was known as Upper Saura Village and the other Lower Saura Village. The Iroquois forced them to move southeast to join the Keyauwee in about 1710, and later they moved to the vicinity of the Pee Dee River. See John R. Swanton, *The Indians of the Southeastern United States* (Washington, D.C., 1946), pp. 109-110.

camped near one of these Indian cornfields, where was excellent food for our horses. Our Indian killed a deer, and the men knocked down no less than four bears and two turkeys, so that this was truly a land of plenty both for man and beast. Dr. Humdrum at this camp first discovered his passion for the delicious flesh of bear.

17. The surveyors moved early and went back at least two miles on the south side of the river before they could get over. Nor was it without difficulty and some danger that they and we crossed this ford, being full of rocks and holes and the current so swift that it made them giddy. However, Heaven be praised, we all got safe on the other side; only one baggage horse stumbled and sopped a little of the bread.

The puzzle in crossing the river and the thick woods hindered our surveyors from carrying the line farther than 2 miles and 250 poles to the banks of Cascade Creek, so called from several waterfalls that are in it. We encamped the sooner because it threatened rain, the wind strong at northeast.

In our way to this place we went over abundance of good land, made so by the river and this creek. Our dogs catched a young cub, and the Indian killed a young buck. Near the creek we found a very good kind of stone that flaked into thin pieces fit for pavement.

About a mile southwest from our camp was a high mount that commanded a full prospect of the mountains and a very extensive view of all the flat country, but being with respect to the mountains no more than a pimple, we called it by that name.

18. The weather clearing up with a brisk northwester, we dispatched the surveyors about nine, who carried the line about 6 miles and 30 poles to a branch of the Dan, which we called the Irvin. We did not follow with the baggage till twelve. We crossed Cascade Creek over a ledge of rocks and marched through a large plain of good land but very thick woods for at least four miles together. We met with no water in all that distance. A little before sunset we crossed the Irvin at a deep ford where the rocks were so slippery the horses could hardly keep their feet. But by the great care of Tom Jones, we all got safe over without any damage to our bread.

We encamped on a pleasant hill in sight of the river, the sand of which is full of shining particles. Bearskin killed a fat doe and came across a bear which had been killed and half devoured by a panther. The last of these brutes reigns king of the woods and often kills the poor bears, I believe, more by surprise than fair fight. They often take them napping, bears being very sleepy animals, and though they be very strong, yet is their strength heavy, and the panthers are much nimbler. The Doctor grutched the panther this dainty morsel, being so fond of bear that he would rise before day to eat a griskin [84] of it.

19. About nine the surveyors took their departure and advanced with the line 5 miles and 135 poles; nor was this a small day's work, considering the way was more uneven and full of thickets than ever. We did not follow them till twelve, because some of the bread horses were missing. Astrolabe would have fain sent out two of the men to find out where the Dan and the Irvin forked, but I would not consent to it for fear they should fall into some disaster, we being now near the path which the northern Indians take when they march against those of the south.

Something more than four miles from our camp we crossed Matrimony Creek, which received its name from being very noisy, the water murmuring everlastingly amongst the rocks. Half a mile beyond this creek we discovered five miles to the northwest of the line a small mountain, which we called the Wart.

We would willingly have marched to a good place for our horses, which began to grow very weak, but, night coming on, we were obliged to encamp on very uneven ground, so overgrown with bushes and saplings that we could with difficulty see ten yards before us. Here our horses met with short commons, and so should we too if we had not brought a horseload of meat along with us. All that our hunters could kill was only one turkey, which helped however to season the broth.

20. This being Sunday, I washed off all my week's dirt and refreshed myself with clean linen. We had prayers and a sermon. We began here to fall from five to four pounds of bread a man for the following week, computing we had enough at that rate to last a month longer. Our Indian had the luck to kill a monstrous fat bear, which

[84] Chop or steak.

came very seasonably, for our men, having nothing else to do, had eat up all their meat and began to look very pensive. But our starved horses had no such good fortune, meeting with no other food but a little wild rosemary that grows on the high ground. This they love very well if they had had enough of it, but it grew only in thin tufts here and there. Tom Short brought me a hatful of very good wild grapes, which were plentiful all over these woods.

Our men, when the service was over, thought it no breach of the Sabbath to wash their linen and put themselves in repair, being a matter of indispensable necessity. Meanwell was very handy at his needle, having learnt the use of that little implement at sea, and flourished his thread with as good a grace as any merchant tailor.

21. Our surveyors got to work about nine and carried the line 4 miles and 270 poles, great part of that distance being very hilly and grown up with thickets, but we could not follow them till after two. Both Hamilton and his horse were missing, and though I sent out several men in quest of them, they were able to find neither. At last, fearing we should not overtake the surveyors, I left Tom Jones and another man to beat all the adjacent woods for them. We passed through intolerable thickets, to the great danger of our eyes and damage of our clothes, insomuch that I had enough to do to keep my patience and sweet temper. With all our diligence we could fight our way through the bushes no farther than two and a half miles before sunset, so that we could not reach the surveyors. This was a sensible grief to us, because they had no bedding with them and probably no victuals. And even in the last article we were not mistaken, for though our Indian killed a bear, he had left it on the line for us to pick up. Thus our dear friends run a risk of being doubly starved both with cold and hunger. I knew this would ill agree with Orion's delicate constitution, but Astrolabe I was in less pain for, because he had more patience and could subsist longer upon licking his paws.

We had the comfort to encamp where our horses fared well, and we drank health to our absent friends in pure element. Just as it was dark, Tom Jones brought poor Hamilton to us without his horse. He had contrived to lose himself, being no great woodsman, but pretended that he was only bogged. He looked very melancholy for the loss of his horse till I promised to employ my interest to procure him satisfaction. For want of venison broth for supper we contented ourselves with some greasy soup *de jambon*, which, though it slipped down well enough, sat not very easy on our stomachs. So soon as we encamped, I dispatched John Evans to look for the surveyors, but he returned without success, being a little too sparing of his trouble. We saw a small mountain to the northwest, which we called the Wart.

22. This morning early, I sent John Evans with Hamilton back to our last camp to make a farther search for the stray horse, with orders to spend a whole day about it. At the same time I dispatched Richard Smith to the surveyors with some provisions to stop their mouths as well as their stomachs. It was eleven o'clock before we could get up all the horses, when we followed our surveyors and in a mile and a half reached the camp where they had lain. The woods were extremely thick in the beginning of this day's march but afterwards grew pretty open. As we rode along we found no less than three bears and a half a deer left upon the line, with which we loaded our light horses.

We came up with the surveyors on the banks of the western branch of the Irvin, which we called the Mayo. Here they had halted for us, not knowing the reason why we stayed behind so long. And this was the cause they proceeded no farther with the line than 1 mile and 230 poles. About a mile before we reached this river we crossed a small creek, which we called Miry Creek because several of the branches of it were miry. We passed the Mayo just below a ledge of rocks, where Meanwell's horse slipped and fell upon one of his legs and would have broke it if his half-jacks [85] had not guarded it. As it was, his ankle was bruised very much, and he halted several days upon it.

After the tent was pitched, Astrolabe, Humdrum, and I clambered up a high hill to see what we could discover from thence. On the brow of the hill we spied a young cub on the top of a high tree at supper upon some acorns. We were so indiscreet as to take no gun with us and therefore were obliged to halloo to the men to bring one.

[85] Boots like jack boots but of shorter length.

When it came, Astrolabe undertook to fetch the bear down but missed him. However, the poor beast, hearing the shot rattle about his ears, came down the tree of his own accord and trusted to his heels. It was a pleasant race between Bruin and our grave surveyor, who, I must confess, runs much better than he shoots; yet the cub outran him, even downhill, where bears are said to sidle lest their guts should come out of their mouths. But our men had better luck and killed no less than six of these unwieldy animals.

We sent our horses back to Miry Creek for the benefit of the canes and winter grass, which they eat very greedily. There was a waterfall in the river just by our camp, the noise of which gave us poetical dreams and made us say our prayers in meter when we awaked.

23. Our surveyors moved forward and proceeded with the line 4 miles and 69 poles. At the distance of 62 poles from our camp we passed over another branch of the Irvin with difficulty, about half a mile from where it forked. It was extremely mountainous great part of the way, and the last mile we encountered a dreadful thicket interlaced with briers and grapevines. We crossed a large creek no less than five times with our line, which for that reason we called Crooked Creek; the banks of it were steep in many places and bordered with canes. With great luck for our horses we encamped where these canes were plentiful. This refreshment was very seasonable after so tiresome a journey, in which these poor beasts had clambered up so many precipices.

About sunset Evans and Hamilton came up with us, but had been so unlucky as not to find the horse. Our men eat up a horseload of bear, which was very unthrifty management, considering we could meet with no game all this day. But woodsmen are good Christians in one respect: by never taking care for the morrow but letting the morrow care for itself, for which reason no sort of people ought to pray so fervently for their daily bread as they.

24. The men feasted so plentifully last night that some of them paid for it by fasting this morning. One who had been less provident than the rest broke his fast very oddly. He singed all the hair off of a bearskin and boiled the pelt into broth. To this he invited his par-

ticular friends, who eat very heartily and commended the cookery by supping it clean up.

Our surveyors hurried away a little after eight and extended the line 6 miles and 300 poles. We did not follow them till about eleven and crossed a thicket two full miles in breadth without any great trees near it.

The soil seemed very rich and level, having many locust and hickory saplings. The reason why there are no high trees is probably because the woods in these remote parts are burnt but seldom. During those long intervals the leaves and other trash are heaped so thick upon the ground that when they come to be set on fire they consume all before them, leaving nothing either standing or lying upon the ground.

Afterwards our way was mountainous and the woods open for about two and a half miles, then level and overgrown with bushes all the remaining distance. The line crossed Crooked Creek ten times in this day's work, and we encamped upon a branch of it where our horses fared but indifferently. The men came off better, for the Indian killed two bears, on which they feasted till the grease ran out of their mouths. Till this night I had always lain in my nightgown, but upon trial I found it much warmer to strip to my shirt and lie in naked bed with my gown over me. The woodsmen put all off, if they have no more than one blanket to lie in, and agree that 'tis much more comfortable than to lie with their clothes on, though the weather be never so cold.

25. The surveyors got to work soon after eight and run the line 4 miles and 205 poles. We did not follow them till near two, by reason Holmes's horse could not be found. And at last we were forced to leave Robin Hix and William Pool behind to search narrowly for him.

The woods were so intolerably thick for near four miles that they tore the very skins that covered the bread bags. This hindered us from overtaking the surveyors, though we used our utmost diligence to do it. We could reach but four miles and were obliged to encamp near a small run, where our horses came off but indifferently. However, they fared very near as well as their masters, for our Indian met with no game, so we had nothing to entertain ourselves with but the scanty remnant of yesterday's plenty. Nor was there much luxury at the surveyors' camp either in their lodging or diet.

However, they had the pleasure, as well as we, to see the mountains very plain both to the north and south of the line. Their distance seemed to be no more than five or six miles. Those to the north appeared in three or four ledges rising one above another, but those to the south made no more than one single ledge, and that not entire but were rather detached mountains lying near one another in a line. One was prodigiously high and the west end of it a perpendicular precipice. The next to it was lower but had another rising out of the east end of it in the form of a stack of chimneys. We could likewise discern other mountains in the course of the line but at a much greater distance. Till this day we never had a clear view of any of these mountains, by reason the air was very full of smoke. But this morning it cleared up and surprised us with this wild prospect all at once. At night the men brought Holmes's horse.

26. We had ambassadors from our hungry surveyors setting forth their wants, which we supplied in the best manner we could. We moved toward them about eleven and found them at the camp where they lay, near a rivulet which we judged to be the head of Deep River, otherwise called the north branch of Cape Fear.[86] We resolved to encamp here because there was great plenty of canes for the poor horses, which began to grow wondrous thin. However, the surveyors measured three hundred poles this day, which carried the line to the banks of the rivulet. The last line tree they marked is a red oak with the trees around it blazed.

We determined to proceed no farther with the dividing line, because the way to the west grew so mountainous that our jaded horses were not in condition to climb over it. Besides, we had no more bread than would last us a fortnight at short allowance. And the season of the year being far advanced, we had reason to fear we might be intercepted by snow or the swelling of the rivers which lay betwixt us and

[86] It seems unlikely that the party was far enough south to have encountered the head of Deep River in Forsyth County, North Carolina. Boyd suggested that the survey ended at "Peter's Creek, on the border of Stokes County, North Carolina."

home. These considerations checked our inclinations to fix the line in the ledge of mountains and determined us to make the best of our way back the same track we came. We knew the worst of that and had a straight path to carry us the nearest distance, while we were ignorant what difficulties might be encountered if we steered any other course.

We had intended to cross at the foot of the mountains over to the head of James River, that we might be able to describe that natural boundary. But prudence got the better of curiosity, which is always the more necessary when we have other men's welfare to consult as well as our own. Just by our camp we found a pair of elk's horns, not very large, and saw the track of the owner of them. They commonly keep more to the northward, as buffaloes do more to the southward.

In the afternoon we walked up a high hill north of our camp, from whence we discovered an amphitheater of mountains extending from the northeast round by the west to the southeast. 'Twas very unlucky that the mountains were more distant just at the head of our line toward the west by thirty or forty miles.

Our chaplain attempted to climb a tree, but before he got six feet from the ground fear made him cling closer to the tree than love would make him cling to a mistress. Meanwell was more venturesome but more unfortunate, for he bruised his foot in a tender place, by which he got a gentle fit of the gout. This was an improper situation to have the cruel distemper in and put my invention upon contriving some way or other to carry him back. In the meanwhile, he bathed his foot frequently in cold water to repel the humor if possible, for, as the case was, he could neither put on shoe nor boot.

Our men killed two bears, a buck, and a turkey — a very seasonable supply and made us reflect with gratitude on the goodness of Providence. The whole distance from Currituck Inlet, where we began the line, to this rivulet where we ended it, was 241½ miles and 70 poles.[87] In the night the wind blew fresh at southwest with moderate rain.

[87] The recording of distances seems to have been rather careless, or they were carelessly transcribed by the copyist. This total appears on p. 153 as 241¼ miles, 70 poles. The *History* (p. 268) gives the total distance traveled as 240 miles and 230

27. This being Sunday, we gave God thanks for protecting and sustaining us thus far by his divine bounty. We had also a sermon proper for the occasion. It rained small rain in the morning and looked louring all day. Meanwell had the gout in form, his foot being very much swelled, which was not more pain to him than it was disturbance to the rest. I ordered all the men to visit their horses and to drive them up that they might be found more easily the next morning. When the distribution of bread was made among the men, I recommended good husbandry to them, not knowing how long we should be obliged to subsist upon it. I sat by the riverside near a small cascade fed by a stream as clear as liquid crystal, and the murmur it made composed my senses into an agreeable tranquillity. We had a fog after sunset that gave an unpleasant dampness to the air, which we endeavored to correct by a rousing fire. This, with the wetness of the ground where we encamped, made our situation a little unwholesome; yet, thank God, all our company continued in a perfect health.

28. We ordered the horses up very early, but the likelihood of more rain prevented our decamping. And we judged right, for about ten o'clock it began to rain in good earnest. Meanwell made an excellent figure with one boot of leather and the other of flannel. So accoutered, he intended to mount, but the rain came seasonably to hinder him from exposing his foot to be bruised and tormented by the bushes.

We kept snug in the tent all day, spending most of our time in reading; and Dr. Humdrum, being disturbed at Astrolabe's reading *Hudibras* aloud, gabbled an old almanac three times over to drown one noise with another. This trial of lungs lasted a full hour and tired the hearers as much as the readers.

Powell's ague returned, for which I gave him the bark, and Pool took some Anderson's pills to force a passage through his body. This man had an odd constitution: he eat like a horse, but all he eat stayed with him till it was forced downwards by some purging physic. Without this assistance his belly and bowels were so swelled he could

poles (3,795 feet), or less than 241 miles. The journals of the expedition sent to England give still different mileage for the total distance.

hardly breath. Yet he was a strong fellow and used a world of exercise. It was therefore wonderful the peristaltic motion was not more vigorously promoted. Page was muffled up for the toothache, for which distemper I could recommend no medicine but patience, which he seemed to possess a great share of. It rained most part of the night.

29. In the morning we were flattered with all the signs of a fair day, the wind being come about to the northwest. This made us order the horses to be got up very early, but the tent horse could not be found; and 'tis well he stopped us, for about ten all our hopes of fair weather blew over and it rained very smartly for some time. This was all in favor of Meanwell's gouty foot, which was now grown better and the inflammation assuaged. Nor did it need above one day more to bring it down to its natural proportion and make it fit for the boot.

Being confined to the tent till dinner, I had no amusement but reading. But in the afternoon I walked up to a neighboring hill, from whence I could view the mountains to the southward, the highest of which our traders fancied to be the Katawa Mountain,[88] but it seems to be too northerly for that.

Our men went out a-driving and had the luck to kill two bears, one of which was found by our Indian asleep and never waked. Unfortunate Hamilton, straggling from the rest of the company, was lost a second time. We fired at least a dozen guns to direct him by their report to our camp, but all in vain: we could get no tidings of him. I was much concerned lest a disaster might befall him, being alone all night in that doleful wilderness.

30. The clouds were all swept away by a kind northwester, which made it pretty cold. We were all impatient to set our faces toward the east, which made the men more alert than ordinary in catching their horses. About seven our stray man found the way to the camp,

[88] The *History* (p. 274) reads "Kiawan" Mountain, a name that probably derives from that of the Keyauwee Indians. Boyd identified this as Pilot Mountain in Surry County, North Carolina, which seems probable. The Indians may have fancied they were seeing Shepherd Mountain, in Randolph County, near which the site of an Indian village was found in 1936. The name, like that of Pilot Mountain, may indicate that it was used by the Indians as a landmark.

being directed by the horses' bells. Though he had lain on the bare ground without either fire or bedclothes, he catched no cold.

I gave order that four men should set off early and clear the way, that the baggage horses might travel with less difficulty and more expedition. We followed them about eleven, and, the air being clear, we had a fair prospect of the mountains both to the north and south. That very high one to the south with the precipice at the west end we called the Lover's Cure, because one leap from thence would put a sudden period both to his passion and his pain. On the highest ledge, that stretched away to the northeast, rose a mount in the shape of a maiden's breast, which for that reason we called by that innocent name. And the main ledge itself we called Mount Eagle. We marched eleven miles from the end of the line and encamped upon Crooked Creek near a thicket of canes. In the front of our camp was a very beautiful hill which bounded our prospect at a mile's distance, and all the intermediate space was covered with green canes. Firewood was scanty with us, which was the harder because 'twas very cold. Our Indian killed a deer that was extremely fat, and we picked his bones as clean as a score of turkey buzzards could have done.

By the favor of a very clear night we made another essay of the variation and found it much the same as formerly, 2° 30′.

This being His Majesty's birthday, we drank his health in a dram of excellent cherry brandy but could not afford one drop for the Queen and the royal issue. We therefore remembered them in water as clear as our wishes. And because all loyal rejoicings should be a little noisy, we fired canes instead of guns, which made a report as loud as a pistol, the heat expanding the air shut up within the joints of this vegetable and making an explosion.

The woods being cleared before us by the pioneers and the way pretty level, we traveled with pleasure, increased by the hopes of making haste home.

31. We dispatched away our pioneers early to clear away the bushes but did not follow them till eleven o'clock. We crossed Crooked Creek several times, the banks of which, being very steep, jaded our poor horses very much. Meanwell's baggage horse gave out the first,

and next to him one of the bread horses, so that we were obliged to drop them both by the way. The second time we crossed Crooked Creek, by endeavoring to step off my horse's back upon the shore, I fell all along in the water. I wet myself all over and bruised the back part of my head, yet made no complaint but was the merriest of the company at my own disaster. Our dreamer Orion had a revelation about it the night before and foretold it fairly to some of the company.

The ground was so mountainous and our horses so weak that with all our diligence we could not exceed four miles. Indeed, we spent some time in crossing the Dan and the Mayo, the fords being something deeper than when we came up. We took up our camp at Miry Creek and regaled ourselves with one buck and two bears, which our men killed in their march. Here we promoted our chaplain from the deanery of Pip to the bishopric of Beardom. For as those countries where Christians inhabit are called Christendom, so those where bears take up their residence may not improperly go by the name of Beardom. And I wish other bishops loved their flock as entirely as our Doctor loves his.

### NOVEMBER

1. The pioneers were sent away about nine o'clock, but we were detained till near two by reason John Evans his horse could not be found, and at last we were obliged to leave four men behind to look for him. However, we made a shift to go six miles and by the way had the fortune to kill a brace of does, two bears, and one turkey. Meanwell's riding horse tired too by the way, so that we were obliged to drop him about a mile short of the camp. Many more of our horses were so weak they staggered under their riders, so that in compassion to the poor animals we walked great part of the way, notwithstanding the path was very rough and in many places uneven. For the same good-natured reason we left our bears behind, choosing rather to carry the venison, for which our bishop had like to have mutinied. We endeavored about noon to observe the latitude, but our observation was something imperfect, the wind blowing too fresh. By such a one as we could make, we found the latitude no more than 36° 20′.

In this camp our horses had short commons and, had they been able to speak like Balaam's ass, would have bemoaned themselves very much.

2. We lost all the morning in hunting for Powell's mare, so that it was two o'clock before we decamped. Our zeal to make the best of our way made us set out when it was very like to rain, and it rained in good earnest before we had marched a mile. We bore it patiently while it was moderate and repassed Matrimony Creek about one and a half miles from our camp. But soon after the rain fell more violently and obliged us to take up our quarters upon an eminence, that we might not be drowned.

This was the only time we were catched in the rain upon the road during the whole journey. It used to be so civil as to fall in the night, as it did while Herod was building the temple, or on a Sunday, or else to give us warning enough to encamp before it fell. But now it took us upon the way and made our lodging uncomfortable, because we were obliged to pitch the tent upon wet ground. The worst circumstance of all was that there was hardly any picking for the horses, which were now grown so lean and so weak that the turkey buzzards began to follow them. It continued raining till three o'clock in the morning, when, to our great joy, it cleared up with a northwester.

3. It was my opinion to rest in our camp, bad as it was, because it was Sunday, but everybody was against me. They urged the danger of starving the horses and the short march we made yesterday, which might justify making a Sabbath Day's journey today. I held out against all these arguments on account of resting the horses, which they greatly needed, as well as because of the duty of the day, till at last the chaplain came with a casuistical face and told me it was a case of necessity that obliged us to remove from a place that would famish all our horses, that charity to those poor animals would excuse a small violation of the Fourth Commandment. I answered that the horses would lose as much by the fatigue of traveling as they would gain by the bettering their food, that the water was raised in the river Irvin and we should be forced to stay till it was fallen again, and so should gain no distance by traveling on the Sunday. However, on

condition the Doctor would take the sin upon himself, I agreed to move three or four miles, which carried us to the banks of the Irvin.

By the way our Indian killed four deer and a bear. When we came to the river, we found the water three or four foot higher than when we came up, so that there was no likelihood of getting over under two days. This made good my argument and put our hasty gentlemen into the vapors, especially Orion, who was more impatient than anybody. I could find no other reason for it but because he had dreamt that Colonel Beverley [89] was dead and imagined his absence might hinder him from making interest for his place of Surveyor General.

In the evening we perceived the water began to fall in the river, which gave some of the company the vain hopes of getting over the next day.

4. In the morning we measured the marks we had set up at the river and found the water had not fallen above a foot; by this we were convinced that we should be obliged to halt there a day longer. We sent some men to endeavor to bring up two horses which tired on Saturday, but the horses were too well pleased with their liberty to come along with them. One of these manumitted horses belonged to Abraham Jones, and, being pricked in the mouth, he bled himself quite off his legs.

There being great plenty in our camp, the men kept eating all day to keep them out of idleness. In the evening it looked very dark and menaced us with more rain, to our great mortification, but after a few drops, I thank God, it blew over. Orion sighed heavily while it lasted, apprehending we should take up our winter quarters in the woods.

John Ellis, who was one of the men we had sent to bring up the tired horses, told us a romantic adventure which he had with a bear on Saturday last. He had straggled from his company and treed a young cub. While he was new priming his gun to shoot at it, the old gentlewoman appeared, who, seeing her heir apparent in distress, came up to his relief. The bear advanced very near to her enemy, reared up on her posteriors, and put herself in guard. The man pre-

[89] William Beverley, son of Robert Beverley the historian, and Byrd's nephew.

sented his piece at her, but, unfortunately, it only snapped, the powder being moist. Missing his fire in this manner, he offered to punch her with the muzzle of his gun, which Mother Bruin, being aware of, seized the weapon with her paws and by main strength wrenched it out of his hand. Being thus fairly disarmed and not knowing in the fright but the bear might turn his own cannon upon him, he thought it prudent to retire as fast as his legs could carry him. The brute, being grown more bold by the flight of her adversary, immediately pursued, and for some time it was doubtful whether fear made one run faster or fury the other. But after a fair course of forty yards, the poor man had the mishap to stumble over a stump and fell down at his full length. He now would have sold his life a pennyworth, but the bear, apprehending there might be some trick in this fall, instantly halted and looked very earnestly to observe what the man could mean. In the meantime, he had with much presence of mind resolved to make the bear believe he was dead by lying breathless on the ground, upon the hopes that the bear would be too generous to kill him over again. He acted a corpse in this manner for some time, till he was raised from the dead by the barking of a dog belonging to one of his companions. Cur came up seasonably to his rescue and drove the bear from her pursuit of the man to go and take care of her innocent cub, which she now apprehended might fall into a second distress.

5. We found this morning that the river had fallen no more than four inches the whole night, but a northwester had swept away all the clouds. About ten we resolved to pass the river, which we did very safely, thank God, only Tom Short's horse fell with him and sopped him all over. In the distance of six miles we crossed Cascade Creek and from thence proceeded in near three miles to the Dan, which we forded with some difficulty because the water was deeper than when we came over it before. Unfortunate Mr. Short was ducked a second time by the fall of his horse but received no hurt. My horse made a false step so that his head was all under water but recovered himself with much ado.

Having day enough left, we proceeded as far as Lowland Creek, where we took up our quarters and had great plenty both of canes and winter grass for the horses, but Whitlock's horse tired two miles off and so did one of Astrolabe's. The truth of it is we made a long journey, not less than fourteen miles in the roundabout distance we came, though it did not exceed ten upon the line. I favored my steed by walking great part of the way on foot; it being level and well cleared made the fatigue more tolerable. The Indian killed a young buck, the bones of which we picked very clean, but want of bear made Dr. Humdrum less gay than he used to be where that delicious food was plenty.

6. We set not out till near twelve and passed over very uneven ground, though our comfort was that it was open and clear of bushes. We avoided crossing the Dan twice by going round the bent of it. About three we passed by Mount Pleasant and proceeded along the riverside to Sable Creek, which we crossed, and encamped a little beyond it near the banks of the Dan. The horses fared sumptuously here upon canes and grass.

Hamilton wounded a buck, which made him turn upon the dogs and even pursue them forty yards with great fury. But he got away from us, choosing rather to give the wolves a supper than to more cruel man. However, our other gunners had better fortune in killing a doe and a two-year-old cub. Thus Providence supplied us every day with food sufficient for us, making the barren wilderness a theater of plenty.

The wind blew very cold and produced a hard frost. Our journey this day did not exceed five miles, great part of which in compliment to my horse I performed on foot, notwithstanding the way was mountainous and the leaves that covered the hills as slippery as ice.

7. After dispatching away our pioneers at eight o'clock, we followed them at ten. The ground was very hilly and full of underwood, but our pioneers had helped that inconvenience. Our journey was eight miles by the lines but near ten by our path, which was not quite so straight. The hunters were more fortunate than ordinary, killing no less than four deer and as many turkeys. This made them impatient to encamp early, that they might enjoy the fruits of their good luck.

We arrived at two o'clock on the banks of the Dan, where we

marked out our quarters, where the horses had as great plenty as ourselves. However, they were now grown so weak that they staggered when we dismounted, and those which had been used to the stable and dry food throve least upon grass and canes and were much sooner jaded than the rest.

8. The pioneers took their departure about nine, and we set out upon their track at ten and found the ground rising and falling all the way between the two fords of the river. The first of these we passed at first setting-out, but Robin Hix and the Indian undertook to go round the bent of the river without crossing it all. This they performed, making the distance no more than twelve miles. About a mile from our camp they met with a creek whose banks were fortified with high cliffs, which gained it the name of Cliff Creek. Near three miles beyond that they forded over another creek, on whose margin grew plenty of canes. And this was called Hix's Creek from the name of the discoverer. Between these two creeks lies a level of exceeding good land, full of large trees and a black mold.

We that marched upon the line passed over Cane Creek something more than four miles from the camp, and three miles beyond that we forded the Dan for the last time, passing through a forest of canes before we got at it. It was no small joy to us to find ourselves safe over all the waters that might retard our journey home. Our distance upon the line was seven miles, and where we encamped afforded good forage for the horses, which we had favored by walking the greater part of the way. The Indian brought us the primings[90] of a fat doe, which he had killed too far off for him to carry the whole. This and two turkeys that our men shot made up our bill of fare this evening.

9. Dr. Humdrum got up so early that it made him quite peevish, especially now we were out of the latitude of fat bear, with which he used to keep up his good humor. It was necessary to hurry out the pioneers by eight o'clock, because great part of the journey was overgrown with bushes. However, about five miles of this day's work were very open and tolerably level. The distance in all was twelve

[90] Prime parts.

miles by the line, though we made fifteen of it by picking our way. Of this I footed it at least eight miles, notwithstanding my servant had scorched my boots by holding them too near the fire. The length of our march harassed the horses much, so that Page was obliged to leave his two miles short of our journey's end, and several others had much ado to drag one leg after another.

In less than half a mile from the Dan we crossed Cockade Creek, so called from our beginning there to wear the turkey beard in our hats by way of cockade. This we made one of the badges of a new order called the Order of Maosti, signifying in the Saponi language a turkey's beard. The other badge is a wild turkey in gold with the wings expanded and a collar round its neck, with this motto engraven upon it: *vice coturnicum.*[91] As most orders have been religious in their original, so this was devised in grateful remembrance of our having been supported in the barren wilderness so many weeks with wild turkeys instead of quails.

From thence we continued our march to Buffalo Creek, on which we encamped. Here our horses made better cheer than we, for the Indian killed nothing but one turkey. However, with what remained of our former good fortune, this was sufficient to keep famine out of the camp.

10. This being Sunday, we observed the Fourth Commandment; only our hunters went out to provide a dinner for the rest, which was matter of necessity. They fired the woods in a ring, which burning inwards drove the deer to the center, where they were easily killed. This sport is called fire-hunting and is much practiced by the Indians and some English as barbarous as Indians. Three deer were slaughtered in this manner, of which they brought one to the camp and were content only to prime[92] the other two. Besides these, Thomas Short brought in a doe, which made us live in luxury.

William Pool complained that though his stomach was good and he eat a great deal yet he hardly ever went to stool without the help of physic. This made him very full and uneasy, giving him pains both

[91] "In place of quail." Byrd refers to the Lord's provision of quail to feed the starving Children of Israel in the Wilderness (Ex. 16:13).
[92] Select the best parts.

139

in his stomach and bowels. First I gave him a dose of Anderson's pills, which afforded him very little ease. Then I prescribed a small dose of ipecacuanha to be taken in hot broth well seasoned with salt, which took off the emetic quality and turned it downwards. This not only employed him and gave him ease but brought him to be very regular in his evacuations, by being now and then repeated. Page went out in quest of his horse and brought him to the camp pretty well recruited. The absence of most of the men diminished our congregation so much that we who remained behind were contented with prayers. I read a great deal and then wrote a letter with design to send an express with it so soon as we got amongst the inhabitants.

11. By the favor of good weather and the impatience of being at home, we decamped early. But there was none of the company so very hasty as Orion. He could not have been more uneasy even though he had a mistress at Williamsburg. He found much fault with my scrupulous observing the Sabbath. I reproved him for his uneasiness, letting him understand that I had both as much business and as much inclination to be at home as he had, but for all that was determined to make no more haste than good speed.

We crossed Hycootomony Creek twice in this march and traversed very thick and very uneven woods as far as Sugartree Creek. This was no more than seven miles but equal in fatigue to double that distance on good ground. Near this creek our men killed a young buffalo of two years old that was as big as a large ox. He had short legs and a deep body, with shagged hair on his head and shoulders. His horns were short and very strong. The hair on the shoulders is soft, resembling wool, and may be spun into thread. The flesh is arrant beef; all the difference is that the fat of it inclines more to be yellow. The species seems to be the same, because a calf produced betwixt tame cattle and these will propagate. Our people were so well pleased with buffalo beef that the gridiron was upon the fire all night. In this day's march I lost one of the gold buttons out of my sleeve, which I bore the more patiently because that and the burning of my boots were all the damage I had suffered.

12. We could not decamp before eleven, the people being so much

engaged with their beef; I found it always a rule that the greater our plenty the later we were in fixing out. We avoided two miles of very uneven ground by leaving the line on our left and keeping upon the ridge. Something less than three miles' distance from the camp we passed over Bluewing Creek and five miles beyond this over that of Tewahominy. Thence we traversed a very large level of rich, high land near two miles in breadth and encamped on a branch three and a half miles beyond the last-named creek, so that our whole distance this day was more than eleven miles.

Here was very scanty fare for the horses, who could pick only here and there a sprig of wild rosemary, which they are fond of; the misfortune was there was not enough of it. John Ellis killed a bear in revenge for the fright one of that species had lately put him into. Nor was this revenge sweeter to him than a griskin of it was to the Doctor, who of all worldly food conceives this to be the best. Though, in truth, 'tis too rich for a single man and inclines the eater of it strongly to the flesh, insomuch that whoever makes a supper of it will certainly dream of a woman or the devil, or both.

13. This morning I wrote a letter to the Governor, intending to dispatch it away by an express from the outermost inhabitants. We mounted about ten, and after proceeding three miles crossed a large branch and two miles farther reached Ohimpamony Creek. Beyond that three and a quarter miles we came to Yapatsco or Beaver Creek. Here those industrious animals had dammed up the water in such a manner that we could with difficulty ford over it. However, we all got happily over and continued our march three miles farther to Massamony Creek, so that the day's journey was in all eleven and a quarter miles. But to make the horses some amends, we encamped in the midst of good forage. Both Meanwell's horses could hardly carry their saddles, no more being required of them; nor was it much better with many others in the company. On our way we had the fortune to kill a deer and a turkey, sufficient for our day's subsistence; nor need anyone despair of his daily bread whose faith is but half so big as his stomach.

14. About eight in the morning, I dispatched two men to Miles

Riley's and by the way to hire John Davis to carry my letters to Major Mumford's with all expedition. I also gave them orders to get a beef killed and likewise some meal ground to refresh the men on their arrival amongst the inhabitants.

We decamped after them at eleven o'clock and at the end of seven and a quarter miles crossed Nutbush Creek. From thence we proceeded about four miles farther to a beautiful branch of Great Creek, where we arrived in good order about four o'clock in the afternoon. We encamped on a rising ground that overlooked a large extent of green reeds with a crystal stream serpenting through the middle of them. The Indian killed a fawn and one of the other men a raccoon, the flesh of which is like pork, but truly we were better fed than to eat it. The clouds gathered and threatened rain, but a brisk northwester swept them all away before morning.

15. We were ready to march about ten o'clock and at the distance of six miles passed Great Creek. Then, after traversing very barren grounds for near five miles, we crossed the trading path used by our traders when they carry goods to the southwest Indians. In less than a mile from thence we had the pleasure to discover a house, though a very poor one, the habitation of our friend Nat on Major Mumford's plantation. As agreeable a sight as a house was, we chose our tent to lie in as much the cleanlier lodging. However, we vouchsafed to eat in the house, where nothing went down so sweetly as potatoes and milk. In order for that, a whole ovenful of potatoes were provided, which the men devoured unmercifully.

Here all the company but myself were told that my little son was dead. This melancholy news they carefully concealed from me for fear of giving me uneasiness. Nothing could be more good-natured and is a proof that more than thirty people may keep a secret. And what makes the wonder the greater is that three women were privy to this my supposed misfortune.

I drew out the men after dinner and harangued them on the subject of our safe return in the following terms:

"Friends and fellow travelers, it is with abundance of pleasure that I now have it in my power to congratulate your happy arrival among the inhabitants. You will give me leave to put you in mind how manifestly Heaven has engaged in our preservation. No distress, no disaster, no sickness of any consequence has befallen any one of us in so long and so dangerous a journey. We have subsisted plentifully on the bounty of Providence and been day by day supplied in the barren wilderness with food convenient for us. This is surely an instance of divine goodness never to be forgotten, and, that it may still be more complete, I heartily wish that the same protection may have been extended to our families during our absence. But lest amidst so many blessings there may be some here who may esteem themselves a little unfortunate in the loss of their horses, I promise faithfully I will do my endeavor to procure satisfaction for them. And as a proof that I am perfectly satisfied with your service, I will receive your pay and cause a full distribution to be made of it as soon as possible. Lastly, as well to gratify your impatience to see your several families as to ease the expense of the government, I will agree to your discharge so fast as we shall approach the nearest distance to your respective habitations."

16. It was noon before we could disengage ourselves from the charms of Madam Nat and her entertainments. I tipped her a pistole for her civilities and ordered the horses to the ford, while we and the baggage were paddled over in the canoe. While the horses were marching round, Meanwell and I made a visit to Cornelius Keith, who lived rather in a pen than a house with his wife and six children. I never beheld such a scene of poverty in this happy part of the world. The hovel they lay in had no roof to cover those wretches from the injuries of the weather, but when it rained or was colder than ordinary the whole family took refuge in a fodder stack. The poor man had raised a kind of a house, but for want of nails it remained uncovered. I gave him a note on Major Mumford for nails for that purpose and so made a whole family happy at a very small expense. The man can read and write very well and by way of a trade can make and set up quernstones,[93] and yet is poorer than any Highland Scot or bogtrotting Irishman. When the horses came up, we moved forward to Miles

[93] Grinding stones for hand mills.

143

Riley's, another of Major Mumford's quarters. Here was a young steer killed for us and meal ground, and everything also provided that the place afforded. There was a huge consumption of potatoes, milk, and butter, which we found in great plenty.

This day I discharged Robin Hix, Thomas Wilson, and Charles Kimball, allowing them two days to reach their homes. I also dismissed our honest Indian Bearskin, after presenting him with a note of £3 on Major Mumford, a pound of powder with shot in proportion. He had, besides, the skins of all the deer he had killed in the whole journey and had them carried for him into the bargain. Nothing could be happier than this honest fellow was with all these riches, besides the great knowledge he had gained of the country. He killed a fat buck, great part of which he left us by way of legacy; the rest he cut into pieces, toasted them before the fire, and then strung them upon his girdle to serve him for his provisions on his way to Christanna Fort, where his nation lived.

We lay in the tent, notwithstanding there was a clean landlady and good beds, which gave the men an opportunity of getting a house over their heads after having for two months had no covering but the firmament.

17. Being Sunday, besides performing the duties of the day, we christened Thomas Page, one of our men who had been bred a Quaker, and Meanwell and I were his gossips.[94] Several of the neighbors came, partly out of curiosity and partly out of devotion. Amongst the rest came a young woman which lives in comfortable fornication with Cornelius Cargill and has several children by him. Meanwell bought a horse of this man, in which he was jockeyed. Our eyes as well as our taste were blest with a sirloin of roast beef, and we drank pleasure to our wives in a glass of shrub. Not content with this moderate refreshment, my friends carried on the joke with bombo made of execrable brandy, the manufacture of the place. I preached against it, though they minded me as little at night as they had Humdrum in the morning, but most of them paid for it by being extremely sick. This day I discharged John Holmes and Thomas Page with a reasonable allowance of days for their return home.

[94] Godparents or sponsors.

18. This day we endeavored to set out early but were hindered by Powell's not finding some of his horses. This man had almost[95] been negligent in that particular but amongst the inhabitants was more careless than ordinary. It was therefore thought high time to discharge him and carry our baggage as well as we could to Cornelius Cargill's, who lived about seven miles off, and there hire his cart to transport it as far as Major Mumford's. We made the best shift we could and, having crossed Mrs. Riley's hand with a pistole, we moved toward Cargill's, where we arrived about two o'clock. Here we put the heavy baggage into the cart, though I ordered mine to continue on my own horses lest some disaster might happen to this frail vehicle. Then, appointing a guard to attend the baggage, we proceeded five miles farther to George Hix's plantation, where preparation was made to entertain us.

By the way we met John Davis, that brought me letters from home and from Major Mumford in answer to those I had sent to them by this express. He had indeed been almost as expeditious as a carrier pigeon, for he went from Miles Riley's on Saturday, and he met us this day, being Monday, early in the afternoon, three miles before we got to George Hix's. By the letters he brought I had the pleasure to hear that all my family was well, that my heir apparent had been extremely ill but was recovered; nevertheless, the danger he had been in gave birth to the report that he was dead. All my company expected that now the bad news would be confirmed. This made Meanwell take a convenient station to observe with how much temper I should receive such melancholy tidings. But not finding any change in my countenance, he ventured to ask me how it fared with my family. And I must gratefully own that both he and the whole company discovered a great deal of satisfaction that the report proved false. They then told me with how much care they had concealed from me the fame of his being dead, being unwilling to make me uneasy upon so much incertainty.

We got to George Hix's before four o'clock, and both he and his

[95] So in the manuscript, possibly in error for "always." The fragment of the "Secret History" in the Blathwayt Papers at Colonial Williamsburg has the word "ever" crossed out in this place and a partially blotted word that may be either "almost" or "always" written above it.

lively little wife received us courteously. His house stands on an eminence, from whence is a good prospect. Everything looked clean and wholesome, which made us resolve to quit the tent and betake ourselves to the house.

All the grandees of the Saponi nation waited here to see us, and our fellow traveler, Bearskin, was amongst the gravest of them. Four ladies of quality graced their visit, who were less besmeared with grease and dirt than any copper-colored beauties I had ever seen. The men too had an air of decency very uncommon, and, what was a greater curiosity, most of the company came on horseback. The men rode more awkwardly than sailors, and the women, who sat astride, were so bashful they would not mount their ponies till they were quite out of sight.

Christanna Fort, where these Indians live, lies three miles from George Hix's plantation. He has considerable dealings with them and supplies them too plentifully with rum, which kills more of them than the northern Indians do and causes much disorder amongst them.

Major Mumford was so good as to send me a horse, believing that mine was sufficiently jaded, and Colonel Bolling [96] sent me another. With the last I complimented Orion, who had marched on foot good part of the way from the mountains. When we saluted Mrs. Hix, she bobbed up her mouth with more than ordinary elasticity and gave us a good opinion of her other motions. Captain Embry, who lives on Nottoway River, met us here and gave us an invitation to make our next stage at his house. Here I discharged John Evans, Stephen Evans, William Pool, George Tilman, George Hamilton, and James Petillo, allowing them for their distance home. Our course from Miles Riley's inwards held generally about northeast and the road level.

19. We dispatched away the cart under a guard by nine o'clock,

[96] Boyd: "Colonel John Bolling (1700–1757), son of Major John Bolling (1676–1729) and grandson of Robert Bolling (1646–1709) who came to Virginia in 1660 and married Jane Rolfe, grand-daughter of John Rolfe and Pocahontas. The residence referred to was 'Cobbe' in Chesterfield, now Henrico County. See 'The Ancestors and Descendants of John Rolfe' (*Virginia Mag. Hist. and Biog.*, Vol. XXII, p. 103)."

and, after complimenting our landlord with a pistole for feeding us and our horses, we followed about eleven. About a mile from the house we crossed Meherrin River, which, being very low, was not more than twenty yards wide. About five miles farther we passed Meherrin Creek, almost as wide as the river. From thence eight miles we went over Sturgeon Run, and six miles beyond that we came upon Waqua Creek, where the stream is swift and tumbles over the rocks very solemnly; this makes broad, low grounds in many places and abundance of rich land.

About two miles more brought us to our worthy friend Captain Embry's habitation, where we found the housekeeping much better than the house. In that the noble Captain is not very curious, his castle containing of one dirty room with a dragging door to it that will neither open nor shut. However, my landlady made us amends by providing a supper sufficient for a battalion. I was a little shocked at our first alighting with a sight I did not expect. Most of the men I discharged yesterday were got here before us and within a few good downs of being drunk. I showed so much concern at this that they had the modesty to retire.

Mr. Walker met us here and kindly invited us to his house, being about five miles wide of this place. I should have been glad to accept of his civility but could not with decency put a slur upon our good friend the Captain, who had made abundant provision for us. For this reason we chose to drink water and stow thick in a dirty room rather than give our black-eyed landlady the trouble of making a feast to no purpose. She had set all her spits, pots, frying pans, gridirons, and ovens to work to pamper us up after fasting so long in the wilderness. The worst point of her civility was that she made us eat part of everything, which obliged two of the nine that lay in the room to rise at a very unseasonable time of night.

20. Mr. Walker came to us again in the morning and was[97] so kind as to bring us some wine and cider along with him. He also lent Meanwell [a] horse for himself and me another for one of my

[97] The text from "so" here through "thankful" (p. 149) is supplied from the fragment in the Blathwayt Papers preserved by Colonial Williamsburg, Inc.

men. We had likewise a visit from Colonel Bolling, who had been surveying in the neighborhood. Our landlord, who is a dealer in rum, let me have some for the men and had the humility, though a captain, to accept of a pistole for our entertainment. I discharged John Ellis and James Whitlock at this place.

It was twelve o'clock before we could get loose from hence, and then we passed Nottoway River just below Captain Embry's house, where it was about fifteen yards over. This river divides Prince George County from Brunswick. We had the company of Colonel Bolling and Mr. Walker along with us, who could not heartily approve of our Lithuanian custom of walking part of the way.

At the distance of eleven miles we crossed Stony Creek, and five miles farther we went over Gravelly Run, which is wide enough to merit the name of a creek. We passed by Sapony Chapel and after thirty good miles arrived safe at Colonel Bolling's, where we were entertained with much plenty and civility. Among abundance of other good things he regaled us with excellent cider.

While Meanwell and I fared deliciously here, our two surveyors and the Reverend Doctor, in compliment to their horses, stuck close to the baggage. They reached no farther than eighteen miles and took up their quarters at James Hudson's, where their horses were better provided for than their masters. There was no more than one bed to pig into, with one cotton sheet and the other of brown Osnaburgs,[98] made browner by a month's perspiration. This mortified Orion to the soul, so that the other two were happy enough in laughing at him; though I think they ought all to have been perfectly satisfied with the man's hospitality who was content to lie out of his own bed to make room for them.

21. These gentlemen quitted their sweet lodging so early that they reached Colonel Bolling's time enough for breakfast. Mr. Mumford's pretty wife was very ill here, which had altered her pretty face beyond all knowledge. I took upon me to prescribe to her and my advice succeeded well, as I understood afterwards.

About eleven o'clock we took leave and proceeded to Major Mum-

[98] A kind of coarse linen originally made in Osnabrück.

ford's, when I discharged the cart and the few men that remained with me, assuring them that their behavior had engaged me to do them any service that lay in my power. I had no sooner settled these affairs but my wife and eldest daughter[99] arrived in the chair to meet me. Besides the pleasure of embracing them, they made me happy by letting me understand the rest of the family were extremely well. Our treatment was as civil as possible in this good family. I wrote a letter to send by Orion to the Governor, and the evening we spent giving an account of our travels and drinking the best cider I ever tasted.

22. I sent away Meanwell's baggage and my own about ten o'clock, he intending to take Westover in his way home. When we had fortified ourselves with a meat breakfast, we took leave about twelve. My wife and I rode in the chair and my daughter on an easy pad she had borrowed. Mrs. Mumford was so kind as to undertake to spin my buffalo's hair in order to knit me a pair of stockings. Orion took the nearest way to Williamsburg, Astrolabe to Goochland, and Humdrum to Mount Misery. We called on Mr. Fitzgerald to advise him what method to take with his sick child, but nature had done the business before we came.

We arrived at Coggins Point about four, where my servants attended with boats in order to transport us to Westover. I had the happiness to find all the family well. This crowned all my other blessings and made the journey truly prosperous, of which I hope I shall ever retain a grateful remembrance. Nor was it all that my people were in good health, but my business was likewise in good order. Everyone seemed to have done their duty, by the joy they expressed at my return. My neighbors had been kind to my wife, when she was threatened with the loss of her son and heir. Their assistance was kind as well as seasonable, when her child was threatened with fatal symptoms and her husband upon a long journey exposed to great variety of perils. Thus, surrounded with the most fearful apprehensions, Heaven was pleased to support her spirits and bring back her child from the grave and her husband from the mountains, for which blessings may we be all sincerely thankful.

[99] Evelyn Byrd.

149

THE NAMES OF THE COMMISSIONERS TO DIRECT THE RUNNING OF THE
LINE BETWEEN VIRGINIA AND NORTH CAROLINA

Steddy  
Firebrand } Commissioners for Virginia  
Meanwell  

Judge Jumble  
Shoebrush  
Plausible } Commissioners for North Carolina  
Puzzlecause  

Orion  
Astrolabe } Surveyors for Virginia  

Plausible  
Boötes } Surveyors for North Carolina  

The Reverend Doctor Humdrum        Chaplain

---

NAMES OF THE MEN EMPLOYED ON THE PART OF VIRGINIA TO RUN
THE LINE BETWEEN THAT COLONY AND NORTH CAROLINA

| *On the first expedition* | *On the second expedition* |
|---|---|
| 1. Peter Jones | Peter Jones |
| 2. Thomas Short | Thomas Short |
| 3. Thomas Jones | Thomas Jones |
| 4. Robert Hix | Robert Hix |
| 5. John Evans | John Evans |
| 6. Stephen Evans | Stephen Evans |
| 7. John Ellis | John Ellis |
| 8. Thomas Wilson | Thomas Wilson |
| 9. George Tilman | George Tilman |
| 10. Charles Kimball | Charles Kimball |
| 11. George Hamilton | George Hamilton |
| 12. Robert Allen | Edward Powell |
| 13. Thomas Jones, Junior | Thomas Jones, Junior |
| 14. John Ellis, Junior | William Pool |

| | |
|---|---|
| 15. James Petillo | James Petillo |
| 16. Richard Smith | Richard Smith |
| 17. John Rice | Abraham Jones |
| | 18. William Calvert |
| | 19. James Whitlock |
| | 20. Thomas Page [100] |

---

ACCOUNT OF EXPENSE OF RUNNING THE LINE BETWEEN

VIRGINIA AND NORTH CAROLINA

| | | | |
|---|---|---|---|
| To the men's wages in current money | £277 | 10 | 0 |
| To sundry disbursements for provisions, etc. | 174 | 1 | 6 |
| To paid the men for seven horses lost | 44 | 0 | 0 |
| | £495 | 11 | 6 |
| The sum of £495 11s.6d. current money reduced at 15% to sterling amounts to | £430 | 8 | 10 |
| To paid Steddy | 142 | 5 | 7 |
| To paid Meanwell | 142 | 5 | 7 |
| To paid Firebrand | 94 | 0 | 0 |
| To paid the Chaplain Humdrum | 20 | 0 | 0 |
| To paid Orion | 75 | 0 | 0 |
| To paid Astrolabe | 75 | 0 | 0 |
| To paid for a tent and marquee | 20 | 0 | 0 |
| | £1000 | 0 | 0 [101] |

This sum was discharged by a warrant out of His Majesty's quit-rents from the lands in Virginia.

---

THE DISTANCES OF PLACES MENTIONED IN THE FOREGOING HISTORY

OF THE DIVIDING LINE BETWEEN VIRGINIA AND NORTH CAROLINA

| | M | Q | P [102] |
|---|---|---|---|
| From Currituck Inlet to the Dismal | 21 | 2 | 16 |
| The course through the Dismal | 15 | 0 | 0 |

[100] The *History* lists twenty-one men on the second expedition, including John Ellis, Jr., who is omitted from this list.

[101] The total is actually £999 rather than £1,000.

[102] The "Q" possibly stands for *quarentena*, a measure equaling a furlong (forty rods, perches, or poles). The "P" probably stands for *perca* or poles. But the totals of the columns (224 miles, 71 furlongs, 2,084 poles) do not convert to a figure equaling the total given. See note 86 for comment on discrepancies in figures.

| | | | |
|---|---|---|---|
| To the east side of Blackwater River | 20 | 1 | 43 |
| We came down Blackwater to the mouth of Not- toway 176 poles, from whence to Meherrin | 13 | 2 | 46 |
| To Meherrin River again | | 1 | 67 |
| To Meherrin River again | 2 | 0 | 40 |
| To the ferry road | 1 | 2 | 60 |
| To Meherrin again | | | 22 |
| To Meherrin the fifth and last time | 2 | 3 | 66 |
| To the middle of Jack's Swamp | 11 | 0 | 25 |
| To a road | 1 | 2 | 52 |
| To Beaver Pond Creek the first time | 3 | 3 | 8 |
| To a road from Bedding Field southward | 11 | 0 | 37 |
| To Pea Hill Creek | 3 | 1 | 33 |
| To a road | 2 | 0 | 30 |
| To Lizard Creek | | 3 | 38 |
| To Pigeon Roost Creek | 3 | 1 | 72 |
| To Cocke's Creek | 2 | 3 | 24 |
| To Roanoke River | | 2 | 48 |
| To the west side of D⁰ [ditto] | | | 49 |
| To the Indian trading path | 8 | 0 | 20 |
| To Great Creek | 4 | 3 | 28 |
| To Nutbush Creek | 7 | 0 | 6 |
| To Massamony Creek | 7 | 1 | 4 |
| To Yapatsco Creek | 3 | 0 | 30 |
| To Ohimpamony Creek | 3 | 1 | 38 |
| To Tewahominy Creek | 8 | 2 | 54 |
| To Bluewing Creek | 4 | 3 | 10 |
| To Sugartree Creek | 2 | 3 | 10 |
| To Hycootomony Creek | 3 | 1 | 76 |
| To the same | | | 18 |
| To the same | | 2 | 64 |
| To the same | | 2 | 66 |
| To the same again | | | 42[?] |
| To Buffalo Creek | 1 | 8 | 40 |
| To Cockade Creek | 11 | 3 | 6[?] |
| To the south branch of Roanoke called the Dan | | 1 | 26 |
| To the west side including the island | | | 34 |
| To Cane Creek | 2 | 2 | 42 |
| To Dan River the second time | 4 | 1 | 38 |
| To the west side of D⁰ [ditto] | | | 24 |

| | | | |
|---|---|---|---|
| To Dan River the third time | 8 | o | 68 |
| To the northwest side aslant | | | 53 |
| To the Dan River the fourth time | 1 | o | 7 |
| To the west side | | | 21 |
| To Lowland Creek | 3 | 2 | 50 |
| To Dan River the fifth time | 1 | o | 18 |
| To the northwest side aslant | | | 66 |
| To Cascade Creek | 2 | 3 | 10 |
| To Irvin River, a branch of the Dan | 6 | o | 30 |
| To Matrimony Creek | 4 | o | 31 |
| To Miry Creek | 7 | 1 | 68 |
| To Mayo River, another branch of the Dan | | 1 | 36 |
| To Dan River the sixth and last time | | 1 | 2 |
| To Crooked Creek the first time | 2 | 1 | 77 |
| To Ne plus ultra Camp | 13 | o | 35 |
| To a red oak, marked on three sides with four notches and the trees blazed about it, on the east bank of a rivulet supposed to be either a branch of Roanoke or Deep River | | 3 | 60 |
| | | | |
| The whole distance | 241 | 2 | 70 |

# HISTORY OF THE
# DIVIDING LINE

*betwixt Virginia and North Carolina*
*Run in the Year of Our Lord 1728*

*B*EFORE I enter upon the journal of the line between Virginia and North Carolina, it will be necessary to clear the way to it by showing how the other British colonies on the main have, one after another, been carved out of Virginia by grants from His Majesty's royal predecessors. All that part of the northern American continent now under the dominion of the King of Great Britain and stretching quite as far as the Cape of Florida went at first under the general name of Virginia.

The only distinction in those early days was that all the coast to the southward of Chesapeake Bay was called South Virginia and all to the northward of it North Virginia.

The first settlement of this fine country was owing to that great ornament of the British nation, Sir Walter Raleigh, who obtained a grant thereof from Queen Elizabeth, of ever-glorious memory, by letters patent dated March 25, 1584.

But whether that gentleman ever made a voyage thither himself is uncertain, because those who have favored the public with an account of his life mention nothing of it. However, thus much may be depended on, that Sir Walter invited sundry persons of distinction to share in his charter and join their purses with his in the laudable project of fitting out a colony to Virginia.

Accordingly, two ships were sent away that very year, under the command of his good friends Amadas and Barlow,[1] to take possession of the country in the name of his royal mistress, the Queen of England.

These worthy commanders, for the advantage of the trade winds, shaped their course first to the Caribbee Islands, thence, stretching away by the Gulf of Florida, dropped anchor not far from Roanoke Inlet. They ventured ashore near that place upon an island now called

[1] Philip Amadas and Arthur Barlow. The latter wrote a narrative of their experiences, which was printed by Richard Hakluyt in *Principal Navigations* (1589), pp. 728–733. D. B. Quinn has recently reprinted it in *The Roanoke Voyages* (London, 1955), I, 91–117 (Hakluyt Society, 2nd Ser., CIV).

Colleton Island,[2] where they set up the arms of England and claimed the adjacent country in right of their sovereign lady, the Queen; and this ceremony being duly performed, they kindly invited the neighboring Indians to traffic with them.

These poor people at first approached the English with great caution, having heard much of the treachery of the Spaniards and not knowing but these strangers might be as treacherous as they. But at length, discovering a kind of good nature in their looks, they ventured to draw near and barter their skins and furs for the baubles and trinkets of the English.

These first adventurers made a very profitable voyage, raising at least a thousand per cent upon their cargo. Amongst other Indian commodities, they brought over some of that bewitching vegetable, tobacco. And this being the first that ever came to England, Sir Walter thought he could do no less than make a present of some of the brightest of it to his royal mistress for her own smoking. The Queen graciously accepted of it, but finding her stomach sicken after two or three whiffs, 'twas presently whispered by the Earl of Leicester's faction that Sir Walter had certainly poisoned her. But Her Majesty, soon recovering her disorder, obliged the Countess of Nottingham and all her maids to smoke a whole pipe out amongst them.

As it happened some ages before to be the fashion to saunter to the Holy Land and go upon other Quixote adventures, so it was now grown the humor to take a trip to America. The Spaniards had lately discovered rich mines in their part of the West Indies, which made their maritime neighbors eager to do so too. This modish frenzy, being still more inflamed by the charming account given of Virginia by the first adventurers, made many fond of removing to such a Paradise.

Happy was he, and still happier she, that could get themselves transported, fondly expecting their coarsest utensils in that happy place would be of massy silver.

This made it easy for the Company to procure as many volunteers as they wanted for their new colony, but, like most other undertakers who

[2] Named for Sir John Colleton, one of the Lords Proprietors. The name has now become corrupted to "Colington."

have no assistance from the public, they starved the design by too much frugality; for, unwilling to launch out at first into too much expense, they shipped off but few people at a time, and those but scantily provided. The adventurers were, besides, idle and extravagant and expected they might live without work in so plentiful a country.

These wretches were set ashore not far from Roanoke Inlet, but by some fatal disagreement or laziness were either starved or cut to pieces by the Indians.

Several repeated misadventures of this kind did for some time allay the itch of sailing to this new world, but the distemper broke out again about the year 1606. Then it happened that the Earl of Southampton and several other persons eminent for their quality and estates were invited into the Company, who applied themselves once more to people the then almost abandoned colony. For this purpose they embarked about an hundred men, most of them reprobates of good families and related to some of the Company who were men of quality and fortune.

The ships that carried them made a shift to find a more direct way to Virginia and ventured through the capes into the Bay of Chesapeake. The same night they came to an anchor at the mouth of Powhatan, the same as James River, where they built a small fort at a place called Point Comfort.

This settlement stood its ground from that time forward, in spite of all the blunders and disagreement of the first adventurers and the many calamities that befell the colony afterwards. The six gentlemen who were first named of the Company by the Crown and who were empowered to choose an annual president from among themselves were always engaged in factions and quarrels, while the rest detested work more than famine. At this rate the colony must have come to nothing had it not been for the vigilance and bravery of Captain Smith, who struck a terror into all the Indians round about. This gentleman took some pains to persuade the men to plant Indian corn, but they looked upon all labor as a curse. They chose rather to depend upon the musty provisions that were sent from England; and when they failed they were forced to take more pains to seek for wild fruits in the woods than they would have taken in tilling the ground. Besides, this exposed them to be knocked in the head by the Indians and gave them fluxes into the bargain, which thinned the plantation very much. To supply this mortality, they were reinforced the year following with a greater number of people, amongst which were fewer gentlemen and more laborers, who, however, took care not to kill themselves with work. These found the first adventurers in a very starving condition but relieved their wants with the fresh supply they brought with them. From Kecoughtan [3] they extended themselves as far as Jamestown, where, like true Englishmen, they built a church that cost no more than fifty pounds and a tavern that cost five hundred.

They had now made peace with the Indians, but there was one thing wanting to make that peace lasting. The natives could by no means persuade themselves that the English were heartily their friends so long as they disdained to intermarry with them. And, in earnest, had the English consulted their own security and the good of the colony, had they intended either to civilize or convert these gentiles, they would have brought their stomachs to embrace this prudent alliance.

The Indians are generally tall and well proportioned, which may make full amends for the darkness of their complexions. Add to this that they are healthy and strong, with constitutions untainted by lewdness and not enfeebled by luxury. Besides, morals and all considered, I cannot think the Indians were much greater heathens than the first adventurers, who, had they been good Christians, would have had the charity to take this only method of converting the natives to Christianity. For, after all that can be said, a sprightly lover is the most prevailing missionary that can be sent amongst these or any other infidels.

Besides, the poor Indians would have had less reason to complain that the English took away their land if they had received it by way of a portion with their daughters. Had such affinities been contracted in the beginning, how much bloodshed had been prevented and how populous would the country have been, and, consequently, how considerable! Nor would the shade of the skin have been any reproach at

[3] Modern Hampton, Virginia.

this day, for if a Moor may be washed white in three generations, surely an Indian might have been blanched in two.

The French, for their parts, have not been so squeamish in Canada, who upon trial find abundance of attraction in the Indians. Their late grand monarch thought it not below even the dignity of a Frenchman to become one flesh with this people and therefore ordered 100 livres for any of his subjects, man or woman, that would intermarry with a native.

By this piece of policy we find the French interest very much strengthened amongst the savages and their religion, such as it is, propagated just as far as their love. And I heartily wish this well-concerted scheme don't hereafter give the French an advantage over His Majesty's good subjects on the northern continent of America.

About the same time New England was pared off from Virginia by letters patent bearing date April 10, 1608. Several gentlemen of the town and neighborhood of Plymouth obtained this grant, with the Lord Chief Justice Popham at their head.

Their bounds were specified to extend from 38 to 45 degrees of northern latitude, with a breadth of one hundred miles from the seashore. The first fourteen years this company encountered many difficulties and lost many men, though, far from being discouraged, they sent over numerous recruits of Presbyterians every year, who for all that had much ado to stand their ground, with all their fighting and praying.

But about the year 1620 a large swarm of dissenters fled thither from the severities of their stepmother, the church. These saints, conceiving the same aversion to the copper complexion of the natives with that of the first adventurers to Virginia, would on no terms contract alliances with them, afraid, perhaps, like the Jews of old, lest they might be drawn into idolatry by those strange women.

Whatever disgusted them I can't say, but this false delicacy, creating in the Indians a jealousy that the English were ill affected toward them, was the cause that many of them were cut off and the rest exposed to various distresses.

This reinforcement was landed not far from Cape Cod, where for their greater security they built a fort and near it a small town, which, in honor of the proprietors, was called New Plymouth. But they still had many discouragements to struggle with, though by being well supported from home they by degrees triumphed over them all.

Their brethren, after this, flocked over so fast that in a few years they extended the settlement one hundred miles along the coast, including Rhode Island and Martha's Vineyard.

Thus the colony throve apace and was thronged with large detachments of Independents and Presbyterians who thought themselves persecuted at home.

Though these people may be ridiculed for some pharisaical particularities in their worship and behavior, yet they were very useful subjects, as being frugal and industrious, giving no scandal or bad example, at least by any open and public vices. By which excellent qualities they had much the advantage of the southern colony, who thought their being members of the established church sufficient to sanctify very loose and profligate morals. For this reason New England improved much faster than Virginia, and in seven or eight years New Plymouth, like Switzerland, seemed too narrow a territory for its inhabitants.

For this reason, several gentlemen of fortune purchased of the company that canton of New England now called Massachusetts Colony. And King James confirmed the purchase by his royal charter dated March 4, 1628.[4] In less than two years after, above one thousand of the Puritanical sect removed thither with considerable effects, and these were followed by such crowds that a proclamation issued in England forbidding any more of His Majesty's subjects to be shipped off. But this had the usual effect of things forbidden and served only to make the willful Independents flock over the faster. And about this time it was that Messrs. Hampden and Pym, and, some say, Oliver Cromwell, to show how little they valued the King's authority, took a trip to New England.[5]

[4] The charter was, of course, confirmed by Charles I, not James, and dated March 4, 1628 (Old Style).

[5] Byrd here repeats an unconfirmed tale that was already in circulation in the seventeenth century. Hampden and Pym were among the recipients of a grant of

In the year 1630, the famous city of Boston was built in a commodious situation for trade and navigation, the same being on a peninsula at the bottom of Massachusetts Bay.

This town is now the most considerable of any on the British continent, containing at least 8,000 houses and 40,000 inhabitants.[6] The trade it drives is very great to Europe and to every part of the West Indies, having near 1,000 ships and lesser vessels belonging to it.

Although the extent of the Massachusetts Colony reached near 110 miles in length and half as much in breadth, yet many of its inhabitants, thinking they wanted elbowroom, quitted their old seats in the year 1636 and formed two new colonies: that of Connecticut and New Haven. These King Charles II erected into one government in 1644[7] and gave them many valuable privileges, and among the rest that of choosing their own governors. The extent of these united colonies may be about seventy miles long and fifty broad.

Besides these several settlements, there sprang up still another, a little more northerly, called New Hampshire. But that, consisting of no more than two counties and not being in condition to support the charge of a distinct government, was glad to be incorporated with that of Massachusetts, but upon condition, however, of being named in all public acts, for fear of being quite lost and forgot in the coalition.

In like manner New Plymouth joined itself to Massachusetts — except only Rhode Island, which, though of small extent, got itself erected into a separate government by a charter from King Charles II soon after the Restoration and continues so to this day.

These governments all continued in possession of their respective rights and privileges till the year 1683, when that of Massachusetts was made void in England by a *quo warranto*.

In consequence of which, the King was pleased to name Sir Ed-

---

land at Saybrook, Connecticut, made in March 1632 by the Earl of Warwick, President of the New England Council. Pym in particular interested himself in furthering overseas settlement where freedom of religion could be practiced. There is no evidence, however, that either Pym or Hampden ever actually visited New England.

[6] Byrd's figures are exaggerated. Boston had a population of 10,567 according to a census of 1722, 13,000 by a census of 1730. See Evarts B. Greene and Virginia D. Harrington, *American Population before the Federal Census of 1790* (New York, 1932), p. 22.

[7] Actually as of April 23, 1662.

mund Andros his first governor of that colony. This gentleman, it seems, ruled them with a rod of iron till the Revolution, when they laid unhallowed hands upon him and sent him prisoner to England.

This undutiful proceeding met with an easy forgiveness at that happy juncture. King William and his royal consort were not only pleased to overlook this indignity to their governor but, being made sensible how unfairly their charter had been taken away, most graciously granted them a new one.

By this some new franchises were given them as an equivalent for those of coining money and electing a governor, which were taken away. However, the other colonies of Connecticut and Rhode Island had the luck to remain in possession of their original charters, which to this day have never been called in question.

The next county dismembered from Virginia was New Scotland, claimed by the crown of England in virtue of the first discovery by Sebastian Cabot.[8] By color of this title, King James I granted it to Sir William Alexander by patent dated September 10, 1621.

But this patentee never sending any colony thither, and the French, believing it very convenient for them, obtained a surrender of it from their good friend and ally, King Charles II, by the Treaty of Breda. And to show their gratitude, they stirred up the Indians soon after to annoy their neighbors of New England. Murders happened continually to His Majesty's subjects by their means, till Sir William Phips took their town of Port Royal in the year 1690. But as the English are better at taking than keeping strong places, the French retook it soon and remained masters of it till 1710, when General Nicholson wrested it once more out of their hands.

Afterwards the Queen of Great Britain's right to it was recognized and confirmed by the Treaty of Utrecht.

Another limb lopped off from Virginia was New York, which the Dutch seized very unfairly on pretense of having purchased it from Captain Hudson, the first discoverer. Nor was their way of taking possession of it a whit more justifiable than their pretended title. Their West India Company tampered with some worthy English skippers,

[8] Really John Cabot, although his son, Sebastian, may have been with him.

who had contracted with a swarm of English dissenters to transport them to Hudson River, by no means to land them there but to carry 'em some leagues more northerly.

This Dutch finesse took exactly and gave the Company time soon after to seize Hudson River for themselves. But Sir Samuel Argall, then Governor of Virginia, understanding how the King's subjects had been abused by these republicans, marched thither with a good force and obliged them to renounce all pretensions to that country. The worst of it was, the knight depended on their parole to ship themselves for Brazil but took no measures to make this slippery people as good as their word.

No sooner was the good governor retired but the honest Dutch began to build forts and strengthen themselves in their ill-gotten possessions; nor did any of the King's liege people take the trouble to drive these intruders thence. The civil war in England and the confusions it brought forth allowed no leisure for such distant considerations. Though 'tis strange that the Protector, who neglected no occasion to mortify the Dutch, did not afterwards call them to account for this breach of faith. However, after the Restoration the King sent a squadron of his ships of war, under the command of Sir Robert Carr, and reduced that province to his obedience.

Some time after, His Majesty was pleased to grant that country to His Royal Highness the Duke of York by letters patent dated March 12, 1664. But to show the modesty of the Dutch to the life, though they had no shadow of right to New York, yet they demanded Surinam, a more valuable country, as an equivalent for it, and our able ministers at that time had the generosity to give it them.

But what wounded Virginia deepest was the cutting off Maryland from it by charter from King Charles I to Sir George Calvert, afterwards Lord Baltimore, bearing date the twentieth of June, 1632. The truth of it is, it begat much speculation in those days how it came about that a good Protestant king should bestow so beautiful a grant upon a zealous Roman Catholic. But 'tis probable it was one fatal instance amongst many other of His Majesty's complaisance to the Queen.

165

However that happened, 'tis certain this province afterwards proved a commodious retreat for persons of that communion. The memory of the Gunpowder Treason Plot was still fresh in everybody's mind and made England too hot for papists to live in without danger of being burnt with the Pope every fifth of November; for which reason legions of them transplanted themselves to Maryland in order to be safe, as well from the insolence of the populace as the rigor of the government.

Not only the Gunpowder Treason but every other plot, both pretended and real, that has been trumped up in England ever since, has helped to people His Lordship's propriety. But what has proved most serviceable to it was the grand rebellion against King Charles I, when everything that bore the least tokens of popery was sure to be demolished and every man that professed it in jeopardy of suffering the same kind of martyrdom the Romish priests do in Sweden.

Soon after the reduction of New York the Duke was pleased to grant out of it all that tract of land included between Hudson and Delaware Rivers to the Lord Berkeley and Sir George Carteret by deed dated June 24, 1664. And when these grantees came to make partition of this territory, His Lordship's moiety was called West Jersey and that to Sir George, East Jersey.

But before the date of this grant the Swedes began to gain footing in part of that country, though after they saw the fate of New York, they were glad to submit to the King of England on the easy terms of remaining in their possessions and rendering a moderate quitrent. Their posterity continue there to this day and think their lot cast in a much fairer land than Dalecarlia.[9]

The proprietors of New Jersey, finding more trouble than profit in their new dominions, made over their right to several other persons, who obtained a fresh grant from His Royal Highness dated March 14, 1682.[10]

Several of the grantees, being Quakers and Anabaptists, failed not to encourage many of their own persuasion to remove to this peaceful region. Amongst them were a swarm of Scots Quakers, who were not tolerated to exercise the gifts of the spirit in their own country.

[9] A region in west-central Sweden.
[10] March 14, 1683, New Style.

Besides the hopes of being safe from persecution in this retreat, the new proprietors inveigled many over by this tempting account of the country: that it was a place free from those three great scourges of mankind, priests, lawyers, and physicians. Nor did they tell them a word of a lie, for the people were yet too poor to maintain these learned gentlemen, who everywhere love to be well paid for what they do and, like the Jews, can't breathe in a climate where nothing is to be got.

The Jerseys continued under the government of these proprietors till the year 1702, when they made a formal surrender of the dominion to the Queen, reserving, however, the property of the soil to themselves. So soon as the bounds of New Jersey came to be distinctly laid off, it appeared there was still a narrow slip of land lying betwixt that colony and Maryland. Of this William Penn, a man of much worldly wisdom and some eminence among the Quakers, got early notice and, by the credit he had with the Duke of York, obtained a patent for it dated March 4, 1680.[11]

It was a little surprising to some people how a Quaker should be so much in the good graces of a popish prince, though, after all, it may be pretty well accounted for. This ingenious person had not been bred a Quaker but, in his early days, had been a man of pleasure about the town. He had a beautiful form and very taking address, which made him successful with the ladies, and particularly with a mistress of the Duke of Monmouth. By this gentlewoman he had a daughter, who had beauty enough to raise her to be a duchess and continued to be a toast full thirty years. But this amour had like to have brought our fine gentleman in danger of a duel, had he not discreetly sheltered himself under this peaceable persuasion.[12] Besides, his father having been a flag officer in the navy while the Duke of York was Lord High Admiral might recommend the son to his favor. This piece of secret history I thought proper to mention to wipe off the suspicion of his having been popishly inclined.

This gentleman's first grant confined him within pretty narrow

[11] March 14, 1681, New Style.
[12] Boyd: "This is a piece of gossip not found elsewhere; it calls to mind other calumnies against Penn perpetuated by Macaulay, which are refuted in Dixon's *William Penn*, pp. 338–357." *William Byrd's Histories of the Dividing Line betwixt Virginia and North Carolina*, edited by William K. Boyd (Raleigh, N.C., 1929).

bonds, giving him only that portion of land which contains Bucking-
ham, Philadelphia, and Chester Counties. But to get these bounds a
little extended, he pushed his interest still farther with His Royal
Highness and obtained a fresh grant of the three lower counties called
Newcastle, Kent, and Sussex, which still remained within the New
York patent and had been luckily left out of the grant of New Jersey.
The six counties being thus incorporated, the proprietor dignified the
whole with the name of Pennsylvania.

The Quakers flocked over to this country in shoals, being averse to
go to Heaven the same way with the bishops. Amongst them were not
a few of good substance, who went vigorously upon every kind of improvement; and thus much I may truly say in their praise, that by diligence and frugality, for which this harmless sect is remarkable, and by
having no vices but such as are private, they have in a few years made
Pennsylvania a very fine country. The truth is, they have observed
exact justice with all the natives that border upon them; they have
purchased all their lands from the Indians, and though they paid but
a trifle for them it has procured them the credit of being more righteous
than their neighbors. They have likewise had the prudence to treat
them kindly upon all occasions, which has saved them from many wars
and massacres wherein the other colonies have been indiscreetly in-
volved. The truth of it is, a people whose principles forbid them to
draw the carnal sword were in the right to give no provocation.

Both the French and Spaniards had, in the name of their respective
monarchs, long ago taken possession of that part of the northern continent that now goes by the name of Carolina; but, finding it produced
neither gold nor silver, as they greedily expected, and meeting such returns from the Indians as their own cruelty and treachery deserved,
they totally abandoned it. In this deserted condition that country lay
for the space of ninety years, till King Charles II, finding it a derelict,
granted it away to the Earl of Clarendon and others by his royal charter
dated March 24, 1663. The boundary of that grant toward Virginia
was a due-west line from Luck Island (the same as Colleton Island),
lying in 36 degrees of north latitude, quite to the South Sea.

But afterwards Sir William Berkeley, who was one of the grantees and at that time Governor of Virginia, finding a territory of thirty-one miles in breadth between the inhabited part of Virginia and the above-mentioned boundary of Carolina, advised the Lord Clarendon of it. And His Lordship had interest enough with the King to obtain a second patent to include it, dated June 30, 1665.

This last grant describes the bounds between Virginia and Carolina in these words: "To run from the north end of Currituck Inlet due west to Weyanoke Creek, lying within or about the degree of thirty-six and thirty minutes of northern latitude, and from thence west in a direct line as far as the South Sea." Without question this boundary was well known at the time the charter was granted, but in a long course of years Weyanoke Creek lost its name, so that it became a controversy where it lay. Some ancient persons in Virginia affirmed it was the same with Wiccacon, and others again in Carolina were as positive it was Nottoway River.

In the meantime, the people on the frontiers entered for land and took out patents by guess, either from the King or the Lords Proprietors. But the Crown was like to be the loser by this uncertainty because the terms both of taking up and seating land were easier much in Carolina. The yearly taxes to the public were likewise there less burdensome, which laid Virginia under a plain disadvantage.

This consideration put that government upon entering into measures with North Carolina to terminate the dispute and settle a certain boundary between the two colonies. All the difficulty was to find out which was truly Weyanoke Creek. The difference was too considerable to be given up by either side, there being a territory of fifteen miles betwixt the two streams in controversy.

However, till that matter could be adjusted it was agreed on both sides that no lands at all should be granted within the disputed bounds. Virginia observed this agreement punctually, but I am sorry I can't say the same of North Carolina. The great officers of that province were loath to lose the fees accruing from the grants of land, and so private interest got the better of public spirit — and I wish that were the only place in the world where such politics are fashionable.

All the steps that were taken afterwards in that affair will best appear by the report of the Virginia commissioners, recited in the order of the council given at St. James's, March 1, 1710, set down in the appendix.[13]

It must be owned, the report of those gentlemen was severe upon the then commissioners of North Carolina, and particularly upon Mr. M[oseley]. I won't take upon me to say with how much justice they said so many hard things, though it had been fairer play to have given the parties accused a copy of such representation, that they might have answered what they could for themselves.

But since that was not done, I must beg leave to say thus much in behalf of Mr. Moseley: that he was not much in the wrong to find fault with the quadrant produced by the surveyors of Virginia, because that instrument placed the mouth of Nottoway River in the latitude of 37 degrees, whereas by an accurate observation made since it appears to lie in 36° 30′ 30″, so that there was an error of near 30 minutes, either in the instrument or in those who made use of it.

Besides, it is evident the mouth of Nottoway River agrees much better with the latitude wherein the Carolina charter supposed Weyanoke Creek (namely, in or about 36° 30′), than it does with Wiccacon Creek, which is about fifteen miles more southerly.

This being manifest, the intention of the King's grant will be pretty exactly answered by a due-west line drawn from Currituck Inlet to the mouth of Nottoway River; for which reason 'tis probable that was formerly called Weyanoke Creek and might change its name when the Nottoway Indians came to live upon it, which was since the date of the last Carolina charter.

The Lieutenant Governor of Virginia, at that time Colonel Spotswood, searching into the bottom of this affair, made very equitable proposals to Mr. Eden, at that time Governor of North Carolina, in order to put an end to this controversy. These, being formed into preliminaries, were signed by both governors and transmitted to England, where they had the honor to be ratified by His late Majesty and assented to by the Lords Proprietors of Carolina.

Accordingly an order was sent by the late King to Mr. Gooch, afterwards Lieutenant Governor of Virginia, to pursue those preliminaries

[13] See pp. 322-336.

exactly. In obedience thereunto he was pleased to appoint three of the council of that colony to be commissioners on the part of Virginia, who, in conjunction with others to be named by the Governor of North Carolina, were to settle the boundary between the two governments upon the plan of the above-mentioned articles.

Two experienced surveyors were at the same time directed to wait upon the commissioners: Mr. Mayo, who made the accurate map of Barbados, and Mr. Irvin, the mathematic professor of William and Mary College. And because a good number of men were to go upon this expedition, a chaplain was appointed to attend them, and the rather because the people on the frontiers of North Carolina, who have no minister near them, might have an opportunity to get themselves and their children baptized.

Of these proceedings on our part, immediate notice was sent to Sir Richard Everard, Governor of North Carolina, who was desired to name commissioners for that province to meet those of Virginia at Currituck Inlet the spring following. Accordingly he appointed four members of the council of that province to take care of the interests of the Lords Proprietors. Of these, Mr. Moseley was to serve in a double capacity, both as commissioner and surveyor. For that reason there was but one other surveyor from thence, Mr. Swann. All the persons being thus agreed upon, they settled the time of meeting to be at Currituck, March 5, 1728.

In the meantime, the requisite preparations were made for so long and tiresome a journey; and because there was much work to be done and some danger from the Indians in the uninhabited part of the country, it was necessary to provide a competent number of men. Accordingly, seventeen able hands were listed on the part of Virginia, who were most of them Indian traders and expert woodsmen.

FEBRUARY 1728

27. These good men were ordered to come armed with a musket and a tomahawk or large hatchet and provided with a sufficient quantity of ammunition. They likewise brought provisions of their own for ten days, after which time they were to be furnished by the govern-

ment. Their march was appointed to be on the twenty-seventh of February, on which day one of the commissioners met them at their rendezvous and proceeded with them as far as Colonel Allen's. This gentleman is a great economist and skilled in all the arts of living well at an easy expense.

28. They proceeded in good order through Surry County as far as the Widow Allen's, who had copied Solomon's complete housewife exactly. At this gentlewoman's house the other two commissioners had appointed to join them, but were detained by some accident at Williamsburg longer than their appointment.

29. They pursued their march through the Isle of Wight and observed a most dreadful havoc made by a late hurricane, which happened in August, 1726. The violence of it had not reached above a quarter of a mile in breadth but within that compass had leveled all before it. Both trees and houses were laid flat on the ground and several things hurled to an incredible distance. 'Tis happy such violent gusts are confined to so narrow a channel, because they carry desolation wherever they go. In the evening they reached Mr. Godwin's, on the south branch of Nansemond River, where they were treated with abundance [of] primitive hospitality.

March 1. This gentleman was so kind as to shorten their journey by setting them over the river. They coasted the northeast side of the Dismal for several miles together and found all the grounds bordering upon it very full of sloughs. The trees that grew near it looked very reverend with the long moss that hung dangling from their branches. Both cattle and horses eat this moss greedily in winter when other provender is scarce, though it is apt to scour them at first. In that moist soil, too, grows abundance of that kind of myrtle which bears the candleberries. There was likewise here and there a gallbush, which is a beautiful evergreen and may be cut into any shape. It derives its name from its berries turning water black, like the galls of an oak. When this shrub is transplanted into gardens, it will not thrive without frequent watering.

The two other commissioners came up with them just at their journey's end, and that evening they arrived all together at Mr. Crawford's, who lives on the south branch of Elizabeth River over against Norfolk. Here the commissioners left the men with all the horses and heavy baggage and crossed the river with their servants only, for fear of making a famine in the town.

Norfolk has most the air of a town of any in Virginia. There were then near twenty brigantines and sloops riding at the wharves, and oftentimes they have more. It has all the advantages of situation requisite for trade and navigation. There is a secure harbor for a good number of ships of any burden. Their river divides itself into three several branches, which are all navigable. The town is so near the sea that its vessels may sail in and out in a few hours. Their trade is chiefly to the West Indies, whither they export abundance of beef, pork, flour, and lumber. The worst of it is, they contribute much toward debauching the country by importing abundance of rum, which, like gin in Great Britain, breaks the constitutions, vitiates the morals, and ruins the industry of most of the poor people of this country. This place is the mart for most of the commodities produced in the adjacent parts of North Carolina. They have a pretty deal of lumber from the borders on the Dismal, who make bold with the King's land thereabouts without the least ceremony. They not only maintain their stocks upon it but get boards, shingles, and other lumber out of it in great abundance.

The town is built on a level spot of ground upon Elizabeth River, the banks whereof are neither so high as to make the landing of goods troublesome or so low as to be in danger of overflowing. The streets are straight and adorned with several good houses, which increase every day. It is not a town of ordinaries and public houses, like most others in this country, but the inhabitants consist of merchants, ship carpenters, and other useful artisans, with sailors enough to manage their navigation. With all these conveniences it lies under the two great disadvantages that most of the towns in Holland do by having neither good air nor good water. The two cardinal virtues that make a place thrive, industry and frugality, are seen here in perfection; and so long as they can banish luxury and idleness the town will remain in a happy and flourishing condition.

173

The method of building wharves here is after the following manner. They lay down long pine logs that reach from the shore to the edge of the channel. These are bound fast together by cross pieces notched into them, according to the architecture of the log houses in North Carolina. A wharf built thus will stand several years, in spite of the worm, which bites here very much, but may be soon repaired in a place where so many pines grow in the neighborhood.

The commissioners endeavored in this town to list three more men to serve as guides in that dirty part of the country but found that these people knew just enough of that frightful place to avoid it. They had been told that those nether lands were full of bogs, of marshes and swamps, not fit for human creatures to engage in, and this was reason enough for them not to hazard their persons. So they told us, flat and plain, that we might e'en daggle through the mire by ourselves for them.

The worst of it was, we could not learn from anybody in this town what route to take to Currituck Inlet; till at last we had the fortune to meet with a borderer upon North Carolina, who made us a rough sketch of that part of the country. Thus, upon seeing how the land lay, we determined to march directly to Prescot Landing upon Northwest River and proceed from thence by water to the place where our line was to begin.[14]

4. In pursuance of this resolution we crossed the river this morning to Powder Point, where we all took horse; and the grandees of the town, with great courtesy, conducted us ten miles on our way, as far as the long bridge built over the south branch of the river. The parson of the parish, Mr. Marston, a painful apostle from the Society,[15] made one in this ceremonious cavalcade.

At the bridge these gentlemen, wishing us a good deliverance, returned, and then a troop of light horse escorted us as far as Prescot Landing upon Northwest River. Care had been taken beforehand to provide two piraguas to lie ready at that place to transport us to Cur-

[14] In the *Secret History* Byrd relates the activities of the party in Norfolk on March 2 and 3, omitting the detailed description of the town given here (see pp. 51–53).

[15] The Society for the Propagation of the Gospel in Foreign Parts.

rituck Inlet. Our zeal was so great to get thither at the time appointed that we hardly allowed ourselves leisure to eat, which in truth we had the less stomach to by reason the dinner was served up by the land-lord, whose nose stood on such ticklish terms that it was in danger of falling into the dish. We therefore made our repast very short and then embarked with only the surveyors and nine chosen men, leaving the rest at Mr. W[ilso]n's to take care of the horses and baggage. There we also left our chaplain, with the charitable intent that the gentiles round about might have time and opportunity, if they pleased, of getting themselves and their children baptized.

We rowed down Northwest River about eighteen miles, as far as the mouth of it, where it empties itself into Albemarle Sound. It was really a delightful sight, all the way, to see the banks of the river adorned with myrtle, laurel, and bay trees, which preserve their ver-dure the year round, though it must be owned that these beautiful plants sacred to Venus and Apollo grow commonly in a very dirty soil. The river is in most places fifty or sixty yards wide, without spread-ing much wider at the mouth. 'Tis remarkable it was never known to ebb and flow till the year 1713, when a violent storm opened a new inlet about five miles south of the old one; since which convulsion the old inlet is almost choked up by the shifting of the sand and grows both narrower and shoaler every day.

It was dark before we could reach the mouth of the river, where our wayward stars directed us to a miserable cottage. The landlord was lately removed bag and baggage from Maryland, through a strong antipathy he had to work and paying his debts. For want of our tent, we were obliged to shelter ourselves in this wretched hovel, where we were almost devoured by vermin of various kinds. However, we were above complaining, being all philosophers enough to improve such slender distresses into mirth and good humor.

5. The day being now come on which we had agreed to meet the commissioners of North Carolina, we embarked very early, which we could the easier do, having no temptation to stay where we were. We shaped our course along the south end of Knott's Island, there being no passage open on the north. Farther still to the southward of us we

175

discovered two smaller islands that go by the names of Bell's and Church's Isles. We also saw a small New England sloop riding in the sound a little to the south of our course. She had come in at the new inlet, as all other vessels have done since the opening of it. This navigation is a little difficult and fit only for vessels that draw no more than ten feet water. The trade hither is engrossed by the saints of New England, who carry off a great deal of tobacco without troubling themselves with paying that impertinent duty of a penny a pound.

It was just noon before we arrived at Currituck Inlet, which is now so shallow that the breakers fly over it with a horrible sound and at the same time afford a very wild prospect. On the north side of the inlet the high land terminated in a bluff point, from which a spit of sand extended itself toward the southeast full half a mile. The inlet lies between that spit and another on the south of it, leaving an opening of not quite a mile, which at this day is not practicable for any vessel whatsoever. And as shallow as it now is, it continues to fill up more and more, both the wind and waves rolling in the sands from the eastern shoals.

About two o'clock in the afternoon we were joined by two of the Carolina commissioners, attended by Mr. S[wan]n, their surveyor. The other two were not quite so punctual, which was the more unlucky for us because there could be no sport till they came. These gentlemen, it seems, had the Carolina commission in their keeping, notwithstanding which they could not forbear paying too much regard to a proverb fashionable in their country — not to make more haste than good speed.

However, that we who were punctual might not spend our precious time unprofitably, we took the several bearings of the coast. We also surveyed part of the adjacent high land, which had scarcely any trees growing upon it but cedars. Among the shrubs, we were showed here and there a bush of Carolina tea called yaupon, which is one species of the phillyrea. This is an evergreen, the leaves whereof have some resemblance to tea but differ very widely both in taste and flavor. We also found some few plants of the spired-leaf silk grass, which is likewise an evergreen, bearing on a lofty stem a large cluster of flowers

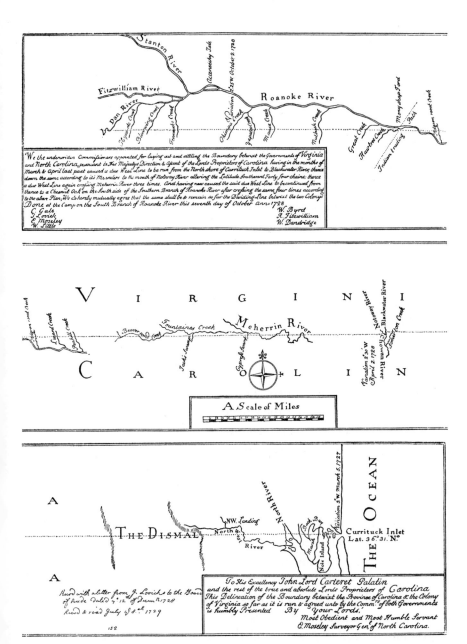

We the underwritten Commissioners appointed for laying out and settling the Boundary betwixt the Governments of Virginia and North Carolina, pursuant to His Majesty's Direction & Consent of the Lords Proprietors of Carolina having in the months of March & April last past caused a due West Line to be run from the North shore of Currituck Inlet to Blackwater River, thence down the same according to its Meanders to the mouth of Nottoway River, altering the Latitude Southward Forty four chains; thence a due West Line again crossing Meherrin River three times. And having now caused the said due West Line to be continued from thence to a Chesnut Oak on the South side of the Southern Branch of Roanoke River after crossing the same four times according to the above Plan, We do hereby mutually agree that the same shall be & remain as far the Dividing-Line betwixt the two Colonys. Done at the Camp on the South Branch of Roanoke River this seventh day of October Anno 1728.

G. Gale
J. Lovick
E. Moseley
W. Little

W. Byrd
R. Fitzwilliam
W. Dandridge

Recd with a letter from J. Lovick to the Board of Trade Dated yr 12 of Decemr 1728
Recd & read July 30th 1729

152

To His Excellency John Lord Carteret Palatin and the rest of the true and absolute Lords Proprietors of Carolina This Delineation of the Boundary betwixt the Province of Carolina & the Colony of Virginia so far as it is run & agreed unto by the Commrs of both Governments is humbly Presented      BY      your Lords.
Most Obedient and Most Humble Servant
E. Moseley Surveyor Genl of North Carolina.

## Surveyor's Map of the Dividing Line Submitted to the Board of Trade

### (reproduced here in three sections)

of a pale yellow. Of the leaves of this plant the people thereabouts twist very strong cordage.

A virtuoso might divert himself here very well in picking up shells of various hue and figure and amongst the rest that species of conch shell which the Indian peak is made of. The extremities of these shells are blue and the rest white, so that peak of both these colors are drilled out of one and the same shell, serving the natives both for ornament and money, and are esteemed by them far beyond gold and silver.

The cedars were of singular use to us in the absence of our tent, which we had left with the rest of the baggage for fear of overloading the piraguas. We made a circular hedge of the branches of this tree, wrought so close together as to fence us against the cold winds. We then kindled a rousing fire in the center of it and lay round it like so many Knights Templars. But, as comfortable as this lodging was, the surveyors turned out about two in the morning to try the variation by a meridian taken from the North Star and found it to be somewhat less than three degrees west.

The commissioners of the neighboring colony came better provided for the belly than the business. They brought not above two men along with them that would put their hands to anything but the kettle and the frying pan. These spent so much of their industry that way that they had as little spirit as inclination for work.

6. At noon, having a perfect observation, we found the latitude of Currituck Inlet to be 36° 31′.

Whilst we were busied about these necessary matters, our skipper rowed to an oyster bank just by and loaded his piragua with oysters as savory and well-tasted as those from Colchester or Walfleet, and had the advantage of them, too, by being much larger and fatter.

About three in the afternoon the two lag commissioners arrived and, after a few decent excuses for making us wait, told us they were ready to enter upon business as soon as we pleased. The first step was to produce our respective powers, and the commission from each governor was distinctly read and copies of them interchangeably delivered.

It was observed by our Carolina friends that the latter part of the

Virginia commission had something in it a little too lordly and positive. In answer to which we told them 'twas necessary to make it thus peremptory lest the present commissioners might go upon as fruitless an errand as their predecessors. The former commissioners were tied down to act in exact conjunction with those of Carolina and so could not advance one step farther or one jot faster than they were pleased to permit them. The memory of that disappointment, therefore, induced the government of Virginia to give fuller powers to the present commissioners by authorizing them to go on with the work by themselves, in case those of Carolina should prove unreasonable and refuse to join with them in carrying the business to execution. And all this was done lest His Majesty's gracious intention should be frustrated a second time.

After both commissions were considered, the first question was where the dividing line was to begin. This begat a warm debate, the Virginia commissioners contending, with a great deal of reason, to begin at the end of the spit of sand, which was undoubtedly the north shore of Currituck Inlet. But those of Carolina insisted strenuously that the point of high land ought rather to be the place of beginning, because that was fixed and certain, whereas the spit of sand was ever shifting and did actually run out farther now than formerly. The contest lasted some hours with great vehemence, neither party receding from their opinion that night. But next morning Mr. M[oseley], to convince us he was not that obstinate person he had been represented, yielded to our reasons and found means to bring over his colleagues.

Here we began already to reap the benefit of those peremptory words in our commission, which in truth added some weight to our reasons. Nevertheless, because positive proof was made by the oaths of two credible witnesses that the spit of sand had advanced two hundred yards toward the inlet since the controversy first began, we were willing for peace's sake to make them that allowance. Accordingly we fixed our beginning about that distance north of the inlet and there ordered a cedar post to be driven deep into the sand for our beginning.

While we continued here, we were told that on the south shore not far from the inlet dwelt a marooner that modestly called himself a hermit, though he forfeited that name by suffering a wanton female to cohabit with him. His habitation was a bower covered with bark after the Indian fashion, which in that mild situation protected him pretty well from the weather. Like the ravens, he neither plowed nor sowed but subsisted chiefly upon oysters, which his handmaid made a shift to gather from the adjacent rocks. Sometimes, too, for change of diet, he sent her to drive up the neighbor's cows, to moisten their mouths with a little milk. But as for raiment, he depended mostly upon his length of beard and she upon her length of hair, part of which she brought decently forward and the rest dangled behind quite down to her rump, like one of Herodotus' East Indian Pygmies. Thus did these wretches live in a dirty state of nature and were mere Adamites, innocence only excepted.

7. This morning the surveyors began to run the dividing line from the cedar post we had driven into the sand, allowing near three degrees for the variation. Without making this just allowance, we should not have obeyed His Majesty's order in running a due-west line. It seems the former commissioners had not been so exact, which gave our friends of Carolina but too just an exception to their proceedings. The line cut Dosier's Island, consisting only of a flat sand with here and there an humble shrub growing upon it. From thence it crossed over a narrow arm of the sound into Knott's Island and there split a plantation belonging to William Harding.

The day being far spent, we encamped in this man's pasture, though it lay very low and the season now inclined people to aguish distempers. He suffered us to cut cedar branches for our enclosure and other wood for firing, to correct the moist air and drive away the damps. Our landlady, in the days of her youth, it seems, had been a laundress in the Temple and talked over her adventures in that station with as much pleasure as an old soldier talks over his battles and distempers and, I believe, with as many additions to the truth.

The soil is good in many places of this island, and the extent of it pretty large. It lies in the form of a wedge: the south end of it is several miles over, but toward the north it sharpens into a point. It is a plentiful place for stock by reason of the wide marshes adjacent to it and because of its warm situation. But the inhabitants pay a little dear for this convenience by losing as much blood in the summer season by the infinite number of mosquitoes as all their beef and pork can recruit in the winter.

The sheep are as large as in Lincolnshire, because they are never pinched by cold or hunger. The whole island was hitherto reckoned to lie in Virginia, but now our line has given the greater part of it to Carolina. The principal freeholder here is Mr. White, who keeps open house for all travelers that either debt or shipwreck happens to cast in his way.

8. By break of day we sent away our largest piragua with the baggage round the south end of Knott's Island, with orders to the men to wait for us in the mouth of North River. Soon after, we embarked ourselves on board the smaller vessel, with intent, if possible, to find a passage round the north end of the island.

We found this navigation very difficult by reason of the continued shoals and often stuck fast aground; for though the sound spreads many miles, yet it is in most places extremely shallow and requires a skillful pilot to steer even a canoe safe over it. It was almost as hard to keep our temper as to keep the channel in this provoking situation. But the most impatient amongst us stroked down their choler and swallowed their curses, lest, if they suffered them to break out, they might sound like complaining, which was expressly forbid as the first step to sedition.

At a distance we descried several islands to the northward of us, the largest of which goes by the name of Cedar Island. Our piragua stuck so often that we had a fair chance to be benighted in this wide water, which must certainly have been our fate had we not luckily spied a canoe that was giving a fortuneteller a cast from Princess Anne County over to North Carolina. But, as conjurers are sometimes mistaken, the man mistrusted we were officers of justice in pursuit of a young wench he had carried off along with him. We gave the canoe chase for more than an hour and when we came up with her threatened to make them all prisoners unless they would direct us into the right channel. By the pilotage of these people we rowed up an arm of the sound called the Back Bay till we came to the head of it. There we were stopped by a miry pocosin full half a mile in breadth, through which we were obliged to daggle on foot, plunging now and then, though we picked our way, up to the knees in mud. At the end of this charming walk we gained the terra firma of Princess Anne County. In that dirty condition we were afterwards obliged to foot it two miles as far as John Heath's plantation, where we expected to meet the surveyors and the men who waited upon them.

While we were performing this tedious voyage, they had carried the line through the firm land of Knott's Island, where it was no more than half a mile wide. After that they traversed a large marsh, that was exceeding miry and extended to an arm of the Back Bay. They crossed that water in a canoe which we had ordered round for that purpose and then waded over another marsh that reached quite to the high land of Princess Anne. Both these marshes together make a breadth of five miles, in which the men frequently sank up to the middle without muttering the least complaint. On the contrary, they turned all these disasters into merriment.

It was discovered by this day's work that Knott's Island was improperly so called, being in truth no more than a peninsula. The northwest side of it is only divided from the main by the great marsh above-mentioned, which is seldom totally overflowed. Instead of that, it might by the labor of a few trenches be drained into firm meadow. capable of grazing as many cattle as Job in his best estate was master of. In the miry condition it now lies, it feeds great numbers in the winter, though when the weather grows warm they are driven from thence by the mighty armies of mosquitoes, which are the plague of the lower part of Carolina as much as the flies were formerly of Egypt (and some rabbis think those flies were no other than mosquitoes).

All the people in the neighborhood flocked to John Heath's to behold such rarities as they fancied us to be. The men left their beloved chimney corners, the good women their spinning wheels, and some, of more curiosity than ordinary, rose out of their sick beds to come and stare at us. They looked upon us as a troop of knights-errant who were running this great risk of our lives, as they imagined, for the public weal; and some of the gravest of them questioned much whether we were not all criminals condemned to this dirty work for offenses against the state. What puzzled them most was what could make our men so very light-hearted under such intolerable drudgery. "Ye have little reason to be merry, my masters," said one of them, with a very solemn face. "I fancy the pocosin you must struggle with tomorrow will make you change your note and try what metal you are made of. Ye are, to be sure, the first of human race that ever had the boldness to attempt it, and I dare say will be the last. If, therefore, you have any worldly goods to dispose of, my advice is that you make your wills this very night, for fear you die intestate tomorrow." But, alas, these frightful tales were so far from disheartening the men that they served only to whet their resolution.

9. The surveyors entered early upon their business this morning and ran the line through Mr. Eyland's plantation, as far as the banks of North River. They passed over it in the piragua and landed in Gibbs's marsh, which was a mile in breadth and tolerably firm. They trudged through this marsh without much difficulty as far as the high land, which promised more fertility than any they had seen in these lower parts. But this firm land lasted not long before they came upon the dreadful pocosin they had been threatened with. Nor did they find it one jot better than it had been painted to them. The beavers and otters had rendered it quite impassable for any creatures but themselves.

Our poor fellows had much ado to drag their legs after them in this quagmire, but, disdaining to be balked, they could hardly be persuaded from pressing forward by the surveyors, who found it absolutely necessary to make a traverse in the deepest place to prevent their sticking fast in the mire and becoming a certain prey to the turkey buzzards.

This horrible day's work ended two miles to the northward of Mr. Merchant's plantation, divided from Northwest River by a narrow swamp which is causewayed over. We took up our quarters in the open field not far from the house, correcting by a fire as large as a Roman funeral pile the aguish exhalations arising from the sunken grounds that surrounded us.

The neck of land included betwixt North River and Northwest

River, with the adjacent marsh, belonged formerly to Governor Gibbs[16] but since his decease to Colonel Bladen,[17] in right of his first lady, who was Mr. Gibbs's daughter. It would be a valuable tract of land in any country but North Carolina, where, for want of navigation and commerce, the best estate affords little more than a coarse subsistence.

10 The Sabbath happened very opportunely, to give some ease to our jaded people, who rested religiously from every work but that of cooking the kettle. We observed very few cornfields in our walks and those very small, which seemed the stranger to us because we could see no other tokens of husbandry or improvement. But upon further inquiry we were given to understand people only made corn for themselves and not for their stocks, which know very well how to get their own living. Both cattle and hogs ramble into the neighboring marshes and swamps, where they maintain themselves the whole winter long and are not fetched home till the spring. Thus these indolent wretches during one half of the year lose the advantage of the milk of their cattle, as well as their dung, and many of the poor creatures perish in the mire, into the bargain, by this ill management. Some who pique themselves more upon industry than their neighbors will now and then, in compliment to their cattle, cut down a tree whose limbs are loaded with the moss afore-mentioned. The trouble would be too great to climb the tree in order to gather this provender, but the shortest way (which in this country is always counted the best) is to fell it, just like the lazy Indians, who do the same by such trees as bear fruit and so make one harvest for all. By this bad husbandry milk is so scarce in the winter season that were a big-bellied woman to long for it she would tax her longing. And, in truth, I believe this is often the case, and at the same time a very good reason why so many people in this province are marked with a custard complexion.

The only business here is raising of hogs, which is managed with

---

[16] Boyd: "John Gibbs, of the Currituck region, who, in 1690, claimed to be Governor of North Carolina and resisted the authority of Philip Ludwell, the appointee of the Proprietors."

[17] Boyd: "Martin Bladen (1680–1746), Whig politician, and member of the Board of Trade from 1717 to his death. His wife was Mary Gibbs."

the least trouble and affords the diet they are most fond of. The truth of it is, the inhabitants of North Carolina devour so much swine's flesh that it fills them full of gross humors. For want, too, of a constant supply of salt, they are commonly obliged to eat it fresh, and that begets the highest taint of scurvy. Thus, whenever a severe cold happens to constitutions thus vitiated, 'tis apt to improve into the yaws, called there very justly the country distemper. This has all the symptoms of the pox, with this aggravation, that no preparation of mercury will touch it. First it seizes the throat, next the palate, and lastly shows its spite to the poor nose, of which 'tis apt in a small time treacherously to undermine the foundation. This calamity is so common and familiar here that it ceases to be a scandal, and in the disputes that happen about beauty the noses have in some companies much ado to carry it. Nay, 'tis said that once, after three good pork years, a motion had like to have been made in the House of Burgesses that a man with a nose should be incapable of holding any place of profit in the province; which extraordinary motion could never have been intended without some hopes of a majority.

Thus, considering the foul and pernicious effects of eating swine's flesh in a hot country, it was wisely forbid and made an abomination to the Jews, who lived much in the same latitude with Carolina.

11. We ordered the surveyors early to their business, who were blessed with pretty dry grounds for three miles together. But they paid dear for it in the next two, consisting of one continued frightful pocosin, which no creatures but those of the amphibious kind ever had ventured into before. This filthy quagmire did in earnest put the men's courage to a trial, and though I can't say it made them lose their patience, yet they lost their humor for joking. They kept their gravity like so many Spaniards, so that a man might then have taken his opportunity to plunge up to the chin without danger of being laughed at. However, this unusual composure of countenance could not fairly be called complaining.

Their day's work ended at the mouth of Northern's Creek, which empties itself into Northwest River; though we chose to quarter a little higher up the river near Mossy Point. This we did for the convenience of an old house to shelter our persons and baggage from the rain, which threatened us hard. We judged the thing right, for there fell an heavy shower in the night that drove the most hardy of us into the house. Though indeed our case was not much mended by retreating thither, because, that tenement having not long before been used as a pork store, the moisture of the air dissolved the salt that lay scattered on the floor and made it as wet withindoors as without. However, the swamps and marshes we were lately accustomed to had made such beavers and otters of us that nobody caught the least cold.

We had encamped so early that we found time in the evening to walk near half a mile into the woods. There we came upon a family of mulattoes that called themselves free, though by the shyness of the master of the house, who took care to keep least in sight, their freedom seemed a little doubtful. It is certain many slaves shelter themselves in this obscure part of the world, nor will any of their righteous neighbors discover them. On the contrary, they find their account in settling such fugitives on some out-of-the way corner of their land to raise stocks for a mean and inconsiderable share, well knowing their condition makes it necessary for them to submit to any terms. Nor were these worthy borderers content to shelter runaway slaves, but debtors and criminals have often met with the like indulgence. But if the government of North Carolina have encouraged this unneighborly policy in order to increase their people, it is no more than what ancient Rome did before them, which was made a city of refuge for all debtors and fugitives and from that wretched beginning grew up in time to be mistress of great part of the world. And, considering how Fortune delights in bringing great things out of small, who knows but Carolina may, one time or other, come to be the seat of some other great empire?

12. Everything had been so soaked with the rain that we were obliged to lie by a good part of the morning and dry them. However, that time was not lost, because it gave the surveyors an opportunity of platting off their work and taking the course of the river. It likewise helped to recruit the spirits of the men, who had been a little harassed with yesterday's march. Notwithstanding all this, we crossed the river

before noon and advanced our line three miles. It was not possible to make more of it by reason good part of the way was either marsh or pocosin. The line cut two or three plantations, leaving part of them in Virginia and part of them in Carolina. This was a case that happened frequently, to the great inconvenience of the owners, who were therefore obliged to take out two patents and pay for a new survey in each government.

In the evening we took up our quarters in Mr. Ballance's pasture, a little above the bridge built over Northwest River. There we discharged the two piraguas, which in truth had been very serviceable in transporting us over the many waters in that dirty and difficult part of our business. Our landlord had a tolerable good house and clean furniture, and yet we could not be tempted to lodge in it. We chose rather to lie in the open field, for fear of growing too tender. A clear sky, spangled with stars, was our canopy, which, being the last thing we saw before we fell asleep, gave us magnificent dreams. The truth of it is, we took so much pleasure in that natural kind of lodging that I think at the foot of the account mankind are great losers by the luxury of feather beds and warm apartments.

The curiosity of beholding so new and withal so sweet a method of encamping brought one of the Senators of North Carolina to make us a midnight visit. But he was so very clamorous in his commendations of it that the sentinel, not seeing his quality either through his habit or behavior, had like to have treated him roughly. After excusing the unseasonablness of his visit and letting us know he was a parliament man, he swore he was so taken with our lodging that he would set fire to his house as soon as he got home and teach his wife and children to lie like us in the open field.

13. Early this morning our chaplain repaired to us with the men we had left at Mr. Wilson's. We had sent for them the evening before to relieve those who had the labor oar from Currituck Inlet. But to our great surprise, they petitioned not to be relieved, hoping to gain immortal reputation by being the first of mankind that ventured through the Great Dismal. But the rest being equally ambitious of the same honor, it was but fair to decide their pretensions by lot. After For-

tune had declared herself, those which she had excluded offered money to the happy persons to go in their stead. But Hercules would have as soon sold the glory of cleansing the Augean stables, which was pretty near the same sort of work. No sooner was the controversy at an end but we sent those unfortunate fellows back to their quarters whom chance had condemned to remain upon firm land and sleep in a whole skin. In the meanwhile, the surveyors carried the line three miles, which was no contemptible day's work, considering how cruelly they were entangled with briers and gallbushes. The leaf of this last shrub bespeaks it to be of the alaternus family.

Our work ended within a quarter of a mile of the Dismal above-mentioned, where the ground began to be already full of sunken holes and slashes, which had, here and there, some few reeds growing in them. 'Tis hardly credible how little the bordering inhabitants were acquainted with this mighty swamp, notwithstanding they had lived their whole lives within smell of it. Yet, as great strangers as they were to it, they pretended to be very exact in their account of its dimensions and were positive it could not be above seven or eight miles wide, but knew no more of the matter than stargazers know of the distance of the fixed stars. At the same time, they were simple enough to amuse our men with idle stories of the lions, panthers, and alligators they were likely to encounter in that dreadful place. In short, we saw plainly there was no intelligence of this *Terra Incognita* to be got but from our own experience. For that reason it was resolved to make the requisite dispositions to enter it next morning. We allotted every one of the surveyors for this painful enterprise, with twelve men to attend them. Fewer than that could not be employed in clearing the way, carrying the chain, marking the trees, and bearing the necessary bedding and provisions. Nor would the commissioners themselves have spared their persons on this occasion but for fear of adding to the poor men's burden, while they were certain they could add nothing to their resolution.

We quartered with our friend and fellow traveler, William Wilkins, who had been our faithful pilot to Currituck and lived about a mile from the place where the line ended. Everything looked so very clean and the furniture so neat that we were tempted to lodge withindoors. But the novelty of being shut up so close quite spoiled our rest, nor did we breathe so free by abundance as when we lay in the open air.

14. Before nine of the clock this morning the provisions, bedding, and other necessaries were made up into packs for the men to carry on their shoulders into the Dismal. They were victualed for eight days at full allowance, nobody doubting but that would be abundantly sufficient to carry them through that inhospitable place; nor indeed was it possible for the poor fellows to stagger under more. As it was, their loads weighed from sixty to seventy pounds, in just proportion to the strength of those who were to bear them. 'Twould have been un-conscionable to have saddled them with burdens heavier than that, when they were to lug them through a filthy bog which was hardly practicable with no burden at all. Besides this luggage at their backs, they were obliged to measure the distance, mark the trees, and clear the way for the surveyors every step they went. It was really a pleasure to see with how much cheerfulness they undertook and with how much spirit they went through all this drudgery. For their greater safety, the commissioners took care to furnish them with Peruvian bark,[18] rhubarb, and ipecacuanha, in case they might happen, in that wet journey, to be taken with fevers or fluxes.

Although there was no need of example to inflame persons already so cheerful, yet to enter the people with the better grace, the author and two more of the commissioners accompanied them half a mile into the Dismal. The skirts of it were thinly planted with dwarf reeds and gallbushes, but when we got into the Dismal itself we found the reeds grew there much taller and closer and, to mend the matter, were so interlaced with bamboo briers that there was no scuffling through them without the help of pioneers. At the same time we found the ground moist and trembling under our feet like a quagmire, insomuch that it was an easy matter to run a ten-foot pole up to the head in it without exerting any uncommon strength to do it. Two of the men whose burdens were the least cumbersome had orders to march before with their tomahawks and clear the way in order to make an opening

[18] Cinchona, used as a specific for malaria and other fevers.

189

for the surveyors. By their assistance we made a shift to push the line half a mile in three hours and then reached a small piece of firm land about a hundred yards wide, standing up above the rest like an island. Here the people were glad to lay down their loads and take a little refreshment, while the happy man whose lot it was to carry the jug of rum began already, like Aesop's bread carriers, to find it grow a good deal lighter.

After reposing about an hour, the commissioners recommended vigor and constancy to their fellow travelers, by whom they were answered with three cheerful huzzas, in token of obedience. This ceremony was no sooner over but they took up their burdens and attended the motion of the surveyors, who, though they worked with all their might, could reach but one mile farther, the same obstacles still attending them which they had met with in the morning. However small this distance may seem to such as are used to travel at their ease, yet our poor men, who were obliged to work with an unwieldy load at their backs, had reason to think it a long way; especially in a bog where they had no firm footing but every step made a deep impression which was instantly filled with water. At the same time they were laboring with their hands to cut down the reeds, which were ten feet high, their legs were hampered with briers. Besides, the weather happened to be warm, and the tallness of the reeds kept off every friendly breeze from coming to refresh them. And indeed it was a little provoking to hear the wind whistling among the branches of the white cedars, which grew here and there amongst the reeds, and at the same time not to have the comfort to feel the least breath of it.

In the meantime the three commissioners returned out of the Dismal the same way they went in and, having joined their brethren, proceeded that night as far as Mr. Wilson's. This worthy person lives within sight of the Dismal, in the skirts whereof his stocks range and maintain themselves all the winter, and yet he knew as little of it as he did of *Terra Australis Incognita*. He told us a Canterbury tale of a North Briton whose curiosity spurred him a long way into this great desert, as he called it, near twenty years ago, but he, having no compass nor seeing the sun for several days together, wandered about till he was almost famished; but at last he bethought himself of a secret his countrymen make use of to pilot themselves in a dark day. He took a fat louse out of his collar and exposed it to the open day on a piece of white paper, which he brought along with him for his journal. The poor insect, having no eyelids, turned himself about till he found the darkest part of the heavens and so made the best of his way toward the North. By this direction he steered himself safe out and gave such a frightful account of the monsters he saw and the distresses he underwent that no mortal since has been hardy enough to go upon the like dangerous discovery.

15. The surveyors pursued their work with all diligence but still found the soil of the Dismal so spongy that the water oozed up into every footstep they took. To their sorrow, too, they found the reeds and briers more firmly interwoven than they did the day before. But the greatest grievance was from large cypresses which the wind had blown down and heaped upon one another. On the limbs of most of them grew sharp snags, pointing every way like so many pikes, that required much pains and caution to avoid. These trees, being evergreens and shooting their large tops very high, are easily overset by every gust of wind, because there is no firm earth to steady their roots. Thus many of them were laid prostrate, to the great encumbrance of the way. Such variety of difficulties made the business go on heavily, insomuch that from morning till night the line could advance no farther than one mile and thirty-one poles.

Never was rum, that cordial of life, found more necessary than it was in this dirty place. It did not only recruit the people's spirits, now almost jaded with fatigue, but served to correct the badness of the water and at the same time to resist the malignity of the air. Whenever the men wanted to drink, which was very often, they had nothing more to do but make a hole and the water bubbled up in a moment. But it was far from being either clear or well tasted and had, besides, a physical effect from the tincture it received from the roots of the shrubs and trees that grew in the neighborhood.

While the surveyors were thus painfully employed, the commissioners discharged the long score they had with Mr. Wilson for the men and horses which had been quartered upon him during our expedition to Currituck. From thence we marched in good order along the east side of the Dismal and passed the long bridge that lies over the south branch of Elizabeth River. At the end of eighteen miles we reached Timothy Ivy's plantation, where we pitched our tent for the first time and were furnished with everything the place afforded. We perceived the happy effects of industry in this family, in which every one looked tidy and clean and carried in their countenances the cheerful marks of plenty. We saw no drones there, which are but too common, alas, in that part of the world. Though, in truth, the distemper of laziness seizes the men oftener much than the women. These last spin, weave, and knit, all with their own hands, while their husbands, depending on the bounty of the climate, are slothful in everything but getting of children, and in that only instance make themselves useful members of an infant colony.

There is but little wool in that province, though cotton grows very kindly and, so far south, is seldom nipped by the frost. The good women mix this with their wool for their outer garments; though, for want of fulling, that kind of manufacture is open and sleazy. Flax likewise thrives there extremely, being perhaps as fine as any in the world, and I question not might with a little care and pains be brought to rival that of Egypt; and yet the men are here so intolerably lazy they seldom take the trouble to propagate it.

16. The line was this day carried one mile and an half and sixteen poles. The soil continued soft and miry but fuller of trees, especially white cedars. Many of these, too, were thrown down and piled in heaps, high enough for a good Muscovite fortification. The worst of it was, the poor fellows began now to be troubled with fluxes, occasioned by bad water and moist lodging, but chewing of rhubarb kept that malady within bounds.

In the meantime, the commissioners decamped early in the morning and made a march of twenty-five miles, as far as Mr. Andrew Meade's, who lives upon Nansemond River. They were no sooner got under the shelter of that hospitable roof but it began to rain hard and continued so to do great part of the night. This gave them much pain for their friends in the Dismal, whose sufferings spoiled their taste for the good cheer wherewith they were entertained themselves. However, late that evening these poor men had the fortune to come upon another terra firma, which was the luckier for them because the lower ground, by the rain that fell, was made a fitter lodging for tadpoles than men. In our journey we remarked that the north side of this great swamp lies higher than either the east or the west, nor were the approaches to it so full of sunken grounds.

We passed by no less than two Quaker meetinghouses, one of which had an awkward ornament on the west end of it that seemed to ape a steeple. I must own I expected no such piece of foppery from a sect of so much outside simplicity. That persuasion prevails much in the lower end of Nansemond County, for want of ministers to pilot the people a decenter way to Heaven. The ill reputation of tobacco planted in those lower parishes makes the clergy unwilling to accept of them, unless it be such whose abilities are as mean as their pay. Thus, whether the churches be quite void or but indifferently filled, the Quakers will have an opportunity of gaining proselytes. 'Tis a wonder no popish missionaries are sent from Maryland to labor in this neglected vineyard, who we know have zeal enough to traverse sea and land on the meritorious errand of making converts. Nor is it less strange that some wolf in sheep's clothing arrives not from New England to lead astray a flock that has no shepherd. People uninstructed in any religion are ready to embrace the first that offers. 'Tis natural for helpless man to adore his Maker in some form or other, and were there any exception to this rule, I should suspect it to be among the Hottentots of the Cape of Good Hope and of North Carolina.

There fell a great deal of rain in the night, accompanied with a strong wind. The fellow feeling we had for the poor Dismalites, on account of this unkind weather, rendered the down we laid upon uneasy. We fancied them half-drowned in their wet lodging, with the trees blowing down about their ears. These were the gloomy images our fears suggested, though 'twas so much uneasiness clear gains. They happened to come off much better, by being luckily encamped on the dry piece of ground afore-mentioned.

17. They were, however, forced to keep the Sabbath in spite of their teeth, contrary to the dispensation our good chaplain had given them. Indeed, their short allowance of provision would have justified their making the best of their way without distinction of days. 'Twas certainly a work both of necessity and self-preservation to save themselves from starving. Nevertheless, the hard rain had made everything so thoroughly wet that it was quite impossible to do any business. They therefore made a virtue of what they could not help and contentedly rested in their dry situation.

Since the surveyors had entered the Dismal, they had laid eyes on no living creature: neither bird nor beast, insect nor reptile came in view. Doubtless the eternal shade that broods over this mighty bog and hinders the sunbeams from blessing the ground makes it an uncomfortable habitation for anything that has life. Not so much as a Zeeland frog could endure so aguish a situation. It had one beauty, however, that delighted the eye, though at the expense of all the other senses: the moisture of the soil preserves a continual verdure and makes every plant an evergreen; but at the same time the foul damps ascend without ceasing, corrupt the air, and render it unfit for respiration. Not even a turkey buzzard will venture to fly over it, no more than the Italian vultures will over the filthy Lake Avernus, or the birds in the Holy Land over the Salt Sea where Sodom and Gomorrah formerly stood.

In these sad circumstances the kindest thing we could do for our suffering friends was to give them a place in The Litany. Our chaplain, for his part, did his office and rubbed us up with a seasonable sermon. This was quite a new thing to our brethren of North Carolina, who live in a climate where no clergyman can breathe, any more than spiders in Ireland.

For want of men in holy orders, both the members of the council and justices of the peace are empowered by the laws of that country to marry all those who will not take one another's word; but, for the ceremony of christening their children, they trust that to chance. If a parson come in their way, they will crave a cast of his office, as they call it; else they are content their offspring should remain as arrant pagans as themselves. They account it among their greatest advantages that they are not priest-ridden, not remembering that the clergy is rarely guilty of bestriding such as have the misfortune to be poor. One thing may be said for the inhabitants of that province, that they are not troubled with any religious fumes and have the least superstition of any people living. They do not know Sunday from any other day, any more than Robinson Crusoe did, which would give them a great advantage were they given to be industrious. But they keep so many Sabbaths every week that their disregard of the seventh day has no manner of cruelty in it, either to servants or cattle.

18. It was with some difficulty we could make our people quit the good cheer they met with at this house, so it was late before we took our departure; but to make us amends our landlord was so good as to conduct us ten miles on our way, as far as the Cypress Swamp, which drains itself into the Dismal. Eight miles beyond that we forded the waters of Corapeake, which tend the same way as do many others on that side. In six miles more we reached the plantation of Mr. Thomas Speight, a grandee of North Carolina. We found the good man upon his crutches, being crippled with the gout in both his knees. Here we flattered ourselves we should by this time meet with good tidings of the surveyors but had reckoned, alas! without our host: on the contrary, we were told the Dismal was at least thirty miles wide in that place. However, as nobody could say this on his own knowledge, we ordered guns to be fired and a drum to be beaten, but received no answer, unless it was from that prating nymph, Echo, who, like a loquacious wife, will always have the last word and sometimes return three for one. It was indeed no wonder our signal was not heard at that time by the people in the Dismal, because, in truth, they had then not penetrated one third of their way. They had that morning fallen to work with great vigor and, finding the ground better than ordinary, drove on the line two miles and thirty-eight poles. This was reckoned an Herculean day's work, and yet they would not have stopped there had not an impenetrable cedar thicket checked their industry.

Our landlord had seated himself on the borders of this Dismal for the advantage of the green food his cattle find there all winter and for the rooting that supports his hogs. This, I own, is some convenience to his purse, for which his whole family pay dear in their persons, for they are devoured by mosquitoes all the summer and have agues every spring and fall, which corrupt all the juices of their bodies, give them a cadaverous complexion and, besides, a lazy, creeping habit, which they never get rid of.

19. We ordered several men to patrol on the edge of the Dismal, both toward the north and toward the south, and to fire guns at proper distances. This they performed very punctually but could hear nothing in return nor gain any sort of intelligence. In the meantime, whole flocks of women and children flew hither to stare at us with as much curiosity as if we had lately landed from Bantam or Morocco. Some borderers, too, had a great mind to know where the line would come out, being for the most part apprehensive lest their lands should be taken into Virginia. In that case they must have submitted to some sort of order and government; whereas, in North Carolina, everyone does what seems best in his own eyes. There were some good women that brought their children to be baptized, but brought no capons along with them to make the solemnity cheerful. In the meantime, it was strange that none came to be married in such a multitude, if it had only been for the novelty of having their hands joined by one in holy orders. Yet so it was that though our chaplain christened above an hundred, he did not marry so much as one couple during the whole expedition. But marriage is reckoned a lay contract in Carolina, as I said before, and a country justice can tie the fatal knot there as fast as an archbishop.

None of our visitors could, however, tell us any news of the surveyors, nor indeed was it possible any of them should at that time, they being still laboring in the midst of the Dismal. It seems they were able to carry the line this day no farther than one mile and sixty-one poles, and that whole distance was through a miry cedar bog, where the ground trembled under their feet most frightfully. In many places, too, their passage was retarded by a great number of fallen trees that lay horsing upon one another.

Though many circumstances concurred to make this an unwholesome situation, yet the poor men had no time to be sick, nor can one conceive a more calamitous case than it would have been to be laid up in that uncomfortable quagmire. Never were patients more tractable or willing to take physic than these honest fellows, but it was from a dread of laying their bones in a bog that would soon spew them up again. That consideration also put them upon more caution about their lodging. They first covered the ground with square pieces of cypress bark, which now, in the spring, they could easily slip off the tree for that purpose. On this they spread their bedding, but, unhappily, the weight and warmth of their bodies made the water rise up betwixt the joints of the bark, to their great inconvenience. Thus they lay not only moist but also exceedingly cold, because their fires were continually going out. For no sooner was the trash upon the surface burnt away but immediately the fire was extinguished by the moisture of the soil, insomuch that it was great part of the sentinel's business to rekindle it again in a fresh place every quarter of an hour. Nor could they indeed do their duty better, because cold was the only enemy they had to guard against in a miserable morass where nothing can inhabit.

20. We could get no tidings yet of our brave adventurers, notwithstanding we dispatched men to the likeliest stations to inquire after them. They were still scuffling in the mire and could not possibly forward the line this whole day more than one mile and sixty-four chains. Every step of this day's work was through a cedar bog, where the trees were somewhat smaller and grew more into a thicket. It was now a great misfortune to the men to find their provisions grow less as their labor grew greater; they were all forced to come to short allowance and consequently to work hard without filling their bellies. Though this was very severe upon English stomachs, yet the people were so far from being discomfited at it that they still kept up their good humor and merrily told a young fellow in the company, who looked very plump and wholesome, that he must expect to go first to pot if matters should come to extremity. This was only said by way of jest, yet it made him thoughtful in earnest. However, for the present he returned them a very civil answer, letting them know that, dead or

alive, he should be glad to be useful to such worthy good friends. But, after all, this humorous saying had one very good effect, for that younker, who before was a little inclined by his constitution to be lazy, grew on a sudden extremely industrious, that so there might be less occasion to carbonade him for the good of his fellow travelers.

While our friends were thus embarrassed in the Dismal, the commissioners began to lie under great uneasiness for them. They knew very well their provisions must by this time begin to fall short, nor could they conceive any likely means of a supply. At this time of the year both cattle and hogs had forsaken the skirts of the Dismal, invited by the springing grass on the firm land. All our hopes were that Providence would cause some wild game to fall in their way or else direct them to a wholesome vegetable for subsistence. In short, they were haunted with so many frights on this occasion that they were in truth more uneasy than the persons whose case they lamented.

We had several visitors from Edenton, in the afternoon, that came with Mr. Gale, who had prudently left us at Currituck to scuffle through that dirty country by ourselves. These gentlemen, having good noses, had smelt out, at thirty miles' distance, the precious liquor with which the liberality of our good friend Mr. Meade had just before supplied us. That generous person had judged very right that we were now got out of the latitude of drink proper for men in affliction and therefore was so good as to send his cart loaden with all sorts of refreshments, for which the commissioners returned him their thanks and the chaplain his blessing.

21. The surveyors and their attendants began now in good earnest to be alarmed with apprehensions of famine, nor could they forbear looking with some sort of appetite upon a dog which had been the faithful companion of their travels. Their provisions were now near exhausted. They had this morning made the last distribution, that so each might husband his small pittance as he pleased. Now it was that the fresh-colored young man began to tremble every joint of him, having dreamt the night before that the Indians were about to barbecue him over live coals. The prospect of famine determined the people at last, with one consent, to abandon the line for the present, which

advanced but slowly, and make the best of their way to firm land. Accordingly they set off very early and, by the help of the compass which they carried along with them, steered a direct westerly course. They marched from morning till night and computed their journey to amount to about four miles, which was a great way, considering the difficulties of the ground. It was all along a cedar swamp, so dirty and perplexed that if they had not traveled for their lives they could not have reached so far. On their way they espied a turkey buzzard that flew prodigiously high to get above the noisome exhalations that ascend from that filthy place. This they were willing to understand as a good omen, according to the superstition of the ancients, who had great faith in the flight of vultures. However, after all this tedious journey they could yet discover no end of their toil, which made them very pensive, especially after they had eat the last morsel of their provisions. But to their unspeakable comfort, when all was hushed in the evening, they heard the cattle low and the dogs bark very distinctly, which, to men in that distress, was more delightful music than Faustina [19] or Farinelli [20] could have made.

In the meantime the commissioners could get no news of them from any of their visitors, who assembled from every point of the compass. But the good landlord had visitors of another kind while we were there, that is to say, some industrious masters of ships that lay in Nansemond River. These worthy commanders came to bespeak tobacco from these parts to make up their loadings, in contempt of the Virginia law which positively forbade their taking in any made in North Carolina. Nor was this restraint at all unreasonable, because they have no law in Carolina either to mend the quality or lessen the quantity of tobacco, or so much as to prevent the turning out of seconds, all which cases have been provided against by the laws of Virginia. Wherefore, there can be no reason why the inhabitants of that province should have the same advantage of shipping their tobacco in our parts when they will by no means submit to the same restrictions that we do.

22. Our patrol happened not to go far enough to the northward

---

[19] Faustina Bordoni (1693–1783), an Italian soprano.
[20] Carlo Broschi Farinelli (1705–1782), a famous *castrato*.

this morning; if they had, the people in the Dismal might have heard the report of their guns. For this reason they returned without any tidings, which threw us into a great though unnecessary perplexity. This was now the ninth day since they entered into that inhospitable swamp, and consequently we had reason to believe their provisions were quite spent. We knew they worked hard and therefore would eat heartily so long as they had wherewithal to recruit their spirits, not imagining the swamp so wide as they found it. Had we been able to guess where the line would come out, we would have sent men to meet them with a fresh supply; but as we could know nothing of that, and as we had neither compass nor surveyor to guide a messenger on such an errand, we were unwilling to expose him to no purpose; therefore, all we were able to do for them, in so great an extremity, was to recommend them to a merciful Providence.

However long we might think the time, yet we were cautious of showing our uneasiness for fear of mortifying our landlord. He had done his best for us, and therefore we were unwilling he should think us dissatisfied with our entertainment. In the midst of our concern, we were most agreeably surprised, just after dinner, with the news that the Dismalites were all safe. These blessed tidings were brought us by Mr. Swann, the Carolina surveyor, who came to us in a very tattered condition. After very short salutations, we got about him as if he had been a Hottentot and began to inquire into his adventures. He gave us a detail of their uncomfortable voyage through the Dismal and told us particularly they had pursued their journey early that morning, encouraged by the good omen of seeing the crows fly over their heads; that after an hour's march over very rotten ground they on a sudden began to find themselves among tall pines that grew in the water, which in many places was knee deep. This pine swamp, into which that of Corapeake drained itself, extended near a mile in breadth; and though it was exceedingly wet, yet was much harder at bottom than the rest of the swamp; that about ten in the morning they recovered firm land, which they embraced with as much pleasure as shipwrecked wretches do the shore.

After these honest adventurers had congratulated each other's deliverance, their first inquiry was for a good house where they might satisfy the importunity of their stomachs. Their good genius directed them to Mr. Brinkley's, who dwells a little to the southward of the line. This man began immediately to be very inquisitive, but they declared they had no spirits to answer questions till after dinner. "But pray, gentlemen," said he, "answer me one question at least: what shall we get for your dinner?" To which they replied, "No matter what, provided it be but enough." He kindly supplied their wants as soon as possible, and by the strength of that refreshment they made a shift to come to us in the evening, to tell their own story. They all looked very thin and as ragged as the Gibeonite ambassadors did in the days of yore.

Our surveyors told us they had measured ten miles in the Dismal and computed the distance they had marched since to amount to about five more, so they made the whole breadth to be fifteen miles in all.

23. It was very reasonable that the surveyors and the men who had been sharers in their fatigue should now have a little rest. They were all, except one, in good health and good heart, blessed be God! notwithstanding the dreadful hardships they had gone through. It was really a pleasure to see the cheerfulness wherewith they received the order to prepare to re-enter the Dismal on the Monday following in order to continue the line from the place where they had left off measuring, that so we might have the exact breadth of that dirty place. There were no more than two of them that could be persuaded to be relieved on this occasion or suffer the other men to share the credit of that bold undertaking; neither would these have suffered it had not one of them been very lame and the other much indisposed.

By the description the surveyors gave of the Dismal, we were convinced that nothing but the exceeding dry season we had been blessed with could have made the passing of it practicable. It is the source of no less than five several rivers which discharge themselves southward into Albemarle Sound and of two that run northerly into Virginia. From thence 'tis easy to imagine that the soil must be thoroughly

201

soaked with water or else there must be plentiful stores of it underground to supply so many rivers, especially since there is no lake or
any considerable body of that element to be seen on the surface. The
rivers that head in it from Virginia are the south branch of Nansemond and the west branch of Elizabeth, and those from Carolina are
Northwest River, North River, Pasquotank, Little River, and Perquimans.

There is one remarkable part of the Dismal, lying to the south of
the line, that has few or no trees growing on it but contains a large
tract of tall reeds. These, being green all the year round and waving
with every wind, have procured it the name of the Green Sea. We
are not yet acquainted with the precise extent of the Dismal, the
whole having never been surveyed; but it may be computed at a
medium to be about thirty miles long and ten miles broad, though
where the line crossed it, 'twas completely fifteen miles wide. But it
seems to grow narrower toward the north, or at least does so in many
places.

The exhalations that continually rise from this vast body of mire
and nastiness infect the air for many miles round and render it very
unwholesome for the bordering inhabitants. It makes them liable
to agues, pleurisies, and many other distempers that kill abundance
of people and make the rest look no better than ghosts. It would require a great sum of money to drain it, but the public treasure could
not be better bestowed than to preserve the lives of His Majesty's
liege people and at the same time render so great a tract of swamp
very profitable, besides the advantage of making a channel to transport by water carriage goods from Albemarle Sound into Nansemond
and Elizabeth rivers in Virginia.

24. This being Sunday, we had a numerous congregation, which
flocked to our quarters from all the adjacent country. The news that
our surveyors were come out of the Dismal increased the number
very much, because it would give them an opportunity of guessing,
at least, whereabouts the line would cut, whereby they might form
some judgment whether they belonged to Virginia or Carolina. Those
who had taken up land within the disputed bounds were in great

pain lest it should be found to lie in Virginia; because this being done contrary to an express order of that government, the patentees had great reason to fear they should in that case have lost their land. But their apprehensions were now at an end when they understood that all the territory which had been controverted was like to be left in Carolina.

In the afternoon, those who were to re-enter the Dismal were furnished with the necessary provisions and ordered to repair the overnight to their landlord, Peter Brinkley's, that they might be ready to begin their business early on Monday morning. Mr. Irvin was excused from the fatigue in compliment to his lungs; but Mr. Mayo and Mr. Swann were robust enough to return upon that painful service, and, to do them justice, they went with great alacrity. The truth was, they now knew the worst of it and could guess pretty near at the time when they might hope to return to land again.

25. The air was chilled this morning with a smart northwest wind, which favored the Dismalites in their dirty march. They returned by the path they had made in coming out and with great industry arrived in the evening at the spot where the line had been discontinued. After so long and laborious a journey, they were glad to repose themselves on their couches of cypress bark, where their sleep was as sweet as it would have been on a bed of Finland down.

In the meantime, we who stayed behind had nothing to do but to make the best observations we could upon that part of the country. The soil of our landlord's plantation, though none of the best, seemed more fertile than any thereabouts, where the ground is near as sandy as the deserts of Africa and consequently barren. The road leading from thence to Edenton, being in distance about twenty-seven miles, lies upon a ridge called Sandy Ridge, which is so wretchedly poor that it will not bring potatoes. The pines in this part of the country are of a different species from those that grow in Virginia: their bearded leaves are much longer and their cones much larger. Each cell contains a seed of the size and figure of a black-eyed pea, which, shedding in November, is very good mast for hogs and fattens them in a short time. The smallest of these pines are full of cones which are eight or nine inches long, and each affords commonly sixty or seventy seeds. This kind of mast has the advantage of all other by being more constant and less liable to be nipped by the frost or eaten by the caterpillars.

The trees also abound more with turpentine and consequently yield more tar than either the yellow or the white pine and for the same reason make more durable timber for building. The inhabitants hereabouts pick up knots of lightwood in abundance, which they burn into tar and then carry it to Norfolk or Nansemond for a market. The tar made in this method is the less valuable because it is said to burn the cordage, though it is full as good for all other uses as that made in Sweden and Muscovy.

Surely there is no place in the world where the inhabitants live with less labor than in North Carolina. It approaches nearer to the description of Lubberland[21] than any other, by the great felicity of the climate, the easiness of raising provisions, and the slothfulness of the people. Indian corn is of so great increase that a little pains will subsist a very large family with bread, and then they may have meat without any pains at all, by the help of the low grounds and the great variety of mast that grows on the high land. The men, for their parts, just like the Indians, impose all the work upon the poor women. They make their wives rise out of their beds early in the morning, at the same time that they lie and snore till the sun has risen one-third of his course and dispersed all the unwholesome damps. Then, after stretching and yawning for half an hour, they light their pipes, and, under the protection of a cloud of smoke, venture out into the open air; though if it happen to be never so little cold they quickly return shivering into the chimney corner. When the weather is mild, they stand leaning with both their arms upon the cornfield fence and gravely consider whether they had best go and take a small heat at the hoe but generally find reasons to put it off till another time. Thus they loiter away their lives, like Solomon's sluggard, with their arms across, and at the winding up of the year scarcely have bread to eat.

[21] Cockaigne, a fabulous land of ease and plenty, subject of a thirteenth-century fabliau.

To speak the truth, 'tis a thorough aversion to labor that makes people file off to North Carolina, where plenty and a warm sun confirm them in their disposition to laziness for their whole lives.

26. Since we were like to be confined to this place till the people returned out of the Dismal, 'twas agreed that our chaplain might safely take a turn to Edenton to preach the Gospel to the infidels there and christen their children. He was accompanied thither by Mr. Little, one of the Carolina commissioners, who, to show his regard for the church, offered to treat him on the road with a fricassee of rum. They fried half a dozen rashers of very fat bacon in a pint of rum, both which being dished up together served the company at once both for meat and drink.

Most of the rum they get in this country comes from New England and is so bad and unwholesome that it is not improperly called "kill-devil." It is distilled there from foreign molasses, which, if skillfully managed, yields near gallon for gallon. Their molasses comes from the same country and has the name of "long sugar" in Carolina, I suppose from the ropiness of it, and serves all the purposes of sugar, both in their eating and drinking. When they entertain their friends bountifully, they fail not to set before them a capacious bowl of bombo, so called from the admiral of that name. This is a compound of rum and water in equal parts, made palatable with the said long sugar. As good humor begins to flow and the bowl to ebb they take care to replenish it with sheer rum, of which there always is a reserve under the table.

But such generous doings happen only when that balsam of life is plenty; for they have often such melancholy times that neither landgraves nor caciques can procure one drop for their wives when they lie in or are troubled with the colic or vapors. Very few in this country have the industry to plant orchards, which, in a dearth of rum, might supply them with much better liquor. The truth is, there is one inconvenience that easily discourages lazy people from making this improvement: very often, in autumn, when the apples begin to ripen, they are visited with numerous flights of parakeets,[22] that bite

[22] Spelled "paroquets" in the manuscript. Byrd refers to the Carolina parakeet, a bird now extinct.

all the fruit to pieces in a moment for the sake of the kernels. The havoc they make is sometimes so great that whole orchards are laid waste, in spite of all the noises that can be made or mawkins [23] that can be dressed up to fright 'em away. These ravenous birds visit North Carolina only during the warm season and so soon as the cold begins to come on retire back toward the sun. They rarely venture so far north as Virginia, except in a very hot summer, when they visit the most southern parts of it. They are very beautiful but, like some other pretty creatures, are apt to be loud and mischievous.

27. Betwixt this [plantation] [24] and Edenton there are many huckleberry slashes,[25] which afford a convenient harbor for wolves and foxes. The first of these wild beasts is not so large and fierce as they are in other countries more northerly. He will not attack a man in the keenest of his hunger but run away from him, as from an animal more mischievous than himself. The foxes are much bolder and will sometimes not only make a stand but likewise assault anyone that would balk them of their prey. The inhabitants hereabouts take the trouble to dig abundance of wolf pits, so deep and perpendicular that when a wolf is once tempted into them he can no more scramble out again than a husband who has taken the leap can scramble out of matrimony.

Most of the houses in this part of the country are log houses, covered with pine or cypress shingles, three feet long and one broad. They are hung upon lathes with pegs, and their doors, too, turn upon wooden hinges and have wooden locks to secure them, so that the building is finished without nails or other ironwork. They also set up their pales without any nails at all, and, indeed, more securely than those that are nailed. There are three rails mortised into the posts, the lowest of which serves as a sill, with a groove in the middle big enough to receive the end of the pales; the middle part of the pale rests against the inside of the next rail, and the top of it is brought forward to the outside of the uppermost. Such wreathing of the pales

---

[23] An obsolete form of "malkin," a scarecrow.
[24] Added from the manuscript of the "History" in the American Philosophical Society.
[25] Swamps.

in and out makes them stand firm and much harder to unfix than when nailed in the ordinary way.

Within three or four miles of Edenton the soil appears to be a little more fertile, though it is much cut with slashes, which seem all to have a tendency toward the Dismal. This town is situate on the north side of Albemarle Sound, which is there about five miles over. A dirty slash runs all along the back of it, which in the summer is a foul annoyance and furnishes abundance of that Carolina plague, mosquitoes. There may be forty or fifty houses, most of them small and built without expense. A citizen here is counted extravagant if he has ambition enough to aspire to a brick chimney. Justice herself is but indifferently lodged, the courthouse having much of the air of a common tobacco house. I believe this is the only metropolis in the Christian or Mahometan world where there is neither church, chapel, mosque, synagogue, or any other place of public worship of any sect or religion whatsoever. What little devotion there may happen to be is much more private than their vices. The people seem easy without a minister as long as they are exempted from paying him. Sometimes the Society for Propagating the Gospel has had the charity to send over missionaries to this country; but, unfortunately, the priest has been too lewd for the people, or, which oftener happens, they too lewd for the priest. For these reasons these reverend gentlemen have always left their flocks as arrant heathen as they found them. Thus much, however, may be said for the inhabitants of Edenton, that not a soul has the least taint of hypocrisy or superstition, acting very frankly and aboveboard in all their exercises.

Provisions here are extremely cheap and extremely good, so that people may live plentifully at a trifling expense. Nothing is dear but law, physic, and strong drink, which are all bad in their kind, and the last they get with so much difficulty that they are never guilty of the sin of suffering it to sour upon their hands. Their vanity generally lies not so much in having a handsome dining room as a handsome house of office: in this kind of structure they are really extravagant. They are rarely guilty of flattering or making any court to their governors but treat them with all the excesses of freedom and familiarity.

They are of opinion their rulers would be apt to grow insolent if they grew rich, and for that reason take care to keep them poorer and more dependent, if possible, than the saints in New England used to do their governors. They have very little coin, so they are forced to carry on their home traffic with paper money. This is the only cash that will tarry in the country, and for that reason the discount goes on increasing between that and real money and will do so to the end of the chapter.

28. Our time passed heavily in our quarters, where we were quite cloyed with the Carolina felicity of having nothing to do. It was really more insupportable than the greatest fatigue and made us even envy the drudgery of our friends in the Dismal. Besides, though the men we had with us were kept in exact discipline and behaved without reproach, yet our landlord began to be tired of them, fearing they would breed a famine in his family. Indeed, so many keen stomachs made great havoc amongst the beef and bacon which he had laid in for his summer provision, nor could he easily purchase more at that time of the year with the money we paid him, because people having no certain market seldom provide any more of these commodities than will barely supply their own occasions. Besides the weather was now grown too warm to lay in a fresh stock so late in the spring. These considerations abated somewhat of that cheerfulness with which he bid us welcome in the beginning and made him think the time quite as long as we did till the surveyors returned.

While we were thus all hands uneasy, we were comforted with the news that this afternoon the line was finished through the Dismal. The messenger told us it had been the hard work of three days to measure the length of only five miles and mark the trees as they passed along; and by the most exact survey they found the breadth of the Dismal in this place to be completely fifteen miles. How wide it may be in other parts, we can give no account, but believe it grows narrower toward the north; possibly toward Albemarle Sound it may be something broader, where so many rivers issue out of it. All we know for certain is that from the place where the line entered the Dismal to where it came out we found the road round that portion of it which belongs to Virginia to be about sixty-five miles. How great the distance may be from each of those points round that part that falls within the bounds of Carolina we had no certain information, though 'tis conjectured it cannot be so little as thirty miles. At which rate the whole circuit must be about an hundred. What a mass of mud and dirt is treasured up within this filthy circumference, and what a quantity of water must perpetually drain into it from the rising ground that surrounds it on every side! Without taking the exact level of the Dismal, we may be sure that it declines toward the places where the several rivers take their rise, in order to carrying off the constant supplies of water. Were it not for such discharges, the whole swamp would long since have been converted into a lake. On the other side this declension must be very gentle, else it would be laid perfectly dry by so many continual drains; whereas, on the contrary, the ground seems everywhere to be thoroughly drenched even in the driest season of the year. The surveyors concluded this day's work with running twenty-five chains up into the firm land, where they waited farther orders from the commissioners.

29. This day the surveyors proceeded with the line no more than one mile and fifteen chains, being interrupted by a mill swamp, through which they made no difficulty of wading in order to make their work more exact. Thus, like Norway mice,[26] these worthy gentlemen went right forward, without suffering themselves to be turned out of the way by any obstacle whatever. We are told by some travelers that those mice march in mighty armies, destroying all the fruits of the earth as they go along. But something peculiar to those obstinate little animals is that nothing stops them in their career, and if a house happen to stand in their way, disdaining to go an inch about, they crawl up one side of it and down the other, or if they meet with any river or other body of water they are so determined that they swim directly over it, without varying one point from their course for the sake of any safety or convenience. The surveyors were also hindered some time by setting up posts in the great road to show the bounds between the two colonies.

[26] Byrd describes the migrations of the lemming in periods of food scarcity.

Our chaplain returned to us in the evening from Edenton in company with the Carolina commissioners. He had preached there in the courthouse, for want of a consecrated place, and made no less than nineteen of Father Hennepin's Christians.[27]

By the permission of the Carolina commissioners, Mr. Swann was allowed to go home as soon as the survey of the Dismal was finished; he met with this indulgence for a reason that might very well have excused his coming at all: namely, that he was lately married. What remained of the drudgery for this season was left to Mr. Moseley, who had hitherto acted only in the capacity of a commissioner. They offered to employ Mr. Joseph Mayo as their surveyor in Mr. Swann's stead, but he thought it not proper to accept of it, because he had hitherto acted as a volunteer in behalf of Virginia and did not care to change sides, though it might have been to his advantage.

30. The line was advanced this day six miles and thirty-five chains, the woods being pretty clear and interrupted with no swamp or other wet ground. The land hereabouts had all the marks of poverty, being for the most part sandy and full of pines. This kind of ground, though unfit for ordinary tillage, will however bring cotton and potatoes in plenty, and consequently food and raiment to such as are easily contented and, like the wild Irish, find more pleasure in laziness than luxury. It also makes a shift to produce Indian corn, rather by the felicity of the climate than by the fertility of the soil. They who are more industrious than their neighbors may make what quantity of tar they please, though indeed they are not always sure of a market for it. The method of burning tar in Sweden and Muscovy succeeds not well in this warmer part of the world. It seems they kill the pine trees by barking them quite round at a certain height, which in those cold countries brings down the turpentine into the stump in a year's

---

[27] The Franciscan friar Louis Hennepin, who accompanied LaSalle on his western expedition in 1678, reported pessimistically on the prospect of converting the American Indians: "They will suffer themselves to be baptized ten times a Day for a Glass of Brandy, or a Pipe of Tobacco, and offer their children to be baptiz'd, but all without any Religious Motive" (quoted from *A New Discovery of a West Country in America,* edited by Reuben G. Thwaites [Chicago, 1903], II, 460). Hennepin's original narrative was entitled *Description de la Louisiane* (Paris, 1683); an English edition appeared in 1696.

time. But experience has taught us that in warm climates the turpentine will not so easily descend but is either fixed in the upper parts of the tree or fried out by the intense heat of the sun.

Care was taken to erect a post in every road that our line ran through, with Virginia carved on the north side of it and Carolina on the south, that the bounds might everywhere appear. In the evening the surveyors took up their quarters at the house of one Mr. Parker, who, by the advantage of a better spot of land than ordinary and a more industrious wife, lives comfortably and has a very neat plantation.

31. It rained a little this morning, but this, happening again upon a Sunday, did not interrupt our business. However the surveyors made no scruple of protracting and platting off their work upon that good day, because it was rather an amusement than a drudgery. Here the men feasted on the fat of the land and, believing the dirtiest part of their work was over, had a more than ordinary gaiety of heart. We christened two of our landlord's children, which might have remained infidels all their lives had not we carried Christianity home to his own door. The truth of it is, our neighbors of North Carolina are not so zealous as to go much out of their way to procure this benefit for their children; otherwise, being so near Virginia, they might without exceeding much trouble make a journey to the next clergyman upon so good an errand. And, indeed, should the neighboring ministers, once in two or three years, vouchsafe to take a turn among these gentiles to baptize them and their children, 'twould look a little apostolical, and they might hope to be requited for it hereafter, if that be not thought too long to tarry for their reward.

#### APRIL

1. The surveyors, getting now upon better ground quite disengaged from underwoods, pushed on the line almost twelve miles. They left Somerton Chapel near two miles to the northward, so that there was now no place of public worship left in the whole province of North Carolina.

The high land of North Carolina was barren and covered with a deep sand, and the low grounds were wet and boggy, insomuch that several of our horses were mired and gave us frequent opportunities to show our horsemanship.

The line cut William Speight's plantation in two, leaving little more than his dwelling house and orchard in Virginia. Sundry other plantations were split in the same unlucky manner, which made the owners accountable to both governments. Wherever we passed we constantly found the borderers laid it to heart if their land was taken into Virginia; they chose much rather to belong to Carolina, where they pay no tribute, either to God or to Caesar. Another reason was that the government there is so loose and the laws are so feebly executed that, like those in the neighborhood of Sidon formerly, everyone does just what seems good in his own eyes. If the Governor's hands have been weak in that province, under the authority of the Lords Proprietors, much weaker, then, were the hands of the magistrate, who, though he might have had virtue enough to endeavor to punish offenders, which very rarely happened, yet that virtue had been quite impotent for want of ability to put it in execution. Besides, there might have been some danger, perhaps, in venturing to be so rigorous, for fear of undergoing the fate of an honest justice in Currituck precinct. This bold magistrate, it seems, taking upon him to order a fellow to the stocks for being disorderly in his drink, was for his intemperate zeal carried thither himself and narrowly escaped being whipped by the rabble into the bargain.

This easy day's work carried the line to the banks of Somerton Creek, that runs out of Chowan River a little below the mouth of Nottoway.

2. In less than a mile from Somerton Creek the line was carried to Blackwater, which is the name of the upper part of Chowan, running some miles above the mouth of Nottoway. It must be observed that Chowan, after taking a compass round the most beautiful part of North Carolina, empties itself into Albemarle Sound a few miles above Edenton. The tide flows seven or eight miles higher than where the river changes its name and is navigable thus high for any small vessel. Our line intersected it exactly half a mile to the northward of the mouth of Nottoway. However, in obedience to His Majesty's command, we directed the surveyors to come down the river as far as the

mouth of Nottoway in order to continue our true-west line from thence. Thus we found the mouth of Nottoway to lie no more than half a minute farther to the northward than Mr. Lawson[28] had formerly done. That gentleman's observation, it seems, placed it in 36° 30', and our working made it out to be 36° 30½' — a very inconsiderable variance.

The surveyors crossed the river over against the middle of the mouth of Nottoway, where it was about eighty yards wide. From thence they run the line about half a mile through a dirty pocosin as far as an Indian field. Here we took up our lodging in a moist situation, having the pocosin above-mentioned on one side of us and a swamp on the other.

In this camp three of the Meherrin Indians made us a visit. They told us that the small remains of their nation had deserted their ancient town, situated near the mouth of the Meherrin River, for fear of the Catawbas, who had killed fourteen of their people the year before; and the few that survived that calamity had taken refuge amongst the English on the east side of Chowan. Though if the complaint of these Indians were true, they are hardly used by our Carolina friends. But they are the less to be pitied because they have ever been reputed the most false and treacherous to the English of all the Indians in the neighborhood.

Not far from the place where we lay, I observed a large oak which had been blown up by the roots, the body of which was shivered into perfect strings and was, in truth, the most violent effect of lightning I ever saw.

But the most curious instance of that dreadful meteor happened at York, where a man was killed near a pine tree in which the lightning made a hole before it struck the man and left an exact figure of the tree upon his breast, with all its branches, to the wonder of all that beheld it; in which I shall be more particular hereafter.

We made another trial of the variation in this place and found it

[28] John Lawson, Surveyor General of North Carolina, was one of the North Carolina commissioners who made an effort to determine the boundary line between Virginia and North Carolina in 1710. Lawson wrote a narrative first published in London in 1709, *A New Voyage to Carolina*, which contains valuable information about the physical terrain and the North Carolina Indians. Byrd reports Lawson's ultimate fate at the hands of the Indians, who felt he had cheated them, on p. 303.

some minutes less than we had done at Currituck Inlet; but so small a difference might easily happen through some defect in one or other of the observations, and therefore we altered not our compass for the matter.

3. By the advantage of clear woods the line was extended twelve miles and three-quarters, as far as the banks of Meherrin. Though the mouth of this river lie fifteen miles below the mouth of Nottoway, yet it winds so much to the northward that we came upon it after running this small distance.

During the first seven miles we observed the soil to be poor and sandy, but as we approached Meherrin it grew better, though there it was cut to pieces by sundry miry branches which discharge themselves into that river. Several of our horses plunged up to the saddle skirts and were not disengaged without difficulty.

The latter part of our day's work was pretty laborious because of the unevenness of the way and because the low ground of the river was full of cypress snags, as sharp and dangerous to our horses as so many *chevaux de frise*. We found the whole distance from the mouth of Nottoway to Meherrin River, where our line intersected it, thirteen miles and a quarter.

It was hardly possible to find a level large enough on the banks of the river whereupon to pitch our tent. But though the situation was, on that account, not very convenient for us, yet it was for our poor horses, by reason of the plenty of small reeds on which they fed voraciously. These reeds are green here all the year round and will keep cattle in tolerable good plight during the winter. But whenever the hogs come where they are they destroy them in a short time by plowing up their roots, of which, unluckily, they are very fond.

The river was in this place about as wide as the river Jordan, that is, forty yards, and would be navigable very high for flat-bottom boats and canoes, if it were not choked up with large trees brought down by every fresh. Though the banks were full twenty feet high from the surface of the water, yet we saw certain marks of their having been overflowed. These narrow rivers that run high up into the country are subject to frequent inundations, when the waters are rolled down with such violence as to carry all before them. The logs that are then floated are very fatal to the bridges built over these rivers, which can hardly be contrived strong enough to stand against so much weight and violence joined together.

The Isle of Wight County begins about three miles to the east of Meherrin River, being divided from that of Nansemond only by a line of marked trees.

4. The river was here hardly fordable, though the season had been very dry. The banks, too, were so steep that our horses were forced to climb like mules to get up them. Nevertheless we had the luck to recover the opposite shore without damage.

We halted for half an hour at Charles Anderson's, who lives on the western banks of the river, in order to christen one of his children. In the meantime, the surveyors extended the line two miles and thirty-nine chains,[29] in which small distance Meherrin River was so serpentine that they crossed it three times. Then we went on to Mr. Kinchen's, a man of figure and authority in North Carolina, who lives about a mile to the southward of the place where the surveyors left off. By the benefit of a little pains and good management, this worthy magistrate lives in much affluence. Amongst other instances of his industry, he had planted a good orchard, which is not common in that indolent climate; nor is it at all strange that such improvident people, who take no thought for the morrow, should save themselves the trouble to make improvements that will not pay them for several years to come. Though if they could trust futurity for anything, they certainly would for cider, which they are so fond of that they generally drink it before it has done working lest the fermentation might unluckily turn it sour.

It is an observation which rarely fails of being true, both in Virginia and Carolina, that those who take care to plant good orchards are in their general characters industrious people. This held good in our landlord, who had many houses built on this plantation and every one kept in decent repair. His wife, too, was tidy, his furniture clean, his pewter bright, and nothing seemed to be wanting to make his home comfortable.

Mr. Kinchen made us the compliment of his house, but because we

[29] The surveyor's chain measures four rods.

were willing to be as little troublesome as possible, we ordered the tent to be pitched in his orchard, where the blossoms of the apple trees contributed not a little to the sweetness of our lodging.

5. Because the spring was now pretty forward and the rattlesnakes began to crawl out of their winter quarters and might grow dangerous both to the men and their horses, it was determined to proceed no farther with the line till the fall. Besides, the uncommon fatigue the people had undergone for near six weeks together and the inclination they all had to visit their respective families made a recess highly reasonable.

The surveyors were employed great part of the day in forming a correct and elegant map of the line from Currituck Inlet to the place where they left off. On casting up the account in the most accurate manner, they found the whole distance we had run to amount to seventy-three miles and thirteen chains. Of the map they made two fair copies, which, agreeing exactly, were subscribed by the commissioners of both colonies, and one of them was delivered to those on the part of Virginia and the other to those on the part of North Carolina.

6. Thus we finished our spring campaign, and having taken leave of our Carolina friends and agreed to meet them again the tenth of September following at the same Mr. Kinchen's in order to continue the line, we crossed Meherrin River near a quarter of a mile from the house. About ten miles from that we halted at Mr. Kindred's plantation, where we christened two children.

It happened that some of Isle of Wight militia were exercising in the adjoining pasture, and there were females enough attending that martial appearance to form a more invincible corps. Ten miles farther we passed Nottoway River at Bolton's Ferry and took up our lodgings about three miles from thence at the house of Richard Parker, an honest planter whose labors were rewarded with plenty, which, in this country, is the constant portion of the industrious.

7. The next day being Sunday, we ordered notice to be sent to all the neighborhood that there would be a sermon at this place and an opportunity of christening their children. But the likelihood of rain

got the better of their devotion and, what perhaps might still be a stronger motive, of their curiosity. In the morning we dispatched a runner to the Nottoway town to let the Indians know we intended them a visit that evening, and our honest landlord was so kind as to be our pilot thither, being about four miles from his house. Accordingly, in the afternoon we marched in good order to the town, where the female scouts, stationed on an eminence for that purpose, had no sooner spied us but they gave notice of our approach to their fellow citizens by continual whoops and cries, which could not possibly have been more dismal at the sight of their most implacable enemies. This signal assembled all their great men, who received us in a body and conducted us into the fort.

This fort was a square piece of ground, enclosed with substantial puncheons or strong palisades about ten feet high and leaning a little outwards to make a scalade more difficult. Each side of the square might be about a hundred yards long, with loopholes at proper distances through which they may fire upon the enemy. Within this enclosure we found bark cabins sufficient to lodge all their people in case they should be obliged to retire thither. These cabins are no other but close arbors made of saplings, arched at the top and covered so well with bark as to be proof against all weather. The fire is made in the middle, according to the Hibernian fashion, the smoke whereof finds no other vent but at the door and so keeps the whole family warm, at the expense both of their eyes and complexion. The Indians have no standing furniture in their cabins but hurdles to repose their persons upon which they cover with mats or deerskins. We were conducted to the best apartments in the fort, which just before had been made ready for our reception and adorned with new mats that were very sweet and clean.

The young men had painted themselves in a hideous manner, not so much for ornament as terror. In that frightful equipage they entertained us with sundry war dances, wherein they endeavored to look as formidable as possible. The instrument they danced to was an Indian drum, that is, a large gourd with a skin braced taut[30] over the mouth

---

[30] The manuscript reads "tort," an erroneous variant form of "taut."

of it. The dancers all sang to this music, keeping exact time with their feet while their head and arms were screwed into a thousand menacing postures.

Upon this occasion the ladies had arrayed themselves in all their finery. They were wrapped in their red and blue matchcoats, thrown so negligently about them that their mahogany skins appeared in several parts, like the Lacedaemonian damsels of old. Their hair was braided with white and blue peak and hung gracefully in a large roll upon their shoulders.

This peak consists of small cylinders cut out of a conch shell, drilled through and strung like beads. It serves them both for money and jewels, the blue being of much greater value than the white for the same reason that Ethiopian mistresses in France are dearer than French, because they are more scarce. The women wear necklaces and bracelets of these precious materials when they have a mind to appear lovely. Though their complexions be a little sad-colored, yet their shapes are very straight and well proportioned. Their faces are seldom handsome, yet they have an air of innocence and bashfulness that with a little less dirt would not fail to make them desirable. Such charms might have had their full effect upon men who had been so long deprived of female conversation but that the whole winter's soil was so crusted on the skins of those dark angels that it required a very strong appetite to approach them. The bear's oil with which they anoint their persons all over makes their skins soft and at the same time protects them from every species of vermin that use to be troublesome to other uncleanly people.

We were unluckily so many that they could not well make us the compliment of bedfellows according to the Indian rules of hospitality, though a grave matron whispered one of the commissioners very civilly in the ear that if her daughter had been but one year older she should have been at his devotion. It is by no means a loss of reputation among the Indians for damsels that are single to have intrigues with the men; on the contrary, they account it an argument of superior merit to be liked by a great number of gallants. However, like the ladies that game,[31] they are a little mercenary in their amours and seldom bestow

[31] Engage in prostitution.

their favors out of stark love and kindness. But after these women have once appropriated their charms by marriage, they are from thenceforth faithful to their vows and will hardly ever be tempted by an agreeable gallant or be provoked by a brutal or even by a fumbling husband to go astray.

The little work that is done among the Indians is done by the poor women, while the men are quite idle or at most employed only in the gentlemanly diversions of hunting and fishing. In this, as well as in their wars, they now use nothing but firearms, which they purchase of the English for skins. Bows and arrows are grown into disuse, except only amongst their boys. Nor is it ill policy, but on the contrary very prudent, thus to furnish the Indians with firearms, because it makes them depend entirely upon the English, not only for their trade but even for their subsistence. Besides, they were really able to do more mischief while they made use of arrows, of which they would let silently fly several in a minute with wonderful dexterity, whereas now they hardly ever discharge their firelocks more than once, which they insidiously do from behind a tree and then retire as nimbly as the Dutch horse used to do now and then formerly in Flanders.

We put the Indians to no expense but only of a little corn for our horses, for which in gratitude we cheered their hearts with what rum we had left, which they love better than they do their wives and children. Though these Indians dwell among the English and see in what plenty a little industry enables them to live, yet they choose to continue in their stupid idleness and to suffer all the inconveniences of dirt, cold, and want rather than disturb their heads with care or defile their hands with labor.

The whole number of people belonging to the Nottoway town, if you include women and children, amount to about two hundred. These are the only Indians of any consequence now remaining within the limits of Virginia. The rest are either removed or dwindled to a very inconsiderable number, either by destroying one another or else by the smallpox and other diseases. Though nothing has been so fatal to them as their ungovernable passion for rum, with which, I am sorry to say it, they have been but too liberally supplied by the English that live near them.

2 1 9

And here I must lament the bad success Mr. Boyle's charity has hitherto had toward converting any of these poor heathens to Christianity.[32] Many children of our neighboring Indians have been brought up in the College of William and Mary. They have been taught to read and write and been carefully instructed in the principles of the Christian religion till they came to be men. Yet after they returned home, instead of civilizing and converting the rest, they have immediately relapsed into infidelity and barbarism themselves.

And some of them, too, have made the worst use of the knowledge they acquired among the English by employing it against their benefactors. Besides, as they unhappily forget all the good they learn and remember the ill, they are apt to be more vicious and disorderly than the rest of their countrymen.

I ought not to quit this subject without doing justice to the great prudence of Colonel Spotswood in this affair. That gentleman was Lieutenant Governor of Virginia when Carolina was engaged in a bloody war with the Indians. At that critical time it was thought expedient to keep a watchful eye upon our tributary savages, who we knew had nothing to keep them to their duty but their fears. Then it was that he demanded of each nation a competent number of their great men's children to be sent to the College, where they served as so many hostages for the good behavior of the rest and at the same time were themselves principled in the Christian religion. He also placed a schoolmaster among the Saponi Indians, at the salary of £50 per annum, to instruct their children. The person that undertook that charitable work was Mr. Charles Griffin, a man of a good family, who by the innocence of his life and the sweetness of his temper was perfectly well qualified for that pious undertaking. Besides, he had so much the secret of mixing pleasure with instruction that he had not a scholar who did not love him affectionately. Such talents must needs

[32] Robert Boyle, the English philosopher-scientist, left money in his will to be used for the propagation of Christianity among the heathen. James Blair used his influence with the trustees of Boyle's estate to have the College of William and Mary made the chief beneficiary of the money. Brafferton Hall, where Indians were to be schooled, was built in 1723 from this bequest; see Hugh Jones, *The Present State of Virginia*, edited by Richard L. Morton (Chapel Hill, 1956), pp. 185–186.

have been blest with a proportionable success, had he not been un-luckily removed to the College, by which he left the good work he had begun unfinished. In short, all the pains he had taken among the infidels had no other effect but to make them something cleanlier than other Indians are.

The care Colonel Spotswood took to tincture the Indian children with Christianity produced the following epigram, which was not pub-lished during his administration for fear it might then have looked like flattery.

> Long has the furious priest assayed in vain,
> With sword and faggot, infidels to gain,
> But now the milder soldier wisely tries
> By gentler methods to unveil their eyes.
> Wonders apart, he knew 'twere vain t'engage
> The fixed preventions of misguided age.
> With fairer hopes he forms the Indian youth
> To early manners, probity, and truth.
> The lion's whelp thus, on the Libyan shore,
> Is tamed and gentled by the artful Moor,
> Not the grim sire, inured to blood before.

I am sorry I can't give a better account of the state of the poor In-dians with respect to Christianity, although a great deal of pains has been and still continues to be taken with them. For my part, I must be of opinion, as I hinted before, that there is but one way of converting these poor infidels and reclaiming them from barbarity, and that is charitably to intermarry with them, according to the modern policy of the Most Christian King in Canada and Louisiana. Had the Eng-lish done this at the first settlement of the colony, the infidelity of the Indians had been worn out at this day with their dark complexions, and the country had swarmed with people more than it does with insects. It was certainly an unreasonable nicety that prevented their entering into so good-natured an alliance. All nations of men have the same natural dignity, and we all know that very bright talents may be lodged under a very dark skin. The principal difference between one people and another proceeds only from the different opportunities of improvement. The Indians by no means want understanding and are in their figure tall and well proportioned. Even their copper-colored complexion would admit of blanching, if not in the first, at the farthest in the second, generation. I may safely venture to say, the Indian women would have made altogether as honest wives for the first planters as the damsels they used to purchase from aboard the ships. 'Tis strange, therefore, that any good Christian should have refused a wholesome, straight bedfellow, when he might have had so fair a portion with her as the merit of saving her soul.

8. We rested on our clean mats very comfortably, though alone, and the next morning went to the toilet of some of the Indian ladies, where, what with the charms of their persons and the smoke of their apartments, we were almost blinded. They offered to give us silk-grass baskets of their own making, which we modestly refused, knowing that an Indian present, like that of a nun, is a liberality put out to interest and a bribe placed to the greatest advantage. Our chaplain observed with concern that the ruffles of some of our fellow travelers were a little discolored with puccoon,[33] wherewith the good man had been told those ladies used to improve their invisible charms.

About ten o'clock we march[ed] out of town in good order, and the war captains saluted us with a volley of small arms. From thence we proceeded over Blackwater Bridge to Colonel Henry Harrison's, where we congratulated each other upon our return into Christendom.

Thus ended our progress for this season, which we may justly say was attended with all the success that could be expected. Besides the punctual performance of what was committed to us, we had the pleasure to bring back every one of our company in perfect health. And this we must acknowledge to be a singular blessing, considering the difficulties and dangers to which they had been exposed. We had reason to fear the many waters and sunken grounds through which we were obliged to wade might have thrown the men into sundry acute distempers; especially the Dismal, where the soil was so full of

---

[33] The colonists seemed to apply the term "puccoon," in any number of spellings, to red dye used by the Indians, whatever the source of the coloring. They did not always identify it as a particular plant. Sometimes the Virginia pokeberry or pokeweed seems to be meant by the word. Another plant, *Sanguinaria canadensis*, provided a root which was also used for red dye.

water and the air so full of damps that nothing but a Dutchman could live in them. Indeed, the foundation of all our success was the exceeding dry season. It rained during the whole journey but rarely, and then, as when Herod built his temple, only in the night or upon the Sabbath, when it was no hindrance at all to our progress.

## PART THE SECOND

### SEPTEMBER

The tenth of September being thought a little too soon for the commissioners to meet in order to proceed on the line on account of snakes, 'twas agreed to put it off to the twentieth of the same month, of which due notice was sent to the Carolina commissioners.

19. We, on the part of Virginia, that we might be sure to be punctual, arrived at Mr. Kinchen's, the place appointed, on the nineteenth, after a journey of three days in which nothing remarkable happened. We found three of the Carolina commissioners had taken possession of the house, having come thither by water from Edenton. By the great quantity of provisions these gentlemen brought and the few men they had to eat them, we were afraid they intended to carry the line to the South Sea. They had five hundred pounds of bacon and dried beef and five hundred pounds of biscuit, and not above three or four men. The misfortune was, they forgot to provide horses to carry their good things, or else trusted to the uncertainty of hiring them here, which, considering the place, was leaving too much to that jilt, Hazard.

On our part we had taken better care, being completely furnished with everything necessary for transporting our baggage and provisions. Indeed, we brought no other provisions out with us but a thousand pounds of bread and had faith enough to depend on Providence for our meat, being desirous to husband the public money as much as possible. We had no less than twenty men, besides the chaplain, the surveyors, and all the servants, to be subsisted upon this bread. However, that it might hold out the better, our men had been ordered to provide themselves at home with provision for ten days, in which time we judged we should get beyond the inhabitants, where forest game of all sorts was like to be plenty at that time of the year.

20. This being the day appointed for our rendezvous, great part of it was spent in the careful fixing our baggage and assembling our men, who were ordered to meet us here. We took care to examine their arms and made proof of the powder provided for the expedition. Our provision horses had been hindered by the rain from coming up exactly at the day; but this delay was the less disappointment by reason of the ten days' subsistence the men had been directed to provide for themselves. Mr. Moseley did not join us till the afternoon nor Mr. Swann till several days after.

Mr. Kinchen had unadvisedly sold the men a little brandy of his own making, which produced much disorder, causing some to be too choleric and others too loving; insomuch that a damsel who assisted in the kitchen had certainly suffered what the nuns call martyrdom had she not capitulated a little too soon. This outrage would have called for some severe discipline, had she not bashfully withdrawn herself early in the morning and so carried off the evidence.

21. We dispatched away the surveyors without loss of time, who, with all their diligence, could carry the line no farther than 3 miles and 176 poles, by reason the low ground was one entire thicket. In that distance they crossed Meherrin River the fourth time. In the meanwhile, the Virginia commissioners thought proper to conduct their baggage a farther way about for the convenience of a clearer road.

The Carolina gentlemen did at length, more by fortune than forecast, hire a clumsy vehicle, something like a cart, to transport their effects as far as Roanoke. This wretched machine, at first setting-out, met with a very rude shock that broke a case bottle of cherry brandy in so unlucky a manner that not one precious drop was saved. This melancholy beginning foreboded an unprosperous journey and too quick a return to the persons most immediately concerned.

In our way we crossed Fontaine Creek, which runs into Meherrin River, so called from the disaster of an unfortunate Indian trader who had formerly been drowned in it.[34] We took up our quarters on the plantation of John Hill, where we pitched our tent, with design to tarry till such time as the surveyors could work their way to us.

22. This being Sunday, we had an opportunity of resting from our labors. The expectation of such a novelty as a sermon in these parts brought together a numerous congregation. When the sermon was over, our chaplain did his part toward making eleven of them Christians.

Several of our men had intermitting fevers but were soon restored to their health again by proper remedies. Our chief medicine was dogwood bark, which we used, instead of that of Peru, with good success. Indeed, it was given in large quantity, but then, to make the patients amends, they swallowed much fewer doses.

In the afternoon our provision horses arrived safe in the camp. They had met with very heavy rains but, thank God, not a single biscuit received the least damage thereby. We were furnished by the neighbors with very lean cheese and very fat mutton, upon which occasion 'twill not be improper to draw one conclusion from the evidence of North Carolina, that sheep would thrive much better in the woods than in pasture land, provided a careful shepherd were employed to keep them from straying and, by the help of dogs, to protect them also from the wolves.

23. The surveyors came to us at night, though they had not brought the line so far as our camp, for which reason we thought it needless to go forward till they came up with us. They could run no more than four miles and five poles, because the ground was everywhere grown up with thick bushes. The soil here appeared to be very good, though much broken betwixt Fontaine Creek and Roanoke River. The line crossed Meherrin the fifth and last time; nor were our people sorry to part with a stream the meanders of which had given them so much trouble.

Our hunters brought us four wild turkeys, which at that season began to be fat and very delicious, especially the hens. These birds

---

[34] Possibly John Fontaine, who accompanied Alexander Spotswood on his expedition in 1716 to explore the Virginia hinterland.

seem to be of the bustard kind and fly heavily. Some of them are exceedingly large and weigh upwards of forty pounds; nay, some bold historians venture to say upwards of fifty. They run very fast, stretching forth their wings all the time, like the ostrich, by way of sails to quicken their speed. They roost commonly upon very high trees, standing near some river or creek, and are so stupefied at the sight of fire that, if you make a blaze in the night near the place where they roost, you may fire upon them several times successively before they will dare to fly away. Their spurs are so sharp and strong that the Indians used formerly to point their arrows with them, though now they point them with a sharp white stone. In the spring the turkey cocks begin to gobble, which is the language wherein they make love.

It rained very hard in the night with a violent storm of thunder and lightning, which obliged us to trench in our tent all round to carry off the water that fell upon it.

24. So soon as the men could dry their blankets we sent out the surveyors, who, now meeting with more favorable grounds, advanced the line seven miles and eighty-two poles. However, the commissioners did not think proper to decamp that day, believing they might easily overtake the surveyors the next. In the meantime, they sent out some of their most expert gunners, who brought in four more wild turkeys.

This part of the country being very proper for raising cattle and hogs, we observed the inhabitants lived in great plenty without killing themselves with labor. I found near our camp some plants of that kind of rattlesnake root called star grass. The leaves shoot out circularly and grow horizontally and near the ground. The root is in shape not unlike the rattle of that serpent and is a strong antidote against the bite of it. It is very bitter and where it meets with any poison works by violent sweats, but where it meets with none has no sensible operation but that of putting the spirits into a great hurry and so of promoting perspiration. The rattlesnake hath an utter antipathy to this plant, insomuch that if you smear your hands with the juice of it, you may handle the viper safely. Thus much I can say on my own experience: that once in July, when these snakes are in their greatest vigor, I besmeared a dog's nose with the powder of this root and made him trample on a large snake several times, which, however, was so far from biting him that it perfectly sickened at the dog's approach and turned its head from him with the utmost aversion.

Our chaplain, to show his zeal, made an excursion of six miles to christen two children, but without the least regard to the good cheer at these solemnities.

25. The surveyors, taking the advantage of clear woods, pushed on the line seven miles and forty poles. In the meantime the commissioners marched with the baggage about twelve miles and took up their quarters near the banks of the Beaver Pond (which is one branch of Fontaine Creek), just by the place where the surveyors were to finish their day's work. In our march one of the men killed a small rattlesnake, which had no more than two rattles. Those vipers remain in vigor generally till toward the end of September, or sometimes later if the weather continue a little warm. On this consideration we had provided three several sorts of rattlesnake root, made up into proper doses and ready for immediate use, in case any one of the men or their horses had been bitten. We crossed Fontaine Creek once more in our journey this day and found the grounds very rich, notwithstanding they were broken and stony. Near the place where we encamped, the county of Brunswick is divided from the Isle of Wight. These counties run quite on the back of Surry and Prince George and are laid out in very irregular figures. As a proof the land mended hereabouts, we found the plantations began to grow thicker by much than we had found them lower down.

26. We hurried away the surveyors without loss of time, who extended the line 10 miles and 160 poles, the grounds proving dry and free from underwoods. By the way the chain carriers killed two more rattlesnakes, which I own was a little ungrateful, because two or three of the men had strided over them without receiving any hurt, though one of these vipers had made bold to strike at one of the baggage horses as he went along, but by good luck his teeth only grazed on the hoof without doing him any damage. However, these accidents were, I think, so many arguments that we had very good

reason to defer our coming out till the twentieth of September. We observed abundance of St.-Andrew's-cross in all the woods we passed through, which is the common remedy used by the Indian traders to cure their horses when they are bitten by rattlesnakes. It grows on a straight stem about eighteen inches high and bears a yellow flower on the top that has an eye of black in the middle, with several pairs of narrow leaves shooting out at right angles from the stock over against one another. This antidote grows providentially all over the woods and upon all sorts of soil, that it may be everywhere at hand in case a disaster should happen, and may be had all the hot months while the snakes are dangerous.

About four o'clock in the afternoon we took up our quarters upon Cabin Branch, which also discharges itself into Fontaine Creek. On our way we observed several meadows clothed with very rank grass and branches full of tall reeds, in which cattle keep themselves fat good part of the winter. But hogs are as injurious to both as goats are said to be to vines, and for that reason it was not lawful to sacrifice them to Bacchus. We halted by the way to christen two children at a spring, where their mothers waylaid us for that good purpose.

27. It was ten of the clock before the surveyors got to work, because some of the horses had straggled a great distance from the camp. Nevertheless, meeting with practicable woods, they advanced the line 9 miles and 104 poles. We crossed over Pea Creek about four miles from our quarters and three miles farther Lizard Creek, both which empty their waters into Roanoke River. Between these two creeks a poor man waited for us with five children to be baptized, and we halted till the ceremony was ended. The land seemed to be very good, by the largeness of the trees, though very stony. We proceeded as far as Pigeon Roost Creek, which also runs into Roanoke, and there quartered.

We had not the pleasure of the company of any of the Carolina commissioners in this day's march except Mr. Moseley's, the rest tarrying behind to wait the coming up of their baggage cart, which they had now not seen nor heard (though the wheels made a dismal noise) for several days past. Indeed, it was a very difficult undertaking to conduct a cart through such pathless and perplexed woods, and no wonder if its motion was a little planetary. We would have paid them the compliment of waiting for them, could we have done it at any other expense but that of the public.

In the stony grounds we rode over we found great quantity of the true ipecacuanha, which in this part of the world is called Indian physic. This has several stalks growing up from the same root about a foot high, bearing a leaf resembling that of a strawberry. It is not so strong as that from Brazil but has the same happy effects if taken in somewhat a larger dose. It is an excellent vomit and generally cures intermitting fevers and bloody fluxes at once or twice taking. There is abundance of it in the upper part of the country, where it delights most in a stony soil intermixed with black mold.

28. Our surveyors got early to work, yet could forward the line but 6 miles and 121 poles because of the uneven grounds in the neighborhood of Roanoke, which they crossed in this day's work. In that place the river is forty-nine poles wide and rolls down a crystal stream of very sweet water, insomuch that when there comes to be a great monarch in this part of the world, he will cause all the water for his own table to be brought from Roanoke, as the great kings of Persia did theirs from the Nile and Choaspes, because the waters of those rivers were light and not apt to corrupt. The same humor prevails at this day in the kings of Denmark, who order all the East India ships of that nation to call at the Cape of Good Hope and take in a butt of water from a spring on the Table Hill and bring it to Copenhagen for Their Majesties' own drinking.

The great falls of Roanoke lie about twenty miles lower, to which a sloop of moderate burden may come up. There are, besides these, many smaller falls above, though none that entirely intercept the passage of the river, as the great ones do by a chain of rocks for eight miles together. The river forks about thirty-six miles higher, and both branches are pretty equal in breadth where they divide, though the southern, now called the Dan, runs up the farthest. That to the north runs away near northwest and is called the Staunton, and heads not far from the source of Appomattox River, while the Dan stretches away pretty near west and runs clear through the great mountains.

We did not follow the surveyors till toward noon, being detained in our camp to christen several more children. We were conducted a nearer way by a famous woodsman called Epaphroditus Bainton. This forester spends all his time in ranging the woods and is said to make great havoc among the deer and other inhabitants of the forest not much wilder than himself.

We proceeded to the canoe landing on Roanoke, where we passed the river with the baggage. But the horses were directed to a ford about a mile higher, called by the Indians Moniseep, which signifies in their jargon "shallow water." This is the ford where the Indian traders used to cross with their horses in their way to the Catawba nation. There are many rocks in the river thereabouts, on which grows a kind of water grass, which the wild geese are fond of and resort to it in great numbers.

We landed on the south side of Roanoke at a plantation of Colonel Mumford's, where by that gentleman's special directions we met with sundry refreshments. Here we pitched our tent, for the benefit of the prospect, upon an eminence that overlooked a broad piece of low ground, very rich, though liable to be overflowed.

By the way one of our men killed another rattlesnake with eleven rattles, having a large gray squirrel in his maw, the head of which was already digested while the body remained still entire. The way these snakes catch their prey is thus: they ogle the poor little animal till by force of the charm he falls down stupefied and senseless on the ground. In that condition the snake approaches and moistens first one ear and then the other with his spawl, and after that the other parts of the head to make all slippery. When that is done, he draws this member into his mouth and after it, by slow degrees, all the rest of the body.

29. This being Sunday, we had divine service and a sermon, at which several of the borderers assisted, and we concluded the duties of the day with christening five children. Our devotion being performed in the open field, like that of Mr. Whitefield's flocks, an unfortunate shower of rain had almost dispersed our congregation.

About four in the afternoon, the Carolina commissioners made a shift to come up with us, whom we had left at Pigeon Roost Creek the Friday before, waiting for their provisions. When their cart came up, they prudently discharged it and rather chose to hire two men to carry some part of their baggage. The rest they had been obliged to leave behind in the crotch of an old tree for want of proper conveniences to transport it any farther.

We found in the low ground several plants of the fern root, which is said to be much the strongest antidote yet discovered against the poison of the rattlesnake. The leaves of it resemble those of fern, from whence it obtained its name. Several stalks shoot from the same root, about six inches long, that lie mostly on the ground. It grows in a very rich soil, under the protection of some tall tree that shades it from the meridian beams of the sun. The root has a faint spicy taste and is preferred by the southern Indians to all other counterpoisons in this country. But there is another sort preferred by the northern Indians that they call Seneca rattlesnake root,[35] to which wonderful virtues are ascribed in the cure of pleurisies, fevers, rheumatisms, and dropsies, besides it being a powerful antidote against the venom of the rattlesnake.

In the evening the messenger we had sent to Christanna returned with five Saponi Indians.[36] We could not entirely rely on the dexterity of our own men, which induced us to send for some of the Indians. We agreed with two of the most expert of them upon reasonable terms to hunt for us the remaining part of our expedition. But one of them falling sick soon after, we were content to take only the other, whose hunting name was Bearskin. This Indian, either by his skill or good luck, supplied us plentifully all the way with meat, seldom discharging his piece in vain. By his assistance, therefore, we were able to keep our men to their business, without suffering them to straggle about the woods on pretense of furnishing us with necessary food.

30. It had rained all night and made everything so wet that our surveyors could not get to their work before noon. They could there-

[35] *Polygala senega.*
[36] Byrd has not mentioned this in the *History*; but see p. 101 of the *Secret History*.

fore measure no more than 4 miles and 220 poles, which, according to the best information we could get, was near as high as the uppermost inhabitant at that time.

We crossed the Indian trading path above-mentioned about a mile from our camp and a mile beyond that forded Hawtree Creek. The woods we passed through had all the tokens of sterility, except a small poisoned field on which grew no tree bigger than a slender sapling. The larger trees had been destroyed either by fire or caterpillar, which is often the case in the upland woods, and the places where such desolation happens are called poisoned fields. We took up our quarters upon a branch of Great Creek, where there was tolerable good grass for the poor horses. These poor animals, having now got beyond the latitude of corn, were obliged to shift as well as they could for themselves.

On our way the men roused a bear, which being the first we had seen since we came out, the poor beast had many pursuers. Several persons contended for the credit of killing him, though he was so poor he was not worth the powder. This was some disappointment to our woodsmen, who commonly prefer the flesh of bears to every kind of venison. There is something indeed peculiar to this animal, namely, that its fat is very firm and may be eaten plentifully without rising in the stomach. The paw (which when stripped of the hair looks like a human foot) is accounted a delicious morsel by all who are not shocked at the ungracious resemblance it bears to a human foot.

### OCTOBER

1. There was a white frost this morning on the ground, occasioned by a northwest wind, which stood our friend in dispersing all aguish damps and making the air wholesome at the same time that it made it cold. Encouraged, therefore, by the weather, our surveyors got to work early and, by the benefit of clear woods and level ground, drove the line twelve miles and twelve poles.

At a small distance from our camp we crossed Great Creek and about seven miles farther Nutbush Creek, so called from the many hazel trees growing upon it. By good luck, many branches of these creeks were full of reeds, to the great comfort of our horses. Near five miles from thence we encamped on a branch that runs into Nutbush Creek, where those reeds flourished more than ordinary. The land we marched over was for the most part broken and stony and in some places covered over with thickets almost impenetrable.

At night the surveyors, taking advantage of a very clear sky, made a third trial of the variation and found it still something less than three degrees; so that it did not diminish by advancing toward the west or by approaching the mountains, nor yet by increasing our distance from the sea, but remained much the same we had found it at Currituck Inlet.

One of our Indians killed a large fawn, which was very welcome, though, like Hudibras' horse, it had hardly flesh enough to cover its bones.

In the low grounds the Carolina gentlemen showed us another plant, which they said was used in their country to cure the bite of the rattlesnake. It put forth several leaves in figure like a heart and was clouded so like the common Asarabacca that I conceived it to be of that family.

2. So soon as the horses could be found, we hurried away the surveyors, who advanced the line 9 miles and 254 poles. About three miles from the camp they crossed a large creek, which the Indians called Massamony, signifying in their language "Paint Creek," because of the great quantity of red ocher found in its banks. This in every fresh tinges the water, just as the same mineral did formerly, and to this day continues to tinge, the famous river Adonis in Phoenicia, by which there hangs a celebrated fable.

Three miles beyond that we passed another water with difficulty called Yapatsco or Beaver Creek. Those industrious animals had dammed up the water so high that we had much ado to get over. 'Tis hardly credible how much work of this kind they will do in the space of one night. They bite young saplings into proper lengths with their foreteeth, which are exceeding strong and sharp, and afterwards drag them to the place where they intend to stop the water. Then they know how to join timber and earth together with so much skill that their work is able to resist the most violent flood that can happen. In this they are qualified to instruct their betters, it being certain their dams will stand firm when the strongest that are made by men will be carried down the stream. We observed very broad, low grounds upon this creek, with a growth of large trees and all the other signs of fertility, but seemed subject to be everywhere overflowed in a fresh. The certain way to catch these sagacious animals is this: squeeze all the juice out of the large pride of the beaver and six drops out of the small pride. Powder the inward bark of sassafras and mix it with this juice; then bait therewith a steel trap and they will eagerly come to it and be taken.

About three miles and an half farther we came to the banks of another creek, called in the Saponi language Ohimpamony, signifying "Jumping Creek," from the frequent jumping of fish during the spring season.

Here we encamped, and by the time the horses were hobbled our hunters brought us no less than a brace and an half of deer, which made great plenty and consequently great content in our quarters. Some of our people had shot a great wildcat, which was that fatal moment making a comfortable meal upon a fox squirrel, and an ambitious sportsman of our company claimed the merit of killing this monster after it was dead. The wildcat is as big again as any household cat and much the fiercest inhabitant of the woods. Whenever it is disabled, it will tear its own flesh for madness. Although a panther will run away from a man, a wildcat will only make a surly retreat, now and then facing about if he be too closely pursued, and will even pursue in his turn if he observe the least sign of fear or even of caution in those that pretend to follow him. The flesh of this beast, as well as of the panther, is as white as veal and altogether as sweet and delicious.

3. We got to work early this morning and carried the line 8 miles and 160 poles. We forded several runs of excellent water and afterwards traversed a large level of high land, full of lofty walnut, poplar, and white oak trees, which are certain proofs of a fruitful soil. This level was near two miles in length and of an unknown breadth, quite

out of danger of being overflowed, which is a misfortune most of the low grounds are liable to in those parts. As we marched along, we saw many buffalo tracks and abundance of their dung very fresh but could not have the pleasure of seeing them. They either smelt us out, having that sense very quick, or else were alarmed at the noise that so many people must necessarily make in marching along. At the sight of a man they will snort and grunt, cock up their ridiculous short tails, and tear up the ground with a sort of timorous fury. These wild cattle hardly ever range alone but herd together like those that are tame. They are seldom seen so far north as forty degrees of latitude, delighting much in canes and reeds which grow generally more southerly.

We quartered on the banks of a creek that the inhabitants call Tewahominy or Tuskarooda [37] Creek, because one of that nation had been killed thereabouts and his body thrown into the creek.

Our people had the fortune to kill a brace of does, one of which we presented to the Carolina gentlemen, who were glad to partake of the bounty of Providence at the same time that they sneered at us for depending upon it.

4. We hurried away the surveyors about nine this morning, who extended the line 7 miles and 160 poles, notwithstanding the ground was exceedingly uneven. At the distance of five miles we forded a stream to which we gave the name of Bluewing Creek because of the great number of those fowls that then frequented it. [38] About two and a half miles beyond that, we came upon Sugartree Creek, so called from the many trees of that kind that grow upon it. By tapping this tree in the first warm weather in February, one may get from twenty to forty gallons of liquor, very sweet to the taste and agreeable to the stomach. This may be boiled into molasses first and afterwards into very good sugar, allowing about ten gallons of liquor to make a pound. There is no doubt, too, that a very fine spirit may be distilled from the molasses, at least as good as rum. The sugar tree delights only in rich ground, where it grows very tall, and by the softness and sponginess

[37] The manuscript gives variant spellings of this Indian name, now normalized to Tuscarora.
[38] The bluewinged teal.

of the wood should be a quick grower. Near this creek we discovered likewise several spice trees, the leaves of which are fragrant and the berries they bear are black when dry and of a hot taste, not much unlike pepper. The low grounds upon the creek are very wide, sometimes on one side, sometimes on the other, though most commonly upon the opposite shore the high land advances close to the bank, only on the north side of the line it spreads itself into a great breadth of rich low ground on both sides the creek for four miles together, as far as this stream runs into Hyco River, whereof I shall presently make mention. One of our men spied three buffaloes, but his piece being loaded only with goose shot, he was able to make no effectual impression on their thick hides; however, this disappointment was made up by a brace of bucks and as many wild turkeys killed by the rest of the company. Thus Providence was very bountiful to our endeavors, never disappointing those that faithfully rely upon it and pray heartily for their daily bread.

5. This day we met with such uneven grounds and thick underwoods that with all our industry we were able to advance the line but 4 miles and 312 poles. In this small distance it intersected a large stream four times, which our Indian at first mistook for the south branch of Roanoke River; but, discovering his error soon after, he assured us 'twas a river called Hycootomony, or Turkey Buzzard River, from the great number of those unsavory birds that roost on the tall trees growing near its banks.

Early in the afternoon, to our very great surprise, the commissioners of Carolina acquainted us with their resolution to return home. This declaration of theirs seemed the more abrupt because they had not been so kind as to prepare us by the least hint of their intention to desert us. We therefore let them understand they appeared to us to abandon the business they came about with too much precipitation, this being but the fifteenth day since we came out the last time. But although we were to be so unhappy as to lose the assistance of their great abilities, yet we, who were concerned for Virginia, determined, by the grace of God, not to do our work by halves but, all deserted as we were like to be, should think it our duty to push the line quite to the mountains; and if their government should refuse to be bound by so much of the line as was run without their commissioners, yet at least it would bind Virginia and stand as a direction how far His Majesty's lands extend to the southward. In short, these gentlemen were positive, and the most we could agree upon was to subscribe plats of our work as far as we had acted together; though at the same time we insisted these plats should be got ready by Monday noon at farthest, when we on the part of Virginia intended, if we were alive, to move forward without farther loss of time, the season being then too far advanced to admit of any unnecessary or complaisant delays.

6. We lay still this day, being Sunday, on the bank of Hyco River and had only prayers, our chaplain not having spirits enough to preach. The gentlemen of Carolina assisted not at our public devotions, because they were taken up all the morning in making a formidable protest against our proceeding on the line without them. When the divine service was over, the surveyors set about making the plats of so much of the line as we had run this last campaign. Our pious friends of Carolina assisted in this work with some seeming scruple, pretending it was a violation of the Sabbath, which we were the more surprised at because it happened to be the first qualm of conscience they had ever been troubled with during the whole journey. They had made no bones of staying from prayers to hammer out an unnecessary protest, though divine service was no sooner over but an unusual fit of godliness made them fancy that finishing the plats, which was now matter of necessity, was a profanation of the day. However, the expediency of losing no time, for us who thought it our duty to finish what we had undertaken, made such a labor pardonable.

In the afternoon, Mr. Fitzwilliam, one of the commissioners for Virginia, acquainted his colleagues it was his opinion that by His Majesty's order they could not proceed farther on the line but in conjunction with the commissioners of Carolina; for which reason he intended to retire the next morning with those gentlemen. This looked a little odd in our brother commissioner; though, in justice to him as well as to our Carolina friends, they stuck by us as long as our good liquor lasted and were so kind to us as to drink our good journey to the mountains in the last bottle we had left.

7. The duplicates of the plats could not be drawn fair this day

before noon, where they were countersigned by the commissioners of each government. Then those of Carolina delivered their protest, which was by this time licked into form and signed by them all. And we have been so just to them as to set it down at full length in the Appendix, that their reasons for leaving us may appear in their full strength. After having thus adjusted all our affairs with the Carolina commissioners and kindly supplied them with bread to carry them back, which they hardly deserved at our hands, we took leave both of them and our colleague, Mr. Fitzwilliam. This gentleman had still a stronger reason for hurrying him back to Williamsburg, which was that neither the General Court might lose an able judge nor himself a double salary, not despairing in the least but he should have the whole pay of commissioner into the bargain, though he did not half the work. This, to be sure, was relying more on the interest of his friends than on the justice of his cause; in which, however, he had the misfortune to miscarry when it came to be fairly considered.

It was two o'clock in the afternoon before these arduous affairs could be dispatched, and then, all forsaken as we were, we held on our course toward the west. But it was our misfortune to meet with so many thickets in this afternoon's work that we could advance no further than 2 miles and 260 poles. In this small distance we crossed the Hyco the fifth time and quartered near Buffalo Creek, so named from the frequent tokens we discovered of that American behemoth. Here the bushes were so intolerably thick that we were obliged to cover the bread bags with our deerskins, otherwise the joke of one of the Indians must have happened to us in good earnest: that in a few days we must cut up our house to make bags for the bread and so be forced to expose our backs in compliment to our bellies. We computed we had then biscuit enough left to last us, with good management, seven weeks longer; and this being our chief dependence, it imported us to be very careful both in the carriage and the distribution of it.

We had now no other drink but what Adam drank in Paradise, though to our comfort we found the water excellent, by the help of which we perceived our appetites to mend, our slumbers to sweeten, the stream of life to run cool and peaceably in our veins, and if ever we dreamt of women, they were kind.

Our men killed a very fat buck and several turkeys. These two kinds of meat boiled together, with the addition of a little rice or French barley, made excellent soup, and, what happens rarely in other good things, it never cloyed, no more than an engaging wife would do, by being a constant dish. Our Indian was very superstitious in this matter and told us, with a face full of concern, that if we continued to boil venison and turkey together we should for the future kill nothing, because the spirit that presided over the woods would drive all the game out of our sight. But we had the happiness to find this an idle superstition, and though his argument could not convince us, yet our repeated experience at last, with much ado, convinced him.

We observed abundance of coltsfoot and maidenhair in many places and nowhere a larger quantity than here. They are both excellent pectoral plants and seem to have greater virtues much in this part of the world than in more northern climates; and I believe it may pass for a rule in botanics that where any vegetable is planted by the hand of Nature it has more virtue than in places whereto it is transplanted by the curiosity of man.

8. Notwithstanding we hurried away the surveyors very early, yet the underwoods embarrassed them so much that they could with difficulty advance the line four miles and twenty poles. Our clothes suffered extremely by the bushes, and it was really as much as both our hands could do to preserve our eyes in our heads. Our poor horses, too, could hardly drag their loads through the saplings, which stood so close together that it was necessary for them to draw and carry at the same time. We quartered near a spring of very fine water, as soft as oil and as cold as ice, to make us amends for the want of wine. And our Indian knocked down a very fat doe, just time enough to hinder us from going supperless to bed.

The heavy baggage could not come up with us because of the excessive badness of the ways. This gave us no small uneasiness, but it went worse with the poor men that guarded it. They had nothing in the world with them but dry bread, nor durst they eat any of that for fear of inflaming their thirst in a place where they could find no water to quench it. This was, however, the better to be endured because it was the first fast anyone had kept during the whole journey, and then, thanks to the gracious guardian of the woods, there was no more than a single meal lost to a few of the company.

We were entertained this night with the yell of a whole family of wolves, in which we could distinguish the treble, tenor, and bass very clearly. These beasts of prey kept pretty much upon our track, being tempted by the garbage of the creatures we killed every day, for which we were serenaded with their shrill pipes almost every night. This beast is not so untamable as the panther, but the Indians know how to gentle their whelps and use them about their cabins instead of dogs.

9. The thickets were hereabouts so impenetrable that we were obliged, at first setting-off this morning, to order four pioneers to clear the way before the surveyors. But after about two miles of these rough woods, we had the pleasure to meet with open grounds, and not very uneven, by the help of which we were enabled to push the line about six miles. The baggage that lay short of our camp last night came up about noon, and the men made heavy complaints that they had been half-starved, like Tantalus in the midst of plenty, for the reason above-mentioned.

The soil we passed over this day was generally very good, being clothed with large trees of poplar, hickory, and oak. But another certain token of its fertility was that wild angelica grew plentifully upon it. The root of this plant, being very warm and aromatic, is coveted by woodsmen extremely as a dry dram, that is, when rum, that cordial for all distresses, is wanting.

Several deer came into our view as we marched along, but none into the pot, which made it necessary for us to sup on the fragments we had been so provident as to carry along with us. This, being but a temperate repast, made some of our hungry fellows call the place we lodged at that night Bread-and-Water Camp.

A great flock of cranes flew over our quarters, that were exceeding clamorous in their flight. They seem to steer their course toward the south (being birds of passage) in quest of warmer weather. They only took this country in their way, being as rarely met with in this part of the world as a highwayman or a beggar. These birds travel generally in flocks, and when they roost they place sentinels upon some of the highest trees, which constantly stand upon one leg to keep themselves waking. Nor are these birds the only animals that appoint scouts to keep the main body from being surprised. For the baboons, whenever they go upon any mischievous expedition, such as robbing an orchard, they place sentinels to look out toward every point of the compass and give notice of any danger. Then, ranking themselves in one file that reaches from the mountain where they harbor to the orchard they intend to rob, some of them toss the fruit from the trees to those that stand nearest; these throw them to the next, and so from one to tother till the fruit is all secured in a few minutes out of harm's way. In the meantime, if any of the scouts should be careless at their posts and suffer any surprise, they are torn to pieces without mercy. In case of danger, these sentinels set up a fearful cry, upon which the rest take the alarm and scour away to the mountains as fast as they can.

Our Indian killed nothing all day but a mountain partridge, which a little resembled the common partridge in the plumage but was near as large as a dunghill hen. These are very frequent toward the mountains, though we had the fortune to meet with very few. They are apt to be shy and consequently the noise of so great a number of people might easily scare them away from our sight. We found what we conceived to be good limestone in several places and a great quantity of blue slate.

10. The day began very fortunately by killing a fat doe and two brace of wild turkeys; so the plenty of the morning made amends for the short commons overnight. One of the new men we brought out with us the last time was unfortunately heard to wish himself at home and for that show of impatience was publicly reprimanded at the head of the men, who were all drawn up to witness his disgrace. He was asked how he came so soon to be tired of the company of so many

brave fellows and whether it was the danger or the fatigue of the journey that disheartened him? This public reproof from thenceforward put an effectual stop to all complaints, and not a man amongst us after that pretended so much as to wish himself in Paradise.

A small distance from our camp we crossed a pleasant stream of water called Cockade Creek, and something more than a mile from thence our line intersected the south branch of Roanoke River the first time, which we called the Dan. It was about two hundred yards wide where we forded it, and when we came over to the west side we found the banks lined with a forest of tall canes that grew more than a furlong in depth. So that it cost us abundance of time and labor to cut a passage through them wide enough for our baggage.

In the meantime, we had leisure to take a full view of this charming river. The stream, which was perfectly clear, ran down about two knots, or two miles, an hour when the water was at the lowest. The bottom was covered with a coarse gravel, spangled very thick with a shining substance that almost dazzled the eye, and the sand upon either shore sparkled with the same splendid particles. At first sight, the sunbeams, giving a yellow cast to these spangles, made us fancy them to be gold dust and consequently that all our fortunes were made. Such hopes as these were the less extravagant because several rivers lying much about the same latitude with this have formerly abounded with fragments of that tempting metal. Witness the Tagus in Portugal, the Heber [39] in Thrace, and the Pactolus in Lesser Asia; not to mention the rivers on the Gold Coast in Africa, which lie in a more southern climate. But we soon found ourselves mistaken, and our gold dust dwindled into small flakes of isinglass. However, though this did not make the river so rich as we could wish, yet it made it exceedingly beautiful.

We marched about two miles and a half beyond this river as far as Cane Creek, so called from a prodigious quantity of tall canes that fringed the banks of it. On the west side of this creek we marked out our quarters and were glad to find our horses fond of the canes, though they scoured them smartly at first and discolored their dung. This

[39] The Hebrus.

beautiful vegetable grows commonly from thirteen to sixteen feet high, and some of them as thick as a man's wrist. Though these appeared large to us, yet they are no more than spires of grass, if compared to those which some curious travelers tell us grow in the East Indies, one joint of which will make a brace of canoes if sawed in two in the middle. Ours continue green through all the seasons during the space of six years and the seventh shed their seed, wither away, and die. The spring following they begin to shoot again and reach their former stature the second or third year after. They grow so thick and their roots lace together so firmly that they are the best guard that can be of the riverbank, which would otherwise be washed away by the frequent inundations that happen in this part of the world. They would also serve excellently well to plant on the borders of fishponds and canals to secure their sides from falling in; though I fear they would not grow kindly in a cold country, being seldom seen here so northerly as thirty-eight degrees of latitude.

11. At the distance of four miles and sixty poles from the place where we encamped, we came upon the river Dan a second time, though it was not so wide in this place as where we crossed it first, being not above 150 yards over. The west shore continued to be covered with the canes above-mentioned but not to so great a breadth as before, and 'tis remarkable that these canes are much more frequent on the west side of the river than on the east, where they grow generally very scattering. It was still a beautiful stream, rolling down its limpid and murmuring waters among the rocks, which lay scattered here and there to make up the variety of the prospect.

It was about two miles from this river to the end of our day's work, which led us mostly over broken grounds and troublesome underwoods. Hereabout, from one of the highest hills we made the first discovery of the mountains on the northwest of our course. They seemed to lie off at a vast distance and looked like ranges of blue clouds rising one above another.

We encamped about two miles beyond the river, where we made good cheer upon a very fat buck that luckily fell in our way. The Indian likewise shot a wild turkey but confessed he would not bring it us lest we should continue to provoke the guardian of the forest by cooking the beasts of the field and the birds of the air together in one vessel. This instance of Indian superstition, I confess, is countenanced in some measure by the Levitical law, which forbade the mixing things of a different nature together in the same field or in the same garment, and why not, then, in the same kettle? But, after all, if the jumbling of two sorts of flesh together be a sin, how intolerable an offense must it be to make a Spanish olla, that is, a hotchpotch of every kind of thing that is eatable? And the good people of England would have a great deal to answer for for beating up so many different ingredients into a pudding.

12. We were so cruelly entangled with bushes and grapevines all day that we could advance the line no farther than five miles and twenty-eight poles. The vines grew very thick in these woods, twining lovingly round the trees almost everywhere, especially to the saplings. This makes it evident how natural both the soil and climate of this country are to vines, though I believe most to our own vines. The grapes we commonly met with were black, though there be two or three kinds of white grapes that grow wild. The black are very sweet but small, because the strength of the vine spends itself in wood, though without question a proper culture would make the same grapes both larger and sweeter. But, with all these disadvantages, I have drunk tolerable good wine pressed from them, though made without skill.[40] There is then good reason to believe it might admit of great improvement if rightly managed.

Our Indian killed a bear, two years old, that was feasting on these grapes. He was very fat, as they generally are in that season of the year. In the fall the flesh of this animal has a high relish different from

[40] The English colonists made continuing efforts to develop a wine industry. The first explorers of the American continent were impressed by the abundance of grapes, and from the time of Raleigh's expeditions until the end of the colonial period efforts were made to plant vineyards and produce wine. Byrd's brother-in-law, Robert Beverley, attempted to establish a vineyard, as did other Virginians, including Byrd himself. See William Strachey, *Historie of Travell into Virginia Britania*, edited by Louis B. Wright and Virginia Freund (London, 1953), pp. 121–122; for Beverley, Hugh Jones, *Present State of Virginia*, pp. 91, 140; *American Husbandry* (1775), edited by Harry J. Carman (New York, 1939), pp. 192–193, 194; and Louis B. Wright, *The Dream of Prosperity in Colonial America* (New York, 1965), *passim*.

that of other creatures, though inclining nearest to that of pork, or rather of wild boar. A true woodsman prefers this sort of meat to that of the fattest venison, not only for the *haut goût*, but also because the fat of it is well tasted and never rises in the stomach. Another proof of the goodness of this meat is that it is less apt to corrupt than any other we are acquainted with.

As agreeable as such rich diet was to the men, yet we who were not accustomed to it tasted it at first with some sort of squeamishness, that animal being of the dog kind, though a little use soon reconciled us to this American venison. And that its being of the dog kind might give us the less disgust, we had the example of that ancient and polite people, the Chinese, who reckon dog's flesh too good for any under the quality of a mandarin. This beast is in truth a very clean feeder, living, while the season lasts, upon acorns, chestnuts, and chinquapins, wild honey and wild grapes. They are naturally not carnivorous, unless hunger constrain them to it after the mast is all gone and the product of the woods quite exhausted. They are not provident enough to lay up any hoard like the squirrels, nor can they, after all, live very long upon licking their paws, as Sir John Mandeville and some travelers tell us, but are forced in the winter months to quit the mountains and visit the inhabitants. Their errand is then to surprise a poor hog at a pinch to keep them from starving. And to show that they are not flesh eaters by trade, they devour their prey very awkwardly. They don't kill it right out and feast upon its blood and entrails, like other ravenous beasts, but, having, after a fair pursuit, seized it with their paws, they begin first upon the rump and so devour one collop after another till they come to the vitals, the poor animal crying all the while for several minutes together. However, in so doing, Bruin acts a little imprudently, because the dismal outcry of the hog alarms the neighborhood, and 'tis odds but he pays the forfeit with his life before he can secure his retreat.

But bears soon grow weary of this unnatural diet, and about January, when there is nothing to be gotten in the woods, they retire into some cave or hollow tree, where they sleep away two or three months very comfortably. But then they quit their holes in March, when the fish begin to run up the rivers, on which they are forced to keep Lent till some fruit or berry comes in season. But bears are fondest of chestnuts, which grow plentifully toward the mountains, upon very large trees, where the soil happens to be rich. We were curious to know how it happened that many of the outward branches of those trees came to be broke off in that solitary place and were informed that the bears are so discreet as not to trust their unwieldy bodies on the smaller limbs of the tree that would not bear their weight, but after venturing as far as is safe, which they can judge to an inch, they bite off the end of the branch, which falling down, they are content to finish their repast upon the ground. In the same cautious manner they secure the acorns that grow on the weaker limbs of the oak. And it must be allowed that in these instances a bear carries instinct a great way and acts more reasonably than many of his betters, who indiscreetly venture upon frail projects that won't bear them.

13. This being Sunday, we rested from our fatigue and had leisure to reflect on the signal mercies of Providence.

The great plenty of meat wherewith Bearskin furnished us in these lonely woods made us once more shorten the men's allowance of bread from five to four pounds of biscuit a week. This was the more necessary because we knew not yet how long our business might require us to be out.

In the afternoon our hunters went forth and returned triumphantly with three brace of wild turkeys. They told us they could see the mountains distinctly from every eminence, though the atmosphere was so thick with smoke that they appeared at a greater distance than they really were.

In the evening we examined our friend Bearskin concerning the religion of his country, and he explained it to us without any of that reserve to which his nation is subject. He told us he believed there was one supreme god, who had several subaltern deities under him. And that this master god made the world a long time ago. That he told the sun, the moon, and stars their business in the beginning, which they, with good looking-after, have faithfully performed ever since. That the same power that made all things at first has taken care to keep them in the same method and motion ever since. He believed that God had formed many worlds before he formed this, but that those worlds either grew old and ruinous or were destroyed for the dishonesty of the inhabitants. That God is very just and very good, ever well pleased with those men who possess those godlike qualities. That he takes good people into his safe protection, makes them very rich, fills their bellies plentifully, preserves them from sickness and from being surprised or overcome by their enemies. But all such as tell lies and cheat those they have dealings with he never fails to punish with sickness, poverty, and hunger and, after all that, suffers them to be knocked on the head and scalped by those that fight against them.

He believed that after death both good and bad people are conducted by a strong guard into a great road, in which departed souls travel together for some time till at a certain distance this road forks into two paths, the one extremely level and the other stony and mountainous. Here the good are parted from the bad by a flash of lightning, the first being hurried away to the right, the other to the left. The right-hand road leads to a charming, warm country, where the spring is everlasting and every month is May; and as the year is always in its youth, so are the people, and particularly the women are bright as stars and never scold. That in this happy climate there are deer, turkeys, elks, and buffaloes innumerable, perpetually fat and gentle, while the trees are loaded with delicious fruit quite throughout the four seasons. That the soil brings forth corn spontaneously, without the curse of labor, and so very wholesome that none who have the happiness to eat of it are ever sick, grow old, or die. Near the entrance into this blessed land sits a venerable old man on a mat richly woven, who examines strictly all that are brought before him, and if they have behaved well, the guards are ordered to open the crystal gate and let them enter into the land of delight. The left-hand path is very rugged and uneven, leading to a dark and barren country where it is always winter. The ground is the whole year round covered with snow, and nothing is to be seen upon the trees but icicles. All the people are hungry yet have not a morsel of anything to eat except a bitter kind of potato, that gives them the dry gripes and fills their whole body with loathsome ulcers that stink and are insupportably painful. Here all the women are old and ugly, having claws like a panther with which they fly upon the men that slight their passion. For it seems these haggard old furies are intolerably fond and expect a vast deal of cherishing. They talk much and exceedingly shrill, giving exquisite pain to the drum of the ear, which in that place of the torment is so tender that every sharp note wounds it to the quick. At the end of this path sits a dreadful old woman on a monstrous toadstool, whose head is covered with rattlesnakes instead of tresses, with glaring white eyes that strike a terror unspeakable into all that behold her. This hag pronounces sentence of woe upon all the miserable wretches that hold up their hands at her tribunal. After this they are delivered over to huge turkey buzzards, like harpies, that fly away with them to the place above-mentioned. Here, after they have been tormented a certain number of years according to their several degrees of guilt, they are again driven back into this world to try if they will mend their manners and merit a place the next time in the regions of bliss.

This was the substance of Bearskin's religion and was as much to the purpose as could be expected from a mere state of nature, without one glimpse of revelation or philosophy. It contained, however, the three great articles of natural religion: the belief of a god, the moral distinction betwixt good and evil, and the expectation of rewards and punishments in another world. Indeed, the Indian notion of a future happiness is a little gross and sensual, like Mahomet's Paradise. But how can it be otherwise in a people that are contented with Nature as they find her and have no other lights but what they receive from purblind tradition?

14. There having been great signs of rain yesterday evening, we had taken our precautions in securing the bread and trenching in our tent. The men had also stretched their blankets upon poles, penthouse fashion, against the weather, so that nobody was taken unprepared. It began to fall heavily about three o'clock in the morning and held not up till near noon. Everything was so thoroughly soaked that we laid aside all thoughts of decamping that day.

This gave leisure to the most expert of our gunners to go and try their fortunes, and they succeeded so well that they returned about noon with three fat deer and four wild turkeys. Thus Providence took care of us, and however short the men might be in their bread, 'tis certain they had meat at full allowance. The cookery went on merrily all night long, to keep the damps from entering our pores; and, in truth, the impressions of the air are much more powerful upon empty stomachs. In such a glut of provisions, a true woodsman when he has nothing else to do, like our honest countrymen the Indians, keeps eating on, to avoid the imputation of idleness; though in a scarcity the Indian will fast with a much better grace than they. They can subsist several days upon a little rockahominy, which is parched Indian corn reduced to powder. This they moisten in the hollow of their hands with a little water, and 'tis hardly credible how small a quantity of it will support them. 'Tis true they grow a little lank upon it, but to make themselves feel full they gird up their loins very tight with a belt, taking up a hole every day. With this slender subsistence they are able to travel very long journeys; but then, to make themselves amends, when they do meet with better cheer they eat without ceasing till they have ravened themselves into another famine.

This was the first time we had ever been detained a whole day in our camp by the rain and therefore had reason to bear it with the more patience.

As I sat in the tent, I overheard a learned conversation between one of our men and the Indian. He ask[ed] the Englishman what it was that made that rumbling noise when it thundered. The man told him merrily that the god of the English was firing his great guns upon the god of the Indians, which made all that roaring in the clouds, and that the lightning was only the flash of those guns. The Indian, carrying on the humor, replied very gravely he believed that might be the case indeed, and that the rain which followed upon the thunder must be occasioned by the Indian god's being so scared he could not hold his water.

The few good husbands amongst us took some thought of their backs as well as their bellies and made use of this opportunity to put their habiliments in repair, which had suffered woefully by the bushes.

The horses got some rest by reason of the bad weather, but very little food, the chief of their forage being a little wild rosemary, which resembles the garden rosemary pretty much in figure but not at all in taste or smell. This plant grows in small tufts here and there on the barren land in these upper parts, and the horses liked it well, but the misfortune was, they could not get enough of it to fill their bellies.

15. After the clouds brake away in the morning, the people dried their blankets with all diligence. Nevertheless, it was noon before we were in condition to move forward and then were so puzzled with passing the river twice in a small distance that we could advance the line in all no farther than one single mile and three hundred poles. The first time we passed the Dan this day was 240 poles from the place where we lay, and the second time was one mile and seven poles beyond that. This was now the fourth time we forded that fine river, which still tended westerly, with many short and returning reaches.

The surveyors had much difficulty in getting over the river, finding it deeper than formerly. The breadth of it here did not exceed fifty yards. The banks were about twenty feet high from the water and beautifully beset with canes. Our baggage horses crossed not the river here at all but, fetching a compass, went round the bent of it. On our way we forded Sable Creek, so called from the dark color of the water, which happened, I suppose, by its being shaded on both sides with canes.

In the evening we quartered in a charming situation near the angle of the river, from whence our eyes were carried down both reaches, which kept a straight course for a great way together. This prospect was so beautiful that we were perpetually climbing up to a neighboring eminence that we might enjoy it in more perfection.

Now the weather grew cool, the wild geese began to direct their flight this way from Hudson's Bay and the lakes that lay northwest of us. They are very lean at their first coming but fatten soon upon a sort of grass that grows on the shores and rocks of this river. The Indians call this fowl "cohunks," from the hoarse note it has, and begin the year from the coming of the cohunks, which happens in the beginning of October. These wild geese are guarded from cold by a down that is exquisitely soft and fine, which makes them much more valuable for their feathers than for their flesh, which is dark and coarse.

The men chased a bear into the river, that got safe over, notwithstanding the continual fire from the shore upon him. He seemed to swim but heavily, considering it was for his life. Where the water is shallow 'tis no uncommon thing to see a bear sitting in the summertime on a heap of gravel in the middle of the river, not only to cool himself but likewise for the advantage of fishing, particularly for a small shellfish that is brought down with the stream. In the upper part of James River I have observed this several times, and wondered very much at first how so many heaps of small stones came to be piled up in the water, till at last we spied a bear sitting upon one of them, looking with great attention on the stream and raking up something with his paw, which I take to be the shellfish above-mentioned.

16. It was ten o'clock this morning before the horses could be found, having hid themselves among the canes, whereof there was great plenty just at hand. Not far from our camp we went over a brook whose banks were edged on both sides with these canes. But three miles farther we forded a larger stream, which we called Lowland Creek by reason of the great breadth of low grounds enclosed between that and the river.

The high land we traveled over was very good, and the low grounds promised the greatest fertility of any I had ever seen. At the end of 4 miles and 311 poles from where we lay, the line intersected the Dan the fifth time. We had day enough to carry it farther, but the surveyors could find no safe ford over the river. This obliged us to ride two miles up the river in quest of a ford, and by the way we traversed several small Indian fields, where we conjectured the Sauros had been used to plant corn, the town where they had lived lying seven or eight miles more southerly upon the eastern side of the river. These Indian fields produced a sweet kind of grass, almost knee-high, which was excellent forage for the horses. It must be observed, by the way, that Indian towns, like religious houses, are remarkable for a fruitful situation; for, being by nature not very industrious, they choose such a situation as will subsist them with the least labor.

The trees grew surprisingly large in this low ground, and amongst the rest we observed a tall kind of hickory, peculiar to the upper parts of the country. It is covered with a very rough bark and produces a nut with a thick shell that is easily broken. The kernel is not so rank as that of the common hickory but altogether as oily. And now I am upon the subject of these nuts, it may not be improper to remark that a very great benefit might be made of nut oil in this colony. The walnuts, the hickory nuts, and pignuts contain a vast deal of oil that might be pressed out in great abundance with proper machines. The trees grow very kindly [41] and may be easily propagated. They bear plenty of nuts every year that are now of no other use in the world but to feed hogs. 'Tis certain there is a large consumption of this oil in several of our manufactures, and in some parts of France, as well as in other countries, it is eaten instead of oil olive, being tolerably sweet and wholesome.

The Indian killed a fat buck, and the men brought in four bears and a brace of wild turkeys, so that this was truly a land of plenty both for man and beast.

17. We detached a party of men this morning early in search of a ford, who after all could find none that was safe; though, dangerous as it was, we determined to make use of it to avoid all farther delay. Accordingly we rode over a narrow ledge of rocks, some of which lay below the surface of the water and some above it. Those that lay under the water were as slippery as ice; and the current glided over them so swiftly that though it was only water it made us perfectly drunk. Yet we were all so fortunate as to get safe over to the west shore with no other damage than the sopping some of our bread by the flouncing of the horses. The tedious time spent in finding out this ford and in getting all the horses over it prevented our carrying the line more than 2 miles and 250 poles.

This was the last time we crossed the Dan with our line, which now began to run away more southerly with a very flush and plentiful stream, the description whereof must be left to future discoveries, though we are well assured by the Indians that it runs through the

[41] Naturally, spontaneously.

252

mountains. We conducted the baggage a roundabout way for the benefit of evener grounds, and this carried us over a broad level of exceeding rich land, full of large trees with vines married to them, if I may
be allowed to speak so poetically.

We untreed a young cub in our march that made a brave stand
against one of the best of our dogs. This and a fawn were all the game
that came in our way.

In this day's journey, as in many others before, we saw beautiful
marble of several colors, and particularly that of the purple kind with
white streaks, and in some places we came across large pieces of pure
alabaster.

We marked out our quarters on the banks of a purling stream, which
we called Cascade Creek by reason of the multitude of waterfalls that
are in it. But, different from all other falls that ever I met with, the
rocks over which the water rolled were soft and would split easily into
broad flakes, very proper for pavement; and some fragments of it
seemed soft enough for hones and the grain fine enough.

Near our camp we found a prickly shrub rising about a foot from
the ground, something like that which bears the barberry though
much smaller. The leaves had a fresh, agreeable smell, and I am persuaded the ladies would be apt to fancy a tea made of them, provided
they were told how far it came and at the same time were obliged to
buy it very dear.[42]

About a mile to the southwest of our camp rose a regular mount
that commanded a full prospect of the mountains and an extensive
view of the flat country. But being, with respect to the high mountains, no more than a pimple, we called it by that name.

Presently, after sunset, we discovered a great light toward the west,
too bright for a fire and more resembling the aurora borealis. This, all
our woodsmen told us, it was a common appearance in the highlands
and generally foreboded bad weather. Their explanation happened
to be exactly true, for in the night we had a violent gale of wind, accompanied with smart hail that rattled frightfully amongst the trees,
though it was not large enough to do us any harm.

[42] Byrd refers to the proverbial saying "Dear-bought and far-fetched are dainties
for ladies."

18. We crossed Cascade Creek over a ledge of smooth rocks and then scuffled through a mighty thicket at least three miles long. The whole was one continued tract of rich high land, the woods whereof had been burnt not long before. It was then overgrown with saplings of oak, hickory, and locust, interlaced with grapevines. In this fine land, however, we met with no water, till at the end of three miles we luckily came upon a crystal stream which, like some lovers of conversation, discovered everything committed to its faithless bosom. Then we came upon a piece of rich low ground, covered with large trees, of the extent of half a mile, which made us fancy ourselves not far from the river; though after that we ascended gently to higher land, with no other trees growing upon it except butterwood, which is one species of white maple.

This, being a dead level without the least declivity to carry off the water, was moist in many places and produced abundance of grass. All our woodsmen call these flat grounds highland ponds and in their trading journeys are glad to halt at such places for several days together to recruit their jaded horses, especially in the winter months, when there is little or no grass to be found in other places. This highland pond extended above two miles, our palfreys snatching greedily at the tufts of grass as they went along.

After we got over this level, we descended some stony hills for about half a mile and then came upon a large branch of the river which we christened the Irvin, in honor of our learned professor. This river we forded with much difficulty and some danger, by reason of the hollow spaces betwixt the rocks, into which our horses plunged almost every step. The Irvin runs into the Dan about four miles to the southward of the line and seemed to roll down its waters from the north-north-west in a very full and limpid stream, and the murmur it made in tumbling over the rocks caused the situation to appear very romantic and had almost made some of the company poetical, though they drank nothing but water.

We encamped on a pleasant hill overlooking the river, which seemed to be deep everywhere except just where we forded. In the meantime, neither that chain of rocks nor any other that we could observe in this stream was so uninterrupted but that there were several breaks where a canoe, or even a moderate flat-bottomed boat, might shear clear. Nor have we reason to believe there are any other falls (except the great ones thirty miles below Moniseep Ford) that reach quite across so as to interrupt the navigation for small craft. And I have been informed that, even at those great falls, the blowing up a few rocks would open a passage at least for canoes, which certainly would be an unspeakable convenience to the inhabitants of all that beautiful part of the country.

The Indian killed a very fat doe and came across a bear, which had been put to death and was half devoured by a panther. The last of these brutes reigns absolute monarch of the woods and in the keenness of his hunger will venture to attack a bear; though then 'tis ever by surprise, as all beasts of the cat kind use to come upon their prey. Their play is to take the poor bears napping, they being very drowsy animals, and though they be exceedingly strong yet their strength is heavy, while the panthers are too nimble and cunning to trust themselves within their hug. As formidable as this beast is to his fellow brutes, he never hath the confidence to venture upon a man but retires from him with great respect, if there be a way open for his escape. However, it must be confessed his voice is a little contemptible for a monarch of the forest, being not a great deal louder nor more awful than the mewing of a household cat. Some authors who have given an account of the southern continent of America would make the world believe there are lions; but in all likelihood they were mistaken, imagining these panthers to be lions. What makes this probable is that the northern and southern parts of America being joined by the Isthmus of Darien, if there were lions in either they would find their way into the other, the latitudes of each being equally proper for that generous animal.

In South Carolina they call this beast a tiger, though improperly, and so they do in some parts of the Spanish West Indies. Some of their authors, a little more properly, compliment it with the name of a leopard. But none of these are the growth of America, that we know of.

The whole distance the surveyors advanced the line this day amounted to six miles and thirty poles, which was no small journey, considering the grounds we had traversed were exceedingly rough and uneven and in many places intolerably entangled with bushes.

All the hills we ascended were encumbered with stones, many of which seemed to contain a metallic substance, and the valleys we crossed were interrupted with miry branches. From the top of every hill we could discern distinctly, at a great distance to the northward, three or four ledges of mountains, rising one above another, and on the highest of all rose a single mountain, very much resembling a woman's breast.

19. About four miles beyond the river Irvin we forded Matrimony Creek, called so by an unfortunate married man because it was exceedingly noisy and impetuous. However, though the stream was clamorous, yet like those women who make themselves plainest heard, it was likewise perfectly clear and unsullied. Still half a mile farther we saw a small mountain about five miles to the northwest of us, which we called the Wart because it appeared no bigger than a wart in comparison of the great mountains which hid their haughty heads in the clouds.

We were not able to extend the line farther than 5 miles and 135 poles, notwithstanding we began our march early in the morning and did not encamp till it was almost dark. We made it the later by endeavoring to quarter in some convenient situation either for grass or canes. But night surprising us, we were obliged to lodge at last upon high and uneven ground, which was so overgrown with shrubs and saplings that we could hardly see ten yards around us. The most melancholy part of the story was that our horses had short commons. The poor creatures were now grown so weak that they staggered when we mounted them. Nor would our own fare have been at all more plentiful, had we not been so provident as to carry a load of meat along with us. Indeed, the woods were too thick to show us any sort of game but one wild turkey, which helped to enrich our soup. To make us amends, we found abundance of very sweet grapes, which, with the help of bread, might have furnished out a good Italian repast in the absence of more savory food.

The men's mouths watered at the sight of a prodigious flight of wild pigeons, which flew high over our heads to the southward.[43] The

[43] Many observers in early America commented on the numerous flights of passenger pigeons, which were easily killed by pot hunters and are now extinct.

flocks of these birds of passage are so amazingly great sometimes that they darken the sky, nor is it uncommon for them to light in such numbers in the larger limbs of mulberry trees and oaks as to break them down. In their travels they make vast havoc amongst the acorns and berries of all sorts that they waste whole forests in a short time and leave a famine behind them for most other creatures; and under some trees where they light, it is no strange thing to find the ground covered three inches thick with their dung. These wild pigeons commonly breed in the uninhabited parts of Canada and as the cold approaches assemble their armies and bend their course southerly, shifting their quarters, like many of the winged kind, according to the season. But the most remarkable thing in their flight, as we are told, is that they never have been observed to return to the northern countries the same way they came from thence but take another route, I suppose for their better subsistence. In these long flights they are very lean and their flesh is far from being white or tender, though good enough upon a march, when hunger is the sauce and makes it go down better than truffles and morels would do.

20. It was now Sunday, which we had like to have spent in fasting as well as prayer; for our men, taking no care for the morrow, like good Christians but bad travelers, had improvidently devoured all their meat for supper. They were ordered in the morning to drive up their horses, lest they should stray too far from the camp and be lost in case they were let alone all day. At their return they had the very great comfort to behold a monstrous fat bear, which the Indian had killed very seasonably for their breakfast. We thought it still necessary to make another reduction of our bread, from four to three pounds a week to every man, computing that we had still enough in that proportion to last us three weeks longer.

The atmosphere was so smoky all round us that the mountains were again grown invisible. This happened not from the haziness of the sky but from the firing of the woods by the Indians, for we were now near the route the northern savages take when they go out to war against the Catawbas and other southern nations. On their way, the fires they make in their camps are left burning, which, catching the dry leaves that lie near, soon put the adjacent woods into a flame. Some of our men in search of their horses discovered one of those Indian camps, where not long before they had been a-furring and dressing their skins.

And now I mention the northern Indians, it may not be improper to take notice of their implacable hatred to those of the south. Their wars are everlasting, without any peace, enmity being the only inheritance among them that descends from father to son, and either party will march a thousand miles to take their revenge upon such hereditary enemies. These long expeditions are commonly carried on in the following manner: some Indian remarkable for his prowess, that has raised himself to the reputation of a war captain, declares his intention of paying a visit to some southern nation; hereupon as many of the young fellows as have either a strong thirst of blood or glory list themselves under his command. With these volunteers he goes from one confederate town to another, listing all the rabble he can till he has gathered together a competent number for mischief. Their arms are a gun and tomahawk, and all the provisions they carry from home is a pouch of rockahominy. Thus provided and accoutered, they march toward the enemy's country, not in a body or by a certain path but straggling in small numbers for the greater convenience of hunting and passing along undiscovered. So soon as they approach the grounds on which the enemy is used to hunt, they never kindle any fire themselves for fear of being found out by the smoke, nor will they shoot at any kind of game, though they should be half famished, lest they might alarm their foes and put them upon their guard. Sometimes, indeed, while they are still at some distance, they roast either venison or bear till it is very dry and, then, having strung it on their belts, wear it round their middle, eating very sparingly of it because they know not when they shall meet with a fresh supply. But coming nearer, they begin to look all round the hemisphere to watch if any smoke ascends and listen continually for the report of guns, in order to make some happy discovery for their own advantage. 'Tis amazing to see their sagacity in discerning the track of a human foot, even amongst dry leaves, which to our shorter sight is quite undiscoverable. If by one or more of those signs they be able to find out the camp of any southern Indians, they squat down in some thicket and keep themselves hush and snug till it is dark; then, creeping up softly, they approach near enough to observe all the motions of the enemy. And about two o'clock in the morning, when they conceive them to be in a profound sleep, for they never keep watch and ward, pour in a volley upon them, each singling out his man. The moment they have discharged their pieces they rush in with their tomahawks and make sure work of all that are disabled. Sometime, when they find the enemy asleep round their little fire, they first pelt them with little stones to wake them, and when they get up, fire in upon them, being in that posture a better mark than when prostrate on the ground.

They that are killed of the enemy or disabled, they scalp: that is, they cut the skin all round the head just below the hair, and then, clapping their feet to the poor mortal's shoulders, pull the scalp off clean and carry it home in triumph, being as proud of those trophies as the Jews used to be of the foreskins of the Philistines. This way of scalping was practiced by the ancient Scythians, who used these hairy scalps as towels at home and trappings for their horses when they went abroad. They also made cups of their enemies' skulls, in which they drank prosperity to their country and confusion to all their foes.

The prisoners they happen to take alive in these expeditions generally pass their time very scurvily. They put them to all the tortures that ingenious malice and cruelty can invent. And (what shows the baseness of the Indian temper in perfection) they never fail to treat those with greatest inhumanity that have distinguished themselves most by their bravery, and if he be a war captain, they do him the honor to roast him alive and distribute a collop to all that had a share in stealing the victory. Though who can reproach the poor Indians for this, when Homer makes his celebrated hero, Achilles, drag the body of Hector at the tail of his chariot for having fought gallantly in defense of his country? Nor was Alexander the Great, with all his famed generosity, less inhuman to the brave Tyrians, two thousand of which he ordered to be crucified in cold blood for no other fault but for having defended their city most courageously against him during a siege of seven months. And what was still more brutal, he dragged —— alive at the tail of his chariot through all the streets, for defending the town with so much vigor.

They are very cunning in finding out new ways to torment their unhappy captives, though, like those of hell, their usual method is by fire. Sometimes they barbecue them over live coals, taking them off every now and then to prolong their misery; at other times they will stick sharp pieces of lightwood all over their bodies and, setting them on fire, let them burn down into the flesh to the very bone. And when they take a stout fellow that they believe able to endure a great deal, they will tear all the flesh off his bones with red-hot pincers. While these and suchlike barbarities are practicing, the victors are so far from being touched with tenderness and compassion that they dance and sing round these wretched mortals, showing all the marks of pleasure and jollity. And if such cruelties happen to be executed in their towns, they employ their children in tormenting the prisoners, in order to extinguish in them betimes all sentiments of humanity. In the meantime, while these poor wretches are under the anguish of all this inhuman treatment, they disdain so much as to groan, sigh, or show the least sign of dismay or concern so much as in their looks; on the contrary, they make it a point of honor all the time to soften their features and look as pleased as if they were in the actual enjoyment of some delight; and if they never sang before in their lives, they will be sure to be melodious on this sad and dismal occasion. So prodigious a degree of passive valor in the Indians is the more to be wondered at, because in all articles of danger they are apt to behave like cowards. And what is still more surprising, the very women discover on such occasions as great fortitude and contempt, both of pain and death, as the gallantest of their men can do.

21. The apprehensions we had of losing the horses in these copse-woods were too well founded, nor were the precautions we used yesterday of driving them up sufficient to prevent their straying away afterwards, notwithstanding they were securely hobbled. We therefore ordered the men out early this morning to look diligently for them, but it was late before any could be found. It seems they had

straggled in quest of forage, and, besides all that, the bushes grew thick enough to conceal them from being seen at the smallest distance. One of the people was so bewildered in search of his horse that he lost himself, being no great forester. However, because we were willing to save time, we left two of our most expert woodsmen behind to beat all the adjacent woods in quest of him.

In the meanwhile, the surveyors proceeded vigorously on their business, but were so perplexed with thickets at their first setting-off that their progress was much retarded. They were no sooner over that difficulty but they were obliged to encounter another. The rest of their day's work lay over very sharp hills, where the dry leaves were so slippery that there was hardly any hold for their feet. Such rubs as these prevented them from measuring more than 4 miles and 270 poles. Upon the sides of these hills the soil was rich, though full of stones, and the trees reasonably large.

The smoke continued still to veil the mountains from our sight, which made us long for rain or a brisk gale of wind to disperse it. Nor was the loss of this wild prospect all our concern, but we were apprehensive lest the woods should be burnt in the course of our line before us or happen to take fire behind us, either of which would effectually have starved the horses and made us all foot soldiers. But we were so happy, thank God, as to escape this misfortune in every part of our progress.

We were exceedingly uneasy about our lost man, knowing he had taken no provision of any kind; nor was it much advantage toward his support that he had taken his gun along with him, because he had rarely been guilty of putting anything to death. He had unluckily wandered from the camp several miles, and after steering sundry unsuccessful courses in order to return either to us or to the line, was at length so tired he could go no farther. In this distress he sat himself down under a tree to recruit his jaded spirits and at the same time indulge a few melancholy reflections. Famine was the first phantom that appeared to him and was the more frightful because he fancied himself not quite bear enough to subsist long upon licking his paws. In the meantime, the two persons we had sent after him hunted

261

diligently great part of the day without coming upon his track. They fired their pieces toward every point of the compass but could perceive no firing in return. However, advancing a little farther, at last they made a lucky shot that our straggler had the good fortune to hear, and, he returning the salute, they soon found each other with no small satisfaction. But though they light of [44] the man, they could by no means light of his horse, and therefore he was obliged to be a foot soldier all the rest of the journey.

Our Indian shot a bear so prodigiously fat that there was no way to kill him but by firing in at his ear. The fore part of the skull of that animal, being guarded by a double bone, is hardly penetrable, and when it is very fat, a bullet aimed at his body is apt to lose its force before it reaches the vitals. This animal is of the dog kind, and our Indians, as well as woodsmen, are as fond of its flesh as the Chinese can be of that of the common hound.

22. Early in the morning we sent back two men to make farther search for the horse that was strayed away. We were unwilling the poor man should sustain such a damage as would eat out a large part of his pay or that the public should be at the expense of reimbursing him for it. These foresters hunted all over the neighboring woods and took as much pains as if the horse had been their own property, but all their diligence was to no purpose. The surveyors, in the meantime, being fearful of leaving these men too far behind, advanced the line no farther than 1 mile and 230 poles.

As we rode along we found no less than three bears and a fat doe, that our Indian, who went out before us, had thrown in our course, and we were very glad to pick them up. About a mile from the camp we crossed Miry Creek, so called because several of the horses were mired in its branches. About 230 poles beyond that, the line intersected another river that seemed to be a branch of the Irvin, to which we gave the name of the Mayo in compliment to the other of our surveyors. It was about fifty yards wide where we forded it, being just below a ledge of rocks which reached across the river and made a natural cascade. Our horses could hardly keep their feet over these

[44] Happened upon, came across.

slippery rocks, which gave some of their riders no small palpitation. This river forks about a quarter of a mile below the ford and has some scattering canes growing near the mouth of it.

We pitched our tent on the western banks of the Mayo, for the pleasure of being lulled to sleep by the cascade. Here our hunters had leisure to go out and try their fortunes, and returned loaded with spoil. They brought in no less than six bears, exceedingly fat, so that the frying pan had no rest all night. We had now the opportunity of trying the speed of these lumpish animals by a fair course it had with the nimblest of our surveyors. A cub of a year old will run very fast, because, being upon his growth, he is never encumbered with too much fat; but the old ones are more sluggish and unwieldy, especially when mast is plenty. Then their nimblest gait is only a heavy gallop, and their motion is still slower downhill, where they are obliged to sidle along very awkwardly to keep their lights from rising up into their throat. These beasts always endeavor to avoid a man, except they are wounded or happen to be engaged in the protection of their cubs. By the force of these instincts and that of self-preservation, they will now and then throw off all reverence for their Maker's image. For that reason, excess of hunger will provoke them to the same desperate attack for the support of their being. A memorable instance of the last case is said to have happened not long ago in New England, where a bear assaulted a man just by his own door, and rearing himself upon his haunches, offered to take him lovingly into his hug. But the man's wife, observing the danger her husband was in, had the courage to run behind the bear and thrust her two thumbs into his eyes. This made Bruin quit the man and turn short upon the woman to take his revenge, but she had the presence of mind to spring back with more than female agility, and so both their lives were preserved.

23. At the distance of sixty-two poles from where we lay, we crossed the south branch of what we took for the Irvin, nor was it without difficulty we got over, though it happened to be without damage. Great part of the way after that was mountainous, so that we were no sooner got down one hill but we were obliged to climb up another. Only for the last mile of our stage we encountered a locust

263

thicket, that was level but interlaced terribly with briers and grapevines. We forded a large creek no less than five times, the banks of
which were so steep that we were forced to cut them down with a hoe.
We gave it the name of Crooked Creek because of its frequent
meanders. The sides of it were planted with shrub canes extremely inviting to the horses, which were now quite jaded with clambering up
so many precipices and tugging through so many dismal thickets; notwithstanding which we pushed the line this day four miles, sixty-
nine poles.

The men were so unthrifty this morning as to bring but a small portion of their abundance along with them. This was the more unlucky because we could discover no sort of game the whole livelong
day. Woodsmen are certainly good Christians in one respect at least,
that they always leave the morrow to care for itself; though for that
very reason they ought to pray more fervently for their daily bread than
most of them remember to do.

The mountains were still concealed from our eyes by a cloud of
smoke. As we went along we were alarmed at the sight of a great fire
which showed itself to the northward. This made our small corps
march in closer order than we used to do, lest perchance we might be
waylaid by Indians. It made us look out sharp to see if we could discover any track or other token of these insidious foresters, but found
none. In the meantime, we came often upon the track of bears, which
can't without some skill be distinguished from that of human creatures
made with naked feet. And, indeed, a young woodsman would be
puzzled to find out the difference, which consists principally in a bear's
paws being something smaller than a man's foot and in its leaving
sometimes the mark of its claws in the impression made upon the
ground.

The soil where the locust thicket grew was exceedingly rich, as it
constantly is where that kind of tree is naturally and largely produced.
But the desolation made there lately, either by fire or caterpillars, had
been so general that we could not see a tree of any bigness standing
within our prospect. And the reason why a fire makes such havoc in
these lonely parts is this: the woods are not there burnt every year as

they generally are amongst the inhabitants. But the dead leaves and trash of many years are heaped up together, which, being at length kindled by the Indians that happen to pass that way, furnish fuel for a conflagration that carries all before it.

There is a beautiful range of hills, as level as a terrace walk, that overlooks the valley through which Crooked Creek conveys its spiral stream. This terrace runs pretty near east and west about two miles south of the line and is almost parallel with it. The horses had been too much harassed to permit us to ride at all out of our way for the pleasure of any prospect or the gratification of any curiosity. This confined us to the narrow sphere of our business and is at the same time a just excuse for not animating our story with greater variety.

24. The surveyors went out the sooner this morning by reason the men lost very little time in cooking their breakfast. They had made but a spare meal overnight, leaving nothing but the hide of a bear for the morrow. Some of the keenest of them got up at midnight to cook that nice morsel after the Indian manner. They first singed the hair clean off, that none of it might stick in their throats; then they boiled the pelt into soup, which had a stratum of grease swimming upon it full half an inch thick. However, they commended this dish extremely; though I believe the praises they gave it were more owing to their good stomach than to their good taste.

The line was extended six miles and three hundred poles and in that distance crossed Crooked Creek at least eight times more. We were forced to scuffle through a thicket about two miles in breadth, planted with locusts and hickory saplings as close as they could stand together. Amongst these there was hardly a tree of tolerable growth within view. It was a dead plain of several miles extent and very fertile soil. Beyond that the woods were open for about three miles but mountainous. All the rest of our day's journey was pestered with bushes and grapevines, in the thickest of which we were obliged to take up our quarters near one of the branches of Crooked Creek.

This night it was the men's good fortune to fare very sumptuously. The Indian had killed two large bears, the fattest of which he had taken napping. One of the people, too, shot a raccoon, which is also of the dog kind and as big as a small fox, though its legs are shorter and when fat has a much higher relish than either mutton or kid. 'Tis naturally not carnivorous but very fond of Indian corn and persimmons. The fat of this animal is reckoned very good to assuage swellings and inflammations. Some old maids are at the trouble of breeding them up tame for the pleasure of seeing them play over as many humorous tricks as a monkey. It climbs up small trees, like a bear, by embracing the bodies of them.

Till this night we had accustomed ourselves to go to bed in our nightgowns, believing we should thereby be better secured from the cold, but upon trial found we lay much warmer by stripping to our shirts and spreading our gowns over us. A true woodsman, if he have no more than a single blanket, constantly pulls all off and, lying on one part of it, draws the other over him, believing it much more refreshing to lie so than in his clothes; and if he find himself not warm enough, shifts his lodging to leeward of the fire, in which situation the smoke will drive over him and effectually correct the cold dews that would otherwise descend upon his person, perhaps to his great damage.

25. The air clearing up this morning, we were again agreeably surprised with a full prospect of the mountains. They discovered themselves both to the north and south of us on either side, not distant above ten miles, according to our best computation. We could now see those to the north rise in four distinct ledges one above another, but those to the south formed only a single ledge and that broken and interrupted in many places, or rather they were only single mountains detached from each other. One of the southern mountains was so vastly high it seemed to hide its head in the clouds, and the west end of it terminated in a horrible precipice that we called the Despairing Lover's Leap. The next to it, toward the east, was lower except at one end, where it heaved itself up in the form of a vast stack of chimneys. The course of the northern mountains seemed to tend west-southwest and those to the southward very near west. We could descry other mountains ahead of us, exactly in the course of the line though at a much greater distance. In this point of view, the ledges on the right and left both seemed to close and form a natural amphi-

theater. Thus 'twas our fortune to be wedged in betwixt these two ranges of mountains, insomuch that if our line had run ten miles on either side it had butted before this day either upon one or the other, both of them now stretching away plainly to the eastward of us.

It had rained a little in the night, which dispersed the smoke and opened this romantic scene to us all at once, though it was again hid from our eyes as we moved forward by the rough woods we had the misfortune to be engaged with. The bushes were so thick for near four miles together that they tore the deerskins to pieces that guarded the bread bags. Though, as rough as the woods were, the soil was extremely good all the way, being washed down from the neighboring hills into the plain country. Notwithstanding all these difficulties, the surveyors drove on the line 4 miles and 205 poles.

In the meantime we were so unlucky as to meet with no sort of game the whole day, so that the men were obliged to make a frugal distribution of what little they left in the morning. We encamped upon a small rill, where the horses came off as temperately as their masters. They were by this time grown so thin by hard travel and spare feeding that henceforth, in pure compassion, we chose to perform the greater part of the journey on foot. And as our baggage was by this time grown much lighter, we divided it after the best manner so that every horse's load might be proportioned to the strength he had left. Though after all the prudent measures we could take, we perceived the hills began to rise upon us so fast in our front that it would be impossible for us to proceed much farther.

We saw very few squirrels in the upper parts, because the wildcats devour them unmercifully. Of these there are four kinds: the fox squirrel, the gray, the flying, and the ground squirrel. These last resemble a rat in everything but the tail and the black and russet streaks that run down the length of their little bodies.

26. We found our way grow still more mountainous, after extending the line three hundred poles farther. We came then to a rivulet that ran with a swift current toward the south. This we fancied to be another branch of the Irvin, though some of these men, who had been Indian traders, judged it rather to be the head of Deep River, that dis-

charges its stream into that of Pee Dee, but this seemed a wild conjecture. The hills beyond that river were exceedingly lofty and not to be attempted by our jaded palfreys, which could now hardly drag their legs after them upon level ground. Besides, the bread began to grow scanty and the winter season to advance apace upon us. We had likewise reason to apprehend the consequences of being intercepted by deep snows and the swelling of the many waters between us and home. The first of these misfortunes would starve all our horses and the other ourselves, by cutting off our retreat and obliging us to winter in those desolate woods. These considerations determined us to stop short here and push our adventures no farther. The last tree we marked was a red oak growing on the bank of the river; and to make the place more remarkable, we blazed all the trees around it.

We found the whole distance from Currituck Inlet to the rivulet where we left off to be, in a straight line, 240 miles and 230 poles. And from the place where the Carolina commissioners deserted us, 72 miles and 302 poles. This last part of the journey was generally very hilly, or else grown up with troublesome thickets and underwoods, all which our Carolina friends had the discretion to avoid. We encamped in a dirty valley near the rivulet above-mentioned for the advantage of the canes, and so sacrificed our own convenience to that of our horses. There was a small mountain half a mile to the northward of us, which we had the curiosity to climb up in the afternoon in order to enlarge our prospect. From thence we were able to discover where the two ledges of mountains closed, as near as we could guess about thirty miles to the west of us, and lamented that our present circumstances would not permit us to advance the line to that place, which the hand of Nature had made so very remarkable.

Not far from our quarters one of the men picked up a pair of elk's horns, not very large, and discovered the track of the elk that had shed them. It was rare to find any tokens of those animals so far to the south, because they keep commonly to the northward of thirty-seven degrees, as the buffaloes, for the most part, confine themselves to the southward of that latitude. The elk is full as big as a horse and of the deer kind. The stags only have horns and those exceedingly large and spreading. Their color is something lighter than that of the red deer and their flesh tougher. Their swiftest speed is a large trot, and in that motion they turn their horns back upon their necks and cock their noses aloft in the air. Nature has taught them this attitude to save their antlers from being entangled in the thickets, which they always retire to. They are very shy and have the sense of smelling so exquisite that they wind a man at a great distance. For this reason they are seldom seen but when the air is moist, in which case their smell is not so nice. They commonly herd together, and the Indians say if one of the drove happen by some wound to be disabled from making his escape, the rest will forsake their fears to defend their friend, which they will do with great obstinacy till they are killed upon the spot. Though, otherwise, they are so alarmed at the sight of a man that to avoid him they will sometimes throw themselves down very high precipices into the river.

A misadventure happened here which gave us no small perplexity. One of the commissioners was so unlucky as to bruise his foot against a stump, which brought on a formal fit of the gout. It must be owned there could not be a more unseasonable time, nor a more improper situation for anyone to be attacked by that cruel distemper. The joint was so inflamed that he could neither draw shoe or boot upon it, and to ride without either would have exposed him to so many rude knocks and bruises in those rough woods as to be intolerable even to a stoic. It was happy indeed that we were to rest here the next day, being Sunday, that there might be leisure for trying some speedy remedy. Accordingly, he was persuaded to bathe his foot in cold water in order to repel the humor and assuage the inflammation. This made it less painful and gave us hopes, too, of reducing the swelling in a short time.

Our men had the fortune to kill a brace of bears, a fat buck, and a wild turkey, all which paid them with interest for yesterday's abstinence. This constant and seasonable supply of our daily wants made us reflect thankfully on the bounty of Providence. And that we might not be unmindful of being all along fed by Heaven in this great and solitary wilderness, we agreed to wear in our hats the maosti, which is in Indian the beard of a wild turkey cock, and on our breasts the figure of that fowl with its wings extended and holding in its claws a scroll with this motto, *Vice coturnicum*, meaning that we had been supported by them in the wilderness in the room of quails.

27. This being Sunday, we were not wanting in our thanks to Heaven for the constant support and protection we had been favored with. Nor did our chaplain fail to put us in mind of our duty by a sermon proper for the occasion. We ordered a strict inquiry to be made into the quantity of bread we had left and found no more than would subsist us a fortnight at short allowance. We made a fair distribution of our whole stock and at the same time recommended to the men to manage this, their last stake, to the best advantage, not knowing how long they would be obliged to live upon it. We likewise directed them to keep a watchful eye upon their horses, that none of them might be missing the next morning to hinder our return.

There fell some rain before noon, which made our camp more a bog than it was before. This moist situation began to infect some of the men with fevers and some with fluxes, which however we soon removed with Peruvian bark and ipecacuanha.

In the afternoon we marched up again to the top of the hill to entertain our eyes a second time with the view of the mountains, but a perverse fog arose that hid them from our sight. In the evening we deliberated which way it might be most proper to return. We had at first intended to cross over at the foot of the mountains to the head of James River, that we might be able to describe that natural boundary so far. But, on second thoughts, we found many good reasons against that laudable design, such as the weakness of our horses, the scantiness of our bread, and the near approach of winter. We had cause to believe the way might be full of hills, and the farther we went toward the north, the more danger there would be of snow. Such considerations as these determined us at last to make the best of our way back upon the line, which was the straightest and consequently the shortest way to the inhabitants. We knew the worst of that course and were sure of a beaten path all the way, while we were totally ignorant what difficulties and dangers the other course might be attended with. So prudence got the better for once of curiosity, and the itch for new discoveries gave place to self-preservation.

Our inclination was the stronger to cross over according to the course of the mountains, that we might find out whether James River and Appomattox River head there or run quite through them. 'Tis certain that Potomac passes in a large stream through the main ledge and then divides itself into two considerable rivers. That which stretches away to the northward is called Cohungaroota [45] and that which flows to the southwest hath the name of Sharantow. The course of this last stream is near parallel to the Blue Ridge of mountains, at the distance only of about three or four miles. Though how far it may continue that course has not yet been sufficiently discovered, but some woodsmen pretend to say it runs as far as the source of Roanoke; nay, they are so very particular as to tell us that Roanoke, Sharantow, and another wide branch of Mississippi all head in one and the same mountain. What dependence there may be upon this conjectural geography I won't pretend to say, though 'tis certain that Sharantow keeps close to the mountains, as far as we are acquainted with its tendency. We are likewise assured that the south branch of James River, within less than twenty miles east of the main ledge, makes an elbow and runs due southwest, which is parallel with the mountains on this side. But how far it stretches that way before it returns is not yet certainly known, no more than where it takes its rise.

In the meantime, it is strange that our woodsmen have not had curiosity enough to inform themselves more exactly of these particulars, and it is stranger still that the government has never thought it worth the expense of making an accurate survey of the mountains, that we might be masters of that natural fortification before the French, who in some places have settlements not very distant from it. It therefore concerns His Majesty's service very nearly and the safety of his subjects in this part of the world to take possession of so im-

[45] The manuscript has the following passage added in the margin: "Which by a late survey has been found to extend above two hundred miles before it reaches its source, in a mountain from which Allegheny, one of the branches of the Mississippi, takes it rise, and runs southwest, as this river does southeast." Sharantow is an old name for Shenandoah.

portant a barrier in time, lest our good friends, the French, and the Indians through their means, prove a perpetual annoyance to these colonies. Another reason to invite us to secure this great ledge of mountains is the probability that very valuable mines may be discovered there. Nor would it be at all extravagant to hope for silver mines among the rest, because part of these mountains lie exactly in the same parallel, as well as upon the same continent, with New Mexico and the mines of St. Barb.[46]

28. We had given orders for the horses to be brought up early, but the likelihood of more rain prevented our being overhasty in decamping. Nor were we out in our conjectures, for about ten o'clock it began to fall very plentifully. Our commissioner's pain began now to abate as the swelling increased. He made an excellent figure for a mountaineer, with one boot of leather and the other of flannel. Thus accoutered he intended to mount, if the rain had not happened opportunely to prevent him. Though, in truth, it was hardly possible for him to ride with so slender a defense without exposing his foot to be bruised and tormented by the saplings that stood thick on either side of the path. It was therefore a most seasonable rain for him, as it gave more time for his distemper to abate.

Though it may be very difficult to find a certain cure for the gout, yet it is not improbable but some things may ease the pain and shorten the fits of it. And those medicines are most likely to do this that supple the parts and clear the passage through the narrow vessels that are the seat of this cruel disease. Nothing will do this more suddenly than rattlesnake's oil, which will even penetrate the pores of glass when warmed in the sun. It was unfortunate, therefore, that we had not taken out the fat of those snakes we had killed some time before, for the benefit of so useful an experiment as well as for the relief of our fellow traveler. But lately the Seneca rattlesnake root has been discovered in this country, which, being infused in wine and drank morning and evening, has in several instances had a very happy effect upon the gout, and enabled cripples to throw away their crutches and walk several miles, and, what is stranger still, it takes away the pain in half an hour.

[46] Santa Barbara, Chihuahua, Mexico.

Nor was the gout the only disease amongst us that was hard to cure. We had a man in our company who had too voracious a stomach for a woodsman. He eat as much as any other two, but all he swallowed stuck by him till it was carried off by a strong purge. Without this assistance, often repeated, his belly and bowels would swell to so enormous a bulk that he could hardly breathe, especially when he lay down, just as if he had had an asthma; though, notwithstanding this oddness of constitution, he was a very strong, lively fellow and used abundance of violent exercise, by which 'twas wonderful the peristaltic motion was not more vigorously promoted. We gave this poor man several purges, which only eased him for the present, and the next day he would grow as burly as ever. At last we gave him a moderate dose of ipecacuanha in broth made very salt, which turned all its operation downwards. This had so happy an effect that from that day forward to the end of our journey all his complaints ceased and the passages continued unobstructed.

The rain continued most of the day and some part of the night, which incommoded us much in our dirty camp and made the men think of nothing but eating, even at a time when nobody could stir out to make provision for it.

29. Though we were flattered in the morning with the usual tokens of a fair day, yet they all blew over, and it rained hard before we could make ready for our departure. This was still in favor of our podagrous friend, whose lameness was now grown better and the inflammation fallen. Nor did it seem to need above one day more to reduce it to its natural proportion and make it fit for the boot; and effectually the rain procured this benefit for him and gave him particular reason to believe his stars propitious.

Notwithstanding the falling weather, our hunters sallied out in the afternoon and drove the woods in a ring, which was thus performed: from the circumference of a large circle they all marched inward and drove the game toward the center. By this means they shot a brace of fat bears, which came very seasonably, because we had made clean work in the morning and were in danger of dining with St. Anthony, or His Grace Duke Humphrey.[47] But in this expedition the unhappy

[47] Humphrey, Duke of Gloucester. A statue in old St. Paul's Cathedral, erron-

man who had lost himself once before straggled again so far in pursuit of a deer that he was hurried a second time quite out of his knowledge; and, night coming on before he could recover the camp, he was obliged to lie down without any of the comforts of fire, food, or covering; nor would his fears suffer him to sleep very sound, because, to his great disturbance, the wolves howled all that night and panthers screamed most frightfully.

In the evening a brisk northwester swept all the clouds from the sky and exposed the mountains as well as the stars to our prospect. That which was the most lofty to the southward and which we called the Lover's Leap, some of our Indian traders fondly fancied was the Kiawan Mountain, which they had formerly seen from the country of the Cherokees. They were the more positive by reason of the prodigious precipice that remarkably distinguished the west end of it. We seemed however not to be far enough south for that, though 'tis not improbable but a few miles farther the course of our line might carry us to the most northerly towns of the Cherokees. What makes this the more credible is the northwest course that our traders take from the Catawbas for some hundred miles together, when they carry goods that roundabout way to the Cherokees.

It was a great pity that the want of bread and the weakness of our horses hindered us from making the discovery. Though the great service such an excursion might have been to the country would certainly have made the attempt not only pardonable but much to be commended. Our traders are now at the vast charge and fatigue of traveling above five hundred miles for the benefit of that traffic which hardly quits cost. Would it not then be worth the Assembly's while to be at some charge to find a shorter cut to carry on so profitable a trade, with more advantage and less hazard and trouble than they do at present? For I am persuaded it will not then be half the distance that our traders make it now nor half so far as Georgia lies from the northern clans of that nation. Such a discovery would certainly prove an un-

---

eously identified as that of the Duke, was a meeting place for needy gallants and rogues. A penniless gallant with nowhere to go for dinner was said to "dine with Duke Humphrey," meaning to go dinnerless.

speakable advantage to this colony by facilitating a trade with so considerable a nation of Indians, which have sixty-two towns and more than four thousand fighting men. Our traders at that rate would be able to undersell those sent from the other colonies so much that the Indians must have reason to deal with them preferably to all others. Of late the new colony of Georgia has made an act obliging us to go four hundred miles to take out a license to traffic with these Cherokees, though many of their towns lie out of their bounds and we had carried on this trade eighty years before that colony was thought of.

30. In the morning early the man who had gone astray the day before found his way to the camp by the sound of the bells that were upon the horses' necks.

At nine o'clock we began our march back toward the rising sun, for though we had finished the line yet we had not yet near finished our fatigue. We had, after all, two hundred good miles at least to our several habitations, and the horses were brought so low that we were obliged to travel on foot great part of the way, and that in our boots, too, to save our legs from being torn to pieces by the bushes and briers. Had we not done this, we must have left all our horses behind, which could now hardly drag their legs after them; and with all the favor we could show the poor animals we were forced to set seven of them free not far from the foot of the mountains.

Four men were dispatched early to clear the road, that our lame commissioner's leg might be in less danger of being bruised and that the baggage horses might travel with less difficulty and more expedition. As we passed along, by favor of a serene sky we had still from every eminence a perfect view of the mountains, as well to the north as to the south. We could not forbear now and then facing about to survey them, as if unwilling to part with a prospect which at the same time, like some rakes, was very wild and very agreeable. We encouraged the horses to exert the little strength they had and, being light, they made a shift to jog on about eleven miles.

We encamped on Crooked Creek near a thicket of canes. In the front of our camp rose a very beautiful hill that bounded our view at about a mile's distance, and all the intermediate space was covered with green canes. Though to our sorrow, firewood was scarce, which was now the harder upon us because a northwester blew very cold from the mountains.

The Indian killed a stately, fat buck, and we picked his bones as clean as a score of turkey buzzards could have done. By the advantage of a clear night, we made trial once more of the variation and found it much the same as formerly. This being His Majesty's birthday, we drank all the loyal healths in excellent water, not for the sake of the drink (like many of our fellow subjects), but purely for the sake of the toast. And because all public mirth should be a little noisy, we fired several volleys of canes, instead of guns, which gave a loud report. We threw them into the fire, where the air enclosed betwixt the joints of the canes, being expanded by the violent heat, burst its narrow bounds with a considerable explosion.

In the evening one of the men knocked down an opossum, which is a harmless little beast that will seldom go out of your way, and if you take hold of it will only grin and hardly ever bite. The flesh was well tasted and tender, approaching nearest to pig, which it also resembled in bigness. The color of its fur was a goose gray, with a swine's snout and a tail like a rat, but at least a foot long. By twisting this tail about the arm of a tree, it will hang with all its weight and swing to anything it wants to take hold of. It has five claws on the fore-feet of equal length, but the hinder feet have only four claws and a sort of thumb standing off at a proper distance. Their feet, being thus formed, qualify them for climbing up trees to catch little birds, which they are very fond of. But the greatest particularity of this creature, and which distinguishes it from most others that we are acquainted with, is the false belly of the female, into which her young retreat in time of danger. She can draw the slit, which is the inlet into this pouch, so close that you must look narrowly to find it, especially if she happen to be a virgin. Within the false belly may be seen seven or eight teats, on which the young ones grow from their first formation till they are big enough to fall off like ripe fruit from a tree. This is so odd a method of generation that I should not have believed it without the testimony of mine own eyes. Besides, a knowing and credible person

276

has assured me he has more than once observed the embryo opossums growing to the teat before they were completely shaped, and afterwards watched their daily growth till they were big enough for birth.[48] And all this he could the more easily pry into because the dam was so perfectly gentle and harmless that he could handle her just as he pleased.

I could hardly persuade myself to publish a thing so contrary to the course that nature takes in the production of other animals unless it were a matter commonly believed in all countries where that creature is produced and has been often observed by persons of undoubted credit and understanding. They say that the leather-winged bats produce their young in the same uncommon manner; and that young sharks at sea and young vipers ashore run down the throats of their dams when they are closely pursued.

[31.][49] The frequent crossing of Crooked Creek and mounting the steep banks of it gave the finishing stroke to the foundering our horses, and no less than two of them made a full stop here and would not advance a foot farther, either by fair means or foul. We had a dreamer of dreams amongst us who warned me in the morning to take care of myself or I should infallibly fall into the creek; I thanked him kindly and used what caution I could but was not able, it seems, to avoid my destiny, for my horse made a false step and laid me down at my full length in the water. This was enough to bring dreaming into credit, and I think it much for the honor of our expedition that it was graced not only with a priest but also with a prophet. We were so perplexed with this serpentine creek, as well as in passing the branches of the Irvin, which were swelled since we saw them before, that we could reach but five miles this whole day.

In the evening we pitched our tent near Miry Creek, though an uncomfortable place to lodge in, purely for the advantage of the canes. Our hunters killed a large doe and two bears, which made all other misfortunes easy. Certainly no Tartar ever loved horseflesh or Hottentot guts and garbage better than woodsmen do bear. The truth of it is, it may be proper food perhaps for such as work or ride it off, but, with

[48] Byrd seems to think that the embryos were formed in the pouch, whereas in fact the mother places the immature embryos there after natural birth.
[49] The date has been added from the *Secret History*.

our chaplain's leave, who loved it much, I think it not a very proper diet for saints, because 'tis apt to make them a little too rampant. And, now, for the good of mankind and for the better peopling an infant colony, which has no want but that of inhabitants, I will venture to publish a secret of importance which our Indian disclosed to me. I asked him the reason why few or none of his countrywomen were barren. To which curious question he answered, with a broad grin upon his face, they had an infallible secret for that. Upon my being importunate to know what the secret might be, he informed me that if any Indian woman did not prove with child at a decent time after marriage, the husband, to save his reputation with the women, forthwith entered into a bear diet for six weeks, which in that time makes him so vigorous that he grows exceedingly impertinent to his poor wife, and 'tis great odds but he makes her a mother in nine months. And thus much I am able to say besides for the reputation of the bear diet, that all the married men of our company were joyful fathers within forty weeks after they got home, and most of the single men had children sworn to them within the same time, our chaplain always excepted, who, with much ado, made a shift to cast out that importunate kind of devil by dint of fasting and prayer.

#### NOVEMBER

1. By the negligence of one of the men in not hobbling his horse, he straggled so far that he could not be found. This stopped us all the morning long; yet, because our time should not be entirely lost, we endeavored to observe the latitude at twelve o'clock. Though our observation was not perfect by reason the wind blew a little too fresh, however, by such a one as we could make, we found ourselves in 36° 20′ only. Notwithstanding our being thus delayed and the unevenness of the ground over which we were obliged to walk (for most of us served now in the infantry), we traveled no less than six miles. Though as merciful as we were to our poor beasts, another of 'em tired by the way and was left behind for the wolves and panthers to feast upon.

As we marched along, we had the fortune to kill a brace of bucks, as many bears, and one wild turkey. But this was carrying our sport to wantonness, because we butchered more than we were able to transport. We ordered the deer to be quartered and divided among the horses for the lighter carriage and recommended the bears to our daily attendants, the turkey buzzards. We always chose to carry venison along with us rather than bear, not only because it was less cumbersome but likewise because the people could eat it without bread, which was now almost spent. Whereas the other, being richer food, lay too heavy upon the stomach unless it were lightened by something farinaceous.

This is what I thought proper to remark for the service of all those whose business or diversion shall oblige them to live any time in the woods. And because I am persuaded that very useful matters may be found out by searching this great wilderness, especially the upper parts of it about the mountains, I conceive it will help to engage able men in that good work if I recommend a wholesome kind of food of very small weight and very great nourishment, that will secure them from starving in case they should be so unlucky as to meet with no game. The chief discouragement at present from penetrating far into the woods is the trouble of carrying a load of provisions. I must own, famine is a frightful monster and for that reason to be guarded against as well as we can. But the common precautions against it are so burdensome that people cannot tarry long out and go far enough from home to make any effectual discovery. The portable provisions I would furnish our foresters withal are glue broth and rockahominy: one contains the essence of bread, the other of meat. The best way of making the glue broth is after the following method: take a leg of beef, veal, venison, or any other young meat, because old meat will not so easily jelly. Pare off all the fat, in which there is no nutriment, and of the lean make a very strong broth after the usual manner, by boiling the meat to rags till all the goodness be out. After skimming off what fat remains, pour the broth into a wide stewpan, well tinned, and let it simmer over a gentle, even fire till it come to a thick jelly. Then take it off and set it over boiling water, which is an evener heat and not so apt to burn the broth to the vessel. Over that let it evaporate, stirring it very often till it be reduced, when cold, into a solid substance like glue. Then cut it into small pieces, laying them single in the cold, that they may dry the sooner. When the pieces are perfectly dry, put them into a canister, and they will be good, if kept dry, a whole East India voyage. This glue is so strong that two or three drams, dissolved in boiling water with a little salt, will make half a pint of good broth, and if you should be faint with fasting or fatigue, let a small piece of this glue melt in your mouth and you will find yourself surprisingly refreshed.

One pound of this cookery would keep a man in good heart above a month and is not only nourishing but likewise very wholesome. Particularly it is good against fluxes, which woodsmen are very liable to, by lying too near the moist ground and guzzling too much cold water. But as it will be only used now and then, in times of scarcity when game is wanting, two pounds of it will be enough for a journey of six months.

But this broth will be still more heartening if you thicken every mess with half a spoonful of rockahominy, which is nothing but Indian corn parched without burning and reduced to powder. The fire drives out all the watery parts of the corn, leaving the strength of it behind, and this, being very dry, becomes much lighter for carriage and less liable to be spoilt by the moist air. Thus half a dozen pounds of this sprightly bread will sustain a man for as many months, provided he husband it well and always spare it when he meets with venison, which, as I said before, may be very safely eaten without any bread at all.

By what I have said, a man needs not encumber himself with more than eight or ten pounds of provisions, though he continue half a year in the woods. These and his gun will support him very well during that time, without the least danger of keeping one single fast. And though some of his days may be what the French call *jours maigres*, yet there will happen no more of those than will be necessary for his health and to carry off the excesses of the days of plenty, when our travelers will be apt to indulge their lawless appetites too much.

2. The heavens frowned this morning and threatened abundance of rain, but our zeal for returning made us defy the weather and de-

camp a little before noon. Yet we had not advanced two miles before a soaking shower made us glad to pitch our tent as fast as we could. We chose for that purpose a rising ground half a mile to the east of Matrimony Creek. This was the first and only time we were catched in the rain during the whole expedition. It used before to be so civil as to fall in the night after we were safe in our quarters and had trenched ourselves in, or else it came upon us on Sundays, when it was no interruption to our progress nor any inconvenience to our persons. We had, however, been so lucky in this particular before that we had abundant reason to take our present soaking patiently, and the misfortune was the less because we had taken our precautions to keep all our baggage and bedding perfectly dry.

This rain was enlivened with very loud thunder, which was echoed back by the hills in the neighborhood in a frightful manner. There is something in the woods that makes the sound of this meteor more awful and the violence of the lightning more visible. The trees are frequently shivered quite down to the root and sometimes perfectly twisted. But of all the effects of lightning that ever I heard of the most amazing happened in this country in the year 1736. In the summer of that year a surgeon of a ship, whose name was Davis, came ashore at York to visit a patient. He was no sooner got into the house but it began to rain with many terrible claps of thunder. When it was almost dark there came a dreadful flash of lightning, which struck the surgeon dead as he was walking about the room but hurt no other person, though several were near him. At the same time it made a large hole in the trunk of a pine tree which grew about ten feet from the window. But what was most surprising in this disaster was that on the breast of the unfortunate man that was killed was the figure of a pine tree, as exactly delineated as any limner in the world could draw it, nay, the resemblance went so far as to represent the color of the pine as well as the figure. The lightning must probably have passed through the tree first before it struck the man and by that means have printed the icon of it on his breast. But whatever may have been the cause, the effect was certain and can be attested by a cloud of witnesses who had the curiosity to go and see this wonderful phenomenon.

The worst of it was, we were forced to encamp in a barren place, where there was hardly a blade of grass to be seen; even the wild rosemary failed us here, which gave us but too just apprehensions that we should not only be obliged to trudge all the way home on foot but also to lug our baggage at our backs into the bargain. Thus we learnt by our own experience that horses are very improper animals to use in a long ramble into the woods, and the better they have been used to be fed, they are still the worse. Such will fall away a great deal faster and fail much sooner than those which are wont to be at their own keeping. Besides, horses that have been accustomed to a plain and champaign country will founder presently when they come to clamber up hills and batter their hoofs against continual rocks. We need Welsh runts and Highland Galloways to climb our mountains withal; they are used to precipices and will bite as close as Banstead Down sheep. But I should much rather recommend mules, if we had them, for these long and painful expeditions; though, till they can be bred, certainly asses are the fittest beasts of burden for the mountains. They are sure footed, patient under the heaviest fatigue, and will subsist upon moss or browsing on shrubs all the winter. One of them will carry the necessary luggage of four men without any difficulty and upon a pinch will take a quarter of bear or venison upon their backs into the bargain.

Thus, when the men are light and disengaged from everything but their guns, they may go the whole journey on foot with pleasure. And though my dear countrymen have so great a passion for riding that they will often walk two miles to catch a horse in order to ride one, yet, if they'll please to take my word for it, when they go into the woods upon discovery I would advise them by all means to march afoot, for they will then be delivered from the great care and concern for their horses which takes up too large a portion of their time. Overnight we are now at the trouble of hobbling them out and often of leading them a mile or two to a convenient place for forage, and then in the morning we are some hours in finding them again, because they are apt to stray a great way from the place where they were turned out. Now and then, too, they are lost for a whole day together and are frequently so weak and jaded that the company must lie still several days near some meadow or highland pond to recruit them.

All these delays retard their progress intolerably; whereas, if they had only a few asses they would abide close by the camp and find sufficient food everywhere, and in all seasons of the year. Men would then be able to travel safely over hills and dales, nor would the steepest mountain obstruct their progress. They might also search more narrowly for mines and other productions of nature, without being confined to level grounds in compliment to the jades they ride on. And one may foretell without the spirit of divination that so long as woodsmen continue to range on horseback we shall be strangers to our own country and few or no valuable discoveries will ever be made.

The French *coureurs de bois*, who have run from one end of the continent to the other, have performed it all on foot or else, in all probability, must have continued full as ignorant as we are. Our country has now been inhabited more than 130 years by the English, and still we hardly know anything of the Appalachian Mountains, that are nowhere above 250 miles from the sea. Whereas the French, who are later-comers, have ranged from Quebec southward as far as the mouth of Mississippi in the Bay of Mexico and to the west almost as far as California, which is either way above two thousand miles.

3. A northwest wind having cleared the sky, we were now tempted to travel on a Sunday for the first time, for want of more plentiful forage, though some of the more scrupulous amongst us were unwilling to do evil that good might come of it and make our cattle work a good part of the day in order to fill their bellies at night. However, the chaplain put on his casuistical face and offered to take the sin upon himself. We therefore consented to move a Sabbath Day's journey of three or four miles, it appearing to be a matter of some necessity.

On the way our unmerciful Indian killed no less than two brace of deer and a large bear. We only primed the deer, being unwilling to be encumbered with their whole carcasses. The rest we consigned to the wolves, which in return serenaded us great part of the night. They are very clamorous in their banquets, which we know is the way some other brutes have, in the extravagance of their jollity and sprightliness, of expressing their thanks to Providence.

We came to our old camp in sight of the river Irvin, whose stream was swelled now near four foot with the rain that fell the day before. This made it impracticable for us to ford it, nor could we guess when the water would fall enough to let us go over. This put our mathematical professor, who should have set a better example, into the vapors, fearing he should be obliged to take up his winter quarters in that doleful wilderness. But the rest were not infected with his want of faith but preserved a firmness of mind superior to such little adverse accidents. They trusted that the same good Providence which had most remarkably prospered them hitherto would continue its goodness and conduct them safe to the end of their journey.

However, we found plainly that traveling on the Sunday, contrary to our constant rule, had not thriven with us in the least. We were not gainers of any distance by it, because the river made us pay two days for violating one. Nevertheless, by making this reflection, I would not be thought so rigid an observer of the Sabbath as to allow of no work at all to be done or journeys to be taken upon it. I should not care to lie still and be knocked on the head, as the Jews were heretofore by Antiochus, because I believed it unlawful to stand upon my defense on this good day. Nor would I care, like a certain New England magistrate, to order a man to the whipping post for daring to ride for a midwife on the Lord's Day. On the contrary, I am for doing all acts of necessity, charity, and self-preservation upon a Sunday as well as other days of the week. But, as I think our present march could not strictly be justified by any of these rules, it was but just we should suffer a little for it.

I never could learn that the Indians set apart any day of the week or the year for the service of God. They pray, as philosophers eat, only when they have a stomach, without having any set time for it. Indeed these idle people have very little occasion for a Sabbath to refresh themselves after hard labor, because very few of them ever labor at all. Like the wild Irish, they had rather want than work and are all men of pleasure, to whom every day is a day of rest. Indeed, in their hunting they will take a little pains; but this being only a diversion, their spirits are rather raised than depressed by it and therefore need at most but a night's sleep to recruit them.

4. By some stakes we had driven into the river yesterday, we perceived the water began to fall but fell so slowly that we found we must have patience a day or two longer. And because we were unwilling to lie altogether idle, we sent back some of the men to bring up the two horses that tired the Saturday before. They were found near the place where we had left them, but seemed too sensible of their liberty to come to us. They were found standing indeed, but as motionless as the equestrian statue at Charing Cross.

We had great reason to apprehend more rain by the clouds that drove over our heads. The boldest amongst us were not without some pangs of uneasiness at so very sullen a prospect. However, God be praised, it all blew over in a few hours. If much rain had fallen, we resolved to make a raft and bind it together with grapevines to ferry ourselves and baggage over the river. Though in that case we expected the swiftness of the stream would have carried down our raft a long way before we could have tugged it to the opposite shore.

One of the young fellows we had sent to bring up the tired horses entertained us in the evening with a remarkable adventure he had met with that day. He had straggled, it seems, from his company in a mist and made a cub of a year old betake itself to a tree. While he was new-priming his piece with intent to fetch it down, the old gentlewoman appeared and, perceiving her heir apparent in distress, advanced open-mouthed to his relief. The man was so intent upon his game that she had approached very near him before he perceived her. But finding his danger, he faced about upon the enemy, which immediately reared upon her posteriors and put herself in battle array. The man, admiring at the bear's assurance, endeavored to fire upon her, but by the dampness of the priming his gun did not go off. He cocked it a second time and had the same misfortune. After missing fire twice, he had the folly to punch the beast with the muzzle of his piece; but Mother Bruin, being upon her guard, seized the weapon with her paws and by main strength wrenched it out of the fellow's hands. The man, being thus fairly disarmed, thought himself no longer a match for the enemy and therefore retreated as fast as his legs could carry him. The brute naturally grew bolder upon the flight of her adversary and pursued him with all her heavy speed. For some time it was doubtful whether fear made one run faster or fury the other. But after an even course of about fifty yards, the man had the mishap to stumble over a stump and fell down at his full length. He now would have sold his life a pennyworth; but the bear, apprehending there might be some trick in the fall, instantly halted and looked with much attention on her prostrate foe. In the meanwhile, the man had with great presence of mind resolved to make the bear believe he was dead by lying breathless on the ground, in hopes that the beast would be too generous to kill him over again. To carry on the farce, he acted the corpse for some time without daring to raise his head to see how near the monster was to him. But in about two minutes, to his unspeakable comfort, he was raised from the dead by the barking of a dog belonging to one of his companions, who came seasonably to his rescue and drove the bear from pursuing the man to take care of her cub, which she feared might now fall into a second distress.

5. We judged the waters were assuaged enough this morning to make the river fordable. Therefore about ten we tried the experiment, and everybody got over safe except one man, whose horse slipped from a rock as he forded over and threw him into the river. But, being able to swim, he was not carried down the stream very far before he recovered the north shore. At the distance of about six miles we passed Cascade Creek, and three miles farther we came upon the banks of the Dan, which we crossed with much difficulty, by reason the water was risen much higher than when we forded it before. Here the same unlucky person happened to be ducked a second time and was a second time saved by swimming. My own horse, too, plunged in such a manner that his head was more than once under water but with much ado recovered his feet, though he made so low an obeisance that the water ran fairly over my saddle.

We continued our march as far as Lowland Creek, where we took up our lodging for the benefit of the canes and winter grass that grew upon the rich grounds thereabouts. On our way thither we had the misfortune to drop another horse, though he carried nothing the whole day but his saddle. We showed the same favor to most of our horses, for fear, if we did not do it, we should in a little time be turned into a Rock, as he forded over, and threw him into the River. But being able to swim, he was not carryd down the Stream very far, before he recoverd the North Shoar.

At the Distance of about 6 miles we past Cascade Creek, and 3 Miles farther we came upon the Banks of the Dan, which we crost with much Difficulty, by reason the Water was risen much higher than when we forded it before.

Here the same unlucky Person happend to be duckt a Second time, and was a Second time Savd by Swiming. My own Horse too plunged in such a Manner, that his Head was more than once under Water: but with much ado recoverd his Feet, tho' he made so low an Obeisance, that the water ran fairly over my Saddle.

We continued our March as far as Low-Land-Creek, where we took up our Lodging for the benefit of the Canes, and Winter Grass, that grew upon the rich Ground thereabouts. On our way thither we had the misfortune to drop another Horse, tho' he carryd nothing the whole Day but his Saddle. We shewd the same favour to most of our Horses, for fear, if we did not do it, we should in a little time be turnd into Beasts of Burthen our selves.

Custom had now made travelling on foot so familiar, that we were able to walk ten Miles with Pleasure. This we could do in our Boots, notwithstanding our way lay over rough Woods, and uneven Grounds.

Our learning to walk in heavy Boots was the same advantage to us, that learning to Dance High-Dances in wooden Shoes, is to the French, it made us most exceeding nimble without them.

The Indians, who have no way of travelling but on the Hoof, make nothing of going 25 Miles a day, and carrying their little Necessaries at their backs, and sometimes a stout Pack of Skins into the Bargain. And very often they laugh at the English, who can't Stir to a next Neighbour without a Horse, and say that 2 Legs are too much for such lazy people, who cant visit their next neighbour without Six.

For their Parts, they were utter Strangers to all our Beasts of Burthen or Carriage, before the Slothfull Europeans came amongst them. They had no part of the American Continent, or in any of the Islands, either Horses or Asses, Camels, Dromedaries, or Elephants to ease the Legs of the Original Inhabitants, or to lighten their Labour.

Indeed in South America, and particularly in Chili, they have an usefull Animal calld Paco. This Creature resembles a Sheep, not by much, only in the Length of the Neck, and figure of the Head is more like a Camel. It is very near as high as an Ass, and the Indians there make use of it for carrying moderate Burthens.

The Fleece that grows upon it, is very Valuable for the fineness, length, and Glossiness of the Wool. It has one remarkable Singularity that the Hoofs of its fore feet have three Clefts, and those behind no more than one. The Flesh of this Animal is Sweet

A Page from the Westover Manuscript of *The History of the Dividing Line*

(The pointer indicates a line with an insertion probably in Byrd's hand.)

beasts of burden ourselves. Custom had now made traveling on foot so familiar that we were able to walk ten miles with pleasure. This we could do in our boots, notwithstanding our way lay over rough woods and uneven grounds. Our learning to walk in heavy boots was the same advantage to us that learning to dance high dances in wooden shoes is to the French: it made us most exceeding nimble without them.

The Indians, who have no way of traveling but on the hoof, make nothing of going twenty-five miles a day and carrying their little necessaries at their backs, and sometimes a stout pack of skins into the bargain. And very often they laugh at the English, who can't stir to a next neighbor without a horse, and say that two legs are too much for such lazy people, who can't visit their next neighbor without six. For their parts, they were utter strangers to all our beasts of burden or carriage before the slothful Europeans came amongst them. They had on no part of the American continent, or in any of the islands, either horses or asses, camels, dromedaries, or elephants to ease the legs of the original inhabitants or to lighten their labor. Indeed, in South America, and particularly in Chile, they have a useful animal called "paco." This creature resembles a sheep pretty much, only in the length of the neck and figure of the head it is more like a camel. It is very near as high as the ass, and the Indians there make use of it for carrying moderate burdens. The fleece that grows upon it is very valuable for the fineness, length, and glossiness of the wool. It has one remarkable singularity, that the hoofs of its forefeet have three clefts and those behind no more than one. The flesh of this animal is something drier than our mutton but altogether as well tasted. When it is angry, it has no way of resenting its wrongs but by spitting in the face of those that provoke it, and if the spawl happen to light on the bare skin of any person, it first creates an itching and afterwards a scab, if no remedy be applied. The way to manage these pacos and make them tractable is to bore a hole in their ears, through which they put a rope and then guide them just as they please. In Chile they weave a beautiful kind of stuff with thread made of this creature's wool, which has a gloss superior to any camlet and is sold very dear in that country.

6. The difficulty of finding the horses among the tall canes made it late before we decamped. We traversed very hilly grounds but, to make amends, it was pretty clear of underwood. We avoided crossing the Dan twice by taking a compass round the bent of it. There was no passing by the angle of the river without halting a moment to entertain our eyes again with that charming prospect. When that pleasure was over, we proceeded to Sable Creek and encamped a little to the east of it. The river thereabouts had a charming effect, its banks being adorned with green canes sixteen feet high, which make a spring all the year as well as plenty of forage all the winter.

One of the men wounded an old buck that was gray with years and seemed by the reverend marks he bore upon him to confirm the current opinion of that animal's longevity. The smart of his wound made him not only turn upon the dogs but likewise pursue them to some distance with great fury. However he got away at last, though by the blood that issued from his wound he could not run far before he fell and without doubt made a comfortable repast for the wolves. However, the Indian had better fortune and supplied us with a fat doe and a young bear two years old. At that age they are in their prime and, if they be fat withal, are a morsel for a cardinal.

All the land we traveled over this day and the day before, that is to say, from the river Irvin to Sable Creek, is exceedingly rich, both on the Virginia side of the line and that of Carolina.[50] Besides whole forests of canes, that adorn the banks of the river and creeks thereabouts, the fertility of the soil throws out such a quantity of winter grass that horses and cattle might keep themselves in heart all the cold season without the help of any fodder. Nor have the low grounds only this advantage but likewise the higher land, and particularly that which we call the Highland Pond, which is two miles broad and of a length unknown.

I question not but there are thirty thousand acres at least, lying all

[50] Boyd comments: "Byrd is here describing the lands which he purchased from the North Carolina commissioners, who had secured them in payment for their services. Byrd called the region the Land of Eden. He inserted in the manuscript of *The Journey to the Land of Eden* a map of his purchases, which was published in Wynne's version and is here reproduced." See p. 413 of this edition.

together, as fertile as the lands were said to be about Babylon, which yielded, if Herodotus tells us right, an increase of no less than two or three hundred for one. But this hath the advantage of being a higher, and consequently a much healthier, situation than that. So that a colony of one thousand families might, with the help of moderate industry, pass their time very happily there. Besides grazing and tillage, which would abundantly compensate their labor, they might plant vineyards upon the hills, in which situation the richest wines are always produced. They might also propagate white mulberry trees, which thrive exceedingly in this climate, in order to the feeding of silkworms and making of raw silk. They might too produce hemp, flax, and cotton in what quantity they pleased, not only for their own use but likewise for sale. Then they might raise very plentifully orchards both of peaches and apples, which contribute as much as any fruit to the luxury of life. There is no soil or climate will yield better rice than this, which is a grain of prodigious increase and of very wholesome nourishment. In short, everything will grow plentifully here to supply either the wants or wantonness of man. Nor can I so much as wish that the more tender vegetables might grow there, such as orange, lemon, and olive trees, because then we should lose the much greater benefit of the brisk northwest winds, which purge the air and sweep away all the malignant fevers which hover over countries that are always warm. The soil would also want the advantages of frost and snow, which by their nitrous particles contribute not a little to its fertility. Besides, the inhabitants would be deprived of the variety and sweet vicissitude of the seasons, which is much more delightful than one dull and constant succession of warm weather diversified only by rain and sunshine.

There is also another convenience that happens to this country by cold weather: it destroys a great number of snakes and other venomous reptiles and troublesome insects, or at least lays them to sleep for several months, which otherwise would annoy us the whole year round and multiply beyond all enduring. Though oranges and lemons are desirable fruits and useful enough in many cases, yet when the want of them is supplied by others more useful we have no cause to complain. There is no climate that produces everything since the Deluge wrenched the poles of the world out of their place, nor is it fit it should be so, because it is the mutual supply one country receives from another which creates a mutual traffic and intercourse amongst men. And in truth, were it not for this correspondence in order to make up each other's wants, the wars betwixt bordering nations, like those of the Indians and other barbarous people, would be perpetual and irreconciliable.

As to olive trees, I know by experience they will never stand the sharpness of our winters; but their place may be supplied by the plant called sesamum, which yields an infinite quantity of large seed from whence a sweet oil is pressed that is very wholesome and in use amongst the people of Lesser Asia. Likewise it is used in Egypt, preferably to oil olive, being not so apt to make those that eat it constantly break out into scabs, as they do in many parts of Italy. This would grow very kindly here and has already been planted with good success in North Carolina by way of experiment.

7. After crossing the Dan, we made a march of eight miles over hills and dales as far as the next ford of that river. And now we were by practice become such very able footmen that we easily outwalked our horses and could have marched much farther, had it not been in pity to their weakness. Besides here was plenty of canes, which was reason enough to make us shorten our journey. Our gunners did great execution as they went along, killing no less than two brace of deer and as many wild turkeys.

Though practice will soon make a man of tolerable vigor an able footman, yet, as a help to bear fatigue, I used to chew a root of ginseng [51] as I walked along. This kept up my spirits and made me trip away as nimbly in my half-jack boots as younger men could do in their shoes. This plant is in high esteem in China, where it sells for its weight in silver. Indeed it does not grow there but in the mountains of Tartary, to which place the Emperor of China sends ten thousand men every year on purpose to gather it. But it grows so scatteringly there that even so

---

[51] Byrd was enthusiastic about ginseng for various ills and, like many others, regarded it as an aphrodisiac.

many hands can bring home no great quantity. Indeed, it is a vegetable of so many virtues that Providence has planted it very thin in every country that has the happiness to produce it. Nor, indeed, is mankind worthy of so great a blessing, since health and long life are commonly abused to ill purposes. This noble plant grows likewise at the Cape of Good Hope, where it is called "kanna" and is in wonderful esteem among the Hottentots. It grows also on the northern continent of America, near the mountains, but as sparingly as truth and public spirit. It answers exactly both to the figure and virtues of that which grows in Tartary, so that there can be no doubt of its being the same. Its virtues are that it gives an uncommon warmth and vigor to the blood and frisks the spirits beyond any other cordial. It cheers the heart even of a man that has a bad wife and makes him look down with great composure on the crosses of the world. It promotes insensible per-spiration, dissolves all phlegmatic and viscous humors, that are apt to obstruct the narrow channels of the nerves. It helps the memory and would quicken even Helvetian dullness. 'Tis friendly to the lungs, much more than scolding itself. It comforts the stomach and strength-ens the bowels, preventing all colics and fluxes. In one word, it will make a man live a great while, and very well while he does live. And what is more, it will even make old age amiable, by rendering it lively, cheerful, and good humored. However, 'tis of little use in the feats of love, as a great prince once found, who, hearing of its invigorating quality, sent as far as China for some of it, though his ladies could not boast of any advantage thereby.

We gave the Indian the skins of all the deer that he shot himself and the men the skins of what they killed. And every evening after the fires were made they stretched them very tight upon sticks and dried them. This, by a nocturnal fire, appeared at first a very odd spectacle, everything being dark and gloomy round about. After they are dried in this manner they may be folded up without damage till they come to be dressed according to art. The Indians dress them with deer's brains, and so do the English here by their example. For ex-pedition's sake, they often stretch their skins over smoke in order to dry them, which makes them smell so disagreeably that a rat must have a good stomach to gnaw them in that condition; nay, it is said, while that perfume continues in a pair of leather breeches, the person that wears them will be in no danger of that villainous little insect the French call *morpion.*

And now I am upon the subject of insects, it may not be improper to mention some few remedies against those that are most vexatious in this climate. There are two sorts withoutdoors that are great nuisances: the ticks and the horseflies. The ticks are either deer ticks or those that annoy the cattle. The first kind are long and take a very strong gripe, being most in remote woods above the inhabitants. The other are round and more gently insinuate themselves into the flesh, being in all places where cattle are frequent. Both these sorts are apt to be troublesome during the warm season, but have such an aversion to pennyroyal that they will attack no part that is rubbed with the juice of that fragrant vegetable. And a strong decoction of this is likewise the most effectual remedy against seed ticks, which bury themselves in your legs when they are so small you can hardly discern them without a microscope.

The horseflies are not only a great grievance to horses but likewise to those that ride them. These little vixens confine themselves chiefly to the woods and are most in moist places. Though this insect be no bigger than an ordinary fly, it bites very smartly, darting its little proboscis into the skin the instant it lights upon it. These are offensive only in the hot months and in the daytime, when they are a great nuisance to travelers; insomuch that it is no wonder they were formerly made use for one of the plagues of Egypt. But dittany, which is to be had in the woods all the while those insects remain in vigor, is a sure defense against them. For this purpose, if you stick a bunch of it on the headstall of your bridle, they will be sure to keep a respectful distance.

Thus, in what part of the woods soever anything mischievous or troublesome is found, kind Providence is sure to provide a remedy. And 'tis probably one great reason why God was pleased to create these and many other vexatious animals, that men should exercise their wits and industry to guard themselves against them.

Bears' oil is used by the Indians as a general defense against every species of vermin. Among the rest, they say it keeps both bugs and mosquitoes from assaulting their persons, which would otherwise devour such uncleanly people. Yet bears' grease has no strong smell, as that plant had which the Egyptians formerly used against mosquitoes, resembling our palma Christi,[52] the juice of which smelt so disagreeably that the remedy was worse than the disease. Against mosquitoes in Egypt, the richer sort used to build lofty towers, with bedchambers in the tops of them, that they might rest undisturbed. 'Tis certain that these insects are no high fliers, because their wings are weak and their bodies so light that if they mount ever so little the wind blows them quite away from their course and they become an easy prey to the martins, East India bats, and other birds that fly about in continual quest of them.

8. As we had twice more to cross the Dan over two fords that lay no more than seven miles from each other, we judged the distance would not be much greater to go round the bent of it. Accordingly, we sent the Indian and two white men that way, who came up with us in the evening, after fetching a compass of about twelve miles. They told us that about a mile from our last camp they passed a creek fortified with steep cliffs, which therefore gained the name of Cliff Creek. Near three miles beyond that they forded a second creek, on the margin of which grew abundance of tall canes, and this was called Hix's Creek from one of the discoverers. Between these two creeks lies a level of exceeding rich land, full of large trees, and covered with black mold, as fruitful, if we believe them, as that which is yearly overflowed by the Nile.

We who marched the nearest way upon the line found the ground rising and falling between the two fords of the Dan, which almost broke our own winds and the hearts of our jaded palfreys. When we had passed the last ford, it was a sensible joy to find ourselves safe over all the waters that might cut off our retreat. And we had the greater reason to be thankful because so late in the year it was very unusual to find the rivers so fordable.

[52] The castor-oil plant.

We catched a large terrapin in the river, which is one kind of turtle. The flesh of it is wholesome and good for consumptive people. It lays a great number of eggs, not larger but rounder than those of pigeons. These are soft but withal so tough that 'tis difficult to break them, yet are very sweet and invigorating, so that some wives recommend them earnestly to their husbands. One of the men, by an overstrain, had unhappily got a running of the reins, for which I gave him every morning a little sweet gum dissolved in water, with good success. This gum distills from a large tree, called the sweet gum tree, very common in Virginia, and is as healing in its virtue as balm of Gilead or the balsams of Tolú and of Peru. It is likewise a most agreeable perfume, very little inferior to ambergris.

And now I have mentioned ambergris, I hope it will not be thought an unprofitable digression to give a faithful account how it is produced, in order to reconcile the various opinions concerning it. It is now certainly found to be the dung of the spermaceti whale, which is at first very black and unsavory. But after having been washed for some months in the sea and blanched in the sun, it comes at length to be of a gray color, and from a most offensive smell contracts the finest fragrancy in the world. Besides the fragrancy of this animal substance, 'tis a very rich and innocent cordial, which raises the spirits without stupefying them afterwards like opium or intoxicating them like wine. The animal spirits are amazingly refreshed by this cordial, without the danger of any ill consequence, and if husbands were now and then to dissolve a little of it in their broth, their consorts might be the better for it as well as themselves. In the Bahama Islands (where a great quantity is found by reason the spermaceti whales resort thither continually), it is used as an antidote against the venomous fish which abound thereabouts, wherewith the people are apt to poison themselves. We are not only obliged to that whale for this rich perfume but also for the spermaceti itself, which is the fat of that fish's head boiled and purged from all its impurities. What remains is of a balsamic and detersive quality, very friendly to the lungs and useful in many other cases.

The Indian had killed a fat doe in the compass he took round the elbow of the river but was contented to prime it only, by reason it was too far off to lug the whole carcass upon his back. This and a brace of wild turkeys which our men had shot made up all our bill of fare this evening but could only afford a philosophical meal to so many craving stomachs. The horses were now so lean that anything would gall those that carried the least burden; no wonder, then, if several of them had sore backs, especially now the pads of the saddles and packs were pressed flat with long and constant use. This would have been another misfortune, had we not been provided with an easy remedy for it. One of the commissioners, believing that such accidents might happen in a far journey, had furnished himself with plasters of strong glue spread pretty thick. We laid on these, after making them running hot, which, sticking fast, never fell off till the sore was perfectly healed. In the meantime, it defended the part so well that the saddle might bear upon it without danger of further injury.

9. We reckoned ourselves now pretty well out of the latitude of bears, to the great grief of most of the company. There was still mast enough left in the woods to keep the bears from drawing so near to the inhabitants. They like not the neighborhood of merciless man till famine compels them to it. They are all black in this part of the world, and so is their dung, but [it] will make linen white, being tolerable good soap, without any preparation but only drying. These bears are of a moderate size, whereas within the polar circles they are white and much larger. Those of the southern parts of Muscovy are of a russet color, but among the Samoyeds,[53] as well as in Greenland and Nova Zembla, they are as white as the snow they converse with and, by some accounts, are as large as a moderate ox. The excessive cold of that climate sets their appetites so sharp, that they will attack a man without ceremony and even climb up a ship's side to come at him. They range about and are very mischievous all the time the sun is above the horizon, which is something more than five months; but after the sun is set for the rest of the year they retire into holes or bury themselves under the snow and sleep away the dark season without any sustenance at all. 'Tis pity our beggars and pickpockets could not do the same.

[53] A Mongoloid tribe of Siberia.

Our journey this day was above twelve miles and more than half the way terribly hampered with bushes. We tired another horse, which we were obliged to leave two miles short of where we encamped, and indeed several others were upon the careen almost every step. Now we wanted one of those celebrated musicians of antiquity who, they tell us, among many other wonders of their art, could play an air which by its animating briskness would make a jaded horse caper and curvet much better than any whip, spur, or even than swearing. Though I fear our poor beasts were so harassed that it would have been beyond the skill of Orpheus himself so much as to make them prick up their ears.

For proof of the marvelous power of music among the ancients, some historians say that one of those skillful masters took upon him to make the great Alexander start up from his seat and handle his javelin, whether he would or not, by the force of a sprightly tune which he knew how to play to him. The king ordered the man to bring his instruments, and then, fixing himself firmly in his chair and determining not to stir, he bade him strike up as soon as he pleased. The musician obeyed and presently roused the hero's spirits with such warlike notes that he was constrained, in spite of all his resolution, to spring up and fly to his javelin with great martial fury.

We can the easier credit these profane stories by what we find recorded in the oracles of truth, where we are told the wonders David performed by sweetly touching his harp. He made nothing of driving the evil spirit out of Saul, though a certain rabbi assures us he could not do so much by his wife, Michal, when she happened to be in her airs.

The greatest instance we have of the power of modern music is that which cures those who in Italy are bit by the little spider called the tarantula, the whole method of which is performed in the following manner: in Apulia 'tis a common misfortune for people to be bit by the tarantula, and most about Taranto and Gallipoli. This is a gray spider, not very large, with a narrow streak of white along the back. It is no wonder there are many of these villainous insects, because, by a ridiculous superstition, 'tis accounted great inhumanity to kill them. They believe, it seems, that if the spider come to a violent death, all those who had been bit by it will certainly have a return of their frenzy every year as long as they live. But if it die a natural death, the patient will have a chance to recover in two or three years.

The bite of the tarantula gives no more pain than the bite of a mosquito and makes little or no inflammation on the part, especially when the disaster happens in April or May; but its venom, increasing with the heat of the season, has more fatal consequences in July and August. The persons who are so unhappy as to be bitten in those warm months fall down on the place in a few minutes and lie senseless for a considerable time, and when they come to themselves feel horrible pains, are very sick at their stomachs, and in a short time break out into foul sores; but those who are bit in the milder months have much gentler symptoms. They are longer before the distemper shows itself, and then they have a small disorder in their senses, are a little sick, and perhaps have some moderate breakings-out.

However, in both cases the patient keeps upon the bed, not caring to stir till he is roused by a tune proper for his particular case. Therefore, as soon as the symptoms discover themselves, a tarantula doctor is sent for, who, after viewing carefully the condition of the person, first tries one tune and then another, till he is so fortunate as to hit the phrenetic turn of the patient. No sooner does this happen but he begins first to wag a finger, then a hand, and afterwards a foot, till at last he springs up and dances round the room with a surprising agility, rolling his eyes and looking wild the whole time. This dancing fit lasts commonly about twenty-five minutes, by which time he will be all in a lather. Then he sits down, falls a-laughing, and returns to his senses. So plentiful a perspiration discharges so much of the venom as will keep off the return of the distemper for a whole year. Then it will visit him again and must be removed in the same merry manner. But three dancing bouts will do the business, unless, peradventure, the spider, according to the vulgar notion, hath been put to a violent death.

The tunes played to expel this whimsical disorder are of the jig kind and exceed not fifteen in number. The Apulians are frequently dancing off the effects of this poison, and no remedy is more commonly applied to any other distemper elsewhere than those sprightly tunes are to the bite of the tarantula in that part of Italy.

It is remarkable that these spiders have a greater spite to the natives of the place than they have to strangers, and women are oftener bit than men. Though there may be a reason for the last, because women are more confined to the house, where these spiders keep, and their coats make them liable to attacks unseen, whereas the men can more easily discover and brush them off their legs. Nevertheless, both sexes are cured the same way and thereby show the wonderful effects of music.

Considering how far we had walked and, consequently, how hungry we were, we found but short commons when we came to our quarters. One brace of turkeys were all the game we could meet with, which almost needed a miracle to enable them to suffice so many voracious appetites. However, they just made a shift to keep famine, and consequently mutiny, out of the camp. At night we lodged upon the banks of Buffalo Creek, where none of us could complain of loss of rest for having eat too heavy and luxurious a supper.

10. In a dearth of provisions our chaplain pronounced it lawful to make bold with the Sabbath and send a party out a-hunting. They fired the dry leaves in a ring of five miles' circumference, which, burning inwards, drove all the game to the center, where they were easily killed. 'Tis really a pitiful sight to see the extreme distress the poor deer are in when they find themselves surrounded with this circle of fire; they weep and groan like a human creature, yet can't move the compassion of those hardhearted people who are about to murder them. This unmerciful sport is called fire-hunting and is much practiced by the Indians and frontier inhabitants, who sometimes, in the eagerness of their diversion, are punished for their cruelty and are hurt by one another when they shoot across at the deer which are in the middle.

What the Indians do now by a circle of fire the ancient Persians performed formerly by a circle of men; and the same is practiced at this day in Germany upon extraordinary occasions when any of the princes of the empire have a mind to make a general hunt, as they call it. At such times they order a vast number of people to surround a whole territory. Then, marching inwards in close order, they at last force all the wild beasts into a narrow compass, that the prince and his company may have the diversion of slaughtering as many as they please with their own hands. Our hunters massacred two brace of deer after this unfair way, of which they brought us one brace whole and only the primings of the rest.

So many were absent on this occasion that we who remained excused the chaplain from the trouble of spending his spirits by preaching to so thin a congregation.

One of the men, who had been an old Indian trader, brought me a stem of silk grass, which was about as big as my little finger. But, being so late in the year that the leaf was fallen off, I am not able to describe the plant. The Indians use it in all their little manufactures, twisting a thread of it that is prodigiously strong. Of this they make their baskets and the aprons which their women wear about their middles for decency's sake. These are long enough to wrap quite round them and reach down to their knees, with a fringe on the under part by way of ornament. They put on this modest covering with so much art that the most impertinent curiosity can't, in the negligentest of their motions or postures, make the least discovery. As this species of silk grass is much stronger than hemp, I make no doubt but sailcloth and cordage might be made of it with considerable improvement.

11. We had all been so refreshed by our day of rest that we decamped earlier than ordinary and passed the several fords of Hyco River. The woods were thick great part of this day's journey, so that we were forced to scuffle hard to advance seven miles, being equal in fatigue to double that distance of clear and open grounds. We took up our quarters upon Sugartree Creek, in the same camp we had lain when we came up, and happened to be entertained at supper with a rarity we had never had the fortune to meet with before during the whole expedition.

A little wide of this creek, one of the men had the luck to meet with a young buffalo of two years old. It was a bull which, notwithstanding he was no older, was as big as an ordinary ox. His legs were very thick and very short and his hoofs exceeding broad. His back rose into a kind of bunch a little above the shoulders, which I believe contributes not a little to that creature's enormous strength. His body is vastly deep from the shoulders to the brisket, sometimes six feet in those that are full grown. The portly figure of this animal is disgraced by a shabby little tail, not above twelve inches long. This he cocks up on end whenever he's in a passion and, instead of lowing or bellowing, grunts with no better grace than a hog. The hair growing on his head and neck is long and shagged and so soft that it will spin into thread not unlike mohair, which might be wove into a sort of camlet. Some people have stockings knit of it that would have served an Israelite during his forty years' march through the wilderness. Its horns are short and strong, of which the Indians make large spoons which they say will split and fall to pieces whenever poison is put into them. Its color is a dirty brown and its hide so thick that it is scarce penetrable. However, it makes very spongy sole leather by the ordinary method of tanning, though this fault might by good contrivance be mended.

As thick as this poor beast's hide was, a bullet made shift to enter it and fetch him down. It was found all alone, which seldom buffaloes are. They usually range about in herds like other cattle, and, though they differ something in figure, are certainly of the same species. There are two reasons for this opinion: the flesh of both has exactly the same taste and the mixed breed betwixt both, they say, will generate. All the difference I could perceive between the flesh of buffalo and common beef was that the flesh of the first was much yellower than that of the other and the lean something tougher. The men were so delighted with this new diet that the gridiron and frying pan had no more rest all night than a poor husband subject to curtain lectures.

Buffaloes may be easily tamed when they are taken young. The best way to catch them is to carry a milch mare into the woods and, when you find a cow and calf, to kill the cow and then, having catched the calf, to suckle it upon the mare. After once or twice sucking her, it will follow her home and become as gentle as another calf. If we could get into a breed of them, they might be made very useful, not only for the dairy, by giving an ocean of milk, but also for drawing vast and cumbersome weights by their prodigious strength. These, with the other advantages I mentioned before, would make this sort of cattle more profitable to the owner than any other we are acquainted with, though they would need a world of provender.

12. Before we marched this morning, every man took care to pack up some buffalo steaks in his wallet, besides what he crammed into his belly. When provisions were plenty, we always found it difficult to get out early, being too much embarrassed with a long-winded breakfast. However, by the strength of our beef, we made a shift to walk about twelve miles, crossing Bluewing and Tewahominy creeks. And because this last stream received its appellation from the disaster of a Tuscarora Indian, 'twill not be straggling much out of the way to say something of that particular nation.[54]

These Indians were heretofore very numerous and powerful, making, within time of memory, at least a thousand fighting men. Their habitation before the war with Carolina was on the north branch of Neuse River, commonly called Connecta Creek,[55] in a pleasant and fruitful country. But now the few that are left of that nation live on the north side of Moratuck, which is all that part of Roanoke below the great falls toward Albemarle Sound. Formerly there were seven towns of these savages, lying not far from each other, but now their number is greatly reduced. The trade they have had the misfortune to

[54] "The Tuscarora [of Iroquoian stock], who lived on the Roanoke and Tar-Pamlico Rivers until their migration northward, were an important people, though comparatively little is known about them . . . The seizure of more and more lands by the settlers led to resentment, and when the whites began to kidnap and enslave the Indians open warfare developed. In 1710 the Tuscarora sent a petition to the provisional government of Pennsylvania embodying their grievances. Eight proposals, each attested by a wampum belt, were framed to cover the relations between Indians and whites. These belts with their pitiful messages were finally sent to the Five Nations of the North. At the beginning of the first war between the Tuscarora and the whites the Indians had 15 towns and a fighting strength of 2,000. The war opened with the capture (September 1711) of Lawson and Baron de Graffenried. Lawson was put to death but de Graffenried was liberated. Five tribes then formed a compact to annihilate the whites, each operating in its own district . . . By 1714 the remnants of the Tuscarora migrated northward to take shelter with the Five Nations" (*North Carolina: A Guide to the Old North State* [Chapel Hill, 1944], pp. 26–27).
[55] This is now called Contentnea Creek, apparently a corruption of the name of Cotechney, a Tuscarora town in this area to which Lawson was taken by his captors in 1711.

drive with the English has furnished them constantly with rum, which they have used so immoderately that, what with the distempers and what with the quarrels it begat amongst them, it has proved a double destruction. But the greatest consumption of these savages happened by the war about twenty-five years ago, on account of some injustice the inhabitants of that province had done them about their lands. It was on that provocation they resented their wrongs a little too severely upon Mr. Lawson, who, under color of being Surveyor General, had encroached too much upon their territories, at which they were so enraged that they waylaid him and cut his throat from ear to ear but at the same time released the Baron de Graffenreid, whom they had seized for company, because it appeared plainly he had done them no wrong.

This blow was followed by some other bloody actions on the part of the Indians which brought on the war, wherein many of 'em were cut off and many were obliged to flee for refuge to the Senecas; so that now there remain so few that they are in danger of being quite exterminated by the Catawbas, their mortal enemies.

These Indians have a very odd tradition amongst them that many years ago their nation was grown so dishonest that no man could keep any of his goods or so much as his loving wife to himself; that, however, their god, being unwilling to root them out for their crimes, did them the honor to send a messenger from Heaven to instruct them and set them a perfect example of integrity and kind behavior toward one another. But this holy person, with all his eloquence and sanctity of life, was able to make very little reformation amongst them. Some few old men did listen a little to his wholesome advice, but all the young fellows were quite incorrigible. They not only neglected his precepts but derided and evil entreated his person. At last, taking upon him to reprove some young rakes of the Conechta[56] clan very sharply for their impiety, they were so provoked at the freedom of his rebukes that they tied him to a tree and shot him with arrows through the heart. But their god took instant vengeance on all who had a hand in that monstrous act by lightning from Heaven, and has ever since

[56] The same name as in "Conneccta Creek" on p. 302.

303

visited their nation with a continued train of calamities; nor will he ever leave off punishing and wasting their people till he shall have blotted every living soul of them out of the world.

Our hunters shot nothing this whole day but a straggling bear, which happened to fall by the hand of the very person who had been lately disarmed and put to flight, for which he declared war against the whole species.

13. We pursued our journey with all diligence and forded Ohimpamony Creek about noon, and from thence proceeded to Yapatsco, which we could not cross without difficulty. The beavers had dammed up the water much higher than we found it at our going-up, so that we were obliged to lay a bridge over a part that was shallower than the rest to facilitate our passage. Beavers have more of instinct, that half brother of reason, than any other animal, especially in matters of self-preservation. In their houses they always contrive a sally port, both toward the land and toward the water, that so they may escape by one if their retreat should happen to be cut off at the other. They perform all their works in the dead of night to avoid discovery and are kept diligently to it by the master beaver, which by his age or strength has gained to himself an authority over the rest. If any of the gang happen to be lazy or will not exert himself to the utmost in felling of trees or dragging them to the place where they are made use of, this superintendent will not fail to chastise him with the flat of the tail, wherewith he is able to give unmerciful strokes. They lie snug in their houses all day, unless some unneighborly miller chance to disturb their repose by demolishing their dams for supplying his mill with water. 'Tis rare to see one of them, and the Indians for that reason have hardly any way to take them but by laying snares near the place where they dam up the water. But the English hunters have found out a more effectual method, by using the following receipt: take the large pride of the beaver, squeeze all the juice out of it, then take the small pride and squeeze out about five or six drops; take the inside of sassafras bark, powder it, and mix it with the liquor, and place this bait conveniently for your steel trap.

The story of biting off their testicles to compound for their lives when they are pursued is a story taken upon trust by Pliny, like many others. Nor is it the beaver's testicles that carry the perfume, but they have a pair of glands just within the fundament as sweet as musk, that perfume their dung and communicate a strong scent to their testicles by being placed near them.

'Tis true several creatures have strange instincts for their preservation, as the Egyptian frog, we are told by Aelian, will carry a whole joint of a reed across its mouth, that it may not be swallowed by the ibis. And this long-necked fowl will give itself a clyster with its beak whenever it finds itself too costive or feverish. The dogs of that country lap the water of the Nile in a full trot, that they may not be snapped by the crocodiles.[57] Both beavers and wolves, we know, when one of their legs is catched in a steel trap, will bite it off, that they may escape with the rest.

The flesh of the beavers is tough and dry, all but the tail, which, like the parrot's tongue, was one of the farfetched rarities with which Heliogabalus used to furnish his luxurious table. The fur of these creatures is very valuable, especially in the more northern countries, where it is longer and finer. This the Dutch have lately contrived to mix with their wool and weave into a sort of drugget that is not only warm but wonderfully light and soft. They also make gloves and stockings of it that keep out the cold almost as well as the fur itself and don't look quite so savage.

There is a deal of rich low ground on Yapatsco Creek, but I believe liable to be overflowed in a fresh. However, it might be proper enough for rice, which receives but little injury from water. We encamped on the banks of Massamony Creek, after a journey of more than eleven

[57] Byrd probably used either the English translation of Claudius Aelianus by Abraham Fleming, printed in 1576 with the title *A Register of Histories*, or the 1665 English translation by Thomas Stanley titled *Claudius Aelianus His Various History*; in both of these editions the note about the frog appears as Chapter iii and that on the Nile dogs as chapter iv, which suggests that Byrd may have referred to the book itself when writing this section. Aelianus' frog uses the reed to protect itself from a snake. Byrd may have deliberately altered this to an ibis in order to be able to introduce the information about the ibis' method of maintaining metabolic regularity, a matter to which he gave great attention in his diary. The item (which Byrd could have found in Pliny) is included in the notes in the manuscript commonplace book in Byrd's hand recently acquired by the Virginia Historical Society.

miles. By the way we shot a fat doe and a wild turkey, which fed us all plentifully. And we have reason to say, by our own happy experience, that no man need to despair of his daily bread in the woods whose faith is but half so large as his stomach.

14. Being at length happily arrived within twenty miles of the uppermost inhabitants, we dispatched two men who had the ablest horses to go before and get a beef killed and some bread baked to refresh their fellow travelers upon their arrival. They had likewise orders to hire an express to carry a letter to the Governor giving an account that we were all returned in safety. This was the more necessary because we had been so long absent that many now began to fear we were by this time scalped and barbecued by the Indians.

We decamped with the rest of the people about ten o'clock and marched near twelve miles. In our way we crossed Nutbush Creek, and four miles farther we came upon a beautiful branch of Great Creek, where we took up our quarters. The tent was pitched on an eminence which overlooked a wide piece of low grounds, covered with reeds and watered by a crystal stream gliding through the middle of it. On the other side of this delightful valley, which was about half a mile wide, rose a hill that terminated the view and in the figure of a semicircle closed in upon the opposite side of the valley. This had a most agreeable effect upon the eye and wanted nothing but cattle grazing in the meadow and sheep and goats feeding on the hill to make it a complete rural landscape.

The Indian killed a fawn which, being upon its growth, was not fat but made some amends by being tender. He also shot an otter, but our people were now better fed than to eat such coarse food. The truth of it is, the flesh of this creature has a rank fishy taste and for that reason might be a proper regale for the Samoyeds, who drink the Czar of Muscovy's health and toast their mistresses in a bumper of train oil.[58] The Carthusians, to save their vow of eating no flesh, pronounce this amphibious animal to be a fish and feed upon it as such without wounding their consciences. The skin of the otter is very soft, and the Swedes make caps and socks of it, not only for warmth but also because

[58] Whale oil.

they fancy it strengthens the nerves and is good against all distempers of the brain. The otter is a great devourer of fish, which are its natural food, and whenever it betakes itself to a vegetable diet it is as some high-spirited wives obey their husbands, by pure necessity. They dive after their prey, though they can't continue long under water but thrust their noses up to the surface now and then for breath. They are great enemies to weirs set up in the rivers to catch fish, devouring or biting to pieces all they find there. Nor is it easy either to fright them from this kind of robbery, or to destroy them. The best way I could ever find was to float an old wheel just by the weir, and so soon as the otter has taken a large fish he will get upon the wheel to eat it more at his ease, which may give you an opportunity of firing upon him from the shore.

One of our people shot a large gray squirrel with a very bushy tail, a singular use of which our merry Indian discovered to us. He said whenever this little animal has occasion to cross a run of water, he launches a chip or piece of bark into the water on which he embarks and, holding up his tail to the wind, sails over very safely. If this be true, 'tis probable men learnt at first the use of sails from these ingenious little animals, as the Hottentots learnt the physical use of most of their plants from the baboons.

15. About three miles from our camp we passed Great Creek, and then, after traversing very barren grounds for five miles together, we crossed the trading path and soon after had the pleasure of reaching the uppermost inhabitant. This was a plantation belonging to Colonel Mumford, where our men almost burst themselves with potatoes and milk. Yet as great a curiosity as a house was to us foresters, yet still we chose to lie in the tent, as being much the cleanlier and sweeter lodging.

The trading path above-mentioned receives its name from being the route the traders take with their caravans when they go to traffic with the Catawbas and other southern Indians. The Catawbas live about 250 miles beyond Roanoke River, and yet our traders find their account in transporting goods from Virginia to trade with them at their own town. The common method of carrying on this Indian commerce is as follows: gentlemen send for goods proper for such a trade from England and then either venture them out at their own risk to the Indian towns or else credit some traders with them of substance and reputation, to be paid in skins at certain price agreed betwixt them. The goods for the Indian trade consist chiefly in guns, powder, shot, hatchets (which the Indians call tomahawks), kettles, red and blue planes,[59] Duffields,[60] Stroudwater blankets,[61] and some cutlery wares, brass rings, and other trinkets.

These wares are made up into packs and carried upon horses, each load being from 150 to 200 pounds, with which they are able to travel about twenty miles a day if forage happen to be plentiful. Formerly a hundred horses have been employed in one of these Indian caravans under the conduct of fifteen or sixteen persons only, but now the trade is much impaired, insomuch that they seldom go with half that number.

The course from Roanoke to the Catawbas is laid down nearest southwest and lies through a fine country that is watered by several beautiful rivers. Those of the greatest note are: first, Tar River, which is the upper part of Pamptico,[62] Flat River, Little River, and Eno River, all three branches of Neuse.

Between Eno and Saxapahaw rivers are the Haw old fields, which have the reputation of containing the most fertile high land in this part of the world, lying in a body of about fifty thousand acres. This Saxapahaw is the upper part of Cape Fear River, the falls of which lie many miles below the trading path. Some mountains overlook this rich spot of land, from whence all the soil washes down into the plain and is the cause of its exceeding fertility. Not far from thence the path crosses Aramanchy River,[63] a branch of Saxapahaw, and about forty

[59] I.e., plain cloth.
[60] Duffels, coarse woolen cloth, named for the town of the same name near Amsterdam.
[61] Coarse woolen blankets, named for Stroud, Gloucestershire, on the Thames and Severn canal.
[62] The old name for Pamlico River.
[63] Now Alamance Creek, in the county of the same name. The fact that most of the early settlers of the country were German led to the conjecture that the name originated from "Allemania." "Allemanni" is one of the spellings found in old records. But it is possible that this is simply a corruption of the original Indian name. An l-r interchange occurred in some Algonquian Indian dialects.

miles beyond that, Deep River, which is the north branch of Pee Dee. Then forty miles beyond that, the path intersects the Yadkin, which is there half a mile over and is supposed to be the south branch of the same Pee Dee.

The soil is exceedingly rich on both sides the Yadkin, abounding in rank grass and prodigious large trees, and for plenty of fish, fowl, and venison, is inferior to no part of the northern continent. There the traders commonly lie still for some days, to recruit their horses' flesh as well as to recover their own spirits. Six miles farther is Crane Creek, so named from its being the rendezvous of great armies of cranes, which wage a more cruel war at this day with the frogs and the fish than they used to do with the pygmies in the days of Homer.

About threescore miles more bring you to the first town of the Catawbas, called Nauvasa, situated on the banks of the Santee River. Besides this town, there are five others belonging to the same nation, lying all on the same stream within the distance of twenty miles. These Indians were all called formerly by the general name of the Usherees and were a very numerous and powerful people. But the frequent slaughters made upon them by the northern Indians and, what has been still more destructive by far, the intemperance and foul distempers introduced amongst them by the Carolina traders have now reduced their numbers to little more than four hundred fighting men, besides women and children. It is a charming place where they live, the air very wholesome, the soil fertile, and the winters are mild and serene.

In Santee River, as in several others of Carolina, a smaller kind of alligator is frequently seen, which perfumes the water with a musky smell. They seldom exceed eight feet in length in these parts, whereas near the equinoctial they come up to twelve or fourteen. And the heat of the climate don't only make them bigger but more fierce and voracious. They watch the cattle there when they come to drink and cool themselves in the river; and because they are not able to drag them into the deep water, they make up by stratagem what they want in force. They swallow great stones, the weight of which, being added to their strength, enables them to tug a moderate cow under water and, as soon as they have drowned her, discharge the stones out of their maw and then feast upon the carcass. However, as fierce and as strong as these monsters are, the Indians will surprise them napping as they float upon the surface, get astride upon their necks, then whip a short piece of wood like a truncheon into their jaws, and holding the ends with their two hands, hinder them from diving by keeping their mouths open; and when they are almost spent, they will make to the shore, where their riders knock them on the head and eat them.[64]

This amphibious animal is a smaller kind of crocodile, having the same shape exactly, only the crocodile of the Nile is twice as long, being when full grown from twenty to thirty feet. This enormous length is the more to be wondered at because the crocodile is hatched from an egg very little larger than that of a goose. It has a long head, which it can open very wide, with very sharp and strong teeth. Their eyes are small, their legs short, with claws upon their feet. Their tail makes half the length of their body, and the whole is guarded with hard impenetrable scales, except the belly, which is much softer and smoother. They keep much upon the land in the daytime but toward the evening retire into the water to avoid the cold dews of the night. They run pretty fast right forward but are very awkward and slow in turning by reason of their unwieldy length. It is an error that they have no tongue, without which they could hardly swallow their food; but in eating they move the upper jaw only, contrary to all other animals. The way of catching them in Egypt is with a strong hook fixed to the end of a chain and baited with a joint of pork, which they are very fond of. But a live hog is generally tied near, the cry of which allures them to the hook. This account of the crocodile will agree in most particulars with the alligator; only the bigness of the last cannot entitle it to the name of "leviathan," which Job gave formerly to the crocodile, and not to the whale as some interpreters would make us believe.

So soon as the Catawba Indians are informed of the approach of the Virginia caravans, they send a detachment of their warriors to bid them welcome and escort them safe to their town, where they are received with great marks of distinction. And their courtesies to the

[64] This method of capturing alligators is attributed by Pliny to a Nile people, who employed it with crocodiles (viii.38).

Virginia traders, I dare say, are very sincere, because they sell them better goods and better pennyworths than the traders of Carolina. They commonly reside among the Indians till they have bartered their goods away for skins, with which they load their horses and come back by the same path they went. There are generally some Carolina traders that constantly live among the Catawbas and pretend to exercise a dictatorial authority over them. These petty rulers don't only teach the honester savages all sorts of debauchery but are unfair in their dealings and use them with all kinds of oppression. Nor has their behavior been at all better to the rest of the Indian nations among whom they reside, by abusing their women and evil entreating their men; and, by the way, this was the true reason of the fatal war which the nations round about made upon Carolina in the year 1713.[65] Then it was that all the neighbor Indians, grown weary of the tyranny and injustice with which they had been abused for many years, resolved to endure their bondage no longer but entered into a general confederacy against their oppressors of Carolina. The Indians opened the war by knocking most of those little tyrants on the head that dwelt amongst them under pretense of regulating their commerce, and from thence carried their resentment so far as to endanger both North and South Carolina.

16. We gave orders that the horses should pass Roanoke River at Moniseep Ford, while most of the baggage was transported in a canoe. We landed at the plantation of Cornelius Keith, where I beheld the wretchedest scene of poverty I had ever met with in this happy part of the world. The man, his wife, and six small children lived in a pen like so many cattle, without any roof over their heads but that of Heaven. And this was their airy residence in the daytime; but then there was a fodder stack not far from this enclosure in which the whole family sheltered themselves anights and in bad weather. However, 'twas almost worth while to be as poor as this man was, to be as perfectly contented. All his wants proceeded from indolence and not from misfortune. He had good land, as well as good health and good limbs to

[65] After the Tuscaroras' massacre of the colonists in 1711 there were intermittent conflicts, culminating in a crushing defeat of the Tuscaroras in 1713.

work it and, besides, had a trade very useful to all the inhabitants round about. He could make and set up quernstones very well and had proper materials for that purpose just at hand if he could have taken the pains to fetch them. There are no other kind of mills in those remote parts, and, therefore, if the man would have worked at his trade, he might have lived very comfortably. The poor woman had a little more industry and spun cotton enough to make a thin covering for her own and her children's nakedness.

I am sorry to say it, but idleness is the general character of the men in the southern parts of this colony as well as in North Carolina. The air is so mild and the soil so fruitful that very little labor is required to fill their bellies, especially where the woods afford such plenty of game. These advantages discharge the men from the necessity of killing themselves with work, and then for the other article, of raiment, a very little of that will suffice in so temperate a climate. But so much as is absolutely necessary falls to the good women's share to provide. They all spin, weave, and knit, whereby they make a good shift to clothe the whole family; and to their credit be it recorded, many of them do it very completely and thereby reproach their husbands' laziness in the most inoffensive way, that is to say, by discovering a better spirit of industry in themselves.

From hence we moved forward to Colonel Mumford's other plantation, under the care of Miles Riley, where by that gentleman's directions we were again supplied with many good things. Here it was we discharged our worthy friend and fellow traveler, Mr. Bearskin, who had so plentifully supplied us with provisions during our long expedition. We rewarded him to his heart's content, so that he returned to his town loaden with riches and the reputation of having been a great discoverer.

17. This being Sunday, we were seasonably put in mind how much we were obliged to be thankful for our happy return to the inhabitants. Indeed, we had great reason to reflect with gratitude on the signal mercies we had received. First, that we had day by day been fed by the bountiful hand of Providence in the desolate wilderness, insomuch that if any of our people wanted one single meal during the

whole expedition, it was entirely owing to their own imprudent management. Secondly, that not one man of our whole company had any violent distemper or bad accident befall him, from one end of the line to the other. The very worst that happened was that one of them gave himself a smart cut on the pan of his knee with a tomahawk, which we had the good fortune to cure in a short time without the help of a surgeon. As for the misadventures of sticking in the mire and falling into rivers and creeks, they were rather subjects of mirth than complaint and served only to diversify our travels with a little farcical variety. And, lastly, that many uncommon incidents have concurred to prosper our undertaking. We had not only a dry spring before we went out, but the preceding winter, and even a year or two before, had been much drier than ordinary. This made not only the Dismal but likewise most of the sunken grounds near the seaside just hard enough to bear us, which otherwise had been quite unpassable. And the whole time we were upon the business, which was in all about sixteen weeks, we were never catched in the rain except once, nor was our progress interrupted by bad weather above three or four days at most.

Besides all this, we were surprised by no Indian enemy, but all of us brought our scalps back safe upon our heads. This cruel method of scalping of enemies is practiced by all the savages in America and perhaps is not the least proof of their original from the northern inhabitants of Asia. Among the ancient Scythians it was constantly used, who carried about these hairy scalps as trophies of victory. They served them too as towels at home and trappings for their horses abroad.[66] But these were not content with the skin of their enemies' heads but also made use of their skulls for cups to drink out of upon high festival days, and made greater ostentation of them than if they had been made of gold or the purest crystal.

Besides the duties of the day, we christened one of our men who had been bred a Quaker. The man desired this of his own mere motion, without being tampered with by the parson, who was willing everyone should go to Heaven his own way. But whether he did it by the conviction of his own reason or to get rid of some troublesome forms

[66] Byrd repeats himself; see p. 259.

and restraints to which the saints of that persuasion are subject, I can't positively say.

18. We proceeded over a level road twelve miles as far as George Hix's plantation on the south side Meherrin River, our course being for the most part northeast. By the way we hired a cart to transport our baggage, that we might the better befriend our jaded horses. Within two miles of our journey's end this day we met the express we had sent the Saturday before to give notice of our arrival. He had been almost as expeditious as [a] carrier pigeon, riding in two days no less than two hundred miles.

All the grandees of the Saponi nation did us the honor to repair hither to meet us, and our worthy friend and fellow traveler, Bearskin, appeared among the gravest of them in his robes of ceremony. Four young ladies of the first quality came with them, who had more the air of cleanliness than any copper-colored beauties I had ever seen; yet we resisted all their charms, notwithstanding the long fast we had kept from the sex and the bear diet we had been so long engaged in. Nor can I say the price they set upon their charms was at all exorbitant. A princess for a pair of red stockings can't, surely, be thought buying repentance much too dear.

The men had something great and venerable in their countenances, beyond the common mien of savages; and indeed they ever had the reputation of being the honestest as well as the bravest Indians we have ever been acquainted with. This people is now made up of the remnant of several other nations, of which the most considerable are the Saponis, the Occaneechis, and Stoukenhocks,[67] who, not finding themselves separately numerous enough for their defense, have agreed to unite into one body, and all of them now go under the name of the Saponis. Each of these was formerly a distinct nation, or rather a several clan or canton of the same nation, speaking the same language and using the same customs. But their perpetual wars against all other Indians in time reduced them so low as to make it necessary to join

[67] Another name for the Stegaraki, a Siouan tribe who were found by the early settlers on the Rappahannock. William Strachey called them the Stegaras and described them as at that time (1608–1609) "contributary" to the Manahoacs and confederates of the Monacans (*Historie of Travell*, p. 107).

their forces together. They dwelt formerly not far below the mountains, upon Yadkin River, about two hundred miles west and by south from the falls of Roanoke. But about twenty-five years ago they took refuge in Virginia, being no longer in condition to make head[68] not only against the northern Indians, who are their implacable enemies, but also against most of those to the south. All the nations round about, bearing in mind the havoc these Indians used formerly to make among their ancestors in the insolence of their power, did at length avenge it home[69] upon them and made them glad to apply to this government for protection. Colonel Spotswood, our then Lieutenant Governor, having a good opinion of their fidelity and courage, settled them at Christanna, ten miles north of Roanoke, upon the belief that they would be a good barrier on that side of the country against the incursion of all foreign Indians. And in earnest they would have served well enough for that purpose if the white people in the neighborhood had not debauched their morals and ruined their health with rum, which was the cause of many disorders and ended at last in a barbarous murder committed by one of these Indians when he was drunk, for which the poor wretch was executed when he was sober. It was matter of great concern to them, however, that one of their grandees should be put to so ignominious a death. All Indians have as great an aversion to hanging as the Muscovites, though perhaps not for the same cleanly reason, these last believing that the soul of one that dies in this manner, being forced to sally out of the body at the postern, must needs be defiled.

The Saponis took this execution so much to heart that they soon after quitted their settlement and removed in a body to the Catawbas. The daughter of the Totero[70] king went away with the Saponis, but, being the last of her nation and fearing she should not be treated according to her rank, poisoned herself, like an old Roman, with the root

[68] Make war.
[69] Completely.
[70] A variant form of Tutelo, originally applied by the Iroquois to all the Siouan tribes of Virginia. Byrd apparently refers, however, to a tribe that migrated from Salem, Virginia, to the junction of the Staunton and the Dan, later to the Yadkin, and in 1714 joined the Saponi and other tribes at Fort Christanna, only to move northward in 1722. They ultimately joined the League of the Iroquois.

of the trumpet plant. Her father died two years before, who was the most intrepid Indian we have been acquainted with. He had made himself terrible to all other Indians by his exploits and had escaped so many dangers that he was esteemed invulnerable. But at last he died of a pleurisy, the last man of his race and nation, leaving only that unhappy daughter behind him, who would not long survive him.

The most uncommon circumstance in this Indian visit was that they all come on horseback, which was certainly intended for a piece of state, because the distance was but three miles and 'tis likely they had walked afoot twice as far to catch their horses. The men rode more awkwardly than any Dutch sailor, and the ladies bestrode their palfreys *à la mode de France* but were so bashful about it that there was no persuading them to mount till they were quite out of our sight. The French women use to ride astraddle, not so much to make them sit firmer in the saddle as from the hopes the same thing might peradventure befall them that once happened to the nun of Orleans, who, escaping out of a nunnery, took post *en cavalier* and in ten miles' hard riding had the good fortune to have all the tokens of a man break out upon her. This piece of history ought to be the more credible because it leans upon much the same degree of proof as the tale of Bishop Burnet's two Italian nuns, who, according to His Lordship's account, underwent the same happy metamorphosis, probably by some other violent exercise.[71]

19. From hence we dispatched the cart with our baggage under a guard and crossed Meherrin River, which was not thirty yards wide in that place. By the help of fresh horses that had been sent us, we now began to mend our pace, which was also quickened by the strong inclinations we had to get home. In the distance of five miles we forded Meherrin Creek, which was very near as broad as the river. About eight miles farther we came to Sturgeon Creek, so called from the dexterity an Occaneechi Indian showed there in catching one of those royal fish, which was performed after the following manner: in the summertime 'tis no unusual thing for sturgeons to sleep on the sur-

[71] Gilbert Burnet, Bishop of Salisbury, *Some Letters Containing an Account of What Seemed Most Remarkable in Switzerland, Italy, etc.* (Rotterdam, 1686), pp. 246–247.

face of the water, and one of them, having wandered up into this creek in the spring, was floating in that drowsy condition. The Indian above-mentioned ran up to the neck into the creek a little below the place where he discovered the fish, expecting the stream would soon bring his game down to him. He judged the matter right, and as soon as it came within his reach, he whipped a running noose over his jowl. This waked the sturgeon, which, being strong in its own element, darted immediately under water and dragged the Indian after him. The man made it a point of honor to keep his hold, which he did to the apparent danger of being drowned. Sometimes both the Indian and the fish disappeared for a quarter of a minute and then rose at some distance from where they dived. At this rate they continued flouncing about, sometimes above and sometimes under water, for a considerable time, till at last the hero suffocated his adversary and haled his body ashore in triumph.

About six miles beyond that, we passed over Wiccoquoi Creek,[72] named so from the multitude of rocks over which the water tumbles in a fresh with a bellowing noise. Not far from where we went over is a rock much higher than the rest that strikes the eye with agreeable horror, and near it a very talkative echo that like a fluent helpmeet will return her goodman seven words for one and after all be sure to have the last. It speaks not only the language of men but also of birds and beasts, and often a single wild goose is cheated into the belief that some of his company are not far off by hearing his own cry multiplied; 'tis pleasant to see in what a flutter the poor bird is when he finds himself disappointed. On the banks of this creek are very broad, low grounds in many places and abundance of good high land, though a little subject to floods.

We had but two miles more to Captain Embry's, where we found the housekeeping much better than the house. Our bountiful landlady had set her oven and all her spits, pots, gridirons, and saucepans to work to diversify our entertainment, though after all it proved but a Mahometan feast, there being nothing to drink but water. The worst of it was we had unluckily outrid the baggage and for that reason were

[72] Waqua Creek. Various spellings of the name appear in the manuscript.

obliged to lodge very sociably in the same apartment with the family, where, reckoning women and children, we mustered in all no less than nine persons, who all pigged lovingly together.

20. In the morning Colonel Bolling, who had been surveying in the neighborhood, and Mr. Walker, who dwelt not far off, came to visit us; and the last of these worthy gentlemen, fearing that our drinking so much water might incline us to pleurisies, brought us a kind supply both of wine and cider. It was noon before we could disengage ourselves from the courtesies of this place, and then the two gentlemen above-mentioned were so good as to accompany us that day's journey, though they could by no means approve of our Lithuanian fashion of dismounting now and then in order to walk part of the way on foot.

We crossed Nottoway River not far from our landlord's house, where it seemed to be about twenty-five yards over. This river divides the county of Prince George from that of Brunswick. We had not gone eight miles farther before our eyes were blessed with the sight of Sapony Chapel, which was the first house of prayer we had seen for more than two calendar months. About three miles beyond that, we passed over Stony Creek, where one of those that guarded the baggage killed a polecat, upon which he made a comfortable repast. Those of his company were so squeamish they could not be persuaded at first to taste, as they said, of so unsavory an animal; but seeing the man smack his lips with more pleasure than usual, they ventured at last to be of his mess, and instead of finding the flesh rank and high tasted they owned it to be the sweetest morsel they had ever eat in their lives. The ill savor of this little beast lies altogether in its urine,[73] which nature had made so detestably ill scented on purpose to furnish a helpless creature with something to defend itself. For as some brutes have horns and hoofs, and others are armed with claws, teeth, and tusks for their defense; and as some spit a sort of poison at their adversaries, like the paco; and others dart quills at their pursuers, like the porcupine; and as some have no weapons to help themselves but their tongues, and others none but their tails; so the poor polecat's safety lies altogether in the irresistible stench of its water, insomuch that

[73] Byrd is mistaken in thinking that the skunk's offensive secretion is urine.

318

when it finds itself in danger from an enemy it moistens its bushy tail plentifully with this liquid ammunition and then, with great fury, sprinkles it like a shower of rain full into the eyes of its assailant, by which it gains time to make its escape. Nor is the polecat the only animal that defends itself by a stink. At the Cape of Good Hope is a little beast called a "stinker," as big as a fox and shaped like [a] ferret, which, being pursued, has no way to save himself but by farting and squittering, and then such a stench ensues that none of its pursuers can possibly stand it.

At the end of thirty good miles, we arrived in the evening at Colonel Bolling's, where first from a primitive course of life we began to relapse into luxury. This gentleman lives within hearing of the falls of Appomattox River, which are very noisy whenever a flood happens to roll a greater stream than ordinary over the rocks. The river is navigable for small craft as high as the falls and at some distance from thence fetches a compass and runs near parallel with James River almost as high as the mountains.

While the commissioners fared sumptuously here, the poor chaplain and two surveyors stopped ten miles short at a poor planter's house in pity to their horses, where they made a St. Anthony's meal, that is, they supped upon the pickings of what stuck in their teeth ever since breakfast. But to make them amends, the good man laid them in his own bed, where they all three nestled together in one cotton sheet and one of brown Osnaburgs, made still something browner by two months' copious perspiration.

21. But those worthy gentlemen were so alert in the morning after their light supper that they came up with us before breakfast and honestly paid their stomachs all they owed them.

We made no more than a Sabbath Day's journey from this to the next hospitable house, namely, that of our great benefactor, Colonel Mumford. We had already been much befriended by this gentleman, who, besides sending orders to his overseers at Roanoke to let us want for nothing, had in the beginning of our business been so kind as to recommend most of the men to us who were the faithful partners of our fatigue. Although in most other achievements those who command are apt to take all the honor to themselves of what perhaps was more owing to the vigor of those who were under them, yet I must be more just and allow these brave fellows their full share of credit for the service we performed and must declare that it was in a great measure owing to their spirit and indefatigable industry that we overcame many obstacles in the course of our line which till then had been esteemed insurmountable. Nor must I at the same time omit to do justice to the surveyors, and particularly to Mr. Mayo, who, besides an eminent degree of skill, encountered the same hardships and underwent the same fatigue that the forwardest of the men did, and that with as much cheerfulness as if pain had been his pleasure and difficulty his real diversion. Here we discharged the few men we had left, who were all as ragged as the Gibeonite ambassadors, though, at the same time, their rags were very honorable by the service they had so vigorously performed in making them so.

22. A little before noon we all took leave and dispersed to our several habitations, where we were so happy as to find all our families well. This crowned all our other blessings and made our journey as prosperous as it had been painful. Thus ended our second expedition, in which we extended the line within the shadow of the Cherokee mountains, where we were obliged to set up our pillars, like Hercules, and return home. We had now, upon the whole, been out about sixteen weeks, including going and returning, and had traveled at least six hundred miles, and no small part of that distance on foot. Below, toward the seaside, our course lay through marshes, swamps, and great waters; and above, over steep hills, craggy rocks, and thickets, hardly penetrable. Notwithstanding this variety of hardship, we may say without vanity that we faithfully obeyed the King's orders and performed the business effectually in which we had the honor to be employed. Nor can we by any means reproach ourselves of having put the Crown to any exorbitant expense in this difficult affair, the whole charge, from beginning to end, amounting to no more than £1,000.[74] But let no one concerned in this painful expedition complain of the

---

[74] As in the *Secret History*, the total of the disbursements enumerated is actually only £999.

scantiness of his pay so long as His Majesty has been graciously pleased to add to our reward the honor of his royal approbation and to declare, notwithstanding the desertion of the Carolina commissioners, that the line by us run shall hereafter stand as the true boundary betwixt the governments of Virginia and North Carolina.

# APPENDIX

to the foregoing journal, containing the second charter to the proprietors of Carolina confirming and enlarging the first and also several other acts to which it refers. These are placed by themselves at the end of the book that they may not interrupt the thread of the story and the reader will be more at liberty whether he will please to read them or not, being something dry and unpleasant.

---

*The second charter granted by King Charles II to the Proprietors of Carolina* [75]

CHARLES, by the grace of God, etc.

Whereas, by our letters patent bearing date the four-and-twentieth day of March in the fifteenth year of our reign we were graciously pleased to grant unto our right trusty and right well-beloved cousin and counselor, Edward, Earl of Clarendon, our High Chancellor of England; our right trusty and right entirely beloved cousin and counselor, George, Duke of Albemarle, Master of our Horse; our right trusty and well-beloved William, now Earl of Craven; [76] our right trusty and well-beloved counselor, Anthony, Lord Ashley, Chancellor of our Exchequer; our right trusty and well-beloved counselor, Sir George Carteret, knight and baronet, Vice Chamberlain of our household; our right trusty and well-beloved Sir John Colleton, knight and baronet; and Sir William Berkeley, knight, all that province, territory, or tract of ground called Carolina, situate, lying, and being within our dominions of America, extending from the north end of the island called Luke Island, which lies in the southern Virginia seas and within six-and-thirty degrees of the northern latitude; and to the west as far as the South Seas; and so respectively as far as the river of Mathias, which bordereth upon the coast of Florida, and within one-and-thirty de-

[75] We have followed the example of previous editors in reprinting only the portion of the charter relevant to the controversy. For the complete document see *North Carolina Charters and Constitutions, 1578–1698,* edited by Mattie E. E. Parker (Raleigh, 1963), pp. 90–104. The transcription of the document as printed therein appears to have several misreadings.

[76] The manuscript inadvertently omits the name of John, Lord Berkeley, following that of the Earl of Craven.

grees of the northern latitude; and so west in a direct line as far as the South Seas aforesaid.

Now know ye that we, at the humble request of the said grantees in the aforesaid letters patent named, and as a further mark of our especial favor toward them, we are graciously pleased to enlarge our said grant unto them according to the bounds and limits hereafter specified; and in favor to the pious and noble purpose of the said Edward, Earl of Clarendon; George, Duke of Albemarle; William, Earl of Craven; John, Lord Berkeley; Anthony, Lord Ashley; Sir George Carteret, Sir John Colleton, and Sir William Berkeley, we do give and grant to them, their heirs and assigns, all that province, territory, or tract of ground situate, lying, and being within our dominions of America aforesaid, extending north and eastward as far as the north end of Currituck River or Inlet, upon a straight westerly line to Weyanoke Creek, which lies within or about the degrees of 36° 30′ northern latitude, and so west in a direct line as far as the South Seas; and south and westward as far as the degrees of twenty-nine inclusive northern latitude, and so west in a direct line as far as the South Seas; together with all and singular ports, harbors, bays, rivers, and inlets belonging unto the province or territory aforesaid. And also, all the soil, lands, fields, woods, mountains, firms, lakes, rivers, bays and inlets situate or being within the bounds or limits last before mentioned; with the fishing of all sorts of fish, whales, sturgeons, and all other royal fishes in the sea, bays, inlets, and rivers within the premises, and the fish therein taken; together with the royalty of the sea, upon the coast within the limits aforesaid. And, moreover, all veins, mines, and quarries, as well discovered as not discovered, of gold, silver, gems, and precious stones, and all other whatsoever, be it of stones, metals, or any other thing found or to be found within the province, territory, inlets, and limits aforesaid. . . .

---

*At the Court of St. James, the first day of March, 1710.*
*Present, the Queen's Most Excellent Majesty in Council*

Upon reading this day at the Board a representation from the Right Honorable the Lords Commissioners for Trade and Plantations, in the words following:

In pursuance of Your Majesty's pleasure, commissioners have been appointed on the part of Your Majesty's colony of Virginia, as likewise on the part of the province of Carolina, for the settling the bounds between those governments; and they have met several times for that purpose but have not agreed upon any one point thereof, by reason of the trifling delays of the Carolina commissioners and of the many difficulties by them raised in relation to the proper observations and survey they were to make. However, the commissioners for Virginia have delivered to Your Majesty's Lieutenant Governor of that colony an account of their proceedings, which account has been under the consideration of Your Majesty's Council of Virginia, and they have made a report thereon to the said Lieutenant Governor, who having lately transmitted unto us a copy of that report, we take leave humbly to lay the substance thereof before Your Majesty, which is as follows.

That the commissioners of Carolina are both of them persons engaged in interest to obstruct the settling the boundaries between that province and the colony of Virginia; for one of them has for several years been Surveyor General of Carolina, has acquired to himself great profit by surveying lands within the controverted bounds, and has taken up several tracts of land in his own name and sold the same to others, for which he stands still obliged [to] obtain patents from the government of Carolina. The other of them is at this time Surveyor General and hath the same prospect of advantage by making future surveys within the said bounds.

That the behavior of the Carolina commissioners has tended visibly to no other end than to protract and defeat the settling this affair; and particularly Mr. Moseley has used so many shifts and excuses to disappoint all conferences with the commissioners of Virginia as plainly show his aversion to proceed in a business that tends so manifestly to his disadvantage. His prevaricating on this occasion has been so undiscreet and so unguarded as to be discovered in the presence of the Lieutenant Governor of Virginia. He started so many objections to the powers granted to the commissioners of that colony, with design to render their conferences ineffectual, that his joint commissioner could hardly find an excuse for him. And when the Lieutenant Governor had with much ado prevailed with the said Mr. Moseley to appoint a time for meeting the commissioners of Virginia and for bringing the necessary instruments to take the latitude of the bounds in dispute, which instruments he owned were ready in Carolina, he not only failed to comply with his own appointment, but, after the commissioners of Virginia had made a journey to his house and had attended him to the places proper for observing the latitude, he would not take the trouble of carrying his own instrument but contented himself to find fault with the quadrant produced by the Virginia commissioners, though that instrument had been approved by the best mathematicians and is of universal use.

From all which it is evident how little hopes there are of settling the boundaries above-mentioned in concert with the present commissioners for Carolina.

That though the bounds of the Carolina charter are in express words limited to Weyanoke Creek, lying in or about 36° 30′ of northern latitude, yet the commissioners for Carolina have not by any of their evidences pretended to prove any such place as Weyanoke Creek, the amount of their evidence reaching no further than to prove which is Weyanoke River, and even that is contradicted by affidavits taken on the part of Virginia; by which affidavits it appears that before the date of the Carolina charter to this day the place they pretend to be Weyanoke River was, and is still, called Nottoway River. But supposing the same had been called Weyanoke River, it can be nothing to their purpose, there being a great difference between a river and a creek. Besides, in that country there are divers rivers and creeks of the same name, as Potomac River and Potomac Creek, Rappahannock River and Rappahannock Creek, and several others, though there are many miles′ distance between the mouths of these rivers and the mouths of these creeks.

It is also observable that the witnesses on the part of Carolina are all very ignorant persons, and most of them of ill fame and reputation, on which account they had been forced to remove from Virginia to Carolina. Further, there appeared to be many contradictions in their testimonies, whereas, on the other hand, the witnesses to prove that the right to those lands is in the government of Virginia are persons of good credit, their knowledge of the lands in question is more ancient than any of the witnesses for Carolina and their evidence fully corroborated by the concurrent testimony of the tributary Indians. And that right is further confirmed by the observations lately taken of the latitude in those parts; by which 'tis plain that the creek proved to be Weyanoke Creek by the Virginia evidences and sometimes called Wiccacon answers best to the latitude described in the Carolina charter, for it lies in 36° 40′, which is ten minutes to the northward of the limits described in the Carolina grant, whereas Nottoway River lies exactly in the latitude of 37° and can by no construction be supposed to be the boundary described in their charter. So that upon the whole matter, if the commissioners of Carolina had no other view than to clear the just right of the Proprietors, such undeniable demonstrations would be sufficient to convince them; but the said commissioners give too much cause to suspect that they mix their own private interest with the claim of the Proprietors and for that reason endeavor to gain time in order to obtain grants for the land already taken up and also to secure the rest on this occasion; we take notice, that they proceed to survey the land in dispute, notwithstanding the assurance given by the government of Carolina to the contrary by their letter of the seventeenth of June, 1707, to the government of Virginia, by which letter they promised that no lands should be taken up within the controverted bounds till the same were settled.

Whereupon we humbly propose that the Lords Proprietors be acquainted with the foregoing complaint of the trifling delays of their commissioners, which delays, 'tis reasonable to believe, have proceeded from the self-interest of those commissioners, and that therefore Your Majesty's pleasure be signified to the said Lords Proprietors, that by the first opportunity they send orders to their Governor or commander in chief of Carolina for the time being to issue forth a new commission, to the purport of that lately issued, thereby constituting two other persons, not having any personal interest in or claim to any of the land lying within the boundaries, in the room of Edward Moseley and John Lawson. The Carolina commissioners to be appointed being strictly required to finish their survey and to make a return thereof in conjunction with the Virginia commissioners within six months, to be computed from the time that due notice shall be given by Your Majesty's Lieutenant Governor of Virginia to the Governor or commander in chief of Carolina of the time and place which Your Majesty's said Lieutenant Governor shall appoint for the first meeting of the commissioners on one part and the other. In order whereunto, we humbly offer that directions be sent to the said Lieutenant Governor to give such notice accordingly; and if, after notice so given, the Carolina commissioners shall refuse or neglect to join with those on the part of Virginia in making such survey, as likewise a return thereof within the time before mentioned, that then and in such case the commissioners on the part of Virginia be directed to draw up an account of the proper observations and survey, which they shall have made for ascertaining the bounds between Virginia and Carolina, and to deliver the same in writing under their hands and seals to the Lieutenant Governor and Council of Virginia, to the end the same may be laid before Your Majesty for Your Majesty's final determination therein, within, with regard to the settling of those boundaries; the Lords Proprietors having, by an instrument under their hands, submitted the same to Your Majesty's royal determination, which instrument, dated in March 1708, is lying in this office.

And lastly, we humbly propose that Your Majesty's further pleasure be signified to the said Lords Proprietors, and in like manner to the Lieutenant Governor of Virginia, that no grants be passed by either of those governments of any of the lands lying within the controverted bounds until such bounds shall be ascertained and settled as aforesaid, whereby it may appear whether those lands do of right belong to Your Majesty or to the Lords Proprietors of Carolina.

Her Majesty in Council, approving of the said representation, is pleased to order, as it is hereby ordered, that the Right Honorable the Lords Commissioners for Trade and Plantations do signify Her Majesty's pleasure herein to Her Majesty's Lieutenant Governor or commander in chief of Virginia for the time being, and to all persons to whom it may belong, as is proposed by Their Lordships in the said representation, and the Right Honorable the Lords Proprietors of Carolina are to do what on their part does appertain.

EDWARD SOUTHWELL

---

*Proposals for determining the controversy relating to the bounds between the governments of Virginia and North Carolina, most humbly offered for His Majesty's royal approbation and for the consent of the Right Honorable the Lords Proprietors of Carolina*

Forasmuch as the dispute between the said two governments about their true limits continues still, notwithstanding the several meetings of the commissioners and all the proceedings of many years past, in order to adjust that affair, and seeing no speedy determination is likely to ensue unless some medium be found out in which both parties may incline to acquiesce: wherefore both the underwritten governors, having met and considered the prejudice both to the King and the Lords Proprietors' interest by the continuance of this contest, and truly endeavoring a decision which they judge comes nearest the intention of royal charter granted to the Lords Proprietors, do, with the advice and consent of their respective councils, propose as follows.

That from the mouth of Currituck River or Inlet, and setting the compass on the north shore thereof, a due-west line be run and fairly marked, and if it happen to cut Chowan River, between the mouths of Nottoway River and Wiccacon Creek, then shall the same direct course be continued toward the mountains and be ever deemed the sole dividing line between Virginia and Carolina.

That if the said west line cuts Chowan River to the southward of Wiccacon Creek, then from point of intersection the bounds shall be allowed to continue up the middle of the said Chowan River to the middle of the entrance into the said Wiccacon Creek, and from thence a due-west line shall divide the said two governments.

That if a due-west line shall be found to pass through islands or to cut out small slips of land, which might much more conveniently be included in one province or the other by natural water bounds, in such cases the persons appointed for running the line shall have power to settle natural

327

bounds, provided the commissioners of both sides agree thereto and that all such variations from the west line be particularly noted in the maps or plats which they shall return to be put upon the records of both governments. All which is humbly submitted by

CHARLES EDEN

A. SPOTSWOOD

———

*Order of the King and Council upon the foregoing proposals, at the Court of St. James, the twenty-eighth day of March, 1729.[77] Present, the King's Most Excellent Majesty in Council*

Whereas it has been represented to His Majesty at the Board that for adjusting the disputes which have subsisted for many years past between the colonies of Virginia and North Carolina concerning their true boundaries, the late governors of the said colonies did some time since agree upon certain proposals for regulating the said boundaries for the future, to which proposals the Lords Proprietors of Carolina have given their assent; and whereas the said proposals were this day presented to His Majesty as proper for his royal approbation,

His Majesty is thereupon pleased, with the advice of his Privy Council, to approve of the said proposals, a copy whereof is hereunto annexed, and to order, as it is hereby ordered, that the Governor or commander in chief of the colony of Virginia do settle the said boundaries in conjunction with the Governor of North Carolina agreeable to the said proposals.

EDWARD SOUTHWELL

———

*The Lieutenant Governor of Virginia's commission in obedience to His Majesty's order*

George the Second, by the grace of God of Great Britain, France, and Ireland King, Defender of the Faith, to our trusty and well-beloved William Byrd, Richard Fitzwilliam, and William Dandridge, Esqrs., members of our Council of the colony and dominion of Virginia, greeting:

Whereas our late royal father of blessed memory was graciously pleased, by order in his Privy Council bearing date the twenty-eighth day of March, 1727, to approve of certain proposals agreed upon by Alexander Spotswood, Esq., late Lieutenant Governor of Virginia, on the one part, and Charles Eden, Esq., late Governor of the province of North Carolina, for determining the controversy relating to the bounds between the said two

[77] A scribal error for "1727."

governments, and was farther pleased to direct and order that the said boundaries should be laid out and settled agreeable to the said proposals. Know ye, therefore, that reposing special trust and confidence in your ability and provident circumspection, [we] have assigned, constituted, and appointed, and by these presents do assign, constitute, and appoint you and every of you, jointly and severally, our commissioners for and on behalf of our colony and dominion of Virginia to meet the commissioners appointed or to be appointed on the part of the province of North Carolina, and in conjunction with them to cause a line or lines of division to be run and marked to divide the said two governments according to the proposals above-mentioned and the order of our late royal father, copies of both which you will herewith receive.

And we do farther give and grant unto you — and in case of the death or absence of any of you, such of you as shall be present — full power and authority to treat and agree with the said commissioners of the province of North Carolina on such rules and methods as you shall judge most expedient for the adjusting and finally determining all disputes or controversies which may arise touching any islands or other small slips of land which may happen to be intersected or cut off by the dividing line aforesaid and which may with more conveniency be included in the one province or the other by natural water bounds agreeable to the proposals afore-mentioned, and generally to do and perform all matters and things requisite for the final determination and settlement of the said boundaries according to the said proposals.

And to the end our service herein may not be disappointed through the refusal or delay of the commissioners for the province of North Carolina to act in conjunction with you in settling the boundaries aforesaid, we do hereby give and grant unto you, or such of you as shall be present at the time and place appointed for running the dividing line aforesaid, full power and authority to cause the said line to be run and marked out, conformable to the said proposals, having due regard to the doing equal justice to us and to the Lords Proprietors of Carolina, any refusal, disagreement, or opposition of the said commissioners of North Carolina notwithstanding. And in that case we do hereby require you to make a true report of your proceedings to our Lieutenant Governor or commander in chief of Virginia, in order to be laid before us for our approbation and final determination herein.

And in case any person or persons whatsoever shall presume to disturb, molest, or resist you, or any of the officers or persons by your direction, in running the said line and executing the powers herein given you, we do by these presents give and grant unto you, or such of you as shall be attending the service aforesaid, full power and authority by warrant under your or any of your hands and seals to order and command all and every the militia officers in our counties of Princess Anne, Norfolk, Nansemond, and Isle of Wight, or other the adjacent counties, together with the sheriff of each of the said counties, or either of them, to raise the militia and posse of the said several counties for the removing all force and opposition which shall or may be made to you in the due execution of this our commission; and we do hereby will and require as well the officers of the said militia as all other our officers and loving subjects within the said counties and all others whom it may concern, to be obedient, aiding, and assisting unto you in all and singular the premises.

And we do in like manner command and require you to cause fair maps and descriptions of the said dividing line and the remarkable places through which it shall pass to be made and returned to our Lieutenant Governor or commander in chief of our said colony for the time being, in order to be entered on record in the proper offices within our said colony. Provided that you do not, by color of this our commission, take upon you or determine any private man's property, in or to the lands which shall by the said dividing line be included within the limits of Virginia, nor of any other matter or thing that doth not relate immediately to the adjusting, settling, and final determination of the boundary aforesaid, conformable to the proposals hereinbefore mentioned and not otherwise. In witness whereof we have caused these presents to be made. Witness our trusty and well-beloved William Gooch, Esq., our Lieutenant Governor and commander in chief of our colony and dominion of Virginia, under the seal of our said colony, at Williamsburg, the fourteenth day of December, 1727, in the first year of our reign.

WILLIAM GOOCH

---

*The Governor of North Carolina's commission in obedi-
ence to His Majesty's order*

Sir Richard Everard, Baronet, Governor, Captain General, Admiral, and Commander in Chief of the said province, to Christopher Gale, Esq., Chief Justice; John Lovick, Esq., Secretary; Edward Moseley, Esq., Surveyor General; and William Little, Esq., Attorney General, greeting:

Whereas many disputes and differences have formerly been between the inhabitants of this province and those of His Majesty's colony of Virginia concerning the boundaries and limits between the said two governments, which having been duly considered by Charles Eden, Esq., late

Governor of this province, and Alexander Spotswood, Esq., late Governor of Virginia, they agreed to certain proposals for determining the said controversy and humbly offered the same for His Majesty's royal approbation and the consent of the true and absolute Lords Proprietors of Carolina. And His Majesty having been pleased to signify his royal approbation of those proposals (consented unto by the true and absolute Lords Proprietors of Carolina) and given directions for adjusting and settling the boundaries as near as may be to the said proposals,

I, therefore, reposing especial trust and confidence in you, the said Christopher Gale, John Lovick, Edward Moseley, and William Little, to be commissioners on the part of the true and absolute Lords Proprietors, and that you, in conjunction with such commissioners as shall be nominated for Virginia, use your utmost endeavors and take all necessary care in adjusting and settling the said boundaries by drawing such a distinct line or lines of division between the said two provinces as near as reasonable you can to the proposals made by the two former governors and the instructions herewith given you.

Given at the council chamber in Edenton, under my hand and the seal of the colony, the twenty-first day of February, anno Domini 1727, and in the first year of the reign of our sovereign lord, King George the Second.

RICHARD EVERARD

---

*The protest of the Carolina commissioners against our*
*proceeding on the line without them*

We, the underwritten commissioners for the government of North Carolina, in conjunction with the commissioners on the part of Virginia, having run the line for the division of the two colonies from Currituck Inlet to the south branch of Roanoke River — being in the whole about 170 miles and near 50 miles without the inhabitants — being of opinion we had run the line as far as would be requisite for a long time, judged the carrying it farther would be a needless charge and trouble. And the grand debate which had so long subsisted between the two governments about Weyanoke River or Creek being settled at our former meeting in the spring, when we were ready on our parts to have gone with the line to the utmost inhabitants, which if it had been done, the line at any time after might have been continued at an easy expense by a surveyor on each side; and if at any time hereafter there should be occasion to carry the line on further than we have now run it — which, we think, will not be in an age or two — it may be done in the same easy manner without the great expense that now attends it. And, on a conference of all the commissioners, we have communicated our sentiments thereon and declared our opinion that we had gone as far as the service required and thought proper to proceed no farther; to which it was answered by the commissioners for Virginia that they should not regard what we did, but if we desisted, they would proceed without us. But we, conceiving by His Majesty's order in council they were directed to act in conjunction with the commissioners appointed for Carolina, and having accordingly run the line jointly so far and exchanged plans, thought they could not carry on the bounds singly but that their proceedings without us would be irregular and invalid and that it would be no boundary, and thought proper to enter our dissent thereto.

Wherefore, for the reasons aforesaid, in the name of His Excellency the Lord Palatine and the rest of the true and absolute Lords Proprietors of Carolina, we do hereby dissent and disallow of any farther proceeding with the bounds without our concurrence, and pursuant to our instructions do give this our dissent in writing.

EDWARD MOSELEY
WILLIAM LITTLE
C. GALE
J. LOVICK

*October 7, 1728*

--------

*The answer of the Virginia commissioners to the foregoing protest*

Whereas on the seventh of October last a paper was delivered to us by the commissioners of North Carolina in the style of a protest against our carrying any farther without them the dividing line between the two governments, we, the underwritten commissioners on the part of Virginia, having maturely considered the reasons offered in the said protest why those gentlemen retired so soon from that service, beg leave to return the following answer:

They are pleased in the first place to allege by way of reason that having run the line near fifty miles beyond the inhabitants, it was sufficient for a long time, in their opinion for an age or two. To this we answer that by breaking off so soon they did but imperfectly obey His Majesty's order, assented to by the Lords Proprietors. The plain meaning of that order was to ascertain the bounds betwixt the two governments as far toward the mountains as we could, that neither the King's grants may hereafter encroach on the Lords Proprietors' nor theirs on the rights of His Majesty.

And though the distance toward the great mountains be not precisely determined, yet surely the west line should be carried as near them as may be, that both the King's lands and those of Their Lordships may be taken up the faster, and that His Majesty's subjects may as soon as possible extend themselves to that natural barrier. This they will certainly do in a few years, when they know distinctly in which government they may enter for the land, as they have already done in the more northern parts of Virginia. So that 'tis strange the Carolina commissioners should affirm that the distance only of fifty miles above the inhabitants would be sufficient to carry the line for an age or two, especially considering that two or three days before the date of their protest Mr. Mayo had entered with them for two thousand acres of land within five miles of the place where they left off. Besides, if we reflect on the richness of the soil in those parts and the convenience for stock, we may foretell, without the spirit of divination, that there will be many settlements higher than those gentlemen went in less than ten years, and perhaps in half that time.

Another reason mentioned in the protest for their retiring so soon from the service is that their going farther would be a needless charge and trouble. And they allege that the rest may be done by one surveyor on a side in an easy manner, whenever it shall be thought necessary.

To this we answer that frugality for the public is a rare virtue, but when the public service must suffer by it, it degenerates into a vice. And this will ever be the case when gentlemen execute the orders of their superiors by halves. But had the Carolina commissioners been sincerely frugal for their government, why did they carry out provisions sufficient to support them and their men for ten weeks when they intended not to tarry half that time? This they must own to be true, since they brought one thousand pounds of provisions along with them. Now, after so great an expense in their preparations, it had been no mighty addition to their charge had they endured the fatigue five or six weeks longer. It would at most have been no more than they must be at whenever they finish their work, even though they should fancy it proper to trust a matter of that consequence to the management of one surveyor. Such a one must have a number of men along with him, both for his assistance and defense, and those men must have provisions to support them.

These are all the reasons these gentlemen think fit to mention in their protest, though they had in truth a more powerful argument for retiring so abruptly, which, because they forgot, it will be neighborly to help them out. The provisions they intended to bring along with them, for want of horses to carry them, were partly dropped by the way, and what they could bring was husbanded so ill that after eighteen days (which was the whole time we had them in our company) they had no more left, by their own confession, than two pounds of biscuit for each man to carry them home. However, though this was an unanswerable reason for gentlemen for leaving the business unfinished, it was none at all for us, who had at that time bread sufficient for seven weeks longer. Therefore, lest their want of management might put a stop to His Majesty's service and frustrate his royal intentions, we judged it our duty to proceed without them and have extended the dividing line so far west as to leave the great mountains on each hand to the eastward of us. And this we have done with the same fidelity and exactness as if the gentlemen had continued with us. Our surveyors (whose integrity I am persuaded they will not call in question) continued to act under the same oath which they had done from the beginning. Yet, notwithstanding all this, if the government of North Carolina should not hold itself bound by that part of the line which we made without the assistance of its commissioners, yet we shall have this benefit in it at least: that His Majesty will know how far his lands reach toward the south, and consequently where his subjects may take it up, and how far they may be granted without injustice to the Lords Proprietors. To this we may also add that, having the authority of our commission to act without the commissioners of Carolina in case of their disagreement or refusal, we thought ourselves bound upon their retreat to finish the line without them, lest His Majesty's service might suffer by any honor [38] or neglect on their part.

WILLIAM DANDRIDGE<br>WILLIAM BYRD

[78] The sense of the word "honor" is not clear; perhaps the scribe wrote "honor" instead of "humor."

| | |
|---|---|
| William Byrd<br>Richard Fitzwilliam<br>William Dandridge | Esquires, commissioners<br>for Virginia |
| Christopher Gale<br>John Lovick<br>Edward Moseley<br>William Little | Esquires, commissioners<br>for Carolina |
| Alexander Irvin<br>William Mayo | Surveyors for Virginia |
| Edward Moseley<br>Samuel Swann | Surveyors for North Carolina |

The Reverend Peter Fontaine, Chaplain

NAMES OF THE MEN EMPLOYED ON THE PART OF VIRGINIA TO RUN THE
LINE BETWEEN THAT COLONY AND NORTH CAROLINA

| On the first expedition | On the second expedition |
|---|---|
| 1. Peter Jones | Peter Jones |
| 2. Thomas Jones | Thomas Jones |
| 3. Thomas Short | Thomas Short |
| 4. Robert Hix | Robert Hix |
| 5. John Evans | John Evans |
| 6. Stephen Evans | Stephen Evans |
| 7. John Ellis | John Ellis |
| 8. John Ellis, Jr. | John Ellis, Jr. |
| 9. Thomas Wilson | Thomas Wilson |
| 10. George Tilman | George Tilman |
| 11. Charles Kimball | Charles Kimball |
| 12. George Hamilton | George Hamilton |
| 13. Robert Allen | Thomas Jones, Jr. |
| 14. Thomas Jones, Jr. | James Petillo |
| 15. James Petillo | Richard Smith |
| 16. Richard Smith | Abraham Jones |
| 17. John Rice | Edward Powell |
| | William Pool |
| | William Calvert |
| | James Whitlock |
| | Thomas Page |

ACCOUNT OF THE EXPENSE OF RUNNING THE LINE BETWEEN VIRGINIA
AND NORTH CAROLINA

| | | | |
|---|---|---|---|
| To the men's wages in current money | £277 | 10 | 0 |
| To sundry disbursements for provisions, etc. | 174 | 1 | 6 |
| To paid the men for seven horses lost | 44 | 0 | 0 |
| | £495 | 11 | 6 |
| | | | |
| The sum of £495 11s.6d. current money reduced | | | |
| at 15% to sterling amounts to | £430 | 8 | 10 |
| To paid to Colonel Byrd | 142 | 5 | 7 |
| To paid to Colonel Dandridge | 142 | 5 | 7 |
| To paid Mr. Fitzwilliam | 94 | 0 | 0 |
| To paid the chaplain, Mr. Fontaine | 20 | 0 | 0 |
| To paid to Mr. William Mayo | 75 | 0 | 0 |
| To paid to Mr. Alexander Irvin | 75 | 0 | 0 |
| To paid for a tent and marquee | 20 | 0 | 0 |
| | £1000 | 0 | 0 |

This sum was discharged by a warrant out of His Majesty's quitrents from the lands in Virginia.

# A PROGRESS TO THE MINES

## IN THE YEAR 1732

## SEPTEMBER 1732

*F*OR the pleasure of the good company of Mrs. Byrd and her little governor, my son, I went about halfway to the falls in the chariot. There we halted, not far from a purling stream, and upon the stump of a propagate oak picked the bones of a piece of roast beef. By the spirit which that gave me I was better able to part with the dear companions of my travels and to perform the rest of my journey on horseback by myself.

I reached Shacco's before two o'clock and crossed the river to the mills.[1] I had the grief to find them both stand as still for the want of water as a dead woman's tongue for want of breath. It had rained so little for many weeks above the falls, that the naiads had hardly water enough left to wash their faces. However, as we ought to turn all our misfortunes to the best advantage, I directed Mr. Booker, my first minister there, to make use of the lowness of the water for blowing up the rocks at the mouth of the canal. For that purpose I ordered iron drills to be made about two foot long, pointed with steel, chisel fashion, in order to make holes into which we put our cartridges of powder, containing each about three ounces. There wanted skill among my engineers to choose the best parts of the stone for boring, that we might blow to the most advantage. They made all their holes quite perpendicular, whereas they should have humored the grain of the stone for the more effectual execution. I ordered the points of the drills to be made chisel

[1] Byrd's father, William Byrd I, inherited land on both sides of the James near the falls from his uncle, Thomas Stegge, Jr. On the south side of the river was developed the Falls plantation. "Shacco's," on the north side, was established as a trading post and an outpost against Indian attack in the time of the first William Byrd. The name derives from an old creek name, probably a corruption of the name of an Indian tribe (either the Shakori or the Shackaconians). A public warehouse at this spot was provided for in a law enacted by the Virginia Assembly in 1730. It was here that Byrd laid out the town of Richmond in 1737; see p. 388. The name survives in Richmond in Shockoe Hill Cemetery and Shockoe Slip.

way, rather than the diamond, that they might need to be seldomer repaired, though in stone the diamond points would make the most dispatch. The water now flowed out of the river so slowly that the miller was obliged to pond it up in the canal by setting open the floodgates at the mouth and shutting those close at the mill. By this contrivance he was able at any time to grind two or three bushels, either for his choice customers or for the use of my plantations.

Then I walked to the place where they broke the flax, which is wrought with much greater ease than the hemp and is much better for spinning. From thence I paid a visit to the weaver, who needed a little of Minerva's inspiration to make the most of a piece of fine cloth. Then I looked in upon my Caledonian spinster, who was mended more in her looks than in her humor. However, she promised much, though at the same time intended to perform little. She is too high-spirited for Mr. Booker, who hates to have his sweet temper ruffled and will rather suffer matters to go a little wrong sometimes than give his righteous spirit any uneasiness. He is very honest and would make an admirable overseer where servants will do as they are bid. But eye-servants, who want abundance of overlooking, are not so proper to be committed to his care.

I found myself out of order and for that reason retired early, yet with all this precaution had a gentle fever in the night, but toward morning Nature set open all her gates and drove it out in a plentiful perspiration.

19. The worst of this fever was that it put me to the necessity of taking another ounce of bark.[2] I moistened every dose with a little brandy and filled the glass up with water, which is the least nauseous way of taking this popish medicine and besides hinders it from purging.

After I had swallowed a few poached eggs, we rode down to the mouth of the canal and from thence crossed over to the broad rock island in a canoe. Our errand was to view some iron ore, which we dug up in two places. That on the surface seemed very spongy and poor, which gave us no great encouragement to search deeper, nor did the

[2] Peruvian (Cinchona) bark, which Byrd mentions on p. 225 of the *History*. There are numerous references in his diary to taking "bark." Byrd calls it "popish medicine" because it was also known as "Jesuit's bark."

quantity appear to be very great. However, for my greater satisfaction I ordered a hand to dig there for some time this winter.

We walked from one end of the island to the other, being about half a mile in length, and found the soil very good and too high for any flood less than that of Deucalion to do the least damage. There is a very wild prospect both upward and downward, the river being full of rocks over which the stream tumbled with a murmur loud enough to drown the notes of a scolding wife. This island would make an agreeable hermitage for any good Christian who had a mind to retire from the world.

Mr. Booker told me how Dr. Ireton had cured him once of a looseness which had been upon him two whole years. He ordered him a dose of rhubarb, with directions to take twenty-five drops of laudanum so soon as he had had two physical stools. Then he rested one day, and the next he ordered him another dose of the same quantity of laudanum to be taken, also after the second stool. When this was done, he finished the cure by giving him twenty drops of laudanum every night for five nights running. The doctor insisted upon the necessity of stopping the operation of the rhubarb before it worked quite off, that what remained behind might strengthen the bowels. I was punctual in swallowing my bark, and that I might use exercise upon it, rode to Prince's Folly and My Lord's islands,[3] where I saw very fine corn.

In the meantime, Vulcan came in order to make the drills for boring the rocks and gave me his parole he would, by the grace of God, attend the works till they were finished, which he performed as lamely as if he had been to labor for a dead horse and not for ready money.

I made a North Carolina dinner upon fresh pork, though we had a plate of green peas after it, by way of dessert, for the safety of our noses.[4] Then my first minister and I had some serious conversation about my affairs, and I find nothing disturbed his peaceable spirit so much as the misbehavior of the spinster above-mentioned. I told him I could not pity a man who had it always in his power to do himself and

[3] Possibly lands belonging to George Hamilton, Earl of Orkney, absentee Governor of Virginia at this time.
[4] See Byrd's reference in the *Secret History* (p. 60) to his belief that too heavy a diet of pork caused yaws, with consequent destruction of the nose.

341

her justice and would not. If she were a drunkard, a scold, a thief, or a slanderer, we had wholesome laws that would make her back smart for the diversion of her other members, and 'twas his fault he had not put those wholesome severities in execution. I retired in decent time to my own apartment and slept very comfortably upon my bark, forgetting all the little crosses arising from overseers and Negroes.

20. I continued the bark and then tossed down my poached eggs with as much ease as some good breeders slip children into the world. About nine I left the prudentest orders I could think of with my vizier and then crossed the river to Shacco's. I made a running visit to three of my quarters, where, besides finding all the people well, I had the pleasure to see better crops than usual both of corn and tobacco. I parted there with my intendant,[5] and pursued my journey to Mr. Randolph's at Tuckahoe [6] without meeting with any adventure by the way.

Here I found Mrs. Fleming, who was packing up her baggage with design to follow her husband the next day, who was gone to a new settlement in Goochland. Both he and she have been about seven years persuading themselves to remove to that retired part of the country, though they had the two strong arguments of health and interest for so doing. The widow smiled graciously upon me and entertained me very handsomely. Here I learnt all the tragical story of her daughter's humble marriage with her uncle's overseer. Besides the meanness of this mortal's aspect, the man has not one visible qualification except impudence to recommend him to a female's inclinations. But there is sometimes such a charm in that Hibernian endowment that frail woman can't withstand it, though it stand alone without any other recommendation. Had she run away with a gentleman or a pretty fellow there might have been some excuse for her, though he were of inferior fortune; but to stoop to a dirty plebeian without any kind of merit is the lowest prostitution. I found the family justly enraged at it, and though I had more good nature than to join in her condemnation, yet

[5] Supervisor.
[6] Tuckahoe, on the creek of the same name, was the plantation of Thomas Randolph, son of William Randolph, who founded the famous Virginia family.

I could devise no excuse for so senseless a prank as this young gentle-woman had played.

Here good drink was more scarce than good victuals, the family be-ing reduced to the last bottle of wine, which was therefore husbanded very carefully. But the water was excellent. The heir of the family did not come home till late in the evening. He is a pretty young man but had the misfortune to become his own master too soon. This puts young fellows upon wrong pursuits before they have sense to judge rightly for themselves, though at the same time they have a strange conceit of their own sufficiency when they grow near twenty years old, especially if they happen to have a small smattering of learning. 'Tis then they fancy themselves wiser than all their tutors and governors, which makes them headstrong to all advice and above all reproof and admoni-tion.

21. I was sorry in the morning to find myself stopped in my career by bad weather brought upon us by a northeast wind. This drives a world of raw, unkindly vapors upon us from Newfoundland, loaden with blights, coughs, and pleurisies. However, I complained not, lest I might be suspected to be tired of the good company, though Mrs. Fleming was not so much upon her guard but mutinied strongly at the rain that hindered her from pursuing her dear husband. I said what I could to comfort a gentlewoman under so sad a disappoint-ment. I told her a husband that stayed so much at home as hers did could be no such violent rarity as for a woman to venture her precious health to go daggling through the rain after him or to be miserable if she happened to be prevented; that it was prudent for married people to fast sometimes from one another, that they might come together again with the better stomach; that the best things in this world, if constantly used, are apt to be cloying, which a little absence and abstinence would prevent. This was strange doctrine to a fond female who fancies people should love with as little reason after marriage as before.

In the afternoon Monsieur Marij,[7] the minister of the parish, came

---

[7] The Reverend James Marye, born a Roman Catholic in Rouen, who came to Virginia via England, where he had been ordained in the Protestant Episcopal Church and had married Letitia Maria Ann Staige. He was called to the parish of

to make me a visit. He had been a Romish priest but found reasons, either spiritual or temporal, to quit that gay religion. The fault of this new convert is that he looks for as much respect from his Protestant flock as is paid to the popish clergy, which our ill-bred Huguenots don't understand. Madam Marij had so much curiosity as to want to come too, but another horse was wanting, and she believed it would have too vulgar an air to ride behind her husband. This woman was of the true Exchange breed, full of discourse but void of discretion,[8] and married a parson with the idle hopes he might some time or other come to be His Grace of Canterbury. The gray mare is the better horse in that family, and the poor man submits to her wild vagaries for peace's sake. She has just enough of the fine lady to run in debt and be of no signification in her household. And the only thing that can prevent her from undoing her loving husband will be that nobody will trust them beyond the sixteen thousand,[9] which is soon run out in a Goochland store. The way of dealing there is for some small merchant or peddler to buy a Scots' pennyworth of goods and clap 150 per cent upon that. At this rate the parson can't be paid much more for his preaching than 'tis worth. No sooner was our visitor retired but the facetious widow was so kind as to let me into all this secret history, but was at the same time exceedingly sorry that the woman should be so indiscreet and the man so tame as to be governed by an unprofitable and fantastical wife.

22. We had another wet day, to try both Mrs. Fleming's patience and my good breeding. The northeast wind commonly sticks by us three or four days, filling the atmosphere with damps, injurious both to man and beast. The worst of it was we had no good liquor to warm

---

St. James' Northam in Goochland County. See Robert A. Brock, *Documents . . . Relating to the Huguenot Emigration to Virginia* (Baltimore, 1962), pp. 183–184.

[8] The Royal Exchange in London was a noted place to meet and gossip, in addition to being a place of business.

[9] Commissary Blair reported to the Bishop of London in a letter of February 10, 1724: "The livings are settled by law at 16,000 lbs. of tobacco per annum, besides glebes and perquisites; and this in the sweet scented parishes is better than £100 sterling; and all the rest about £80." The Virginia Assembly had fixed this salary in 1696 and it remained stationary until the Revolution. See Hugh Jones, *The Present State of Virginia*, edited by Richard L. Morton (Chapel Hill, 1956), p. 99 and pp. 230–231, n. 203.

our blood and fortify our spirits against so strong a malignity. However, I was cheerful under all these misfortunes and expressed no concern but a decent fear lest my long visit might be troublesome. Since I was like to have thus much leisure, I endeavored to find out what subject a dull married man could introduce that might best bring the widow to the use of her tongue. At length I discovered she was a notable quack and therefore paid that regard to her knowledge as to put some questions to her about the bad distemper that raged then in the country. I mean the bloody flux, that was brought us in the Negro ship consigned to Colonel Braxton.[10] She told me she made use of very simple remedies in that case, with very good success. She did the business either with hartshorn drink that had plantain leaves boiled in it, or else with a strong decoction of St.-Andrew's-cross in new milk instead of water. I agreed with her that those remedies might be very good but would be more effectual after a dose or two of Indian physic.

But for fear this conversation might be too grave for a widow, I turned the discourse and began to talk of plays, and, finding her taste lay most toward comedy, I offered my service to read one to her, which she kindly accepted. She produced the second part of *The Beggar's Opera*, which had diverted the town for forty nights successively and gained £4,000 to the author. This was not owing altogether to the wit or humor that sparkled in it but to some political reflections that seemed to hit the ministry. But the great advantage of the author was that his interest was solicited by the Duchess of Queensberry, which no man could refuse who had but half an eye in his head or half a guinea in his pocket.[11] Her Grace, like death, spared nobody but even took My Lord Selkirk in for two guineas, to repair which extravagance he lived upon Scots herrings two months afterwards. But the best story was she made a very smart officer in His Majesty's guards give her a guinea, who swearing at the same time 'twas all he had in the

---

[10] Probably George Braxton, Jr. His importation of Negro slaves is mentioned in Byrd's diary for 1739–1741 (*Another Secret Diary of William Byrd of Westover*, edited by Maud H. Woodfin and Marion Tinling [Richmond, Va., 1942], p. 22).

[11] Catherine Hyde Douglas, Duchess of Queensberry, and her husband were devoted patrons of John Gay, who actually died in the Duke's house in Burlington Gardens in 1732. *The Beggar's Opera*, first printed in 1728, had a fourth edition in the year Byrd wrote.

world, she sent him fifty for it the next day to reward his obedience. After having acquainted my company with the history of the play, I read three acts of it, and left Mrs. Fleming and Mr. Randolph to finish it, who read as well as most actors do at a rehearsal. Thus we killed the time and triumphed over the bad weather.

23. The clouds continued to drive from the northeast and to menace us with more rain. But as the lady resolved to venture through it I thought it a shame for me to venture to flinch. Therefore, after fortifying myself with two capacious dishes of coffee and making my compliments to the ladies, I mounted, and Mr. Randolph was so kind as to be my guide.

At the distance of about three miles, in a path as narrow as that which leads to Heaven but much more dirty, we reached the homely dwelling of the Reverend Mr. Marij. His land is much more barren than his wife and needs all Mr. Bradley's [12] skill in agriculture to make it bring corn. Thence we proceeded five miles farther to a mill of Mr. Randolph's, that is apt to stand still when there falls but little rain and to be carried away when there falls a great deal. Then we pursued a very blind path four miles farther, which puzzled my guide, who I suspect led me out of the way. At length we came into a great road, where he took leave, after giving me some very confused directions, and so left me to blunder out the rest of the journey by myself. I lost myself more than once but soon recovered the right way again. About three [?] miles after quitting my guide, I passed the south branch of Pamunkey River, near fifty yards over and full of stones.

After this I had eight miles to Mr. Chiswell's, [13] where I arrived about two o'clock and saved my dinner. I was very handsomely entertained, finding everything very clean and very good. I had not seen Mrs. Chiswell in twenty-four years, which, alas! had made great havoc with her pretty face and plowed very deep furrows in her fair skin. It was impossible to know her again, so much the flower was

[12] Richard Bradley, author of a number of works on agriculture, such as *New Improvements of Planting and Gardening* (1717), *The Gentleman and Gardener's Calendar* (1720), and *The County Housewife* (1727). Byrd's library contained several of Bradley's works.

[13] Charles Chiswell was clerk of the General Court, 1706. See p. 30 for Byrd's earlier acquaintance with Mrs. Chiswell.

faded. However, though she was grown an old woman, yet she was one of those absolute rarities, a very good old woman.

I found Mr. Chiswell a sensible, well-bred man and very frank in communicating his knowledge in the mystery of making iron, wherein he has had long experience. I told him I was come to spy the land and inform myself of the expense of carrying on an ironwork with effect; that I sought my instruction from him, who understood the whole mystery, having gained full experience in every part of it, only I was very sorry he had bought that experience so dear. He answered that he would with great sincerity let me into the little knowledge he had, and so we immediately entered upon the business.

He assured me the first step I was to take was to acquaint myself fully with the quantity and quality of my ore. For that reason I ought to keep a good pickax man at work a whole year to search if there be a sufficient quantity, without which it would be a very rash undertaking. That I should also have a skillful person to try the richness of the ore. Nor is it great advantage to have it exceeding rich, because then it will yield brittle iron, which is not valuable. But the way to have it tough is to mix poor ore and rich together, which makes the poorer sort extremely necessary for the production of the best iron. Then he showed me a sample of the richest ore they have in England, which yields a full moiety of iron. It was of a pale red color, smooth and greasy, and not exceedingly heavy; but it produced so brittle a metal that they were obliged to melt a poorer ore along with it.

He told me, after I was certain my ore was good and plentiful enough, my next inquiry ought to be how far it lies from a stream proper to build a furnace upon, and again what distance that furnace will be from water carriage; because the charge of carting a great way is very heavy and eats out a great part of the profit. That this was the misfortune of the mines of Fredericksville, where they were obliged to cart the ore a mile to the furnace, and after 'twas run into iron to carry that twenty-four miles over an uneven road to Rappahannock River, about a mile below Fredericksburg, to a plantation the company rented of Colonel Page.[14] If I were satisfied with the situation, I was in the

[14] Probably Colonel Mann Page, of Gloucester County, member of the Virginia Council from 1714 until his death in 1730.

next place to consider whether I had woodland enough near the furnace to supply it with charcoal, whereof it would require a prodigious quantity. That the properest wood for that purpose was that of oily kind, such as pine, walnut, hickory, oak, and in short all that yields cones, nuts, or acorns. That two miles square of wood would supply a moderate furnace, that so what you fell first may have time to grow up again to a proper bigness (which must be four inches over) by that time the rest is cut down.

He told me farther that 120 slaves, including women, were necessary to carry on all the business of an ironwork, and the more Virginians amongst them the better; though in that number he comprehended carters, colliers, and those that planted the corn. That if there should be much carting, it would require 1,600 barrels of corn yearly to support the people and the cattle employed; nor does even that quantity suffice at Fredericksville.

That if all these circumstances should happily concur, and you could procure honest colliers and firemen, which will be difficult to do, you may easily run eight hundred tons of sow iron [15] a year. The whole charge of freight, custom, commission, and other expenses in England, will not exceed 30s. a ton, and 'twill commonly sell for £6, and then the clear profit will amount to £4 10s. So that allowing the 10s. for accidents, you may reasonably expect a clear profit of £4, which being multiplied by eight hundred, will amount to £3,200 a year, to pay you for your land and Negroes. But then it behooved me to be fully informed of the whole matter myself, to prevent being imposed upon; and if any offered to put tricks upon me, to punish them as they deserve.

Thus ended our conversation for this day, and I retired to a very clean lodging in another house and took my bark, but was forced to take it in water, by reason a light-fingered damsel had ransacked my baggage and drank up my brandy. This unhappy girl, it seems, is a baronet's daughter; but her complexion, being red-haired, inclined her so much to lewdness that her father sent her, under the care of the virtuous Mr. Cheep, to seek her fortune on this side the globe.

[15] Iron cast in a mold larger than a pig.

348

24. My friend Mr. Chiswell made me reparation for the robbery of his servant by filling my bottle again with good brandy.

It being Sunday, I made a motion for going to church to see the growth of the parish, but unluckily the sermon happened to be at the chapel, which was too far off. I was unwilling to tire my friend with any farther discourse upon iron and therefore turned the conversation to other subjects. And talking of management, he let me into two secrets worth remembering. He said the quickest way in the world to stop the fermentation of any liquor was to keep a lighted match of brimstone under the cask for some time. This is useful in so warm a country as this, where cider is apt to work itself off both of its strength and sweetness. The other secret was to keep weevils out of wheat and other grain. You have nothing to do, said he, but to put a bag of pepper into every heap or cask, which those insects have such an antipathy to that they will not approach it. These receipts he gave me, not upon report, but upon his own repeated experience. He farther told me he had brewed as good ale of malt made of Indian corn as ever he tasted; all the objection was he could neither by art or standing ever bring it to be fine in the cask. The quantity of corn he employed in brewing a cask of forty gallons was two bushels and a half, which made it very strong and pleasant.

We had a haunch of venison for dinner, as fat and well-tasted as if it had come out of Richmond Park. In these upper parts of the country the deer are in better case than below, though I believe the buck which gave us so good a dinner had eat out his value in peas, which will make deer exceedingly fat.

In the afternoon I walked with my friend to his mill, which is half a mile from his house. It is built upon a rock very firmly, so that 'tis more apt to suffer by too little water (the run not being over plentiful) than too much. On the other side of this stream lie several of Colonel Jones's[16] plantations. The poor Negroes upon them are a kind of Adamites, very scantily supplied with clothes and other necessaries; nevertheless (which is a little incomprehensible), they continue in perfect health and none of them die except it be of age. However, they

[16] Colonel Thomas Jones, a member of the House of Burgesses.

are even with their master and make him but indifferent crops, so that he gets nothing by his injustice but the scandal of it.

And here I must make one remark, which I am a little unwilling to do for fear of encouraging of cruelty, that those Negroes which are kept the barest of clothes and bedding are commonly the freest from sickness. And this happens, I suppose, by their being all face and therefore better proof against the sudden changes of weather to which this climate is unhappily subject.

25. After saying some very civil things to Mrs. Chiswell for my handsome entertainment, I mounted my horse and Mr. Chiswell his phaeton, in order to go to the mines at Fredericksville. We could converse very little by the way, by reason of our different *voitures*. The road was very straight and level the whole journey, which was twenty-five miles, the last ten whereof I rode in the chair and my friend on my horse, to ease ourselves by that variety of motion.

About a mile before we got to Fredericksville we forded over the north branch of Pamunkey, about sixty yards over. Neither this nor the south branch run up near so high as the mountains but many miles below them spread out into a kind of morass, like Chickahominy. When we approached the mines there opened to our view a large space of cleared ground, whose wood had been cut down for coaling.

We arrived here about two o'clock, and Mr. Chiswell had been so provident as to bring a cold venison pasty with which we appeased our appetites without the impatience of waiting. When our tongues were at leisure for discourse, my friend told me there was one Mr. Harrison in England who is so universal a dealer in all sorts of iron that he could govern the market just as he pleased. That it was by his artful management that our iron from the plantations sold for less than that made in England, though it was generally reckoned much better. That ours would hardly fetch £6 a ton, when theirs fetched seven or eight, purely to serve that man's interest. Then he explained the several charges upon our sow iron after it was put on board the ships. That in the first place it paid 7s. 6d. a ton for freight, being just so much clear gain to the ships, which carry it as ballast or wedge it in among the hogsheads. When it gets home, it pays 3s. 9d. custom.

These articles together make no more than 11s. 3d., and yet the merchants, by their great skill in multiplying charges, swell the account up to near 30s. a ton by that time it gets out of their hands, and they are continually adding more and more, as they serve us in our accounts of tobacco.

He told me a strange thing about steel, that the making of the best remains at this day a profound secret in the breast of a very few and therefore is in danger of being lost, as the art of staining of glass and many others have been. He could only tell me they used beechwood in the making of it in Europe and burn it a considerable time in powder of charcoal; but the mystery lies in the liquor they quench it in.

After dinner we took a walk to the furnace, which is elegantly built of brick, though the hearth be of firestone. There we saw the founder, Mr. Derham, who is paid 4s. for every ton of sow iron that he runs, which is a shilling cheaper than the last workman had. This operator looked a little melancholy because he had nothing to do, the furnace having been cold ever since May for want of corn to support the cattle. This was, however, no neglect of Mr. Chiswell, because all the persons he had contracted with had basely disappointed him. But, having received a small supply, they intended to blow very soon. With that view they began to heat the furnace, which is six weeks before it comes to that intense heat required to run the metal in perfection. Nevertheless, they commonly begin to blow when the fire has been kindled a week or ten days.

Close by the furnace stood a very spacious house full of charcoal, holding at least four hundred loads, which will be burnt out in three months. The company has contracted with Mr. Harry Willis to fall the wood, and then maul it and cut it into pieces of four feet in length and bring it to the pits where it is to be coaled. All this he has undertaken to do for 2s. a cord, which must be four foot broad, four foot high, and eight foot long. Being thus carried to the pits, the collier has contracted to coal it for 5s. a load, consisting of 160 bushels. The fire in the furnace is blown by two mighty pair of bellows that cost £100 each, and these bellows are moved by a great wheel of twenty-six foot diameter. The wheel again is carried round by a small stream of water, conveyed about 350 yards overland in a trough, from a pond made by a wooden dam. But there is great want of water in a dry season, which makes the furnace often blow out, to the great prejudice of the works.

Having thus filled my head with all these particulars, we returned to the house, where, after talking of Colonel Spotswood and his stratagems to shake off his partners and secure all his mines to himself, I retired to a homely lodging which, like a homespun mistress, had been more tolerable if it had been sweet.

26. Over our tea, Mr. Chiswell told me the expense which the company had been already at amounted to near £12,000; but then the land, Negroes, and cattle were all included in that charge. However, the money began now to come in, they having run twelve hundred tons of iron, and all their heavy disbursements were over. Only they were still forced to buy great quantities of corn, because they had not strength of their own to make it. That they had not more than eighty Negroes, and few of those Virginia born. That they need forty Negroes more to carry on all the business with their own force. They have 15,000 acres of land, though little of it rich except in iron, and of that they have a great quantity.

Mr. Fitzwilliam took up the mine tract and had the address to draw in the Governor, Captain Pearse, Dr. Nicholas, and Mr. Chiswell to be jointly concerned with him, by which contrivance he first got a good price for the land and then, when he had been very little out of pocket, sold his share to Mr. Nelson for £500; and of these gentlemen the company at present consists. And Mr. Chiswell is the only person amongst them that knows anything of the matter, and has £100 a year for looking after the works, and richly deserves it.

After breaking our fast we took a walk to the principal mine, about a mile from the furnace, where they had sunk in some places about fifteen or twenty feet deep. The operator, Mr. Gordon, raised the ore, for which he was to have by contract 1s. 6d. per cartload of twenty-six hundredweight. This man was obliged to hire all the laborers he wanted for this work of the company, after the rate of 25s. a month, and for all that was able to clear £40 a year for himself.

We saw here several large heaps of ore of two sorts, one of rich, and the other spongy and poor, which they melted together to make the metal more tough. The way of raising the ore was by blowing it up, which operation I saw here from beginning to end. They first drilled a hole in the mine, either upright or sloping, as the grain of it required. This hole they cleansed with a rag fastened to the end of an iron with a worm at the end of it. Then they put in a cartridge of powder containing about three ounces and at the same time a reed full of fuse that reached to the powder. Then they rammed dry clay or soft stone very hard into the hole, and lastly they fired the fuse with a paper that had been dipped in a solution of saltpeter and dried, which, burning slow and sure, gave leisure to the engineer to retire to a proper distance before the explosion. This in the miner's language is called "making a blast," which will loosen several hundredweight of ore at once; and afterwards the laborers easily separate it with pickaxes and carry it away in baskets up to the heap.

At our return we saw near the furnace large heaps of mine with charcoal mixed with it, a stratum of each alternately, beginning first with a layer of charcoal at the bottom. To this they put fire, which in a little time spreads through the whole heap and calcines the ore, which afterwards easily crumbles into small pieces fit for the furnace. Then was likewise a mighty quantity of limestone brought from Bristol by way of ballast, at 2s. 6d. a ton, which they are at the trouble to cart hither from Rappahannock River, but contrive to do it when the carts return from carrying of iron. They put this into the furnace with the iron ore, in the proportion of one ton of stone to ten of ore, with design to absorb the sulphur out of the iron, which would otherwise make it brittle. And if that be the use of it, oyster shells would certainly do as well as limestone, being altogether as strong an alkali, if not stronger. Nor can their being taken out of salt water be any objection, because 'tis pretty certain the West India limestone, which is thrown up by the sea, is even better than that imported from Bristol. But the founders who never tried either of these will by no means be persuaded to go out of their way, though the reason of the thing be never so evident.

I observed the richer sort of mine, being of a dark color mixed with rust, was laid in a heap by itself, and so was the poor, which was of a liver or brick color. The sow iron is in the figure of a half round, about two feet and a half long, weighing sixty or seventy pounds, whereof three thousandweight make a cartload drawn by eight oxen, which are commonly shod to save their hoofs in those stony ways. When the furnace blows, it runs about twenty tons of iron a week. The founders find it very hot work to tend the furnace, especially in summer, and are obliged to spend no small part of their earnings in strong drink to recruit their spirits.

Besides the founder, the collier, and miner, who are paid in proportion to their work, the company have several other officers upon wages: a stocktaker, who weighs and measures everything, a clerk, who keeps an account of all receipts and disbursements; a smith to shoe their cattle and keep all their ironwork in repair; a wheelwright, cartwright, carpenter, and several carters. The wages of all these persons amount to £100 a year; so that including Mr. Chiswell's salary they disburse £200 per annum in standing wages. The provisions, too, are a heavy article, which their plantations don't yet produce in a sufficient quantity, though they are at the charge of a general overseer. But while corn is so short with them, there can be no great increase of stock of any kind.

27. Having now pretty well exhausted the subject of sow iron, I asked my friend some questions about bar iron. He told me we had as yet no forge erected in Virginia, though we had four furnaces. But there was a very good one set up at the head of the bay in Maryland, that made exceeding good work. He let me know that the duty in England upon bar iron was 24s. a ton, and that it sold there from £10 to £16 a ton. This would pay the charge of forging abundantly, but he doubted the parliament of England would soon forbid us that improvement, lest after that we should go farther and manufacture our bars into all sorts of ironware, as they already do in New England and Pennsylvania. Nay, he questioned whether we should be suffered to cast any iron, which they can do themselves at their furnaces.

Thus ended our conversation, and I thanked my friend for being so free in communicating everything to me. Then, after tipping a pistole to the clerk, to drink prosperity to the mines with all the workmen, I accepted the kind offer of going part of my journey in the phaeton.

I took my leave about ten and drove over a spacious level road ten miles to a bridge built over the river Po, which is one of the four branches of Mattaponi, about forty yards wide. Two miles beyond that we passed by a plantation, belonging to the company, of about five hundred acres, where they keep a great number of oxen to relieve those that have dragged their loaded carts thus far. Three miles farther we came to the Germanna road, where I quitted the chair and continued my journey on horseback. I rode eight miles together over a stony road, and had on either side continual poisoned fields, with nothing but saplings growing on them. Then I came into the main county road that leads from Fredericksburg to Germanna,[17] which last place I reached in ten miles more.

This famous town consists of Colonel Spotswood's enchanted castle on one side of the street and a baker's dozen of ruinous tenements on the other, where so many German families had dwelt some years ago, but are now removed ten miles higher, in the fork of Rappahannock, to land of their own. There had also been a chapel about a bowshot from the colonel's house, at the end of an avenue of cherry trees, but some pious people had lately burnt it down, with intent to get another built nearer to their own homes.

Here I arrived about three o'clock and found only Mrs. Spotswood at home, who received her old acquaintance with many a gracious smile. I was carried into a room elegantly set off with pier glasses, the largest of which came soon after to an odd misfortune. Amongst other favorite animals that cheered this lady's solitude, a brace of tame deer

---

[17] Governor Spotswood had secured the Council's approval in 1714 to settle a community of German miners at the falls of the Rappahannock as a barrier against the Indians. The German settlers did not remain satisfied and moved elsewhere. In 1720 the town became the seat of the newly formed Spotsylvania County, but in the year of Byrd's visit Fredericksburg replaced Germanna as the chief settlement of the county. Germanna was described in 1715 as containing "nine houses, built all in a line; and before every house, about twenty feet distant from it, they have small sheds built for their hogs and hens, so that the hog-sties and houses make a street"; quoted from Ann Maury, *Memoirs of a Huguenot Family* (New York, 1872), p. 269, by Leonidas Dodson in *Alexander Spotswood* (Philadelphia, 1932), p. 232.

ran familiarly about the house, and one of them came to stare at me as a stranger; but, unluckily spying his own figure in the glass, he made a spring over the tea table that stood under it and shattered the glass to pieces and, falling back upon the tea table, made a terrible fracas among the china. This exploit was so sudden, and accompanied with such noise, that it surprised me and perfectly frightened Mrs. Spotswood. But 'twas worth all the damage to show the moderation and good humor with which she bore this disaster.

In the evening the noble colonel came home from his mines, who saluted me very civilly, and Mrs. Spotswood's sister, Miss Theky,[18] who had been to meet him *en cavalier*, was so kind too as to bid me welcome. We talked over a legend of old stories, supped about nine, and then prattled with the ladies till 'twas time for a traveler to retire. In the meantime, I observed my old friend to be very uxorious and exceedingly fond of his children. This was so opposite to the maxims he used to preach up before he was married that I could not forbear rubbing up the memory of them. But he gave a very good-natured turn to his change of sentiments by alleging that whoever brings a poor gentlewoman into so solitary a place, from all her friends and acquaintance, would be ungrateful not to use her and all that belongs to her with all possible tenderness.

28. We all kept snug in our several apartments till nine, except Miss Theky, who was the housewife of the family. At that hour we met over a pot of coffee, which was not quite strong enough to give us the palsy.

After breakfast the Colonel and I left the ladies to their domestic affairs and took a turn in the garden, which has nothing beautiful but three terrace walks that fall in slopes one below another. I let him understand that besides the pleasure of paying him a visit I came to be instructed by so great a master in the mystery of making iron, wherein he had led the way and was the Tubal-cain of Virginia. He corrected me a little there by assuring me he was not only the first in

---

[18] Presumably a nickname for "Dorothea," the first name of Mrs. Spotswood's sister. Colonel Spotswood married Anne Butler Brayne of Westminster in 1724 and brought her to Virginia in 1730; see Dodson, *Alexander Spotswood*, p. 299.

this country but the first in North America who had erected a regular furnace. That they ran altogether upon bloomeries in New England and Pennsylvania till his example had made them attempt greater works.[19] But in this last colony, they have so few ships to carry their iron to Great Britain that they must be content to make it only for their own use, and must be obliged to manufacture it when they have done. That he hoped he had done the country very great service by setting so good an example. That the four furnaces now at work in Virginia circulated a great sum of money for provisions and all other necessaries in the adjacent counties. That they took off a great number of hands from planting tobacco and employed them in works that produced a large sum of money in England to the persons concerned, whereby the country is so much the richer. That they are besides a considerable advantage to Great Britain, because it lessens the quantity of bar iron imported from Spain, Holland, Sweden, Denmark, and Muscovy, which use to be no less than twenty thousand tons yearly, though at the same time no sow iron is imported thither from any country but only from the plantations. For most of this bar iron they do not only pay silver, but our friends in the Baltic are so nice they even expect to be paid all in crown pieces. On the contrary, all the iron they receive from the plantations, they pay for it in their own manufactures and send for it in their own shipping.

Then I inquired after his own mines, and hoped, as he was the first that engaged in this great undertaking, that he had brought them to the most perfection. He told me he had iron in several parts of his great tract of land, consisting of forty-five thousand acres. But that the mine he was at work upon was thirteen miles below Germanna. That his ore (which was very rich) he raised a mile from his furnace and was obliged to cart the iron, when it was made, fifteen miles to Massaponax, a plantation he had upon Rappahannock River; but that the road was exceeding good, gently declining all the way, and had no

---

[19] Dodson points out that Spotswood is mistaken, since blast furnaces and forges had been in operation in New England seventy years earlier (*Alexander Spotswood*, p. 296). William B. Weeden, *Economic and Social History of New England, 1620–1780* (Boston and New York, 1890), I, 177–178, describes iron working at Lynn and Braintree. Lynn began smelting, forging, and refining iron in 1643.

more than one hill to go up in the whole journey. For this reason his loaded carts went it in a day without difficulty.

He said it was true his works were of the oldest standing; but that his long absence in England, and the wretched management of Mr. Graeme,[20] whom he had entrusted with his affairs, had put him back very much. That, what with neglect and severity, above eighty of his slaves were lost while he was in England and most of his cattle starved. That his furnace stood still great part of the time, and all his plantations ran to ruin. That, indeed, he was rightly served for committing his affairs to the care of a mathematician, whose thoughts were always among the stars. That nevertheless, since his return he had applied himself to rectify his steward's mistakes and bring his business again into order. That now he had contrived to do everything with his own people, except raising the mine and running the iron, by which he had contracted his expense very much. Nay, he believed that by his directions he could bring sensible Negroes to perform those parts of the work tolerably well.

But at the same time he gave me to understand that his furnace had done no great feats lately, because he had been taken up in building an air furnace at Massaponax, which he had now brought to perfection and should be thereby able to furnish the whole country with all sorts of cast iron as cheap and as good as ever came from England. I told him he must do one thing more to have a full vent for those commodities: he must keep a *chaloupe*[21] running into all the rivers, to carry his wares home to people's own doors. And if he would do that I would set a good example and take off a whole ton of them.

Our conversation on this subject continued till dinner, which was both elegant and plentiful. The afternoon was devoted to the ladies, who showed me one of their most beautiful walks. They conducted me through a shady lane to the landing and by the way made me drink some very fine water that issued from a marble fountain and ran incessantly. Just behind it was a covered bench, where Miss Theky

[20] He had appointed John Graeme, his cousin, manager of his American estate in 1725 (Dodson, *Alexander Spotswood*, p. 298).

[21] The French form of the word anglicized to "shallop," a light open boat, used chiefly on rivers.

often sat and bewailed her virginity. Then we proceeded to the river, which is the south branch of Rappahannock, about fifty yards wide and so rapid that the ferryboat is drawn over by a chain and therefore called the Rapidan. At night we drank prosperity to all the Colonel's projects in a bowl of rack punch and then retired to our devotions.

29. Having employed about two hours in retirement, I sallied out at the first summons to breakfast, where our conversation with the ladies, like whip sillabub, was very pretty but had nothing in it. This it seems was Miss Theky's birthday, upon which I made her my compliments and wished she might live twice as long a married woman as she had lived a maid. I did not presume to pry into the secret of her age, nor was she forward to disclose it, for this humble reason, lest I should think her wisdom fell short of her years. She contrived to make this day of her birth a day of mourning, for, having nothing better at present to set her affections upon, she had a dog that was a great favorite. It happened that very morning the poor cur had done something very uncleanly upon the Colonel's bed, for which he was condemned to die. However, upon her entreaty, she got him a reprieve, but was so concerned that so much severity should be intended on her birthday that she was not to be comforted; and lest such another accident might oust the poor cur of his clergy,[22] she protested she would board out her dog at a neighbor's house, where she hoped he would be more kindly treated.

Then the Colonel and I took another turn in the garden to discourse farther on the subject of iron. He was very frank in communicating all his dear-bought experience to me and told me very civilly he would not only let me into the whole secret but would make a journey to James River and give me his faithful opinion of all my conveniences. For his part, he wished there were many more ironworks in the coun-

[22] Referring to the appeal to "benefit of clergy" by which offenders were enabled to escape the death penalty for a first offense of a capital nature. Originally designed to exempt members of the clergy from secular jurisdiction, the benefit was later extended to all who could prove their literacy by reading a passage that came to be called "neck verse." An act of Parliament in 1707 abolished the literacy test; but by this time most felonies were "non-clergyable." Benefit of clergy itself was abolished in 1827. See Theodore F. T. Plucknett, *A Concise History of the Common Law* (London, 1948), pp. 414–416.

try, provided the parties concerned would preserve a constant harmony among themselves and meet and consult frequently what might be for their common advantage. By this they might be better able to manage the workmen and reduce their wages to what was just and reasonable. After this frank speech he began to explain the whole charge of an ironwork. He said there ought at least to be an hundred Negroes employed in it, and those upon good land would make corn and raise provisions enough to support themselves and the cattle and do every other part of the business. That the furnace might be built for £700 and made ready to go to work, if I went the nearest way to do it, especially since, coming after so many, I might correct their errors and avoid their miscarriages. That if I had ore and wood enough and a convenient stream of water to set the furnace upon, having neither too much nor too little water, I might undertake the affair with a full assurance of success, provided the distance of carting be not too great, which is exceedingly burdensome. That there must be abundance of wheel carriages shod with iron and several teams of oxen provided to transport the wood that is to be coaled, and afterwards the coal and ore to the furnace, and last of all the sow iron to the nearest water carriage, and carry back limestone and other necessaries from thence to the works; and a sloop also would be useful to carry the iron on board the ships, the masters not being always in the humor to fetch it.

Then he enumerated the people that were to be hired, viz.: a founder, a mine-raiser, a collier, a stocktaker, a clerk, a smith, a carpenter, a wheelwright, and several carters. That these altogether will be a standing charge of about £500 a year. That the amount of freight, custom, commission, and other charges in England, comes to 27s. a ton. But that the merchants yearly find out means to inflame the account with new articles, as they do in those of tobacco. That, upon the whole matter, the expenses here and in England may be computed modestly at £3 a ton. And the rest that the iron sells for will be clear gain, to pay for the land and Negroes, which 'tis to be hoped will be £3 more for every ton that is sent over. As this account agreed pretty near with that which Mr. Chiswell had given me, I set it down (notwithstanding it may seem a repetition of the same thing) to prove that both these gentlemen were sincere in their representations.

We had a Michaelmas goose for dinner of Miss Theky's own raising, who was now good-natured enough to forget the jeopardy of her
dog. In the afternoon we walked in a meadow by the riverside, which
winds in the form of a horseshoe about Germanna, making it a peninsula containing about four hundred acres. Rappahannock forks a-
bout fourteen miles below this place, the northern branch being the
larger and consequently must be the river that bounds My Lord
Fairfax's grant of the Northern Neck.[23]

30. The sun rose clear this morning, and so did I, and finished all
my little affairs by breakfast. It was then resolved to wait on the ladies
on horseback, since the bright sun, the fine air, and the wholesome
exercise all invited us to it. We forded the river a little above the ferry
and rode six miles up the neck to a fine level piece of rich land, where
we found about twenty plants of ginseng, with the scarlet berries growing on the top of the middle stalk. The root of this is of wonderful
virtue in many cases, particularly to raise the spirits and promote perspiration, which makes it a specific in colds and coughs. The Colonel
complimented me with all we found in return for my telling him the
virtues of it. We were all pleased to find so much of this king of plants
so near the Colonel's habitation and growing, too, upon his own land,
but were, however, surprised to find it upon level ground, after we
had been told it grew only upon the north side of stony mountains.
I carried home this treasure with as much joy as if every root had been
a graft of the tree of life, and washed and dried it carefully.

This airing made us as hungry as so many hawks, so that, between
appetite and a very good dinner, 'twas difficult to eat like a philosopher.
In the afternoon the ladies walked me about amongst all their little
animals, with which they amuse themselves and furnish the table; the
worst of it is, they are so tender-hearted they shed a silent tear every
time any of them are killed.

At night the Colonel and I quitted the threadbare subject of iron

[23] The portion of Virginia bounded by the Rappahannock and Potomac Rivers.
The original charter of the land had been ambiguously phrased, and Lord Fairfax
claimed a wider extent of land than Virginians were willing to concede. Byrd was
one of the commissioners appointed to represent the King against Fairfax in a review of the matter in 1735. Fairfax ultimately won his case, the boundaries being
set at the southern branch of the Rappahannock and the northern branch of the
Potomac; see Richard L. Morton, *Colonial Virginia* (Chapel Hill, 1960), II, 546–547.

and changed the scene to politics. He told me the ministry[24] had receded from their demand upon New England to raise a standing salary for all succeeding governors, for fear some curious members of the House of Commons should inquire how the money was disposed of that had been raised in the other American colonies for the support of their governors. And particularly what becomes of the 4½ per cent paid in the sugar colonies for that purpose. That duty produces near £20,000 a year, but, being remitted into the Exchequer, not one of the West India governors is paid out of it; but they, like falcons, are let loose upon the people, who are complaisant enough to settle other revenues upon them, to the great impoverishing of those colonies.[25] In the meantime 'tis certain the money raised by the 4½ per cent molders away between the minister's fingers, nobody knows how, like the quitrents of Virginia. And 'tis for this reason that the instructions forbidding all governors to accept of any presents from their assemblies are dispensed with in the Sugar Islands, while 'tis strictly insisted upon everywhere else, where the assemblies were so wise as to keep their revenues among themselves. He said further that if the assembly in New England would stand buff,[26] he did not see how they could be forced to raise money against their will, for if they should direct it to be done by act of Parliament, which they have threatened to do (though it be against the right of Englishmen to be taxed but by their representatives), yet they would find it no easy matter to put such an act in execution.

Then the Colonel read me a lecture upon tar, affirming that it can't be made in this warm climate after the manner they make it in Sweden and Muscovy, by barking the tree two yards from the ground, whereby the turpentine descends all into the stump in a year's time, which is then split in pieces in order for the kiln. But here the sun fries out the turpentine in the branches of the tree, when the leaves

[24] The Board of Trade and Plantations.

[25] Virginians, like other colonists, habitually complained about the avarice of governors, who expected to recoup their fortunes from moneys which they might wring from the colonies; see *An Essay upon the Government of the English Plantations on the Continent of America* (1701), edited by Louis B. Wright (San Marino, Calif., 1945), *passim*.

[26] To stand firm; not to flinch.

are dried, and hinders it from descending. But, on the contrary, those who burn tar of lightwood in the common way and are careful about it, make as good as that which comes from the East Country,[27] nor will it burn the cordage more than that does.

Then we entered upon the subject of hemp, which the Colonel told me he never could raise here from foreign seed but at last sowed the seed of the wild hemp (which is very common in the upper parts of the country) and that came up very thick. That he sent about five hundred pounds of it to England, and that the Commissioners of the Navy, after a full trial of it, reported to the Lords of the Admiralty that it was equal in goodness to the best that comes from Riga. I told him if our hemp were never so good it would not be worth the making here, even though they should continue the bounty. And my reason was because labor is not more than twopence a day in the East Country where they produce hemp, and here we can't compute it at less than tenpence, which being five times as much as their labor, and considering besides that our freight is three times as dear as theirs, the price that will make them rich will ruin us, as I have found by woeful experience. Besides, if the King, who must have the refusal, buys our hemp, the Navy is so long in paying both the price and the bounty that we who live from hand to mouth cannot afford to wait so long for it. And then our good friends the merchants load it with so many charges that they run away with great part of the profit themselves, just like the bald eagle which, after the fishing hawk has been at great pains to catch a fish, powders down [28] and takes it from him.

Our conversation was interrupted by a summons to supper, for the ladies, to show their power, had by this time brought us tamely to go to bed with our bellies full, though we both at first declared positively against it. So very pliable a thing is frail man when women have the bending of him.

OCTOBER

1. Our ladies overslept themselves this morning, so that we did not break our fast till ten. We drank tea made of the leaves of ginseng,

[27] The Baltic area.
[28] Descends hastily.

which has the virtues of the root in a weaker degree and is not disagreeable.

So soon as we could force our inclinations to quit the ladies, we took a turn on the terrace walk and discoursed upon quite a new subject. The Colonel explained to me the difference betwixt the galleons and the flota, which very few people know. The galleons, it seems, are the ships which bring the treasure and other rich merchandise to Cartagena from Portobelo, to which place it is brought overland from Panama and Peru. And the flota is the squadron that brings the treasure, etc., from Mexico and New Spain, which make up at La Vera Cruz. Both these squadrons rendezvous at the Havana, from whence they shoot the Gulf of Florida in their return to Old Spain. That this important port of the Havana is very poorly fortified and worse garrisoned and provided, for which reason it may be easily taken. Besides, both the galleons and flota, being confined to sail through the gulf, might be intercepted by our stationing a squadron of men-of-war at the most convenient of the Bahama Islands. And that those islands are of vast consequence for that purpose. He told me also that the *azogue* ships are they that carry quicksilver to Portobelo and La Vera Cruz to refine the silver, and that in Spanish *azogue* signifies quicksilver.

Then my friend unriddled to me the great mystery why we have endured all the late insolences of the Spaniards so tamely. The *Asiento* Contract [29] and the liberty of sending a ship every year to the Spanish West Indies make it very necessary for the South Sea Company to have effects of great value in that part of the world. Now these, being always in the power of the Spaniards, make the directors of that company very fearful of a breach and consequently very generous in their offers to the ministry to prevent it. For fear these worthy gentlemen should suffer, the English squadron under Admiral Hosier lay idle at the bastimentos till the ship's bottoms were eat out by the worm and the officers and men, to the number of five thousand, died like rotten sheep, without being suffered, by the strictest orders, to strike one stroke, though they

[29] By the Treaty of Utrecht (1713), Great Britain received a 33-year monopoly of selling Negro slaves to the Spanish colonies and the right to send one ship annually to trade with the Spanish Indies; the concessions were to be managed by the South Sea Company.

might have taken both the flota and galleons and made themselves masters of the Havana into the bargain, if they had not been chained up from doing it. All this moderation our peaceable ministry showed even at a time when the Spaniards were furiously attacking Gibraltar and taking all the English ships they could, both in Europe and America, to the great and everlasting reproach of the British nation. That some of the ministry, being tired out with the clamors of the merchants, declared their opinion for war and while they entertained those sentiments they pitched upon him, Colonel Spotswood, to be Governor of Jamaica, that by his skill and experience in the art military they might be the better able to execute their design of taking the Havana. But the courage of these worthy patriots soon cooled and the arguments used by the South Sea directors persuaded them once again into more pacific measures. When the scheme was dropped, his government of Jamaica was dropped at the same time, and then General Hunter was judged fit enough to rule that island in time of peace.

After this the Colonel endeavored to convince me that he came fairly by his place of Postmaster General,[30] notwithstanding the report of some evil-disposed persons to the contrary. The case was this: Mr. Hamilton of New Jersey, who had formerly had that post, wrote to Colonel Spotswood in England to favor him with his interest to get it restored to him. But the Colonel, considering wisely that charity began at home, instead of getting the place for Hamilton, secured it for a better friend; though, as he tells the story, that gentleman was absolutely refused before he spoke the least good word for himself.

2. This being the day appointed for my departure from hence, I packed up my effects in good time; but the ladies, whose dear companies we were to have to the mines, were a little tedious in their equipment. However, we made a shift to get into the coach by ten o'clock; but little master,[31] who is under no government, would by all means

[30] Spotswood was appointed Deputy Postmaster General in 1730 for a term of ten years. By 1732 he had extended to Williamsburg a service which had formerly stopped at Philadelphia. Benjamin Franklin wrote that in 1737 "Colonel Spotswood, . . . being dissatisfied with the conduct of his deputy at Philadelphia respecting some negligence in rendering, and inexactitude of his accounts, took from him the commission and offered it to me" (Dodson, *Alexander Spotswood*, pp. 300–301).

[31] Spotswood had two sons, John (the elder) and Robert.

go on horseback. Before we set out I gave Mr. Russel [32] the trouble of distributing a pistole among the servants, of which I fancy the nurse had a pretty good share, being no small favorite.

We drove over a fine road to the mines, which lie thirteen measured miles from Germanna, each mile being marked distinctly upon the trees. The Colonel has a great deal of land in his mine tract exceedingly barren, and the growth of trees upon it is hardly big enough for coaling. However, the treasure underground makes amends and renders it worthy to be his lady's jointure.

We light[ed] at the mines, which are a mile nearer to Germanna than the furnace. They raise abundance of ore there, great part of which is very rich. We saw his engineer blow it up after the following manner. He drilled a hole about eighteen inches deep, humoring the situation of the mine. When he had dried it with a rag fastened to a worm, he charged it with a cartridge containing four ounces of powder, including the priming. Then he rammed the hole up with soft stone to the very mouth; after that he pierced through all with an iron called a primer, which is taper and ends in a sharp point. Into the hole the primer makes the priming is put, which he fired by a paper moistened with a solution of saltpeter. And this burns leisurely enough, it seems, to give time for the persons concerned to retreat out of harm's way. All the land hereabouts seems paved with iron ore; so that there seems to be enough to feed a furnace for many ages.

From hence we proceeded to the furnace, which is built of rough stone, having been the first of that kind erected in the country. It had not blown for several moons, the Colonel having taken off great part of his people to carry on his air furnace at Massaponax. Here the wheel that carried the bellows was no more than twenty feet [in] diameter but was an overshot wheel that went with little water. This was necessary here, because water is something scarce, notwithstanding 'tis sup-

[32] Possibly this should be Mrs. Russell (Katharine Russell), described "as the niece of Governor Spotswood, [who] presided over his household"; see *The Secret Diary of William Byrd of Westover, 1709–1712*, edited by Louis B. Wright and Marion Tinling (Richmond, Va., 1941), p. 206. However, there was some gossip about her relations with the Governor, which might have made her presence in the household uncomfortable when he brought home a bride, and Byrd calls Miss Theky the "housewife of the family" on p. 356.

plied by two streams, one of which is conveyed 1,900 feet through wooden pipes and the other sixty.

The name of the founder employed at present is one Godfrey of the kingdom of Ireland, whose wages are 3s.6d. per ton for all the iron he runs and his provisions. This man told me that the best wood for coaling is red oak. He complained that the Colonel starves his works out of whimsicalness and frugality, endeavoring to do everything with his own people, and at the same time taking them off upon every vagary that comes into his head. Here the coal carts discharge their load at folding doors, made at the bottom, which is sooner done and shatters the coal less. They carry no more than 110 bushels. The Colonel advised me by all means to have the coal made on the same side the river with the furnace, not only to avoid the charge of boating and bags, but likewise to avoid breaking of the coals and making them less fit for use.

Having picked the bones of a sirloin of beef, we took leave of the ladies and rode together about five miles, where the roads parted. The Colonel took that to Massaponax, which is fifteen miles from his furnace and very level, and I that to Fredericksburg, which can't be less than twenty. I was a little benighted and should not have seen my way, if the lightning, which flashed continually in my face, had not befriended me. I got about seven o'clock to Colonel Harry Willis', a little moistened with the rain; but a glass of good wine kept my pores open and prevented all rheums and defluxions for that time.

3. I was obliged to rise early here that I might not starve my landlord, whose constitution requires him to swallow a beefsteak before the sun blesses the world with its genial rays. However, he was so complaisant as to bear the gnawing of his stomach till eight o'clock for my sake. Colonel Waller, after a score of loud hems to clear his throat, broke his fast along with us.

When this necessary affair was dispatched, Colonel Willis walked me about his town of Fredericksburg. It is pleasantly situated on the south shore of Rappahannock River, about a mile below the falls. Sloops may come up and lie close to the wharf, within thirty yards of the public warehouses, which are built in the figure of a cross. Just by the wharf is a quarry of white stone that is very soft in the ground and hardens in the air, appearing to be as fair and fine-grained as that of Portland. Besides that, there are several other quarries in the river bank, within the limits of the town, sufficient to build a great city. The only edifice of stone yet built is the prison, the walls of which are strong enough to hold Jack Sheppard,[33] if he had been transported hither.

Though this be a commodious and beautiful situation for a town, with the advantages of a navigable river and wholesome air, yet the inhabitants are very few. Besides Colonel Willis, who is the top man of the place, there are only one merchant, a tailor, a smith, and an ordinary keeper; though I must not forget Mrs. Levistone,[34] who acts here in the double capacity of a doctress and coffee woman. And were this a populous city, she is qualified to exercise two other callings. 'Tis said the courthouse and the church are going to be built here, and then both religion and justice will help to enlarge the place.

Two miles from this place is a spring strongly impregnated with alum, and so is the earth all about it. This water does wonders for those that are afflicted with a dropsy. And on the other side the river, in King George County, twelve miles from hence, is another spring of strong steel water as good as that at Tunbridge Wells. Not far from this last spring are England's Iron Mines, called so from the chief manager of them, though the land belongs to Mr. Washington.[35] These mines are two miles from the furnace, and Mr. Washington raises the ore, and carts it thither for 20s. the ton of iron that it yields. The furnace is built on a run, which discharges its waters into Potomac. And when the iron is cast, they cart it about six miles to a landing on that river. Besides Mr. Washington and Mr. England, there are several

[33] A notorious highwayman of the 1720's, a onetime associate of Jonathan Wild. Sheppard made several spectacular escapes from custody, two from Newgate itself, before the authorities finally succeeded in hanging him. For a resumé of his colorful career see Patrick Pringle, *Stand and Deliver* (London, 1951), pp. 200–205.

[34] Mrs. Susanna Levingstone was the widow of the William Levingstone who operated a theater in Williamsburg in about 1717. See Robert H. Land, "The First Williamsburg Theatre," *William and Mary Quarterly*, 3rd Ser., 5:359–374 (July 1948). Byrd implies that she was capable of being a whore as well as an actress.

[35] Augustine Washington, father of George. Washington's iron foundry was operated during the Revolution by James Hunter and furnished the American forces with pots, pans, camp kettles, anchors, and bayonets.

other persons in England concerned in these works. Matters are very well managed there, and no expense is spared to make them profitable, which is not the case in the works I have already mentioned. Mr. England can neither write nor read, but without those helps is so well skilled in ironworks that he don't only carry on his furnace but has likewise the chief management of the works at Principia, at the head of the bay, where they have also erected a forge and make very good bar iron.

Colonel Willis had built a flue to try all sorts of ore in, which was contrived after the following manner. It was built of stone four foot square, with an iron grate fixed in the middle of it for the fire to lie upon. It was open at the bottom, to give a free passage to the air up to the grate. Above the grate was another opening that carried the smoke into a chimney. This makes a draft upward, and the fire, rarefying the air below, makes another draft underneath, which causes the fire to burn very fiercely and melt any ore in the crucibles that are set upon the fire. This was erected by a mason called Taylor, who told me he built the furnace at Fredericksville and came in for that purpose at 3s.6d. a day, to be paid him from the time he left his house in Gloucestershire to the time he returned thither again, unless he chose rather to remain in Virginia after he had done his work.

It happened to be court day here, but the rain hindered all but the most quarrelsome people from coming. The Colonel brought three of his brother justices to dine with us, namely, John Taliaferro,[36] Major Lightfoot,[37] and Captain Green, and in the evening Parson Kenner edified us with his company, who left this parish for a better without any regard to the poor souls he had half saved, of the flock he abandoned.

[36] Probably the son of the Robert "Talifer" from whose house near the falls of the Rappahannock John Lederer set out on his journey of exploration in 1670; see Clarence W. Alvord and Lee Bidgood, *The First Explorations of the Trans-Allegheny Regions* (Cleveland, 1912), p. 163. A well-known Virginia family descended from Robert Taliaferro, who arrived in Virginia in 1657 (*Dictionary of American Biography*, under William Booth Taliaferro). John Taliaferro traded with the Indians up the Rappahannock and to the southwest; see Hugh Jones, *Present State of Virginia*, p. 169, n. 42.
[37] One of the numerous relatives of Colonel Philip Lightfoot of Sandy Point, Charles City County, member of the Council and one of the richest men in Virginia.

4. The sun, rising very bright, invited me to leave this infant city; accordingly, about ten I took leave of my hospitable landlord and persuaded Parson Kenner to be my guide to Massaponax, lying five miles off, where I had agreed to meet Colonel Spotswood.

We arrived there about twelve and found it a very pleasant and commodious plantation. The Colonel received us with open arms and carried us directly to his air furnace, which is a very ingenious and profitable contrivance. The use of it is to melt his sow iron in order to cast it into sundry utensils, such as backs for chimneys, andirons, fenders, plates for hearths, pots, mortars, rollers for gardeners, skillets, boxes for cartwheels; and many other things, which, one with another, can be afforded at 20s. a ton and delivered at people's own homes, and, being cast from the sow iron, are much better than those which come from England, which are cast immediately from the ore for the most part.

Mr. Flowry is the artist that directed the building of this ingenious structure, which is contrived after this manner. There is an opening about a foot square for the fresh air to pass through from without. This leads up to an iron grate that holds about half a bushel of charcoal and is about six feet higher than the opening. When the fire is kindled, it rarefies the air in such a manner as to make a very strong draft from without. About two foot above the grate is a hole [that] leads into a kind of oven, the floor of which is laid shelving toward the mouth. In the middle of this oven, on one side, is another hole that leads into the funnel of a chimney, about forty feet high. The smoke mounts up this way, drawing the flame after it with so much force that in less than an hour it melts the sows of iron that are thrust toward the upper end of the oven. As the metal melts, it runs toward the mouth into a hollow place, out of which the potter lades it in iron ladles, in order to pour it into the several molds just by. The mouth of the oven is stopped close with a movable stone shutter, which he removes so soon as he perceives through the peepholes that the iron is melted. The inside of the oven is lined with soft bricks made of Sturbridge or Windsor clay, because no other will endure the intense heat of the fire. And over the floor of the oven they strew sand taken from the land and not from the waterside. This sand will melt the second heat here, but that which they use in England will bear the fire four or five times. The potter is also obliged to plaster over his ladles with the same sand moistened, to save them from melting. Here are two of these air furnaces in one room, so that in case one wants repair the other may work, they being exactly of the same structure.

The chimneys and other outside work of this building are of free-stone, raised near a mile off on the Colonel's own land, and were built by his servant, whose name is Kerby, a very complete workman. This man disdains to do anything of rough work, even where neat is not required, lest anyone might say hereafter Kerby did it. The potter was so complaisant as to show me the whole process, for which I paid him and the other workmen my respects in the most agreeable way. There was a great deal of ingenuity in the framing of the molds wherein they cast the several utensils, but without breaking them to pieces I found there was no being let into that secret. The flakes of iron that fall at the mouth of the oven are called geets,[38] which are melted over again.

The Colonel told me in my ear that Mr. Robert Cary in England was concerned with him, both in this and his other ironworks, not only to help support the charge but also to make friends to the undertaking at home. His Honor has settled his cousin, Mr. Graeme, here as postmaster, with a salary of £60 a year to reward him for having ruined his estate while he was absent. Just by the air furnace stands a very substantial wharf, close to which any vessel may ride in safety.

After satisfying our eyes with all these sights, we satisfied our stomachs with a sirloin of beef, and then the parson and I took leave of the Colonel and left our blessing upon all his works. We took our way from thence to Major Woodford's[39] seven miles off, who lives upon a high hill that affords an extended prospect, on which account 'tis dignified with the name of Windsor. There we found Rachel Cocke, who stayed with her sister[40] some time, that she might not lose the use

[38] Jets.
[39] William Woodford, whose son William later led the American forces in the first defeat of the British troops on Virginia soil (at Great Bridge) during the Revolution; see *Dictionary of American Biography*.
[40] Major Woodford was married to Anne Cocke, daughter of Dr. William Cocke, secretary of the College of William and Mary.

of her tongue in this lonely place. We were received graciously and the evening was spent in talking and toping, and then the parson and I were conducted to the same apartment, the house being not yet finished.

5. The parson slept very peaceably and gave me no disturbance, so I rose fresh in the morning and did credit to the air by eating a hearty breakfast. Then Major Woodford carried me to the house where he cuts tobacco. He manufactures about sixty hogsheads yearly, for which he gets after the rate of 11d. a pound and pays himself liberally for his trouble. The tobacco he cuts is Long Green, which, according to its name, bears a very long leaf and consequently each plant is heavier than common sweet-scented[41] or Townsend tobacco. The worst of it is, the veins of the leaf are very large, so that it loses its weight a good deal by stemming. This kind of tobacco is much the fashion in these parts, and Jonathan Forward[42] (who has great interest here) gives a good price for it. This sort the Major cuts up and has a man that performs it very handily. The tobacco is stemmed clean in the first place and then laid straight in a box and pressed down hard by a press that goes with a nut. This box is shoved forward toward the knife by a

[41] This variety, more valuable than other tobacco, was comparatively scarce, perhaps because, as the Reverend Hugh Jones declared in his *Present State of Virginia*, it required "particular seed and management," or because it required light, sandy soil to thrive, as was declared by the Reverend John Clayton in 1688; see Jones, *Present State of Virginia*, pp. 197–198. According to the letter of Commissary Blair quoted earlier, a minister's living was worth £20 more per year in a "sweet scented parish" than in other parishes.

[42] Forward was a London merchant who was also active in the trade supplying convicts from Newgate Prison and the home counties for the labor market in Virginia and Maryland. Parliament had passed an act in 1717 "for the further preventing robbery, burglary, and other felonies, and for the more effectual transportation of felons," which conflicted with an act of the Virginia General Court forbidding the importation of convicts. As a result of the act of Parliament, the Virginia Assembly in May 1722 passed a law requiring masters of vessels to give bond not to let the convicts go on shore until they had been disposed of and to guarantee their good behavior for two months thereafter. They were also required to register with the county courts the name of each convict and the offense for which he was transported. Forward, who had made a contract with the Treasury in 1718 to be paid £3 apiece for Newgate felons and £5 for those from the counties, promptly appealed to the Privy Council, pointing out that the Virginia law made the transportation of convicts wholly impracticable, and on August 27, 1723, the Privy Council formally disallowed it. See Abbot E. Smith, *Colonists in Bondage: White Servitude and Convict Labor in America, 1607–1776* (Chapel Hill, 1947), pp. 110–111, 113, 120, and 363, n. 13; Morton, *Colonial Virginia*, II, 494–495.

screw, receiving its motion from a treadle that the engineer sets a-going with his foot. Each motion pushes the box the exact length which the tobacco ought to be of, according to the saffron, or oblong, cut, which it seems yields one penny in a pound more at London than the square cut, though at Bristol they are both of equal price. The man strikes down the knife once at every motion of the screw, so that his hand and foot keep exact pace with each other. After the tobacco is cut in this manner, 'tis sifted first through a sand riddle, and then through a dust riddle, till 'tis perfectly clean. Then 'tis put into a tight hogshead and pressed under the nut, till it weighs about a thousand neat. One man performs all the work after the tobacco is stemmed, so that the charge bears no proportion to the profit.

One considerable benefit from planting Long Green tobacco is that 'tis much hardier and less subject to fire than other sweet-scented, though it smells not altogether so fragrant.

I surprised Mrs. Woodford in her housewifery in the meat house, at which she blushed as if it had been a sin. We all walked about a mile in the woods, where I showed them several useful plants and explained the virtues of them. This exercise and the fine air we breathed in sharpened our appetites so much that we had no mercy on a rib of beef that came attended with several other good things at dinner.

In the afternoon we tempted all the family to go along with us to Major Ben Robinson's, who lives on a high hill called Moon's Mount, about five miles off. On the road we came to an eminence from whence we had a plain view of the mountains, which seemed to be no more than thirty miles from us in a straight line, though to go by the road it was near double that distance. The sun had just time to light us to our journey's end, and the Major received us with his usual good humor. He has a very industrious wife, who has kept him from sinking by the weight of gaming and idleness. But he is now reformed from those ruinous qualities and by the help of a clerk's place in a quarrelsome county will soon be able to clear his old scores.

We drank exceeding good cider here, the juice of the white apple, which made us talkative till ten o'clock, and then I was conducted to a bedchamber where there was neither chair nor table; however I slept sound and waked with strong tokens of health in the morning.

6. When I got up about sunrise I was surprised to find that a fog had covered this high hill; but there's a marsh on the other side the river that sends its filthy exhalation up to the clouds. On the borders of that morass lives Mr. Lomax,[43] a situation fit only for frogs and otters.

After fortifying myself with toast and cider and sweetening my lips with saluting the lady, I took leave and the two majors conducted me about four miles on my way as far as the church. After that, Ben Robinson ordered his East Indian to conduct me to Colonel Martin's. In about ten miles we reached Caroline [County] courthouse, where Colonel Armistead[44] and Colonel Will Beverley have each of 'em erected an ordinary well supplied with wine and other polite liquors for the worshipful bench. Besides these, there is a rum ordinary for persons of a more vulgar taste. Such liberal supplies of strong drink often make Justice nod and drop the scales out of her hands.

Eight miles beyond the ordinary I arrived at Colonel Martin's, who received me with more gravity than I expected. But, upon inquiry, his lady was sick, which had lengthened his face and gave him a very mournful air. I found him in his nightcap and banian,[45] which is his ordinary dress in that retired part of the country. Poorer land I never saw than what he lives upon, but the wholesomeness of the air and the goodness of the roads make some amends. In a clear day the mountains may be seen from hence, which is, in truth, the only rarity of the place.

At my first arrival, the Colonel saluted me with a glass of canary and soon after filled my belly with good mutton and cauliflowers. Two people were as indifferent company as a man and his wife, without a little inspiration from the bottle; and then we were forced to go as far as the kingdom of Ireland to help out our conversation. There, it seems,

[43] Possibly the Lunsford Lomax who acted as one of the commissioners representing the King in a settlement of the dispute concerned with the bounds of Lord Fairfax's estate in 1746 and who was one of the Virginia commissioners in a conference with the Ohio Indians on April 28, 1752, at Logstown, Pennsylvania (Morton, *Colonial Virginia*, II, 547, 615).

[44] Colonel Henry Armistead of Hesse, Gloucester County.

[45] A dressing gown, derived from a loose garment of that name worn in India.

the Colonel had an elder brother, a physician, who threatens him with an estate some time or other; though possibly it might come to him sooner if the succession depended on the death of one of his patients.

By eight o'clock at night we had no more to say, and I gaped wide as a signal for retiring, whereupon I was conducted to a clean lodging, where I would have been glad to exchange one of the beds for a chimney.

7. This morning Mrs. Martin was worse, so that there were no hopes of seeing how much she was altered. Nor was this all, but the indisposition of his consort made the Colonel intolerably grave and thoughtful. I prudently eat a meat breakfast, to give me spirits for a long journey and a long fast.

My landlord was so good as to send his servant along with me to guide me through all the turnings of a difficult way. In about four miles we crossed Mattaponi River at Norman's Ford and then slanted down to King William County road. We kept along that for about twelve miles, as far as the new brick church. After that I took a blind path that carried me to several of Colonel Jones's quarters, which border upon my own. The Colonel's overseers were all abroad, which made me fearful I should find mine as idle as them. But I was mistaken, for when I came to Gravel Hall, the first of my plantations in King William, I found William Snead (that looks after three of them) very honestly about his business. I had the pleasure to see my people all well and my business in good forwardness. I visited all the five quarters on that side, which spent so much of my time that I had no leisure to see any of those on the other side the river; though I discoursed Thomas Tinsley, one of the overseers, who informed me how matters went.

In the evening Tinsley conducted me to Mrs. Syme's house,[46] where I intended to take up my quarters. This lady, at first suspecting I was some lover, put on a gravity that becomes a weed, but so soon as she learnt who I was brightened up into an unusual cheerfulness and serenity. She was a portly, handsome dame, of the family of Esau, and

[46] This was Studley, home of John Syme. Mrs. Syme married John Henry after Syme's death and gave birth to Patrick Henry at Studley in 1736.

seemed not to pine too much for the death of her husband, who was of the family of the Saracens. He left a son by her who has all the strong features of his sire, not softened in the least by any of hers, so that the most malicious of her neighbors can't bring his legitimacy in question, not even the parson's wife, whose unruly tongue, they say, don't spare even the Reverend Doctor, her husband. This widow is a person of a lively and cheerful conversation, with much less reserve than most of her countrywomen. It becomes her very well and sets off her other agreeable qualities to advantage. We tossed off a bottle of honest port, which we relished with a broiled chicken. At nine I retired to my devotions and then slept so sound that fancy itself was stupefied, else I should have dreamt of my most obliging landlady.

8. I moistened my clay with a quart of milk and tea, which I found altogether as great a help to discourse as the juice of the grape. The courteous widow invited me to rest myself there that good day and go to the church with her, but I excused myself by telling her she would certainly spoil my devotion. Then she civilly entreated me to make her house my home whenever I visited my plantations, which made me bow low and thank her very kindly.

From thence I crossed over to Shacco's and took Thomas Tinsley for my guide, finding the distance about fifteen miles. I found everybody well at the Falls, blessed be God, though the bloody flux raged pretty much in the neighborhood. Mr. Booker had received a letter the day before from Mrs. Byrd giving an account of great desolation made in our neighborhood by the death of Mr. Lightfoot, Mrs. Soan, Captain Gerald, and Colonel Henry Harrison. Finding the flux had been so fatal, I desired Mr. Booker to make use of the following remedy, in case it should come amongst my people: to let them blood immediately about eight ounces; the next day to give them a dose of Indian physic, and to repeat the vomit again the day following, unless the symptoms abated. In the meantime, they should eat nothing but chicken broth and poached eggs and drink nothing but a quarter of a pint of milk boiled with a quart of water and medicated with a little mullein root or that of the prickly pear, to restore the mucus of the bowels and heal the excoriation. At the same time, I ordered him to communicate this method to all the poor neighbors, and especially to my overseers, with strict orders to use it on the first appearance of that distemper, because in that and all other sharp diseases delays are very dangerous.

I also instructed Mr. Booker in the way I had learnt of blowing up the rocks, which were now drilled pretty full of holes, and he promised to put it in execution. After discoursing seriously with the father about my affairs, I joked with the daughter in the evening and about eight retired to my castle and recollected all the follies of the day, the little I had learnt and the still less good I had done.

9. My long absence made me long for the domestic delights of my own family, for the smiles of an affectionate wife and the prattle of my innocent children. As soon as I sallied out of my castle, I understood that Colonel Carter's Sam was come, by his master's leave, to show my people to blow up the rocks in the canal. He pretended to great skill in that matter but performed very little, which, however, might be the effect of idleness rather than ignorance. He came upon one of my horses, which he tied to a tree at Shacco's, where the poor animal kept a fast of a night and a day. Though this fellow worked very little at the rocks, yet my man Argalus stole his trade and performed as well as he. For this good turn, I ordered Mr. Samuel half a pistole, all which he laid out with a New England man for rum and made my weaver and spinning woman, who has the happiness to be called his wife, exceedingly drunk. To punish the varlet for all these pranks, I ordered him to be banished from thence forever, under the penalty of being whipped home from constable to constable if he presumed to come again.

I left my memorandums with Mr. Booker of everything I ordered to be done and mounted my horse about ten, and in little more reached Bermuda Hundred and crossed over to Colonel Carter's.[47] He, like an industrious person, was gone to oversee his overseers at North Wales, but his lady was at home and kept me till suppertime before we went to dinner. As soon as I had done justice to my stomach, I made my honors to the good-humored little fairy and made the best of my

[47] Not Robert "King" Carter, who had died in August of this year, but his eldest son, John Carter, who had married Elizabeth Hill, heiress of Shirley on the James River.

way home, where I had the great satisfaction to find all that was dearest to me in good health, nor had any disaster happened in the family since I went away. Some of the neighbors had worm fevers, with all the symptoms of the bloody flux, but, blessed be God, their distempers gave way to proper remedies.

# A JOURNEY TO THE LAND OF

## EDEN ANNO 1733

11. *H*AVING recommended my family to the protection of the Almighty, I crossed the river with two servants and four horses and rode to Colonel Mumford's. There I met my friend, Mr. Banister, who was to be the kind companion of my travels. I stayed dinner with the good Colonel, while Mr. Banister made the best of his way home, to get his equipage ready in order to join me the next day.

After dining plentifully and wishing all that was good to the household, I proceeded to Major Mumford's,[1] who had also appointed to go along with me. I was the more obliged to him because he made me the compliment to leave the arms of a pretty wife to lie on the cold ground for my sake. She seemed to chide me with her eyes for coming to take her bedfellow from her, now the cold weather came on, and to make my peace I was forced to promise to take abundance of care of him, in order to restore him safe and sound to her embraces.

12. After the Major had cleared his pipes in calling with much authority about him, he made a shift to truss up his baggage about nine o'clock. Near the same hour my old friend and fellow traveler, Peter Jones, came to us completely accoutered. Then we fortified ourselves with a beefsteak, kissed our landlady for good luck, and mounted about ten. The Major took one Robin Bolling with him, as squire of his body, as well as conductor of his baggage. Tom Short had promised to attend me but had married a wife and could not come.

We crossed Hatcher's Run, Gravelly Run, Stony Creek, and in the distance of about twenty miles reached Sapony Chapel, where Mr. Banister joined us. Thus agreeably reinforced, we proceeded ten miles further to Major Embry's, on the south side of Nottoway River. The

---

[1] James Mumford, major of militia of Prince George County; see *Another Secret Diary of William Byrd of Westover, 1739-1741*, edited by Maude H. Woodfin and Marion Tinling (Richmond, Va., 1942), p. 153.

Major was ill of a purging and vomiting, attended with a fever which had brought him low, but I prescribed him a gallon or two of chicken broth, which washed him as clean as a gun and quenched his fever. Here Major Mayo met us, well equipped for a march into the woods, bringing a surveyor's tent that would shelter a small troop. Young Tom Jones also repaired hither to make his excuse; but old Tom Jones, by the privilege of his age, neither came nor sent, so that we were not so strong as we intended, being disappointed of three of our ablest foresters.

The entertainment we met with was the less sumptuous by reason of our landlord's indisposition. On this occasion we were as little troublesome as possible, by sending part of our company to Richard Birch's, who lives just by the bridge over the river.

We sent for an old Indian called Shacco-Will,[2] living about seven miles off, who reckoned himself seventy-eight years old. This fellow pretended he could conduct us to a silver mine that lies either upon Eno River or a creek of it, not far from where the Tuscaroras once lived. But by some circumstances in his story, it seems to be rather a lead than a silver mine. However, such as it is, he promised to go and show it to me whenever I pleased. To comfort his heart I gave him a bottle of rum, with which he made himself very happy and all the family very miserable by the horrible noise he made all night.

13. Our landlord had great relief from my remedy and found himself easy this morning. On this account we took our departure with more satisfaction about nine and, having picked up our friends at Mr. Birch's, pursued our journey over Quoique[3] Creek and Sturgeon Run, as far as Brunswick courthouse, about twelve miles beyond Nottoway. By the way I sent a runner half a mile out of the road to Colonel Drury Stith's, who was so good as to come to us. We cheered our hearts

[2] The name may indicate that he was a member of the Shakori tribe, who lived with Eno tribes on the Eno River in 1701 and later united with the Catawbas. The surveyor John Lawson had an Indian guide named Eno Will, for whom the Eno River was named, but who was believed to be a Shakori; this may be the same man. See John R. Swanton, *The Indians of the Southeastern United States* (Washington D.C., 1946), p. 183; and *North Carolina: A Guide to the Old North State* (Chapel Hill, 1944), p. 482.

[3] Waqua; the same creek as that spelled "Wiccoquoi" in the *History* (p. 317) and "Queocky" later in this narrative (p. 410), where we have changed it to "Waqua."

with three bottles of pretty good Madeira, which made Drury talk very hopefully of his copper mine. We easily prevailed with him to let us have his company, upon condition we would take the mine in our way.

From thence we proceeded to Meherrin River, which lies eight miles beyond the courthouse, and in our way forded Great Creek. For fear of being belated, we called not at my quarter, where Don Pedro is overseer and lives in good repute amongst his neighbors. In compliment to the little Major we went out of our way to lie at a settlement of his upon Cox Creek, four miles short of Roanoke. Our fare here was pretty coarse, but Mr. Banister and I took possession of the bed, while the rest of the company lay in bulk upon the floor. This night the little Major made the first discovery of an impatient and peevish temper, equally unfit both for a traveler and a husband.

14. In the morning my friend Tom Wilson made me a visit and gave me his parole that he would meet us at Bluestone Castle.[4] We took horse about nine and in the distance of ten miles reached a quarter of Colonel Stith's, under the management of John Tomasin. This plantation lies on the west side of Stith's Creek, which was so full of water, by reason of a fresh in the river, that we could not ford it, but we and our baggage were paddled over in a canoe and our horses swam by our sides. After staying here an hour, with some of Diana's maids of honor, we crossed Miles Creek a small distance off, and at the end of eight miles were met by a tall, meager figure which I took at first for an apparition, but it proved to be Colonel Stith's miner. I concluded that the unwholesome vapors arising from the copper mine had made this operator such a skeleton, but upon inquiry understood it was sheer famine had brought him so low. He told us his stomach had not been blessed with one morsel of meat for more than three weeks, and that too he had been obliged to short allowance of bread, by reason corn was scarce and to be fetched from Tomasin's, which was ten long miles from the mine where he lived. However, in spite of this spare diet, the man was cheerful and uttered no complaint.

[4] At this time Byrd had a house on this site and refers to it as Bluestone Castle. He later built here a hunting lodge; he mentions marking out the site on p. 408.

Being conducted by him, we reached the mines about five o'clock and pitched our tents for the first time, there being yet no building erected but a log house to shelter the miner and his two Negroes. We examined the mine and found it dipped from east to west and showed but a slender vein, embodied in a hard rock of white spar. The shaft they had opened was about twelve feet deep and six over. I saw no more than one peck of good ore aboveground, and that promised to be very rich. The engineer seemed very sanguine and had not the least doubt but his employer's fortune was made. He made us the compliment of three blasts, and we filled his belly with good beef in return, which in his hungry circumstances was the most agreeable present we could make him.

15. It rained in the morning, which made us decamp later than we intended, but, the clouds clearing away about ten, we wished good luck to the mine and departed. We left Colonel Stith there to keep fast with his miner and directed our course through the woods to Butcher's Creek, which hath its name from an honest fellow that lives upon it. This place is about six miles from Colonel Stith's works and can also boast of a very fair show of copper ore. It is dug out of the side of a hill that rises gradually from the creek to the house. The good man was from home himself, but his wife, who was as old as one of the Sibyls, refreshed us with an ocean of milk. By the strength of that entertainment we proceeded to Mr. Mumford's quarter, about five miles off, where Joseph Colson is overseer. Here our thirsty companions raised their drooping spirits with a cheerful dram, and, having wet both eyes, we rode on seven miles farther to Bluestone Castle, five whereof were through my own land, that is to say, all above Sandy Creek.

My land there in all extends ten miles upon the river, and three charming islands, namely Sappony, Occaneechee, and Totero, run along the whole length of it. The lowest of these islands is three miles long, the next four, and the uppermost three, divided from each other by only a narrow strait. The soil is rich in all of them, the timber large, and a kind of pea, very grateful to cattle and horses, holds green all the winter. Roanoke River is divided by these islands; that part which runs on the north side is about eighty yards and that on the south more than one hundred. A large fresh will overflow the lower part of these islands but never covers all, so that the cattle may always recover a place of security. The middlemost island, called Occaneechee Island, has several fields in it where Occaneechi Indians formerly lived, and there are still some remains of the peach trees they planted. Here grow likewise excellent wild hops without any cultivation. My overseer, Harry Morris, did his utmost to entertain me and my company; the worst of it was, we were obliged all to be littered down in one room, in company with my landlady and four children, one of which was very sick and consequently very fretful.

16. This being Sunday, and the place where we were quite out of Christendom, very little devotion went forward. I thought it no harm to take a Sabbath Day's journey and rode with my overseer to a new entry I had made upon Bluestone Creek, about three miles from the castle, and found the land very fertile and convenient. It consists of low grounds and meadows on both sides the creek. After taking a view of this, we rode two miles farther to a stony place where there were some tokens of a copper mine, but not hopeful enough to lay me under any temptation. Then we returned to the company and found Tom Wilson was come according to his promise in order to proceed into the woods along with us. Joseph Colson likewise entered into pay, having cautiously made his bargain for a pistole. There were three Tuscarora Indians (which I understood had been kept on my plantation to hunt for Harry Morris) that with much ado were also persuaded to be of the party.

My landlady could not forbear discovering some broad signs of the fury by breaking out into insolent and passionate expressions against the poor Negroes. And if my presence could not awe her, I concluded she could be very outrageous when I was an hundred miles off. This inference I came afterwards to understand was but too true, for between the husband and the wife the Negroes had a hard time of it.

17. We set off about nine from Bluestone Castle and rode up the river six miles (one half of which distance was on my own land) as far as Major Mumford's quarter, where Master Hogen was tenant upon

halves. Here were no great marks of industry, the weeds being near as high as the corn. My islands run up within a little way of this place, which will expose them to the inroad of the Major's creatures. That called Totero Island lies too convenient not to receive damage that way, but we must guard against it as well as we can.

After the Major had convinced himself of the idleness of his tenant, he returned back to Bluestone, and Harry Morris and I went in quest of a copper mine which he had secured for me in the fork. For which purpose, about a quarter of a mile higher than Hogen's, we crossed a narrow branch of the river into a small island, not yet taken up and, after traversing that, forded a much wider branch into the fork of Roanoke River. Where we landed was near three miles higher up than the point of the fork. We first directed our course easterly toward that point, which was very sharp, and each branch of the river where it divided first seemed not to exceed eighty yards in breadth. The land was broken and barren off from the river till we came within half a mile of the point where the low ground began. The same sort of low ground ran up each branch of the river. That on the Staunton (being the northern branch) was but narrow, but that on the south, which is called the Dan, seemed to carry a width of at least half a mile. After discovering this place, for which I intended to enter, we rode up the midland five miles to view the mine, which in my opinion hardly answered the trouble of riding so far out of our way.

We returned downwards again about four miles and a mile from the point found a good ford over the north branch into the upper end of Totero Island. We crossed the river there and near the head of the island saw a large quantity of wild hops growing that smelt fragrantly and seemed to be in great perfection. At our first landing we were so hampered with brambles, vines, and poke bushes that our horses could hardly force their way through them. However, this difficulty held only about twenty-five yards at each end of the island, all the rest being very level and free from underwood.

We met with old fields where the Indians had formerly lived and the grass grew as high as a horse and his rider. In one of these fields were large duck ponds, very firm at the bottom, to which wild fowl resort in the winter. In the woody part of the island grows a vetch that is green all winter and a great support for horses and cattle, though 'tis to be feared the hogs will root it all up. There is a cave in this island in which the last Totero king, with only eight of his men, defended himself against a great host of northern Indians and at last obliged them to retire.

We forded the strait out of this into Occaneechee Island, which was full of large trees and rich land, and the south part of it is too high for any flood less than Noah's to drown it. We rode about two miles down this island (being half the length of it) where, finding ourselves opposite to Bluestone Castle, we passed the river in a canoe which had been ordered thither for that purpose and joined our friends, very much tired, not so much with the length of the journey as with the heat of the weather.

18. We lay by till the return of the messenger that we sent for the ammunition and other things left at the courthouse. Nor had the Indians yet joined us according to their promise, which made us begin to doubt of their veracity. I took a solitary walk to the first ford of Bluestone Creek, about a quarter of a mile from the house. This creek had its name from the color of the stones which paved the bottom of it and are so smooth that 'tis probable they will burn into lime. I took care to return to my company by dinnertime, that I might not trespass upon their stomachs.

In the afternoon I was paddled by the overseer and one of my servants up the creek but could proceed little farther than a mile because of the shoal water. All the way we perceived the bottom of the creek full of the blue stones above-mentioned, sufficient in quantity to build a large castle. At our return we went into the middle of the river and stood upon a large blue rock to angle, but without any success. We broke off a fragment of the rock and found it as heavy as so much lead.

Discouraged by our ill luck, we repaired to the company, who had procured some pieces of copper ore from Cargill's mine, which seemed full of metal. This mine lies about two miles higher than Major Mumford's plantation and has a better show than any yet discovered. There are so many appearances of copper in these parts that the inhabitants seem to be all mine-mad and neglect making of corn for their present necessities in hopes of growing very rich hereafter.

19. The heavens loured a little upon us in the morning, but, like a damsel ruffled by too bold an address, it soon cleared up again. Because I detested idleness, I caused my overseer to paddle me up the river as far as the strait that divides Occaneechee from Totero Island, which is about twenty yards wide. There runs a swift stream continually out of the south part of the river into the north and is in some places very deep. We crossed the south part to the opposite shore to view another entry I had made, beginning at Buffalo Creek, and running up the river to guard my islands and keep off bad neighbors on that side. The land seems good enough for corn along the river, but a quarter of a mile back 'tis broken and full of stones. After satisfying my curiosity, I returned the way that I came and shot the same strait back again and paddled down the river to the company.

When we got home, we laid the foundation of two large cities: one at Shacco's, to be called Richmond, and the other at the point of Appomattox River, to be named Petersburg. These Major Mayo offered to lay out into lots without fee or reward. The truth of it is, these two places, being the uppermost landing of James and Appomattox rivers, are naturally intended for marts where the traffic of the outer inhabitants must center. Thus we did not build castles only, but also cities in the air.

In the evening our ammunition arrived safe and the Indians came to us, resolved to make part of our company upon condition of their being supplied with powder and shot and having the skins of all the deer they killed to their own proper use.

20. Everything being ready for a march, we left Bluestone Castle about ten. My company consisted of four gentlemen (namely, Major Mayo, Major Mumford, Mr. Banister, and Mr. Jones) and five woodsmen, Thomas Wilson, Henry Morris, Joseph Colson, Robert Bolling, and Thomas Hooper, four Negroes and three Tuscarora Indians. With this small troop we proceeded up the river as far as Hogen's, above which, about a quarter of a mile, we forded into the little island and

from thence into the fork of the river. The water was risen so high that it ran into the top of my boots but without giving me any cold, although I rid in my wet stockings.

We landed three miles above the point of the fork and, after marching three miles farther, reached the tenement of Peter Mitchell, the highest inhabitant on Roanoke River. Two miles above that we forded a water, which we named Birch Creek, not far from the mouth, where it discharges itself into the Dan. From thence we rode through charming low grounds for six miles together to a larger stream, which we agreed to call Banister River. We were puzzled to find a ford, by reason the water was very high, but at lost got safe over about one and a half miles from the banks of the Dan. In our way we killed two very large rattlesnakes, one of fifteen and the other of twelve rattles. They were both fat, but nobody would be persuaded to carry them to our quarters, although they would have added much to the luxury of our supper.

We pitched our tents upon Banister River, where we feasted on a young buck which had the ill luck to cross our way. It rained great part of the night, with very loud thunder, which rumbled frightfully amongst the tall trees that surrounded us in that low ground, but, thank God, without any damage. Our Indians killed three deer but were so lazy they brought them not to the camp, pretending for their excuse that they were too lean.

21. The necessity of drying our baggage prevented us from marching till eleven o'clock. Then we proceeded through low grounds which were tolerably wide for three miles together, as far as a small creek, named by us Morris Creek. This tract of land I persuaded Mr. Banister to enter for, that he might not be a loser by the expedition. The low grounds held good a mile beyond the creek and then the high land came quite to the river and made our traveling more difficult.

All the way we went we perceived there had been tall canes lately growing on the bank of the river but were universally killed; and, inquiring into the reason of this destruction, we were told that the nature of those canes was to shed their seed but once in seven years and the succeeding winter to die and make room for young ones to grow up in their places. Thus much was certain, that four years before we saw canes grow and flourish in several places where they now lay dead and dry upon the ground.

The whole distance we traveled this day by computation was fifteen miles, and then the appearance of a black cloud, which threatened a gust, obliged us to take up our quarters. We had no sooner got our tents over our heads but it began to rain and thunder furiously, and one clap succeeded the lightning the same instant and made all tremble before it. But, blessed be God, it spent its fury upon a tall oak just by our camp.

Our Indians were so fearful of falling into the hands of the Catawbas that they durst not lose sight of us all day, so they killed nothing and we were forced to make a temperate supper upon bread and cheese. It was strange we met with no wild turkeys, this being the season in which great numbers of them used to be seen toward the mountains. They commonly perch on the high trees near the rivers and creeks. But this voyage, to our great misfortune, there were none to be found. So that we could not commit that abomination in the sight of all Indians of mixing the flesh of deer and turkeys in our broth.[5]

22. We were again obliged to dry our baggage, which had thoroughly soaked with the heavy rain that fell in the night. While we stayed for that, our hunters knocked down a brace of bucks, wherewith we made ourselves amends for our scanty supper the aforegoing night. All these matters being duly performed made it near noon before we sounded to horse.

We marched about two miles over fine low grounds to a most pleasant stream which we named the Medway, and by the way discovered a rich neck of high land that lay on the south side of the Dan and looked very tempting. Two miles beyond the Medway we forded another creek, which we called Maosti Creek. The whole distance between these two streams lay exceeding rich lands, and the same continued two miles higher. This body of low ground tempted me to enter

---

[5] This taboo may have been peculiar to the Saponi Indians. The only mention of it in Swanton, *Indians of the Southeastern United States*, is a citation of Byrd's being warned by the Saponis of the evil of mixing meat and fowl.

for it, to serve as a stage between my land at the fork and the Land of Eden.

The heavens looked so menacing that we resolved to take up our quarters two miles above Maosti Creek, where we entrenched ourselves on a rising ground. We had no sooner taken these precautions but it began to rain unmercifully and to put out our fire as fast as we could kindle it; nor was it only a hasty shower but continued with great impetuosity most part of the night. We preferred a dry fast to a wet feast, being unwilling to expose the people to the weather to gratify an unreasonable appetite. However it was some comfort in the midst of our abstinence to dream of the delicious breakfast we intended to make next morning upon a fat doe and two-year-old bear our hunters had killed the evening before. Notwithstanding all the care we could take, several of the men were dripping wet and, among the rest, Harry Morris dabbled so long in the rain that he was seized with a violent fit of an ague that shook him almost out of all his patience.

23. It was no loss of time to rest in our camp according to the duty of the day, because our baggage was so wet it needed a whole day to dry it. For this purpose we kindled four several fires in the absence of the sun, which vouchsafed us not one kind look the whole day. My servant had dropped his greatcoat yesterday, and two of the men were so good-natured as to ride back and look for it today, and were so lucky as to find it.

Our Indians, having no notion of the Sabbath, went out to hunt for something for dinner and brought a young doe back along with them. They laughed at the English for losing one day in seven, though the joke may be turned upon them for losing the whole seven, if idleness and doing nothing to the purpose may be called loss of time.

I looked out narrowly for ginseng, this being the season when it wears its scarlet fruit, but neither now nor any other time during the whole journey could I find one single plant of it. This made me conclude that it delighted not in quite so southerly a climate; and in truth I never heard of its growing on this side of thirty-eight degrees latitude. But to make amends we saw abundance of sugar trees in all these low grounds, which the whole summer long the woodpeckers tap for the sweet juice that flows out of them. Toward the evening a strong norwester was so kind as to sweep all the clouds away that had blackened our sky and moistened our skins for some time past.

24. The rest the Sabbath had given us made everybody alert this morning, so that we mounted before nine o'clock. This diligence happened to be the more necessary by reason the woods we encountered this day were exceedingly bushy and uneven.

At the distance of four miles we forded both branches of Forked Creek, which lay within one thousand paces from each other. My horse fell twice under me but, thank God, without any damage either to himself or his rider; and Major Mayo's baggage horse rolled down a steep hill and ground all his biscuit to rockahominy. My greatest disaster was that in mounting one of the precipices my steed made a short turn and gave my knee an unmerciful bang against a tree, and I felt the effects of it several days after. However, this was no interruption of our journey, but we went merrily on and two miles farther crossed Peter's Creek, and two miles after that Jones's Creek. Between these creeks was a good breadth of low grounds, with which Mr. Jones was tempted, though he shook his head at the distance.

A little above Jones's Creek we met with a pleasant situation where the herbage appeared more inviting than usual. The horses were so fond of it that we determined to camp there, although the sun had not near finished his course. This gave some of our company leisure to go out and search for the place where our line first crossed the Dan, and by good luck they found it within half a mile of the camp. But the place was so altered by the desolation which had happened to the canes (which had formerly fringed the banks of the river a full furlong deep) that we hardly knew it again. Pleased with this discovery, I forgot the pain in my knee, and the whole company eat their venison without any other sauce than keen appetite.

25. The weather now befriending us, we dispatched our little affairs in good time and marched in a body to the line. It was already grown very dim, by reason many of the marked trees were burnt or blown down. However, we made shift, after riding little more than half a mile, to find it and, having once found it, stuck as close to it as we could.

After a march of two miles we got upon Cane Creek, where we saw the same havoc amongst the old canes that we had observed in other places and a whole forest of young ones springing up in their stead. We pursued our journey over hills and dales till we arrived at the second ford of the Dan, which we passed with no other damage than sopping a little of our bread and shipping some water at the tops of our boots. The late rains, having been a little immoderate, had raised the water and made a current in the river.

We drove on four miles farther to a plentiful run of very clear water and quartered on a rising ground a bowshot from it. We had no sooner pitched the tents, but one of our woodsmen alarmed us with the news that he had followed the track of a great body of Indians to the place where they had lately encamped. That there he had found no less than ten huts, the poles whereof had green leaves still fresh upon them. That each of these huts had sheltered at least ten Indians, who by some infallible marks must have been northern Indians. That they must needs have taken their departure from thence no longer ago than the day before, having erected those huts to protect themselves from the late heavy rains.

These tidings I could perceive were a little shocking to some of the company, and, particularly, the little Major, whose tongue had never lain still, was taken speechless for sixteen hours. I put as good a countenance upon the matter as I could, assuring my fellow travelers that the northern Indians were at peace with us, and although one or two of them may now and then commit a robbery or a murder (as other rogues do), yet nationally and avowedly they would not venture to hurt us. And in case they were Catawbas, the danger would be as little from them, because they are too fond of our trade to lose it for the pleasure of shedding a little English blood. But supposing the worst, that they might break through all the rules of self-interest and attack us, yet we ought to stand bravely on our defense and sell our lives as dear as we could. That we should have no more fear of this occasion than just to make us more watchful and better provided to receive the enemy, if they had the spirit to venture upon us.

This reasoning of mine, though it could not remove the panic, yet it abated something of the palpitation and made us double our guard.

However, I found it took off the edge of most of our appetites for everything but the rum bottle, which was more in favor than ever because of its cordial quality. I hurt my other knee this afternoon, but not enough to spoil either my dancing[6] or my stomach.

26. We liked the place so little that we were glad to leave it this morning as soon as we could. For that reason we were all on horseback before nine and after riding four miles arrived at the mouth of Sable Creek. On the eastern bank of that creek, six paces from the mouth and just at the brink of the river Dan, stands a sugar tree, which is the beginning of my fine tract of land in Carolina called the Land of Eden. I caused the initial letters of my name to be cut on a large poplar and beech near my corner, for the more easy finding it another time. We then made a beginning of my survey, directing our course due south from the sugar tree above-mentioned. In a little way we perceived the creek forked and the western branch was wide enough to merit the name of a river. That to the east was much less, which we intersected with this course. We ran southerly a mile and found the land good all the way, only toward the end of it we saw the trees destroyed in such a manner that there were hardly any left to mark my bounds. Having finished this course, we encamped in a charming peninsula formed by the western branch of the creek. It contained about forty acres of very rich land, gradually descending to the creek, and is a delightful situation for the manor house.

My servant had fed so intemperately upon bear that it gave him a scouring, and that was followed by the piles, which made riding worse to him than purgatory. But, anointing with the fat of the same bear, he soon grew easy again.

27. We were stirring early from this enchanting place and ran eight miles of my back line, which tended south 84½ westerly. We found the land uneven but tolerably good, though very thin of trees, and those that were standing fit for little but fuel and fence rails. Some conflagration had effectually opened the country and made room for the air to circulate. We crossed both the branches of Lowland Creek and sundry other rills of fine water. From every eminence we dis-

[6] The calisthenics that Byrd habitually performed.

covered the mountains to the northwest of us, though they seemed to be a long way off. Here the air felt very refreshing and agreeable to the lungs, having no swamps or marshes to taint it. Nor was this the only good effect it had, but it likewise made us very hungry, so that we were forced to halt and pacify our appetites with a frugal repast out of our pockets, which we washed down with water from a purling stream just by.

My knees pained me very much, though I broke not the laws of traveling by uttering the least complaint. Measuring and marking spent so much of our time that we could advance no further than eight miles, and the chain carriers thought that a great way.

In the evening we took up our quarters in the low grounds of the river, which our scouts informed us was but three hundred yards ahead of us. This was no small surprise, because we had flattered ourselves that this back line would not have intersected the Dan at all; but we found ourselves mistaken and plainly perceived that it ran more southerly than we imagined and in all likelihood pierces the mountains where they form an amphitheater.

The venison here was lean; and the misfortune was we met no bear in so open a country to grease the way and make it slip down.

In the night our sentinel alarmed us with an idle suspicion that he heard the Indian whistle (which amongst them is a signal for attacking their enemies). This made everyone stand manfully to our arms in a moment, and I found nobody more undismayed in this surprise than Mr. Banister; but after we had put ourselves in battle array, we discovered this whistle to be nothing but the nocturnal note of a little harmless bird that inhabits those woods. We were glad to find the mistake and, commending the sentinel for his great vigilance, composed our noble spirits again to rest till the morning. However, some of the company dreamed of nothing but scalping all the rest of the night.

28. We snapped up our breakfast as fast as we could, that we might have the more leisure to pick our way over a very bad ford across the river, though, bad as it was, we all got safe on the other side. We were no sooner landed but we found ourselves like to encounter a very rough and almost impassable thicket. However, we scuffled through it

without any dismay or complaint. This was a copse of young saplings, consisting of oak, hickory, and sassafras, which are the growth of a fertile soil.

We gained no more than two miles in three hours in this perplexed place and after that had the pleasure to issue out into opener woods. The land was generally good, though pretty bare of timber, and particularly we traversed a rich level of at least two miles. Our whole day's journey amounted not quite to five miles, by reason we had been so hampered at our first setting-out. We were glad to take up our quarters early in a piece of fine low grounds lying about a mile north of the river. Thus we perceived the river edged away gently toward the south and never likely to come in the way of our course again. Nevertheless, the last time we saw it, it kept much the same breadth and depth that it had where it divided its waters from the Staunton and in all likelihood holds its own quite as high as the mountains.

29. In measuring a mile and a half farther we reached the lower ford of the Irvin, which branches from the Dan about two miles to the south-southeast of this place. This river was very near threescore yards over and in many places pretty deep. From thence in little more than a mile we came to the end of this course, being in length fifteen miles and eighty-eight poles. And so far the land held reasonably good; but when we came to run our northern course of three miles to the place where the country line intersects the same Irvin higher up, we passed over nothing but stony hills and barren grounds, clothed with little timber and refreshed with less water.

All my hopes were in the riches that might lie underground, there being many goodly tokens of mines. The stones which paved the river both by their weight and color promised abundance of metal; but whether it be silver, lead, or copper is beyond our skill to discern. We also discovered many shows of marble, of a white ground, with streaks of red and purple. So that 'tis possible the treasure in the bowels of the earth may make ample amends for the poverty of its surface.

We encamped on the bank of this river, a little below the dividing line and near the lower end of an island half a mile long, which, for the metallic appearances, we dignified with the name of Potosi.[7] In our

[7] The Bolivian city famous for its silver mines.

way to this place we treed a bear of so mighty a bulk that when we fetched her down she almost made an earthquake. But neither the shot nor the fall disabled her so much but she had like to have hugged one of our dogs to death in the violence of her embrace.

We exercised the discipline of the woods by tossing a very careless servant in a blanket for losing one of our axes.

30. This being Sunday, we were glad to rest from our labors; and, to help restore our vigor, several of us plunged into the river, notwithstanding it was a frosty morning. One of our Indians went in along with us and taught us their way of swimming. They strike not out both hands together but alternately one after another, whereby they are able to swim both farther and faster than we do.

Near the camp grew several large chestnut trees very full of chestnuts. Our men were too lazy to climb the trees for the sake of the fruit but, like the Indians, chose rather to cut them down, regardless of those that were to come after. Nor did they esteem such kind of work any breach of the Sabbath so long as it helped to fill their bellies.

One of the Indians shot a bear, which he lugged about half a mile for the good of the company. These gentiles have no distinction of days but make every day a Sabbath, except when they go out to war or a-hunting, and then they will undergo incredible fatigues. Of other work the men do none, thinking it below the dignity of their sex, but make the poor women do all the drudgery. They have a blind tradition amongst them that work was first laid upon mankind by the fault of a female, and therefore 'tis but just that sex should do the greatest part of it. This they plead in their excuse; but the true reason is that the weakest must always go to the wall, and superiority has from the beginning ungenerously imposed slavery on those who are not able to resist it.

### OCTOBER

1. I plunged once more into the river Irvin this morning, for a small cold I had caught, and was entirely cured by it.

We ran the three-mile course from a white oak standing on my corner upon the western bank of the river and intersected the place where we ended the back line exactly, and fixed that corner at a hickory. We steered south from thence about a mile and then came upon the Dan, which thereabouts makes but narrow low grounds. We forded it about a mile and a half to the westward of the place where the Irvin runs into it. When we were over, we determined to ride down the river on that side and for three miles found the high land come close down to it, pretty barren and uneven.

But then on a sudden the scene changed, and we were surprised with an opening of large extent where the Sauro Indians once lived, who had been a considerable nation. But the frequent inroads of the Senecas annoyed them incessantly and obliged them to remove from this fine situation about thirty years ago. They then retired more southerly as far as Pee Dee River and incorporated with the Keyauwees, where a remnant of them is still surviving. It must have been a great misfortune to them to be obliged to abandon so beautiful a dwelling, where the air is wholesome and the soil equal in fertility to any in the world. The river is about eighty yards wide, always confined within its lofty banks and rolling down its waters, as sweet as milk and as clear as crystal. There runs a charming level of more than a mile square that will bring forth like the lands of Egypt, without being overflowed once a year. There is scarce a shrub in view to intercept your prospect but grass as high as a man on horseback. Toward the woods there is a gentle ascent till your sight is intercepted by an eminence that overlooks the whole landscape. This sweet place is bounded to the east by a fine stream called Sauro Creek, which, running out of the Dan and tending westerly, makes the whole a peninsula.

I could not quit this pleasant situation without regret but often faced about to take a parting look at it as far as I could see, and so indeed did all the rest of the company. But at last we left it quite out of sight and continued our course down the river till where it intersects my back line, which was about five miles below Sauro Town.

We took up our quarters at the same camp where we had a little before been alarmed with the supposed Indian whistle, which we could hardly get out of our heads. However, it did not spoil our rest but we dreamt all night of the delights of Tempe and the Elysian fields.

2. We awaked early from these innocent dreams and took our way

along my back line till we came to the corner of it. From thence we slanted to the country line and kept down that as far as the next fording place of the river, making in the whole eighteen miles. We breathed all the way in pure air, which seemed friendly to the lungs and circulated the blood and spirits very briskly. Happy will be the people destined for so wholesome a situation, where they may live to fullness of days and, which is much better still, with much content and gaiety of heart.

On every rising ground we faced about to take our leave of the mountains, which still showed their towering heads. The ground was uneven, rising into hills and sinking into valleys great part of the way, but the soil was good, abounding in most places with a greasy black mold. We took up our quarters on the western bank of the river where we had forded it at our coming up.

One of our men, Joseph Colson by name, a timorous, lazy fellow, had squandered away his bread and grew very uneasy when his own ravening had reduced him to short allowance. He was one of those drones who love to do little and eat much and are never in humor unless their bellies are full. According to this wrong turn of constitution, when he found he could no longer revel in plenty, he began to break the rules by complaining and threatening to desert. This had like to have brought him to the blanket, but his submission reprieved him.

Though bread grew a little scanty with us, we had venison in abundance, which a true woodsman can eat contentedly without any bread at all. But bears' flesh needs something of the farinaceous to make it pass easily off the stomach.

In the night we heard a dog bark at some distance, as we thought, when we saw all our own dogs lying about the fire. This was another alarm, but we soon discovered it to be a wolf, which will sometimes bark very like a dog but something shriller.

3. The fine season continuing, we made the most of it by leaving our quarters as soon as possible. We began to measure and mark the bounds of Major Mayo's land on the south of the country line. In order to do this, we marched round the bent of the river, but, he being obliged to make a traverse, we could reach no farther than four miles.

399

In the distance of about a mile from where we lay, we crossed Cliff Creek, which confined its stream within such high banks that it was difficult to find a passage over. We kept close to the river, and two miles farther came to Hix's Creek, where abundance of canes lay dry and prostrate on the ground, having suffered in the late septennial slaughter of that vegetable.

A mile after that we forded another stream, which we called Hatcher Creek, from two Indian traders of that name who used formerly to carry goods to the Sauro Indians. Near the banks of this creek I found a large beech tree with the following inscription cut upon the bark of it, "JH, HH, BB, lay here the 24th of May, 1673." It was not difficult to fill up these initials with the following names, Joseph Hatcher, Henry Hatcher, and Benjamin Bullington, three Indian traders, [who] had lodged near that place sixty years before in their way to the Sauro town. But the strangest part of the story was this, that these letters cut in the bark should remain perfectly legible so long. Nay, if no accident befalls the tree, which appears to be still in a flourishing condition, I doubt not but this piece of antiquity may be read many years hence. We may also learn from it that the beech is a very long-lived tree, of which there are many exceedingly large in these woods.

The Major took in a pretty deal of rich low ground into his survey, but unhappily left a greater quantity out, which proves the weakness of making entries by guess.

We found the Dan fordable hereabouts in most places. One of the Indians shot a wild goose that was very lousy, which nevertheless was good meat and proved those contemptible tasters to be no bad tasters.[8] However, for those stomachs that were so unhappy as to be squeamish, there was plenty of fat bear, we having killed two in this day's march.

4. I caused the men to use double diligence to assist Major Mayo in fixing the bounds of his land, because he had taken a great deal of pains about mine. We therefore mounted our horses as soon as we had swallowed our breakfast. Till that is duly performed, a woodsman makes a conscience of exposing himself to any fatigue. We proceeded

[8] I.e., proved that the contemptible lice themselves had a taste for good food.

then in this survey and made an end before night, though most of the company were of opinion the land was hardly worth the trouble. It seemed most of it before below the character the discoverers had given him of it.

We fixed his eastern corner on Cockade Creek and then continued our march over the hills and far away along the country line two miles farther. Nor had we stopped there unless a likelihood of rain had obliged us to encamp on an eminence where we were in no danger of being overflowed.

Peter Jones had a smart fit of an ague which shook him severely, though he bore it like a man; but the small Major[9] had a small fever and bore it like a child. He groaned as if he had been in labor and thought verily it would be his fate to die like a mutinous Israelite in the wilderness and be buried under a heap of stones.

The rain was so kind as to give us leisure to secure ourselves against it but came however time enough to interrupt our cookery, so that we supped as temperately as so many philosophers and kept ourselves snug within our tents. The worst part of the story was that the sentinel could hardly keep our fires from being extinguished by the heaviness of the shower.

5. Our invalids found themselves in traveling condition this morning and began to conceive hopes of returning home and dying in their own beds. We pursued our journey through uneven and perplexed woods and in the thickest of them had the fortune to knock down a young buffalo of two years old. Providence threw this vast animal in our way very seasonably just as our provisions began to fail us. And it was the more welcome, too, because it was change of diet, which of all varieties, next to that of bedfellows, is the most agreeable. We had lived upon venison and bear until our stomachs loathed them almost as much as the Hebrews of old did their quails.[10] Our butchers were so unhandy at their business that we grew very lank before we could get our dinner. But when it came, we found it equal in goodness to the best beef. They made it the longer because they kept sucking the

[9] Probably Major Mumford; see the comment on Major Mayo's disposition on p. 410 and the comment on Mumford on p. 383.
[10] Referring to Num. 11:20, 31–33.

water out of the guts, in imitation of the Catawba Indians, upon the belief that it is a great cordial, and will even make them drunk, or at least very gay.

We encamped upon Hyco River pretty high up and had much ado to get our house in order before a heavy shower descended upon us. I was in pain lest our sick men might suffer by the rain but might have spared myself the concern, because it had the effect of a cold bath upon them and drove away their distemper, or rather changed it into a canine appetite that devoured all before it. It rained smartly all night long, which made our situation on the low ground more fit for otters than men.

6. We had abundance of drying work this morning after the clouds broke away and showed the sun to the happy earth. It was impossible for us to strike the tents till the afternoon and then we took our departure and made an easy march of four miles to another branch of Hyco River, which we called Jesuit's Creek because it misled us.

We lugged as many of the dainty pieces of the buffalo along with us as our poor horses could carry, envying the wolves the pleasure of such luxurious diet. Our quarters were taken upon a delightful eminence that scornfully overlooked the creek and afforded us a dry habitation. We made our supper on the tongue and udder of the buffalo, which were so good that a cardinal legate might have made a comfortable meal upon them during the carnival. Nor was this all, but we had still a rarer morsel, the bunch rising up between the shoulders of this animal, which is very tender and very fat. The primings of a young doe, which one of the men brought to the camp, were slighted amidst these dainties, nor would even our servants be fobbed off with cates so common.

The low grounds of this creek are wide in many places and rich but seem to lie within reach of every inundation, and this is commonly the case with most low grounds that lie either on the rivers or the creeks that run into them. So great an inconvenience lessens their value very much and makes high land that is just tolerable of greater advantage to the owner. There he will be more likely to reap the fruits of his industry every year and not run the risk, after all his toil, to see the sweat of his brow carried down the stream and perhaps many of his cattle drowned into the bargain. Perhaps in times to come people may bank their low grounds as they do in Europe, to confine the water within its natural bounds to prevent these inconveniences.

7. The scarcity of bread, joined to the impatience of some of our company, laid us under a kind of necessity to hasten our return home. For that reason we thought we might be excused for making a Sabbath Day's journey of about five miles as far as our old camp upon Sugartree Creek. On our way we forded Buffalo Creek, which also empties its waters into Hyco River. The woods we rode through were open and the soil very promising, great part thereof being low grounds, full of tall and large trees. A she-bear had the ill luck to cross our way, which was large enough to afford us several luxurious meals. I paid for violating the Sabbath by losing a pair of gold buttons.

I pitched my tent on the very spot I had done when we ran the dividing line between Virginia and Carolina. The beech whose bark recorded the names of the Carolina commissioners was still standing, and we did them the justice to add to their names a sketch of their characters.

We got our house in order time enough to walk about and make some slight observations. There were sugar trees innumerable growing in the low grounds of this creek, from which it received its name. They were many of them as tall as large hickories with trunks from fifteen to twenty inches through. The woodpeckers, for the pleasure of the sweet juice which these trees yield, pierce the bark in many places and do great damage, though the trees live a great while under all these wounds. There grows an infinite quantity of maidenhair, which seems to delight most in rich ground. The sorrel tree is frequent there, whose leaves, brewed in beer, are good in dropsies, greensickness, and cachexies. We also saw in this place abundance of papaw trees, the wood whereof the Indians make very dry on purpose to rub fire out of it. Their method of doing it is this: they hold one of these dry sticks in each hand and by rubbing them hard and quick together rarefy the air in such a manner as to fetch fire in ten minutes. Whenever they offer any sacrifice to their god they look upon it as a profanation to make use of a fire already kindled but produce fresh virgin fire for that purpose by rubbing two of these sticks together that never had been used before on any occasion.

8. After fortifying ourself with a bear breakfast, Major Mayo took what help he thought necessary and began to survey the land with which the commissioners of Carolina had presented him upon this creek. After running the bounds, the Major was a little disappointed in the goodness of the land, but as it had cost him nothing it could be no bad pennyworth, as his upper tract really was.

While that business was carrying on, I took my old friend and fellow traveler Tom Wilson and went to view the land I had entered for upon this creek on the north of the country line. We rode down the stream about six miles, crossing it sundry times, and found very wide low grounds on both sides of it, only we observed wherever the low grounds were broad on one side of the creek they were narrow on the other. The high lands we were obliged to pass over were very good and in some places descended so gradually to the edge of the low grounds that they formed very agreeable prospects and pleasant situations for building. About four miles from the line, Sugartree Creek emptied itself into the Hyco, which with that addition swelled into a fine river. In this space we saw the most, and most promising, good land we had met with in all our travels.

In our way we shot a doe, but, she not falling immediately, we had lost our game had not the ravens by their croaking conducted us to the thicket where she fell. We plunged the carcass of the deer into the water, to secure it from these ominous birds till we returned, but an hour afterwards were surprised with the sight of a wolf which had been fishing for it and devoured one side.

We knocked down an ancient she-bear that had no flesh upon her bones, so we left it to the freebooters of the forest. In coming back to the camp we discovered a solitary bull buffalo, which boldly stood his ground, contrary to the custom of that shy animal. We spared his life, from a principle of never slaughtering an innocent creature to no purpose. However, we made ourselves some diversion by trying if he would face our dogs. He was so far from retreating at their approach that he ran at them with great fierceness, cocking up his ridiculous little tail and grunting like a hog. The dogs in the meantime only played about him, not venturing within reach of his horns, and by their nimbleness came off with a whole skin.

All these adventures we related at our return to the camp, and, what was more to the purpose, we carried to them the side of venison which the wolf had vouchsafed to leave us. After we had composed ourselves to rest, our horses ran up to our camp as fast as their hobbles would let them. This was to some of us a certain argument that Indians were near, whose scent the horses can no more endure than they can their figures; though it was more likely they had been scared by a panther or some other wild beast, the glaring of whose eyes are very terrifying to them in a dark night.

9. Major Mayo's survey being no more than half done, we were obliged to amuse ourselves another day in this place. And that the time might not be quite lost, we put our garments and baggage into good repair. I for my part never spent a day so well during the whole voyage. I had an impertinent tooth in my upper jaw that had been loose for some time and made me chew with great caution. Particularly I could not grind a biscuit but with much deliberation and presence of mind. Toothdrawers we had none amongst us, nor any of the instruments they make use of. However, invention supplied this want very happily, and I contrived to get rid of this troublesome companion by cutting a caper. I caused a twine to be fastened round the root of my tooth, about a fathom in length, and then tied the other end to the snag of a log that lay upon the ground in such a manner that I could just stand upright. Having adjusted my string in this manner, I bent my knees enough to enable me to spring vigorously off the ground as perpendicularly as I could. The force of the leap drew out the tooth with so much ease that I felt nothing of it, nor should have believed it was come away unless I had seen it dangling at the end of the string. An under tooth may be fetched out by standing off the ground and fastening your string at due distance above you. And, having so fixed your gear, jump off your standing, and the weight of your body, added to the force of the spring, will prize out your tooth with less pain than

any operator upon earth could draw it. This new way of toothdrawing, being so silently and deliberately performed, both surprised and delighted all that were present, who could not guess what I was going about. I immediately found the benefit of getting rid of this troublesome companion by eating my supper with more comfort than I had done during the whole expedition.

10. In the morning we made an end of our bread, and all the rest of our provision, so that now we began to travel pretty light. All the company were witnesses how good the land was upon Sugartree Creek, because we rode down it four miles till it fell into Hyco River. Then we directed our course over the high land, thinking to shorten our way to Tom Wilson's quarter. Nevertheless, it was our fortune to fall upon the Hyco again, and then kept within sight of it several miles together till we came near the mouth. Its banks were high and full of precipices on the east side, but it afforded some low grounds on the west. Within two miles of the mouth are good shows of copper mines, as Harry Morris told me, but we saw nothing of them. It runs into the Dan just below a large fall, but the chain of rocks don't reach quite cross the river to intercept the navigation. About a mile below lives Aaron Pinston, at a quarter belonging to Thomas Wilson, upon Tewahominy Creek. This man is the highest inhabitant on the south side of the Dan and yet reckons himself perfectly safe from danger. And if the bears, wolves, and panthers were as harmless as the Indians, his stock might be so too.

Tom Wilson offered to knock down a steer for us, but I would by no means accept of his generosity. However, we were glad of a few of his peas and potatoes and some rashers of his bacon, upon which we made good cheer. This plantation lies about a mile from the mouth of Tewahominy and about the same distance from the mouth of Hyco River and contains a good piece of land. The edifice was only a log house, affording a very free passage for the air through every part of it, nor was the cleanliness of it any temptation to lie out of our tents, so we encamped once more, for the last time, in the open field.

11. I tipped our landlady with what I imagined a full reward for the trouble we had given her and then mounted our horses, which

pricked up their ears after the two meals they had eaten of corn. In the distance of about a mile we reached the Dan, which we forded with some difficulty into the fork. The water was pretty high in the river and the current something rapid, nevertheless all the company got over safe, with only a little water in their boots. After traversing the fork, which was there at least two good miles across, we forded the Staunton into a little island and then the narrow branch of the same to the mainland.

We took Major Mumford's tenant in our way, where we moistened our throats with a little milk and then proceeded in good order to Bluestone Castle. My landlady received us with a grim sort of a welcome, which I did not expect, since I brought her husband back in good health, though perhaps that might be the reason. 'Tis sure something or other did tease her, and she was a female of too strong passions to know how to dissemble. However, she was so civil as to get us a good dinner, which I was better pleased with because Colonel Cock [11] and Mr. Mumford came time enough to partake of it. The Colonel had been surveying land in these parts, and particularly that on which Mr. Stith's copper mine lies, as likewise a tract on which Cornelius Cargill has fine appearances. He had but a poor opinion of Mr. Stith's mine, foretelling it would be all labor in vain, but thought something better of Mr. Cargill's.

After dinner these gentlemen took their leaves, and at the same time I discharged two of my fellow travelers, Thomas Wilson and Joseph Colson, after having made their hearts merry and giving each of them a piece of gold to rub their eyes with.

We now returned to that evil custom of lying in a house, and an evil one it is, when ten or a dozen people are forced to pig together in a room, as we did, and were troubled with the squalling of peevish, dirty children into the bargain.

12. We ate our fill of potatoes and milk, which seems delicious fare to those who have made a campaign in the woods. I then took my first

---

[11] The name probably should be Cocke, as he was very likely a member of the Cocke family descended from Richard Cocke, who arrived in Virginia sometime before 1628.

minister, Harry Morris, up the hill, and marked out the place where Bluestone Castle was to stand and overlook the adjacent country. After that I put my friend in mind of many things he had done amiss, which he promised faithfully to reform. I was so much an infidel to his fair speeches (having been many times deceived by them) that I was forced to threaten him with my highest displeasure unless he mended his conduct very much. I also let him know that he was not only to correct his own errors but likewise those of his wife, since the power certainly belonged to him in virtue of his conjugal authority. He scratched his head at this last admonition, from whence I inferred that the gray mare was the better horse.

We gave our heavy baggage two hours' start, and about noon followed them and in twelve miles reached John Butcher's, calling by the way for Master Mumford, in order to take him along with us. Mr. Butcher received us kindly and we had a true Roanoke entertainment of pork upon pork, and pork again upon that. He told us he had been one of the first seated in that remote part of the country and in the beginning had been forced, like the great Nebuchadnezzar, to live a considerable time upon grass. This honest man set a mighty value on the mine he fancied he had in his pasture and showed us some of the ore, which he was made to believe was a gray copper and would certainly make his fortune. But there's a bad distemper rages in those parts that grows very epidemical. The people are all mine-mad and, neglecting to make corn, starve their families in hopes to live in great plenty hereafter. Mr. Stith was the first that was seized with the frenzy, and has spread the contagion far and near. As you ride along the woods, you see all the large stones knocked to pieces, nor can a poor marcasite rest quietly in its bed for these curious inquirers. Our conversation ran altogether upon this darling subject till the hour came for our lying in bulk together.

13. After breaking our fast with a sea of milk and potatoes, we took our leave, and I crossed my landlady's hand with a piece of money. She refused the offer at first but, like a true woman, accepted of it when it was put home to her. She told me the utmost she was able to do for me was a trifle in comparison of some favor I had formerly done her; but

what that favor was neither I could recollect nor did she think proper to explain. Though it threatened rain, we proceeded on our journey and jogged on in the new road for twenty miles, that is as far as it was cleared at that time, and found it would soon come to be a very good one after it was well grubbed.

About nine miles from John Butcher's, we crossed Allen's Creek, four miles above Mr. Stith's mine. Near the mouth of this creek is a good body of rich land, whereof Occaneechee Neck is a part. It was entered for many years ago by Colonel Harrison [12] and Colonel Allen but to this day is held without patent or improvement. And they say Mr. Bolling does the same with a thousand acres lying below John Butcher's.

After beating the new road for twenty miles, we struck off toward Meherrin, which we reached in eight miles farther and then came to the plantation of Joshua Nicholson, where Daniel Taylor lives for halves. There was a poor dirty house, with hardly anything in it but children that wallowed about like so many pigs. It is a common case in this part of the country that people live worst upon good land, and the more they are befriended by the soil and the climate the less they will do for themselves. This man was an instance of it, for though his plantation would make plentiful returns for a little industry, yet he, wanting that, wanted everything. The woman did all that was done in the family, and the few garments they had to cover their dirty hides were owing to her industry. We could have no supplies from such neighbors as these but depended on our own knapsacks, in which we had some remnants of cold fowls that we brought from Bluestone Castle. When my house was in order, the whole family came and admired it, as much as if it had been the Grand Vizier's tent in the Turkish army.

14. The Sabbath was now come round again, and although our horses would have been glad to take the benefit of it, yet we determined to make a Sunday's journey to Brunswick Church, which lay about eight miles off. Though our landlord could do little for us, nevertheless we did him all the good we were able by bleeding his sick Negro and giving him a dose of Indian physic. We got to church in decent time,

---

[12] Benjamin Harrison, owner of Berkeley, a plantation adjoining Westover.

and Mr. Betty, the parson of the parish, entertained us with a good honest sermon, but whether he bought it or borrowed it would have been uncivil in us to inquire. Be that as it will, he is a decent man, with a double chin that sits gracefully over his band, and his parish, especially the female part of it, like him well.

We were not crowded at church, though it was a new thing in that remote part of the country. What women happened to be there were very gim [13] and tidy in the work of their own hands, which made them look tempting in the eyes of us foresters.

When church was done we refreshed our teacher with a glass of wine and then, receiving his blessing, took horse and directed our course to Major Embry's. The distance thither was reputed fifteen miles but appeared less by the company of a nymph of those woods, whom innocence and wholesome flesh and blood made very alluring.

In our way we crossed Sturgeon Creek and Waqua Creek but at our journey's end were so unlucky as not to find either master or mistress at home. However, after two hours of hungry expectation, the good woman luckily found her way home and provided very hospitably for us. As for the Major, he had profited so much by my prescription as to make a journey to Williamsburg, which required pretty good health, the distance being a little short of one hundred miles.

15. After our bounteous landlady had cherished us with roast beef and chicken pie, we thankfully took leave. At the same time we separated from our good friend and fellow traveler, Major Mayo, who steered directly home. He is certainly a very useful, as well as an agreeable, companion in the woods, being ever cheerful and good-humored under all the little crosses, disasters, and disappointments of that rambling life.

As many of us as remained jogged on together to Sapony Chapel, where I thanked Major Mumford and Peter Jones for the trouble that they had taken in this long journey.

That ceremony being duly performed, I filed off with my honest friend Mr. Banister to his habitation on Hatcher Run, which lay about fourteen miles from the chapel above-mentioned. His good-humored

[13] Smart, spruce.

little wife was glad to see her runaway spouse returned in safety and treated us kindly. It was no small pleasure to me that my worthy friend found his family in good health and his affairs in good order. He came into this ramble so frankly that I should have been sorry if he had been a sufferer by it.

In the gaiety of our hearts we drank our bottle a little too freely, which had an unusual effect on persons so long accustomed to simple element. We were both of us raised out of our beds in the same manner and near the same time, which was a fair proof that people who breathe the same air and are engaged in the same way of living will be very apt to fall into the same indispositions. And this may explain why distempers sometimes go round a family, without any reason to believe they are infectious, according to the superstition of the vulgar.

16. After pouring down a basin of chocolate, I wished peace to that house and departed. As long as Mr. Banister had been absent from his family, he was yet so kind as to conduct me to Major Mumford's, and, which was more, his wife very obligingly consented to it. The Major seemed overjoyed at his being returned safe and sound from the perils of the woods, though his satisfaction had some check from the change his pretty wife had suffered in her complexion. The vermilion of her cheeks had given place a little to the saffron, by means of a small tincture of the yellow jaundice. I was sorry to see so fair a flower thus faded and recommended the best remedy I could think of.

After a refreshment of about an hour, we went on to Colonel Bolling's, who was so gracious as to send us an invitation. As much in haste as I was to return to my family, I spent an hour or two at that place, but could by no means be persuaded to stay dinner, nor could even Madam de Graffenried's [14] smiles on one side of her face shake my resolution.

From thence we proceeded to Colonel Mumford's, who seemed to have taken a new lease, were any dependence to be upon looks or any indulgence allowed to the wishes of his friends. An honester a man, a fairer trader, or a kinder friend, this country never produced: God

[14] Mrs. Barbara Graffenried, who taught dancing at Williamsburg; see *Another Secret Diary . . . 1739–1741*, p. 86.

send any of his sons may have the grace to take after him. We took a running repast with this good man and then, bidding adieu both to him and Mr. Banister, I mounted once more and obstinately pursued my journey home, though the clouds threatened and the heavens looked very louring. I had not passed the courthouse before it began to pour down like a spout upon me. Nevertheless, I pushed forward with vigor and got dripping wet before I could reach Merchant's Hope Point. My boat was there luckily waiting for me and wafted me safe over. And the joy of meeting my family in health made me in a moment forget all the fatigues of the journey, as much as if I had been huskanawed.[15] However, the good Providence that attended me and my whole company will, I hope, stick fast in my memory and make me everlastingly thankful.

[15] A ceremony of the Virginia Indians for preparing young men for mature manhood by means of solitary confinement and the use of narcotics. Byrd is thinking of Robert Beverley's description of the aftereffects of fasting and the use of intoxicating roots: "Upon this occasion it is pretended that these poor creatures drink so much of that water of Lethe that they perfectly lose the remembrance of all former things, even of their parents, their treasure, and their language"; *The History and Present State of Virginia*, edited by Louis B. Wright (Chapel Hill, 1947), p. 207.

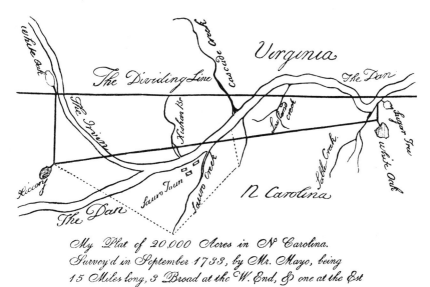

My Plat of 20,000 Acres in N° Carolina.
Survey'd in September 1733, by Mr. Mayo, being
15 Miles long, 3 Broad at the W. End, & one at the Est

William Byrd's Map of his "Land of Eden," from the Westover Manuscripts
(*The lettering at the bottom is not in Byrd's hand.*)

----

*A list of our company of all sorts*

| | | |
|---|---|---|
| Myself | Thomas Wilson | Lawson |
| Major Mayo | Joseph Colson | 3 Indians |
| Major Mumford | Harry Morris | 3 Negroes |
| Mr. Banister | Robert Bolling | 20 horses |
| Mr. Jones | Thomas Hooper | 4 dogs |

----

*An account of the distances of places*

| | miles |
|---|---|
| From Westover to Colonel Mumford's | 16 |
| From Colonel Mumford's to Major Mumford's | 6 |
| From thence to Sapony Chapel | 20 |
| From thence to Major Embry's on Nottoway | 10 |
| From thence to Brunswick courthouse | 15 |

| | |
|---|---|
| From thence to Meherrin River | 8 |
| From thence to the ford on Roanoke | 12 |
| From thence to Colonel Stith's copper mine | 20 |
| From thence to Butcher's Creek | 6 |
| From thence to Bluestone Castle | 12 |
| From thence to the ford into the fork | 7 |
| From thence to Birch's Creek | 5 |
| From thence to Banister River | 6 |
| From thence to Morris Creek | 3 |
| From thence to the Medway | 14 |
| From thence to Maosti Creek | 2 |
| From hence to Forked Creek | 6 |
| From hence to Peter's Creek | 2 |
| From hence to Jones's Creek | 2 |
| From hence to the first ford over the Dan | $1\frac{1}{2}$ |
| From hence to Cane Creek | $2\frac{1}{2}$ |
| From hence to the second ford of the Dan | $4\frac{1}{2}$ |
| From hence to the mouth of Sable Creek | 8 |
| From hence to the southeast corner of my land | 1 |
| From thence to the Dan on my back line | 8 |
| From thence to the Irvin on my back line | 6 |
| From thence to my southwest corner | 1 |
| From thence to my corner on the west of the Irvin | 3 |
| From thence to the Dan along my upper line | $4\frac{1}{2}$ |
| From thence to the mouth of the Irvin | $1\frac{1}{2}$ |
| From thence to Sauro Creek | $2\frac{1}{2}$ |
| From thence to where my back line crosses the Dan | 5 |
| From thence to my southeast corner | 8 |
| From thence to Cliff Creek | 10 |
| From thence to Hix's Creek | 2 |
| From thence to Hatcher's Creek | 1 |
| From thence to Cockade Creek | 5 |
| From thence to the upper ford of Hyco River | 7 |
| From thence to Jesuit's Creek | 4 |
| From thence to where the line cuts Sugartree Creek | 5 |
| From thence to the mouth of Sugartree Creek | 4 |
| From thence to the mouth of Hyco River | 7 |
| From thence to Wilson's quarter on Tewahominy Creek | 1 |
| From thence to the Dan | 1 |
| From thence across the fork to the Staunton | 2 |

| | |
|---|---|
| From thence to Bluestone Castle | 7 |
| From thence to Sandy Creek | 5 |
| From thence to Mr. Mumford's plantation | 2 |
| From thence to Butcher's Creek | 5 |
| From thence to Allen's Creek | 9 |
| From thence to Joshua Nicholson's on Meherrin | 18 |
| From thence to Brunswick courthouse | 8 |
| From thence to Nottoway Bridge | 14 |
| From thence to Sapony Chapel | 10 |
| From thence to Mr. Banister's on Hatcher Run | 12 |
| From thence to Colonel Bolling's plantation | 9 |
| From thence to Colonel Mumford's plantation | 5 |
| From thence to Westover | 16 |
| | —— |
| | 184[16] |

[16] The correct total of this column is 186.

# APPENDIX

Notes on the Text and Provenance of the Byrd Manuscripts

By Kathleen L. Leonard

THE four major prose works of William Byrd II, *The History of the Dividing Line, The Secret History of the Line, A Journey to the Land of Eden*, and *A Progress to the Mines*, are here printed together for the first time. The present edition was encouraged by the Virginia Historical Society's recent purchase of the large Westover folio of miscellaneous Byrd manuscripts. This bound vellum folio, the sole text for *A Journey to the Land of Eden* and *A Progress to the Mines* and the primary source for *The History of the Dividing Line*, has been in the hands of Byrd descendants since his death, and the texts have not been subject to critical re-examination since Thomas Hicks Wynne edited the folio contents in 1866. Not included in the folio is the remaining work, *The Secret History of the Line*. It has been printed only once, by William K. Boyd in 1929, and exists in only one full-length manuscript, located in the library of the American Philosophical Society in Philadelphia. Also in the A.P.S. library is another manuscript version of Byrd's main work, *The History of the Dividing Line*, differing only slightly from the Virginia Historical Society Westover folio copy.

Although the two Byrd manuscripts in the A.P.S. library are in the same scribal hand and on the same octavo-size paper, they seem to have reached the A.P.S. library by different routes. Byrd's manuscript of *The History of the Dividing Line* appears to have been presented to the A.P.S. in 1815 (after the death of William Byrd III's widow, Mary Willing Byrd, in 1814) by Mrs. E. C. Izard of Philadelphia, a "granddaughter of the late deceased Colonel Byrd, son of the Commissioner and author." On July 14, 1815, the "Bird Journal" was referred to the A.P.S. Historical and Literary Committee, consisting of Peter S. DuPonceau, J. Correa de Serra, and Dr. Caspar Wistar, which reported on May 22, 1816:

The journal of the commissioners to fix the limits between Virginia and North Carolina from the library of the late Colonel Bird, is well worthy being published for the important and curious information that it affords, not only on the object of that operation, but more particularly on the state of civilisation of these states about the middle of last century.

# APPENDIX

The manuscript had several pages missing, however, and Peter Du-Ponceau immediately sought means of supplying the lacunae. With the support of Mrs. Izard he wrote to Benjamin Harrison of Berkeley, an executor of Byrd's estate, for assistance in locating the deficient parts of the "Manuscript Journal of the Commissioners appointed by Virginia, in the year 1728, to run the boundary line between that Province and North Carolina, ascribed to the father of the late Dr. Byrd . . ." He described the manuscript ("The Book had the form of a long receipt Book & was written across in a small neat hand") and inquired about other valuable historical papers in Byrd's possession as well. In his reply to Mrs. Izard of April 28, 1816, Mr. Harrison stated that although he had not been serving as actual executor of the Byrd estate he nevertheless had access to the papers. He generously offered to commence an investigation of them, "and such as have any reference to the great objects of the Society shall be forwarded to your literary friends by some safe conveyance."

DuPonceau also apparently consulted Thomas Jefferson early in 1816 but received no real assistance until a year later, when Jefferson wrote on January 26, 1817, that he had obtained from Mr. Harrison a manuscript of the journal of the dividing line and offered to supply the missing parts in DuPonceau's copy. Jefferson's letter reads:

I promised you in my letter of Jan. 22.16. to make enquiry on the subject of the MS. journal of the boundary between Virginia and North Carolina, run in 1728, of which you have a defective transcript. I have since been able to obtain the original for perusal, and now have it in my possession. I call it *original*, because it is that which has been preserved in the Westover family, having probably been copied fair by the Amanuensis of Dr. Byrd from his rough draught . . . This MS. wants pages 155 & 156. The 154th page ending with the words 'our landlord who,' and the 157th beginning with the words 'fortify'd ourselves with a meat breakfast.' You say that your copy wants the first 24 pages, and about a dozen more pages in the middle of the work. Let us concur then in making both compleat.

Jefferson's further description of the manuscript in his possession revealed, however, that it was not a copy of the *History* but rather an entirely different manuscript, the *Secret History*:

In one place the writer identifies himself with the person whom he calls Steddy, and from other passages it is sufficiently evident that

| | | |
|---|---|---|
| Meanwell | is | Fitzwilliam |
| Firebrand | | Dandridge |
| Astrolabe | | Irving |
| Orion | | Mayo |
| Dr. Humdrum | | non constet. |

. . . The MS. is of 162 pages small 8vo., is entitled 'The secret history of the line,' begins with the words "The Governor and Council of Virginia in 1727 received' etc. and ends its narration with the words 'for which blessings may we all be sincerely thankful,' and then subjoins a list of the Commissioners and Surveyors under feigned names, the Virginia attendants by their real names, and a statement of expences and distances.

After DuPonceau and Jefferson discovered that the two manuscripts were not the same, Jefferson's offer to supply the missing segments in the A.P.S. copy was postponed until a later date when it might prove to be of value. Further correspondence indicates that on November 6, 1817, Jefferson instead deposited the *Secret History* manuscript in the A.P.S. collection. This was apparently done with full approval of Benjamin Harrison, who had written Jefferson in July 1817: "I shall approve entirely of any use which you may think proper to make of it, but would recommend its not being published immediately, as I have every reason to hope that I shall be able to obtain a copy of a MS on the same subject & by the same author, which is in the possession of Mr. Harrison of Brandon."

The third manuscript mentioned by Harrison turned out to be the Westover folio, which, according to the inscription on its flyleaf, had been given to "Mrs. Evelyn Taylor Harrison from her Affectionate mother Mary [Willing] Byrd. For Master George Evelyn Harrison of Brandon. Westover May the 12th 1809." By January 17, 1818, Benjamin Harrison had arranged to borrow the folio from its owner, George Evelyn Harrison of Brandon, for Jefferson's use in copying extracts, on the condition that it not be allowed out of his possession. Jefferson immediately notified DuPonceau of the situation and offered again "to extract from the folio what may be necessary to supply the lacunae" in either of his manuscripts. It appears likely that he also enclosed copies of a few sample sheets of the folio manuscript of the *History*, for DuPonceau replied on January 24, 1818, that he believed the folio in Jefferson's hands to be a copy of the *History*, which he preferred to publish:

There is no part in which the two MSS of the line in our possession are both alike defective; what is wanting in the one is supplied by the other as far as they respectively go; but I ought to observe that the MS which you have had the goodness to deposit with us is not so Satisfactory or so full as the other in what relates to the country, its natural history & the manners of its inhabitants, it contains more of the gossip, if I may so speak, of the Commissioners, & less of what Historians or posterity will look for. For this reason, it would be very satisfactory if the larger work [the longer work, the *History*], of which I presume the folio MS. in your hands is a copy, would be completed. The Committee have not the most distant idea of your taking the trouble to supply what is deficient; but it might, perhaps, so happen, that among your numerous Visitors, some young Gentleman might be found, a friend to the Literature of his Country, who for the honor of Virginia would be disposed to undertake the task. In any event, I shall take the liberty of stating the parts of our MS. that are wanting. as the events are related by their dates, the easiest way will be to refer to them.

Whereas the main body of DuPonceau's letter supports his opinion of the *History* as embodying the kind of historical knowledge valued by posterity, his tactful postscript includes some apt commentary on and appreciation of the qualities of the *Secret History*:

P.S. In the comparison I made of the two MSS. I did not mean to disparage the one which you had the goodness to deposit with us. It is highly valuable for the wit & humor with which it abounds, & the insight which it gives into the Characters of the influential men of the day; I only mean to say that the other contains more matter of topographical and general historical information.

Blank sheets the size of the A.P.S. volume were enclosed with DuPonceau's list of missing portions by date, page numbers, and catch phrases, and the supplements were returned by Jefferson on February 19, 1818. The three portions described as missing by DuPonceau almost exactly correspond to the three sections which appear in a different hand in the copy of the *History* now in the A.P.S. library.

1. From the beginning to the passage under the date of the 9th of March which has the words "Bush, which is a beautiful evergreen, & may be cut into any Shape." Our MS begins with the word "Bush." *

2. From the passage in the date 12th Oct: to another in Oct: 15th. The paragraph in Oct. 12 begins "But Bears are fond of Chestnuts" and proceeds a few lines to these words with which our MS ends, "But as far as is safe which they can judge to an inch, they bite off the." Here begins the hiatus in our MSS. Six pages from 122 to 129, which last page begins with the words "that is exquisitely soft & fine," which will be found near the end of a paragraph, under the date Oct. 15th.

3. Part of the dates 20th & 21st Oct. (two pages 139 & 140). Our date 20th Oct. ends with the words: "The Prisoners they happen to take alive in these Expedi-" & that of the 21st begins with "their first setting off, that their progress was much retarded" — which ends a paragraph.

Furthermore, these supplied portions are headed and concluded by catch phrases tying them conclusively to the main text, in still another hand, identified by the editor of the Jefferson papers, Dr. Julian Boyd, as Thomas Jefferson's. Jefferson presumably went over the work after it was copied

---

* The portion supplied by Jefferson actually extends from the beginning of the *History* to March 5 (instead of March 9). DuPonceau seems mistaken about the date his copy starts, for in another place he says it lacks the first twenty-four pages (putting it much closer to March 5 than 9), and Thomas Jefferson was unable to find the catch phrase DuPonceau gave for the March 9 entry.

and added these catch lines himself, for greater clarity and for DuPonceau's convenience.

The hiatus in the *Secret History* manuscript (pp. 155–156) mentioned by Jefferson in his letter to DuPonceau of January 26, 1817, was not so readily supplied. Until recently the A.P.S. copy was thought to be the only existing manuscript of the *Secret History*. Lately, two fragments have appeared: one in the Brock collection at the Huntington Library, including the portion of the journal from the beginning to March 11, and one in the Blathwayt papers at Colonial Williamsburg, covering the period from November 5 to the end of the journal on November 22 (four pages are missing, November 12–16). Both of these *Secret History* fragments are rough drafts containing corrections and interlineations; both are on the same size paper and in the same hand (possibly Byrd's). Fortunately, the two pages (155–156) missing in the A.P.S. manuscript, for the entries November 20–22, are found in the Blathwayt fragment and have been supplied in the present edition, footnoted accordingly.

Although the A.P.S. Historical and Literary Committee expressed interest in the publication of the Byrd journals in 1817–1818, nothing appears to have been done at that time. At some point, presumably for purposes of intended publication, a large sprawling hand marked the A.P.S. copy of the *History*, introducing elegancies of language and crossing out segments to be omitted. For example, the word "cultivate" was in one place substituted for "propagate" (fol. 52), the "Dunghill Hen" was changed to "common" hen (fol. 117), and the descriptive phrase "a single mountain very much resembling a Woman's Breast" (fol. 134) was shortened to "a single conical mountain." Entirely crossed out were the sections on the Indian women as potential bed partners (fols. 87, 92), the effect of bear diet on sexual potency (fols. 161–162), the story of the man who was directed out of the great Dismal Swamp by a louse he plucked from his collar (fols. 49–50), and the comparison of a skinned bear's paw to the human foot (fol. 105) — as well as other items of doubtful scientific accuracy or outdated significance. The delicate sensibility evidenced by this editor is reflected in a report of 1834 by an A.P.S. committee appointed to examine the manuscripts in the Society's library and to report whether any should be published in the second volume of the *Historical and Literary Transactions*:

Among the Mss. in the possession of the Society are two Volumes, containing the History of what took place on the drawing of the line between the Colonies of Virginia and North Carolina in 1728, written by one of the Commissioners from Virginia & communicated to us by Mr. Jefferson; an Extract from those Volumes, judiciously made, or a review of their Contents, might be of some interest; but your Committee are of opinion, that the style and manner in which they are written, forbid their publication as a whole, & that even Extracts or a review of them, tho' they might amuse elsewhere, would not be in their place in the transactions of our Society.

Consequently, not even the more factual *History* was printed in the A.P.S. *Transactions*. The only use of either manuscript by outside editors has been by William K. Boyd when he edited the first and only printing of the *Secret History*, solely from the A.P.S. text. Earlier Byrd editors appear to have been either unaware of the existence of the A.P.S. Byrd journals or unable to consult them. The five editions of *The History of the Dividing Line* prior to the present one have all relied exclusively on the Westover folio. Edmund Ruffin, editing the first publication of the *History* in 1841, stated that the Westover folio contained all the known Byrd works. Thomas Hicks Wynne re-examined the Westover folio and issued a more authentic edition in 1866; in his Introduction to this edition he mentioned the existence of both a "History" and a "Secret History" manuscript in the A.P.S. library but stated that he had not seen the items and suspected that they might even be original or rough drafts. In their editions of the *History* of 1901 and 1929 respectively, John Spencer Bassett and William K. Boyd seem to have followed the text of Wynne's edition; neither mentioned the A.P.S. copy, although Boyd used the A.P.S. manuscript as the source for his edition of the *Secret History* in the same volume. Mark Van Doren in his 1929 edition of the *History* admittedly reprinted Ruffin's text and does not mention the existence of an A.P.S. manuscript.

Although Jefferson and DuPonceau (and possibly later editors) assumed that the A.P.S. octavo copy of the *History* was identical with the Westover folio lent by Harrison, further examination of the manuscripts reveals several textual differences. Some of these are variations in wording, others are phrases existing in the Westover folio but lacking in the A.P.S. copy. Thus, a comparison of the opening sentences of the respective entries for March 14 reveals:

| *Westover folio* | *A.P.S. octavo* |
|---|---|
| We quarter'd with our Friend and Fellow-Traveller William Wilkins, who had been our *faithfull* pilot to Coratuck . . . (fol. 22) | We quarter'd with our Friend and Fellow Traveller William Wilkins, who had been our Pilot to Coratuck . . . (fol. 47) |

So with a passage in the April 7th entries, and the final sentence of the October 17th entries:

| | |
|---|---|
| Within this Inclosure *We found Bark* Cabanes sufficient to lodge all their People . . . (fol. 43) | Within this Enclosure are Cabanes sufficient to lodge all their People . . . (fol. 85) |

| | |
|---|---|
| . . . in the Night we had a Violent Gale of Wind, accompany'd with Smart Hail, that rattled frightfully amongst the Trees, *tho' it was not large enough to do us any Harm* (fol. 69) | . . . in the Night we had a Violent Gale of Wind, accompany'd with smart Hail, that rattled frightfully amongst the Trees. (fol. 132) |

Apart from a few obvious scribal errors, all of the variations in the two manuscripts seem to be the result of erasures and subsequent additions made in the Westover folio, in a darker ink and a different hand, one closely resembling samples of Byrd's own handwriting. While both the A.P.S. and Westover versions appear to be fair copies done by an amanuensis, it seems likely that Byrd himself at a later time may have returned to the Westover folio copy and made corrections in the text that were never entered in the A.P.S. copy. The corrections and additions, all apparently made in the interest of clarity and stylistic refinement, resemble in character the interlineations found on the rough-draft fragments of the *Secret History*, and the paleography of both manuscripts is similar. However, the A.P.S. copyist, in the case of the *Secret History* manuscript, has almost consistently incorporated into his copy of that work all of the interlineations noted on the obviously rough-draft fragments now in Colonial Williamsburg and the Huntington Library. Therefore, since it seems likely that the Westover folio is the final version of Byrd's *History*, the present editor has used that text as the standard for the *History* and has followed the A.P.S. text for the *Secret History*, supplying only the one hiatus from the Williamsburg fragment. As the Westover folio remains the only known source for the two smaller works, *A Progress to the Mines* and *A Journey to the Land of Eden*, the texts for this edition were, of course, transcribed from it.

# INDEX

425

Miry Creek, 125, 126, 133, 153, 262, 277
Mississippi River, 271
Mitchell, Peter, 389
Monacan Indians, 314n
Moniseep Ford, 230, 255, 311
Monmouth, James Scott, Duke of, 167
Montague, Elizabeth, Duchess of, 16
Moon's Mount, 373
Moratuck River, 302
Morris, Harry, 385, 386, 388, 391, 406, 408
Morris, Mrs. Harry, 385, 407, 408
Morris Creek, 389, 414
Morton, Richard L., *Colonial Virginia*, cited, 361n, 374n
Moseley, Edward (Plausible), 42, 43n, 47, 54–55, 55n, 56, 68, 72, 76, 79, 80, 86, 91, 97, 101, 109, 150, 171, 210, 224, 228, 324, 326, 330, 331, 332, 335
Mosquitoes, 182, 207, 294
Moss, Mr., 58
Mossy Point, 60, 185
Mount Eagle, 132
Mount Misery, 149
Mount Pleasant, 121, 137
Mules recommended for mountain travel, 282
Mulloy, W. J., and R. C. Beatty, *William Byrd's Natural History of Virginia*, 17
Mumford, Mr., 100, 101, 408
Mumford, Major James, 100, 142, 143, 144, 145, 146, 148, 381, 383, 385, 386, 387, 388, 393, 401, 407, 410, 411, 413
Mumford, Mrs. James, 381, 411
Mumford, Colonel Robert, 47, 230, 307, 312, 319, 381, 384, 411–412, 413, 415
Mumford, Mrs. Robert, 148, 149
Myrtle, 53, 172, 175

Nansemond County, N.C., 193, 215, 330
Nansemond River, 51, 77, 172, 192, 199, 202
Nat, servant to Major Mumford, 100, 142
Nat's wife, 143
Nauvasa, Catawba town, 309
Ne plus ultra Camp, 153

Nebuchadnezzar, 408
Nelson, Mr., 352
Neuse River, 302, 308
New England: iron manufacture, 354, 357; rum, 205; settlement, 161–164; tobacco trade, 176
New Hampshire colony, 163
New Haven colony, 163
New Jersey settlement, 166–167, 168
New York, 164–165, 166
Newton, Colonel George, 51, 52
Newton, Mrs. George, 51, 53
Nicholas, Dr. George (Dr. Arsmart), 49, 352
Nicholas, Robert Carter, 49n
Nicholson, Francis, Governor of Virginia, 9, 42n, 164
Nicholson, Joshua, 409, 415
Norfolk, Va., 51–53, 173–174
Norfolk County, Va., 330
Norman's Ford, 375
North Carolina: boundary, 19, 27, 169–171 (*see also* Dividing line); charters, 27, 168–171, 322–323; Council, 43, 87, 194; general description, 23–24, 207–208; irreligion, 44, 171, 193, 194–195; lawlessness, 212; laziness of inhabitants, 114, 184–185, 192, 204–205, 226; Lords Proprietors, 43, 87, 169, 212, 322, 331, 332, 334; pork diet, 59–60, 61, 184–185, 341
*North Carolina: A Guide*, cited, 302n, 382n
North Carolina, University of, Byrd notebooks, 7, 33, 35
North River, 58, 181, 183, 202
Northern Indians, 123, 146, 257, 258–260, 309, 393
Northern Neck, 41n, 361
Northern's Creek, 61, 185
Northwest River, 52, 53–54, 59, 174, 175, 183–184, 185, 186, 202
Nottingham, Catherine Howard, Countess of, 158
Nottoway Indians, 81–83, 170, 217–222
Nottoway River, 27, 78, 79, 81, 94, 146, 148, 152, 169, 212, 213, 214, 216, 318, 325, 327, 381, 413, 415
Nottoway Town, 81, 217–219
Nova Scotia, 164
Nuns, sexual transformation of, 316
Nutbush Branch, 103, 233
Nutbush Creek, 103, 142, 152, 232, 233, 306

437

## DATE DUE

| | | | |
|---|---|---|---|
| 5-2-98 | | | |
| ILL# 1949388 | | | |
| | | | |
| | | | |
| | | | |
| | | | |
| | | | |
| | | | |
| | | | |
| | | | |
| | | | |
| | | | |
| | | | |
| | | | |
| | | | |
| | | | |
| GAYLORD | | | PRINTED IN U.S.A. |